CROOKED PRAYERS

A Max Strong Thriller

MIKE DONOHUE

ALSO BY MIKE DONOHUE

MAX STRONG/MICHAEL SULLIVAN PREQUELS

Sleeping Dogs

The Devil's Angel

MAX STRONG THRILLERS

Shaking the Tree

Bottom of the World

Hollow City

Trouble Will Find Me

Burn the Night

SHORT STORIES

October Days

For my grandfather –

I wish I could know you now.

And you were right. I constantly cheated at Go Fish.

God, give me the strength each day
to fight for my family.

— NEHEMIAH 4:14

CROOKED PRAYERS

PART ONE: THEN

CHAPTER ONE

George Keres put his boots up on the bed and swallowed a laugh. He knew the others were looking at him, but that was alright. It played to the dumb hick persona he wanted to cultivate. Better to be underestimated. He sipped his beer. Best not to overdo it. He looked at the dark splatter stain on the mustard-colored coverlet. To his practiced eye, he'd wager on blood. He moved his boots a few inches to the left. His luck might have changed, but the accommodations were still for shit.

Three days ago, he'd been desperate, reduced to looking under his couch cushions for change that wouldn't make a damn bit of difference. Anything he scraped together would just be a tiny chip off an ice bucket full of debt. He'd thought about running, but he knew that was an even worse idea than turning over the cushions. He wouldn't make it 500 miles before Monty ran him down. And then Monty's guys would be pissed that they'd had to chase him. But he couldn't just sit here and wait for it, either. When you had no other options, you could talk yourself into almost anything.

He'd laid on the floor staring at the crumbs and dust

under the couch and tried to think of the best place to disappear. They'd expect him to go south because his mother and brother still lived in Tennessee. Family had to help, right? But they'd never met his mother. Maybe he'd head north instead. Maybe go to Maine or Upstate New York. He'd never been to either place. No connections, no past. Should be easy to get lost up there. Might even slip over the border somewhere into Canada. Plenty of people had hidden in Canada over the years. He'd rummaged through his apartment, figuring out what he might sell and trying to jack himself up on living the rest of his life with moose and maple syrup, when the phone rang. He hadn't paid the bill in months and the fact that the phone company hadn't cutoff service yet surprised him. He almost didn't answer. The chances were high it was someone looking for money, probably not Monty who tended toward the personal touch of in-person visits, it was harder to break fingers over the phone, but maybe Edison or Visa or Mastercard. Someone polite and legit, but with their hand out looking to get paid just the same.

He stood next to the green plastic phone mounted on the wall and let it ring, his mind twitching back and forth. Pick it up, let it ring. Pick it up, let it ring. Keres was a gambler to his marrow. He picked it up.

He pulled the second can off the plastic ring and cracked the top. The head bubbled up, and he sipped it loudly. He flicked the pull tab toward the ashtray on the nightstand and missed. It didn't detract from the decor. Might have added to it. The motel room was cramped and cheap. Water-stained walls matched the stain on the bedspread and the funk seeping up from the thin carpet. Keres locked eyes with the lean guy standing by the dresser. He thought the others were buying his hick shtick, but he wasn't sure about Sullivan.

They'd all made half-hearted introductions at the start. Keres, the last one in the door, found himself the odd man out. He didn't know the other four, but they all appeared to have at least a passing familiarity with each other. Probably done jobs together in the past. That wasn't too unusual for Keres. He rarely worked with the same crew twice. He preferred it that way. It was one of the first things he learned as he worked his way into the heist game. Never trust your partners. If they're already stealing from someone else, what's stopping them from stealing from you too? It made the jobs less steady. And it made Keres less popular. But it also provided a bit of pragmatic self-protection. There was less chance of someone learning too much about you and offering it up to the cops if they got pinched. Better to be the unknown or the unpopular guy than the one who gets double-crossed.

He didn't know if the names of the others were real or not, and didn't care. He didn't need to know them. Especially for this job. He stifled another grin with a burp. The blond looked over with a sour look on her face. John Sullivan and his girlfriend, or wife, or whatever, leaned against the cheap Formica dresser. Did people unpack and put their clothes in there? Maybe when the place was shiny and new, back in the '40s or '50s, but 30 years later, on its last legs, Keres doubted it. Better to leave your things rumpled and wrinkled in your suitcase. Not that he'd noticed many people toting suitcases into these rooms. The Sentinel Motel might charge by the day, but it appeared most guests only used it for a few hours. Best case, someone demolished the place and cheap tract housing took its place. Worst case, the landscape slowly swallowed it up as it fell apart. Which was exactly why Finnegan had picked the Sentinel for the meet. The front desk was happy to take cash and happier still not to ask questions.

A sobering thought hit Keres. If things still went sour for

him and he had no choice but to run, he might spend the rest of his life jumping between beds in places like this. He couldn't let that happen.

He placed his feet back on the ground and felt the room sway slightly. He needed to ease back on the beer. He hadn't eaten anything since breakfast and that was almost 12 hours ago. He'd popped a pill in the parking lot to sharpen up, but now the alcohol and chemicals were threatening to get on top of him.

He let the room settle and forced himself to focus. Sullivan's woman was still staring at him. She looked a little like that tiny, red-haired actress that was in all the teen movies recently except with blond hair and dark eyebrows. Small and elfin, Keres thought she would be attractive if she cracked a smile once in a while.

Standing next to her, Sullivan himself had a stylish haircut, with fashionable clear-framed glasses, and a loud red Hawaiian shirt. He looked like a joker. A guy playing at being a badass, dressing up like Tom Selleck, but his eyes were dark and watchful behind those glasses. Keres didn't think he missed much. Maybe he was playing a part, too.

Finnegan stood in the middle of the room between the beds. He was the guy who called and invited Keres to the meeting. He was thin with a wavy, gray comb-over that he was constantly brushing out of his eyes. There were damp patches under his arms, and Keres noticed he responded to any interruption or question with a nervous stutter. He was not the type to inspire immediate confidence. But Keres knew his rep was solid. If not, he wouldn't have used half of his remaining bankroll to drive to Delaware. Then again, what choice did he have? If this didn't work out, he might as well keep driving until the tank ran dry. The thought made him queasy. He dropped the empty second can on the floor and opened a third.

He looked up to find Sullivan staring at him.

"See something you like, friend?" Keres asked.

Sullivan didn't respond but turned to the guy standing on the far side of the room, closest to the door. "Superman, you ever work with this guy?"

"Nope. Might have heard a thing or two, though."

Superman was a Black guy, short and squat, like a fireplug but with long powerful arms that stretched the cuffs of his shirt. His hair looked painted across his scalp, shaved close. He'd given his name as Jack Justice, which Keres figured was too queer to be anything but real. Keres didn't like Black guys. Keres didn't trust them, and it pissed him off hearing Sullivan ask his opinion of him.

"Me, too," Sullivan said. "Wimpy, we really need him?"

"Hey, who's running this show? I didn't get any invite from you. And I didn't come here just to get insulted," Keres responded.

"Who says you're being insulted? I didn't hear no one disparaging you," Justice said.

"Screw you."

"That the way you roll? Hadn't heard that."

Keres felt his face redden, but Finnegan started talking again and Justice turned away before Keres could respond.

"Y-y-yeah, we need three. No way around it. Two, even you two, leaves too many holes. I wanted Collins, but he's out of town and Rudy just took a fall. Looks like he's headed to Walpole for at least a dime. This job has a short timeframe and the money is too good to pass up." Finnegan shrugged. "Gotta make do, but I understand if you want to pass."

Sullivan pulled his glasses off and pinched his nose but eventually turned to Keres. "You got a problem with alcohol? I don't work with drunks. Or tweakers."

"Three beers doesn't make me a drunk."

"Doesn't make you someone I want to work with either."

"Finnegan's the finger, he set up the string. He's running the show. He's bankrolling it. That right?" Finnegan gave a small nod. "That settles it then. Talk all the shit you want. I'm in. You can walk. I won't stop you."

They all fell silent. The girlfriend put a hand on Sullivan's arm and whispered something only he could hear. Sullivan closed his eyes, then waved at Finnegan to keep going. Finnegan went to a giant suitcase on the bed, unzipped it, and took out a collection of maps and blueprints with hand-drawn notes and annotations. He spread them on the bed.

"A-a-alright. We're hitting a shipping security company. Lir Security. They're based in Dublin and deal with high-value cargo shipped from overseas, typically Western Europe ports to ones on the Eastern U.S. Seaboard."

"What are we talking about exactly?" Justice asked. "I don't want to give up a percent or wait on a fence."

"I don't have a number, but once a month there's a specific shipment that comes in from Belgium. It contains two things: U.S. cash, dollars, all unmarked from foreign banks that are being transferred to domestic banks back here."

"Okay, I like cash. What's the second thing?" Justice said.

"Raw materials for jewelry making."

"Raw materials?"

"Diamonds, gold, silver. It gets distributed up and down the coast to the people who make pieces for retail stores. We'd take a hit on that, but I've got a guy lined up. Shouldn't have to wait."

"How much would we give up?"

"We'd get 25 on the dollar."

"And you don't know how much cash will be there?" Sullivan asked.

"No, it varies a bit by the month, I've been told, but I don't think they're shipping rolls of pennies. It's enough to make it worth the effort and to stomach the fence's cut. My source said the shipment comes in like clockwork, the third Thursday of the month, every month for the last year and a half. And here's the key. It always arrives after the last armored truck leaves the shipping yard, so it's stored overnight in the company's vault and picked up in the morning. That's our window." Finnegan paused and gauged the room's reaction before continuing. "You'll go in after midnight but before four. I figure you'll need more than 30 minutes, but less than an hour. The extra day shift security for the yard comes on at five, but the commercial fisherman a few wharves over will typically be there prepping by four. You'll want to be gone by then."

Finnegan shuffled more papers around on the bed, picked up a sheet and handed it to Sullivan. "I've charted the guard's rounds. One car. Maybe a van. I'll leave the specifics to you, John. No need for shooting. There will be two people inside. One will be the guard. Rent-a-cop. The other will be the overnight cargo manager. He'll have the combination for the vault and can disable any silent alarms. The cash and cargo are all insured. The manager shouldn't need much convincing. I've got a package on him just in case. You secure both men and clean out whatever is in the vault."

Sullivan leaned over the current schematic. "How do we get into the yard?"

Wimpy put a finger down. "This is the main entrance and has a manned booth 24/7. The trucks hauling the containers in and out all pass through that checkpoint. But here and here," he moved his finger, "are employee entrances so they don't get held up in the truck traffic. Gated, but no guard. You want this one, the southern one, so you don't get near the main gate." He pulled a gray piece of plastic out of an envelope and handed it to Sullivan. "This will open the gate."

Sullivan had more questions and Keres let them talk. It wasn't rocket science. The plan relied on the softness of the target and inside information on the timing, and less on skill or tactics. Stick a gun in someone's face and they'll wet themselves, but they'll do what you want. The important thing for Keres was that the plan appeared legit. Legit and profitable. There might even be enough left over after paying Monty that he could take a vacation. Maybe get out to Vegas and see if he could keep this new streak of luck rolling.

Still, as the meeting broke up, his skin prickled as he thought about Sullivan's aloofness and Justice's veiled insults. It bubbled up and bumped the warmth of his good fortune aside. His fingers itched to pull out the gun in his boot and add a few new stains to the walls. Put a shiny piece of brass through those faggy little lenses. But he couldn't pass up the score. And he needed them, at least some of them, to get the money. First the money, then make them beg. He smiled, thinking about it, and felt the warmth return. He looked over at Sullivan and decided when the time came, he'd shoot the woman first.

CHAPTER TWO

Lisa and John Sullivan drove north on Route 1, skirted the small airport in New Castle, picked up 95, accelerated, but then had to slow again in the congestion around the much larger Philadelphia airport. They pushed on, through the end of rush hour, eager to get home, and eventually crossed the Delaware River into Jersey just after 8:00 and took the turnpike north toward Massachusetts.

They stopped once, ducking the cookie-cutter rest-stop chains strung out along the highway for a legit Jersey diner: greasy burgers, salty fries, and to-go coffees. John paused by the rotating case near the register.

"Pie?"

"Anything you can't eat one-handed isn't road food."

"I'm not driving. I could use two hands."

"If you want to wear lemon cream pie the rest of the drive, be my guest."

He settled for a chocolate chip cookie the size of a dinner plate instead and paid the check.

.   .   .

Lisa hesitated in the parking lot.

"Go ahead," John said.

"What? I wasn't..." Then she gave up the pretext and veered toward the phone. It was a battered silver booth tucked under the eaves of the diner next to a plastic bin full of free used car circulars. "I'll be quick," she replied.

She stepped into the small booth and felt something crackle and pop at the back of her brain. She left the door open. The only time she could stomach tight spaces was when she was tucked tight behind the wheel. Those moments didn't bother her. Instead of closing in around her, the world expanded. As long as she could press the pedal down and push the scenery to whip past the windshield, she was okay.

She faced the open door, put the phone against her shoulder, and dialed. A monotone voice requested 85 cents to connect the call and told her it would be an additional 30 cents for each minute. She pulled a pile of change out of her purse and spread it on the small metal tray below the phone. It added up to less than two bucks. She'd make it quick. She was lucky it was evening rates.

She plugged the coins in and waited. There was a pause, then the distant clicks of relays connecting. Her sister picked up on the fourth ring. Lisa could hear a laugh track on the television in the background.

"Joyce? It's Lisa."

"Guessed it was you. On your way back?"

"Yeah, should be back by midnight. Mikey okay?"

She could hear Joyce take a sip of something, probably chardonnay. She'd noticed Joyce had been drinking more lately. The breakup with Martin had hit her hard. Lisa's stomach clenched. She felt like a terrible sister and a terrible friend. She knew she should be there for Joyce, and she would be, she would. She just had to get clear of her own problems first. Then they could have a proper girls' night. Hit the clubs. Leave the kids with John. They all had to hold it together just a little longer. This thing with Wimpy promised to move fast. It would be over in a week. They could make it a week.

"He's fine," Joyce said. "He asked about you this morning, but once he and Danny got wound up, your name didn't come up again until bedtime. I took them down to Carson for most of the afternoon. Not warm enough for the water yet but they didn't mind. They ran around in the sand. Burned off the crazy. They fell right asleep."

"Good, I'm glad he wasn't a problem. I appreciate you watching him."

"You going to need me again this week?" Joyce knew what Lisa and John did but didn't ask for details and Lisa never offered. Far better for Joyce to be able to deny honestly if she was ever confronted. But since Michael had come along, Lisa had needed Joyce when they had to go out of town for work.

Lisa hesitated, but there was no way around it. "I hate to ask again so soon, but is Thursday night okay?"

"Sure. That's fine. You'd think having two in the house would be harder, but it makes it easier in some ways. At least two boys."

"I know what you mean. They bounce off each other instead of you." She paused, again not sure she wanted to ask the next question either but she did. "Listen, I gotta go, but did you hear anything about the other thing?"

Lisa heard Joyce take a long swallow and heard the tink of the wineglass being set down on the glass coffee table. She dropped her head and braced herself. If Joyce needed the Dutch courage to get it out, it wouldn't be good news.

"I'm sorry, Lisa. He said it wouldn't work out. Not right now. Things are tight and there's just no room for someone without more experience."

Lisa put some false cheer in her voice but doubted it fooled Joyce. "Of course. I understand."

"It just takes one."

"I know. You're right. I just felt like this time..." The automated voice popped on and requested 30 more cents, but Lisa had nothing more to say. "Give Mikey a kiss for me," she said quickly. "See you soon."

She got back behind the wheel and chased the bright tunnels of her headlights down the highway. She couldn't even land a simple receptionist gig. So far, she'd resisted going back to waitressing. She was getting too old to put in 12-hour shifts and hustle tips. She didn't want her son to think that was her ceiling. She wanted better. So did John. She believed that. But there were bills to pay and waitressing was honest work. Michael could at least tell his classmates what his mother did. Not like heisting. A waitress didn't have to hide part of herself. She decided to wallow in self-pity for the rest of the ride and then she'd send out more resumes in the morning.

She glanced over at John. He sat quietly in the passenger seat. He'd asked about Michael but not the receptionist job. He didn't have to. He could see it on her face. He reached out and squeezed her hand then settled back in his seat. Occasionally he reached up and adjusted the radio dial as they drifted in and out of station range, picking up New Wave and Brit-pop from WXPN out of UPenn then hair bands and glam rock with WAXQ out of New York. It was just background noise. Neither of them were listening. They hit a dead spot halfway up 84, approaching New Haven, and she reached down and snapped it off.

"What do you think?" Just like him, she didn't need to ask. She already knew what he thought. She could see it in the rigid posture of his shoulders and the way he worked his jaw, but this is what she did when she got stressed, focused on the details, talked it through with John. It made them a good team. And kept them out of jail.

John might be a cipher to most, but Lisa had known him since the first day of third grade. They'd been together since the summer of seventh grade. There wasn't a mood, expression, or thought she hadn't seen cross his face.

"The job itself looks solid. Wimpy sweats the details just like us. I'm not worried about that. It's Keres."

"What was Justice needling him about? What have you heard about him?"

"Nothing that makes me eager to work with the guy and I saw nothing tonight to change my mind. Hot-tempered, excitable. Quick to blow up the plan and quick on the trigger. He hasn't killed anyone, that I've heard about, at least, but probably not for a lack of trying. He doesn't have a steady crew and I can see why."

"He's a ticking time bomb."

"That's right."

She hadn't liked Keres, either. She didn't buy the aw-shucks, good old boy act in the motel room. The man had the flat eyes of a shark. Maybe he hadn't killed anyone, or maybe he just hadn't been caught. But Lisa doubted that killing a person would bother Keres very much.

Michaelades' face jumped into her mind now. She and John had lost two people on jobs they'd worked. An off-duty cop shot Michaelades on the way out of a racetrack job. A wild, lucky shot. Unlucky for Michaelades, however. Turner was killed by a guard after they tripped an alarm that hadn't been on the plans they'd been sold. Neither she nor John had ever shot anyone, and she hoped they never would. John had never fired any weapon on a job. He always told his crews if the shooting started the job was already gone. It was better to just walk away at that point.

"Plus, he had rotten teeth," she added. "You see that hockey mouth? Those chompers were snaggly."

That got a smile out of John. One of her snap judgments about people was always about their teeth. She figured if a person couldn't spare the time to take care of their teeth, how were they going to deal with the rest of life's details?

"I don't know. I thought it improved his hood rat face."

"A rat is a good word to describe George Keres."

"I'm worried he's less a rat and more a weasel. A rat will kill to eat. A weasel will kill for the hell of it."

She suppressed a shudder at that image. "You know anyone we could get to swap in for Keres?" She knew that answer, too, but had to ask.

"No. I'm sure Wimpy tried."

They had slowly cut ties with their heist connections since Michael had been born. They turned down more jobs than they accepted, as they tried to find a way to gently fade out without pissing anyone off. It did them no good to get out if it meant someone eventually came looking for them and their son. That's why this job hurt so much. It was a step forward when they should keep stepping back.

"We're committed," John continued. "We all know the setup. If we try to nudge Keres aside, it would only lead to problems. We just need to keep a close eye on him."

"I don't like it."

"If you buy the house, you buy the cockroaches too."

CHAPTER THREE

Once the questions were done, the meeting broke up. They all agreed to stagger the times they left the motel room. Keres was the first to leave, but he didn't go far. The Sentinel Motel might have been slowly disintegrating, but the strip club a quarter mile up the road, cheekily named The Dancing Bare, was doing just fine. The parking lot was more than half full before sunset.

Keres drove his Chevette hatchback up the road until he was out of sight, then turned around and crept back. He pulled into The Dancing Bare's lot and slotted the little car between a listing plastic fence and a rusting Ford sedan. Looking through the windows of the Ford gave him a good view of the Sentinel. He rolled his window down, lit a smoke, and waited.

They were probably in there talking about him right now. All of them thought they were better than him. Maybe that was true, but he knew his limitations. And his strengths. Maybe that made him the smarter man. He sucked the cigarette down to the filter and dropped it out of the window. They were going to learn none of them were as ruthless as he was. If you didn't watch your own back, who else would? He knew. No one.

Two cigarettes later, he watched Justice exit the Sentinel and walk to a midnight blue Cutlass Supreme with sparkling chrome rims and wide whitewalls. Justice paused at the driver's side door and turned his head left and right, almost like he'd picked up Keres's scent. Keres involuntarily edged himself lower in his seat.

Justice gave one last look around, wiped at a spot on the roof, then climbed into the car. The V8 rumbled to life with a deep, guttural roar Keres could hear from his hiding spot. Justice rolled out of the dirt lot, turned left, and headed north. Thirty seconds later, there was only the distant echo of the engine disappearing up the road.

Keres could afford to let Justice and Sullivan go. He knew where they would be in three days. He needed to take care of Finnegan now. Finnegan wouldn't be on hand for the heist and Keres didn't know where he lived.

For a man who fingered jobs, it surprised Keres that Finnegan had given it all up at the first meet. If it had been Keres, he would have held back something. If you weren't riding shotgun during the heist, you had to continue to provide value, or what good were you? It was a mistake that Keres intended to capitalize on. If he was going to pay off Monty and get a fresh start, he couldn't leave any loose ends.

Fifteen minutes after Justice, the Sullivans left. Unlike the spade, they went for something small and Japanese. Keres wasn't a car guy, they were just replaceable tools, but he didn't mess around with foreign ones, especially from Asia. Those people barely had paved roads. What could they possibly know about cars? When he stole some wheels, he stole American, even if it was a Chevette. He'd taken this one late last night from the back row of the Northbridge casino and Jai Alai after he stopped in to see Monty.

It was a risk, but he didn't want Monty to think he was running. The fat man was at his usual table and Keres had told him he'd have his money by the end of the week. Monty had looked skeptical. Keres couldn't blame him. He would be skeptical, too. He'd fixed his glass eye on Keres for a long time. Keres clenched his fists to keep them from shaking and did his best to keep his gaze steady. In the end, Monty had picked up the four-pound lobster on his plate, snapped off a claw in a way that made Keres wince, and said, "Saturday night or we'll start breaking bones on Sunday."

The Northbridge served a cheap three-dollar chuck wagon buffet. Keres swiped a handful of cold cuts and cheese slices and stuffed them into his mouth as quickly as he could. He was sure his petty crime was on video, but what could they do? He flicked a one-fingered salute at the cameras on the ceiling and walked out.

He could still taste the cheap American cheese and pimento-studded ham slices underneath the cheap beer. He'd driven through the night and most of the day to make it on time. He'd stopped once in Virginia when the lines on the road blurred. He'd slept for 30 minutes, then popped a pill and kept going. He'd sleep when he was dead. Isn't that how the saying went?

Better yet, he'd sleep when Finnegan was dead.

He checked his watch. It had been five minutes since the Sullivans had driven off in their piece of Jap crap. He used his shirtsleeve to wipe down the interior of the car as best he could. He left the keys on the seat and the door unlocked.

Someone would take it. Worst case, the car got towed or impounded and ended up as scrap. But he'd bet on someone stealing it. Probably before last call. It was an upgrade over many of the junkers in the lot.

He walked back to the motel. No cars passed. Nothing moved at the motel. There were three remaining cars in the lot. One Ford Fiesta with a mismatched white driver's side door parked near the office. Probably the desk clerk's. A pickup truck down at the very end and then a silver Celebrity parked halfway down the line, near the road, away from the rooms, under the motel's sign. Keres pegged that one as belonging to Finnegan.

He walked past the office and could hear the television behind the yellowed drapes. He walked on and, after passing a small alcove with a humming Pepsi machine and upright ice maker, tried the door marked 'Housekeeping.' It was unlocked. It was a small space. Shelves lined all three walls. Folded sheets and coverlets on the right. Stacked toilet paper in mini silos to the left. Thin, bleached towels occupied the back. A rolling maid's cart took up the remaining space in the middle. He pulled out the cart and shut the door. He could see a layer of dust covering the small bars of soap and shampoo on top and wondered how often the maid used the cart.

He rolled it toward room eight. He glanced over his shoulder. No movement from the office. He checked his watch again. If Finnegan matched the timing of the others, he'd be leaving soon. Keres thought about the best way to play it. A knock and the maid cart should get the door opened. He wasn't worried about controlling Finnegan. Keres probably had 50 pounds on him, but then what? Even in a shithole like the Sentinel, gunshots would draw attention. Then he stopped. The answer was right there on the wall. His cards kept coming up aces.

They built the entire place on the cheap and that included the flimsy pine boards they'd used for the doors. His knock sounded hollow and too loud for a housekeeper. There was no security peephole, but the window gave a view out. He stepped back and to the side so only the cleaning cart was visible.

"Yeah," he heard Finnegan call from inside.

Keres pitched his voice higher. "Maid service."

"Come back later. I'm leaving in 10 minutes."

Keres knocked again.

"Later," Finnegan replied.

Keres knocked again and now he heard Finnegan approaching the door, too annoyed to be careful. As soon as Keres saw the knob turn, he put his shoulder to the door. Finnegan yelled and fell back. Keres pulled the cart in behind him and pushed the door closed. He looked out the window. No movement, no reaction. He turned back to Finnegan. He was flat on his back on the crusty carpet with a surprised look on his face and a growing red welt where the door had caught him on the forehead.

CHAPTER FOUR

William 'Wimpy' Finnegan knew immediately that he was in a tight spot.

"Keres?" Finnegan said, putting a little whine into his voice. "What the hell? I thought you left."

Finnegan wasted no time on regret. He ran through his options. He wasn't a strong man, not physically, the Wimpy nickname stuck for a reason, but he wasn't a coward either. He'd squeezed his way out of tight spots in the past by using what his mama gave him. In his case, not brawn, but the ability to look pathetic. He could get anyone with a drop of empathy in their soul to take pity on him. Some animals in the wild got camouflage. Some got claws. Some got sharp teeth. Wimpy inherited the droopy eyes and slumped shoulder deference of a lost puppy. What type of person hits a puppy?

"I did," Keres said. "Now I'm back."

"Why?"

"To renegotiate my take."

"What?"

"One less guy means more for me when the cash and jewels get divvied up."

"So, what? You're going to cross all of us? Then what? Word will get around. You won't work again. It's a good score, but it's not retirement money. Not with the fence's cut. How you going to swing that?"

Damn it, he'd seen this coming. But the money...

Wimpy took a sip of orange juice and tried again. "K-keres is like an old stick of dynamite. Unstable and explosive. He's just as likely to blow off his own foot as he is to get the job done."

The man sitting in the dark booth across from him nodded. "I understand, but that's your problem. I'm bringing the job to you, Keres is my only requirement. You can pick the rest of the team."

It was an odd request, and it smelled bad. But Finnegan needed this job. The last two had fallen through, and his funds were getting dangerously low. His line of work required a certain amount of risk. "Alright, Keres is in."

"Good. Did you want to talk about anything else?"

"Give it to me one more time," Finnegan said. The man frowned. "We can't afford to get the day wrong." The man glanced around, but the bar had only been open for 10 minutes and was empty except for the two of them and a bartender polishing glasses 40 yards away as the NPR headlines played on the radio.

"Fine..." and he ran through the details a final time.

"Okay, got it."

"You're sure?" The man didn't hide his sarcasm.

Finnegan ignored the jab and kept the placid, slightly dull look on his face. The man across the table was tighter than a frog's ass. "I'm sure."

The man stood and stalked out of the bar without another word.

Finnegan finished his juice and then waited until the bartender disappeared through the set of swinging doors into the kitchen before he carefully pulled out the small camera hidden in a knot in the booth's wood and put it in his pocket. The low light might make the footage grainy, but Finnegan was confident it would be clear enough if necessary. He'd used the setup before. Risk was one thing, having insurance was another.

"Everything you said it true." Keres pulled out the same chair he'd used earlier and sat down. "Do you know Monty Green?"

"Sure. Not personally, but I heard of him. He runs the casinos down south, right? Along the Florida, Georgia, Alabama line."

"That's right. For the Traficante family. Do you know his nickname? Because all the top mob guys need nicknames, right?"

"No."

"Iron Monty. Know why?"

"No."

"Because he likes to use an iron pipe on his victims. Likes to hear their bones crack. Says it reminds him of eating chicken wings. One of his favorite foods. You believe that?"

"No, not really."

Keres laughed and smiled with those crooked teeth. Finnegan saw the crazy in the man's eyes and felt an icy finger run up his back. His puppy-dog act wouldn't work on a sociopath like Keres.

"Yeah, me either. That man must weigh three large at a minimum. It would take buckets of itty-bitty wings to fill him up." Keres dropped the smile. "But I believe the pipe part.

And that's the problem. See, I'm a gambler, Wimpy. You mind if I call you Wimpy like your friends do? I had a run of bad luck in some of those state line casinos. To his credit, Monty gave me time. Time and credit to turn it around, but the fates weren't on my side."

"How much are you into him?"

"Depends on the day. I lost track of the vig, but it's north of 100, probably closer to 125."

"Shit."

"Yeah, so you can see why I might not care much about the long term. I've got short-term problems and if I don't take care of those, well, retirement money is irrelevant, right?"

"How long you got?"

"Saturday night."

"Lucky I called, huh?" Finnegan tried to fit his source's insistence on using Keres with this new information. Was it part of it? Had he known? He didn't think so. He'd done his research and hadn't tied the guy to the mob. Not even close. That kind of information would have set off alarm bells. He did his best to steer clear of the mob. No, he figured this was just one of life's little fuck yous that he couldn't have anticipated. He slowly slipped a hand into his pocket and felt for the switchblade. His best bet was to keep Keres talking, stretch things out, and wait for an opportunity.

That plan fell apart when Keres stood and pulled an ax out of the bag hanging off the housekeeping cart.

Keres had never been squeamish about blood. He had a thing about spiders ever since his mother used the basement storage closet for punishment, but blood had never bothered him.

But he also knew blood could get him caught. Blood and

DNA were all over the news recently. He didn't fully understand how, but the science geeks could pin a crime on you with just a tiny drop, so he planned to get Finnegan in the bathtub before going to work with the ax. Keres thought that would make the clean-up easier.

But Finnegan surprised him. He pulled a knife from his pocket and lunged at him from the floor. On instinct, Keres dodged back and brought the ax down to defend himself from the jabbing blade. The ax had likely sat, untouched, in the emergency box on the motel's wall for 20 years. The oxidized blade was dull, but it was still sharp enough to go halfway through Finnegan's arm. It embedded in the bicep and the handle vibrated when it hit the bone.

Finnegan's mouth opened as if he wanted to scream, but no sound came out. He was likely in shock. Keres stomped down on Finnegan's hand and the switchblade skittered away under the bed. Then he grabbed the gaping Finnegan by the front of his shirt and dragged him into the bathroom and dropped him into the tub. Keres put a boot to the man's chest and wrenched the ax free. Finnegan's face went a flat white and his eyes rolled back as he groaned. Keres didn't mind if he passed out. It would make the next part easier.

The bathroom was small. He had to choke up on the handle of the ax, but he managed.

Despite his best efforts, there had been some splatter. More than a few drops. Keres went back to the housekeeping cart to grab more towels. He ran the shower for 20 minutes to rinse off the blood and flush the other bits down the drain. He wiped down the outer room even though he was sure the others had all done the same thing, then he retrieved the knife from under the bed and put it with Finnegan in the suitcase. He found a few small spots of blood on the carpet.

He tried to blot them up, but was sure he was leaving something behind. He was also sure hundreds, maybe thousands, had already speckled the room with drips and drabs of various body fluids over the years, so he didn't stress out about it. He did his best and left it at that.

He put the blood-soaked towels in the suitcase and zipped it up and left it by the door. He scooped up the papers and plans that were originally in the suitcase and carried them outside and put them in the back seat of Finnegan's Celebrity. Finally, he returned the maid's cart to the closet and the ax back to the case on the wall.

It was close to 8:oo when he was done. He paused in the breezeway and looked across the road at the sinking sun above the tips of the pines. Still a couple of hours until true dark in this part of the country, at this time of year. He went back inside, closed the door, and threw the security latch. Wimpy had paid for the room, someone might as well use it. He had more work and another long drive ahead of him. He put Finnegan's keys and wallet on the bedside table, pulled the stained coverlet off the bed, laid down, and fell asleep.

He woke up slightly disoriented four hours later. He took a moment to gather himself and then stood and looked out the room's window. As far as he could tell, the only thing that had changed was the glow from the now illuminated neon sign of The Dancing Bare. The Sentinel's sign was dark. Either burned out or not profitable enough to bother turning on. He put the odds at 50/50 as to which was the case.

He gripped the big Samsonite with both hands and carried it outside. If anyone saw him wrestling with the bulging suitcase, he might be memorable, but luck continued to run his way. No cars passed. No one exited their rooms.

The faint blue light flickering against the motel office's drapes was the only movement.

With some effort, he got the suitcase into the trunk of the Celebrity. Wimpy was heavier in pieces than when he was all put together. The suitcase took up most of the roomy trunk. He was lucky Finnegan hadn't been driving a car like the Sullivans. He might have had a problem.

He drove south, away from the highway. Two miles past The Dancing Bare, on a straight isolated stretch, with no other headlights in sight, he pulled to the shoulder and flung Finnegan's wallet, now minus the $220 in cash and his gas card, into the woods. If cops ever found the body, no use making it easy by also providing the ID.

He kept driving. He was looking for a rural fire road or access road for electrical towers. He'd leave the body as deep in the woods as he could get and let nature take its course. No use complicating matters. But now he re-thought that plan. The effort it had taken just to get the suitcase the 20 feet from the room to the trunk had been exhausting. Maybe it would be better to just start flinging parts out the window, as he'd done with the wallet. Maybe not everything, but maybe a few bits to lighten the load. He could then carry the feet, head, and hands deeper in the woods. That sounded like a better plan.

He came around a bend in the road and saw the illustrated sign lit up with double spotlights. A new housing development was nearing completion, and he thought of an even better plan. He turned off his headlights and cruised up the roughly paved road. All the houses were dark and unoccupied, but almost finished. He found what he was looking for near the back. A recently completed house that was still being hooked up to utilities, including the septic tank. A bulldozer sat nearby. The crew would cover the tank in another day or two and the finishing landscaping would begin. Lady Luck again.

He drove the big sedan over the dirt as close as he could get. The yard was full of dozer and tire tracks. No one would blink at the ones he just added. He removed the access cover closest to the trunk and dumped parts of Finnegan into the empty tank before replacing the cover. He was back in the car 10 minutes after pulling into the development. Fifteen minutes after that, he was accelerating onto the highway. He threw Finnegan's suitcase in a dumpster behind a truck stop outside Secaucus. He thought about keeping the switchblade. It was a nice knife, but he had to be smart. He dropped it out the window on the Cross Bronx expressway.

He smiled, thinking that there was now a bit of Finnegan in at least three different states.

CHAPTER FIVE

Lisa stared at the ceiling and tried to will herself back to sleep. It didn't work. She turned on her side and looked at the bedside clock. Not yet 5:00, but not far off either. She slipped carefully out from under the blankets and took her robe from the post on the end of the bed. Michael was almost sideways in the bed. He was almost five now and going through a phase where every time he woke up at night, he'd come into their room and ask to get in bed with them. She knew she should send him back to his own bed, but some nights she didn't have the strength to argue. But it didn't help her sleep any better. Michael fell asleep quickly and became a hot, twitching ball that kicked and elbowed her constantly. John could sleep through an air-raid siren and hardly budge. She looked down at them both now and noted how similar they appeared in repose. Their slack faces, unruly hair, and slightly large ears made the father/son resemblance impossible to miss. She tiptoed out of the room and closed the door.

In the kitchen, she flipped on the coffeemaker and sat down at the kitchen table. The bay window faced east, and the sun was eking up over the horizon. In a half hour, it would light up the water like a blanket of diamonds and make the bronze clock hands of the Custom House Tower glisten like shiny new pennies.

For now, the morning gloaming was peaceful. The neighborhood remained asleep. A few scattered brake lights flared on the expressway, but it was all from a distance. The apartment was on the third floor, in a new building, and had that view from South Boston back across the harbor to downtown. They'd been flush and flying high after a run of successful jobs and had plunked down a good chunk of their savings for the place. It had felt like the grown-up thing to do. Get a nice place, in a good neighborhood, start planning for a future. With hindsight, they'd learned the bitter truth. The grown-up thing would have been to sock the savings away for a rainy day.

And it was pouring now.

She picked up the stack of envelopes they'd collected from the lobby mailbox when they returned home last night. She wished she still smoked, despite how dangerous everyone was saying it was now, just to have something to do with her hands other than flip through the overdue bills. The collection agencies marked each one with increasingly dire warnings (Last chance! Final notice!) on the outside, as if she needed the reminder of what they had to do to get out from under it all.

She and John never set out to be career criminals, and they went out of their way to only do independent jobs. They avoided any connection to the syndicate, mafia, outfit, or whatever else you wanted to call organized crime. They gave the Patriarca crime family down in Providence a very wide berth. The first job was almost a dare. They'd scraped through to the end of high school. They were bored and staring down a lifetime of minimum wage jobs. The Mendon drive-in was showing a *Star Wars* and *Close Encounters* double feature over Memorial Day weekend. Any pro would have sniffed at their profits, but they'd gotten away clean and lived on that money for the rest of the year.

After that, it wasn't a lark. They took it seriously. They'd work one or two jobs a year. Sometimes on their own, sometimes coming in on larger jobs with people they trusted. But never more than four or five people. A crowded job drew too much attention and provided too many opportunities for things to go wrong. It got to be addictive. Many people were into coke in the '80s. Lisa and John got hooked on heists. And they were good at it. They'd never been arrested and, as far as they knew, had no authorities sniffing around. In-between jobs, she'd waitress and John would do some construction to provide the IRS a viable reason for their income. They put some money in the bank and kept the rest in a safe under the bed. When the bankroll ran low, they started looking for the next job. It all started simple enough and... just kept going.

She sometimes wondered if other people's careers worked like that, too. Suddenly you look up, you're north of 30 and have been doing the same thing for the last 10 years. Do you call that a career? She could feel inertia pulling both of them along even after Michael was born. It was tempting to continue. The good times were very good. And having a kid was expensive.

She promised herself they'd save more, be more careful. But she knew she was lying to herself. There were very few old criminals. Armed robbery had a short lifespan and only ended one way. They were good. They were smart. But they'd also been lucky. This upcoming job proved it. Keres was a harbinger, a reminder, a kick in the ass that things had to change.

In the past, they would never have considered a job with a wild card like Keres, but they couldn't afford to drop this one and walk away. The pile of envelopes was a chain around their necks. They needed a chunk of money, had needed it for a while, but all the jobs they'd looked at had been bad and they'd walked. This new one with Wimpy wasn't great, but they were running out of time and options.

They'd looked at declaring bankruptcy, that's what normal people would do, but quickly realized they didn't want the scrutiny that came with that process. So, it came down to two choices. Drop everything and walk away, start over somewhere else. Or do the next job, pay off their debts, and get out of the life. She didn't think she could just leave Joyce behind. Her sister was the only family she had left. Michael was still young, but she didn't think she could uproot him from everything he'd ever known.

It wasn't really a choice at all.

CHAPTER SIX

Lisa turned the knob on the dash and killed the van's headlights as she turned off First Street and onto the access road that fronted the marina and commercial docks.

"Past the marina," John said from the passenger seat.

She didn't respond. They'd spent the last day and a half, after getting the vehicles sorted with Jimmy Swag, doing research and reconnaissance. She knew where to turn. He knew she knew where to turn. It was just nerves. She could practically feel Keres and Justice vibrating on the bench seat behind her.

She drove slowly. It was 2:30 a.m. The docks, as Wimpy had promised, were quiet. The waterfront was a serious operation, but it wasn't large. This wasn't New York, Boston, or Philly. There were nine main wharves jutting out into the Atlantic. The first wharf was a marina for yachts and large personal boats. Charters and wholesale fishing operations took the second and third wharves. The remaining group was for commercial shipping. As she drove, Lisa could see stacked wooden pallets, bags of salt, bait barrels, and lobster traps lining the sides of the wharves next to the long, low cold storage warehouses. Moored boats rocked in the nighttime breeze against the wooden pilings.

The main gated entrance to the shipping docks was on the north side, as Wimpy had mentioned, so trucks could access it off the highway without driving through the downtown business district. Lisa had decided on a southwest approach, avoiding the highway for local surface roads. She spotted the unguarded employee entrance ahead on their right. She checked her mirrors. No cars. She turned and slowed by the gate. As she rolled down the window, the smell of saltwater, rusted metal, and decay wafted through the van. She picked up the keycard from the cupholder and glanced at John. He gave a curt nod. The entire job could sink in the next 10 seconds. They'd scoped out the roads, timed different routes, watched the employees come and go, but they hadn't been able to test their access.

She waved the keycard in front of the electric eye on the post. There was a pause, then a purr as the internal gears engaged and the gate lifted. Lisa drove the truck through the gate and headed for the northeast corner. John pulled down the ski mask that was rolled up to his forehead. She heard the rustling as the others did the same. So far, so good.

John pushed the van's passenger door closed with a quiet click and jogged toward the back door. Justice and Keres followed. He waved the card at the box next to the door. The small light turned from red to green, and he heard a chunking noise as the bolt disengaged. He pulled the door open and stepped inside. John had studied the floor plans from Wimpy's source and knew the layout but paused to let the two-dimensional images in his mind catch up to reality.

The building was a large rectangle with two floors. A

single hallway bisected the building down the middle. There were two sets of stairs, front and back. Management offices and conference rooms were on the second floor. The biggest unknown in the plan was where the overnight manager would be and what his routine was each night. He had an office upstairs, but theoretically, he could be anywhere in the building. His name was Ted Conder and Wimpy's plan included a summary of personal information if they had to push him. Married, with two kids, a boy and a girl, both under 10. He lived a half hour west in the town of Gorham in a raised ranch. He'd worked for Lir Security for five years. First in the warehouse, before he worked his way up to management. John was confident if they could get their hands on him, he would open the vault.

The first floor was spartan and designed strictly for business. John opened the first two doors along the hall and saw office supplies and empty storage racks laid out in plain square rooms with cheap dividers of drywall nailed into metal studs dividing each space. Presumably, the vault was behind one door. The blueprints hadn't specified.

John started down the hall. There was a small reception area upfront. That's where the night guard would be when he wasn't on rounds. The guard sat at reception for the graveyard shift. Beige industrial carpet covered the hallway. It was paper thin but softened the sound of their footfalls. The overhead lights were off, and the only illumination came from the glowing red exit signs above the doors at each end. John stopped halfway down the hallway next to the door marked seven. There was nothing to distinguish it from the other doors other than a keypad installed on the wall to the left of the knob. Wimpy hadn't mentioned a keypad. Everything else had lined up perfectly so far. John felt that uneasy feeling return. He'd been pushing it down, trying to ignore it, but it bubbled up now. These things happened when you rushed a job.

"What's wrong?" Justice hissed.

John just shook his head and kept walking to the end of the hallway. The door had a narrow glass window that allowed a view into the next room.

The guard was behind the desk. They had put a little more money into the public-facing reception area than the back storage area. John figured if you were a security company, it paid to promote an air of stable sanctuary when a potential client walked through the front door. To the right, there was a black leather couch and two matching chairs grouped around a glass coffee table. A framed aerial shot of the Portland port hung on the wall behind the couch. The opposite wall held a Lir Security sign in a fancy script along with four clocks showing various world time zones. The curved reception desk sat in the middle, directly opposite the front entry doors. Built out of dark wood, the desk looked impressively solid. There was a ledge running the full width, convenient for a client to lean against or put down a folio. A vase of fresh flowers, now slightly wilted and waiting to be replaced, sat off to the left. Otherwise, the counter was empty. No clutter. Nothing out of place. Everything safe, stable, and secure.

John adjusted his mask, took a breath, and went through the door.

The guard sat in a padded swivel chair with its own separate workspace below and mostly out of sight. John could see the guard's side of the desk was not free of clutter. A small clock radio sat at the guard's elbow. John could hear the Fine Young Cannibal's *She Drives Me Crazy* leaking through the door. The song had been everywhere that summer. The guard faced the front doors with his back to John and the interior hallway door. He creased and folded the newspaper in front of him into a rectangle. He must have heard the door open, but he spoke without turning.

"Ted, you see this thing about the proposed fishing quotas?"

When there was no response, he spun around in the chair, but Justice was already all over him.

"Wha—"

Justice put his large hands on the back of the chair and turned it back around. John walked around the half-moon reception desk and leaned on it like he was a customer with a simple question. He saw the guard's eyes jump to the gun in his hand and they widened. John actually had a question and he hoped there was a simple answer.

John knew less about the guard than the night manager, but he knew some. The guard's name was Greg Woodman. He'd worked for Lir for just over a year after he'd failed out of the state police academy. They didn't need to know any more. They didn't need leverage on Woodman. They just needed to subdue him, and that was already done. Woodman was young and thin. The uniform, a generic navy sport coat with a sewn-on badge over the left pocket, hung off him like a jacket on a scarecrow. All else being equal, John preferred when the guards were old. No more urges to be a hero. A little more perspective on life. No reason to risk all their lives for something as silly as a corporation.

He waited another moment for Woodman's eyes to stop jitterbugging.

"Greg, let's make this easy on all of us. Can you do that?" Woodman swallowed and nodded, and John continued, "Good, that's fantastic. I just have one question for you. You ready?"

John liked to get them talking, liked them to relax a bit. Woodman nodded again.

"Sorry, Greg, I can't hear you."

"Y-y-yes. I think so. I hope so. I'm just the night watch."

"We know who you are, and I promise you can help. It's not calculus. You know this answer."

"Okay."

"Where's Ted?"

"Ted?"

John smiled. He didn't think Woodman was being coy; he was just nervous. A line of sweat beaded at the kid's hairline. "Yes, the night manager. Ted Conder. Where is he?"

"He was in his office, up on the second floor, when I did my last rounds."

"Have you seen him since?"

"No."

"Does he usually stay up there?"

Woodman was nodding. "Yes, most of the time. Occasionally he'll come down, the vending machine is down here, and we'll chat a little."

"Okay. That's all I needed to know. Thanks, Greg."

"You're welcome."

John smiled, though his ski mask partially hid it. It was a very civil robbery so far.

"Greg, do you have asthma or any other breathing issues?"

"No, I don't think so."

"Good." He nodded and Justice started pulling lengths of thick silver duct tape off a roll. He wrapped them around Woodman's head and mouth. He left his nostrils free and then secured his arms, thighs, and ankles to the chair.

John pointed to Keres. "Stay here. Twitch the radio if you need us." He turned to Justice. "Let's get Conder and bring him down."

They retreated through the hallway door and turned immediately to the right. A set of stairs led up to the second floor. The second-floor hallway was a facsimile of the one downstairs, but the doors had name plaques instead of numbers. It smelled like printer toner and burnt coffee.

Most of the doors were closed, but a few remained open. All were dark, save one at the far end. John glanced inside the open doors as he walked past. One was a conference room. Another was a small kitchenette with a fridge, coffeemaker, sink, and bulletin board papered with flyers. A square of yellow light spilled out in the hall. The same beige corporate carpet was on the floor.

The office with the light was empty. John looked around but there wasn't much to see. It was a small 10 x 10 square. There was nowhere to hide. A coffee cup sat next to the keyboard. He put a hand against it.

"Still warm."

Then they heard the rushing whoosh of a toilet flushing. They backed up into the hall. The bathrooms were next to the kitchenette breakroom in the center of the hall. They took up spots next to the men's room door. They could hear movement behind the door. A faucet running, then someone pulling paper towels from a dispenser. A moment later, the door opened.

"Excuse me," he said automatically as he stepped out and almost bumped into John. It took a moment for Ted Conder's brain to catch up. He took two steps before it all registered. "Wait." He paused, turned, and took in John and Justice with their masks and their guns. To his credit, John thought, he kept it together better than most. Better than Woodman had downstairs. "I'll open it. No reason to hurt either of us." He caught on quick, too.

"Couldn't have said it better myself," John replied.

CHAPTER SEVEN

Justice picked up the next box. The vault was a square, 20 x 20 feet. No adornments inside. No shelves or tables. Just a sealed concrete box. Crude, but effective. Lir had stacked the overnight boxes in the center of the room. John came in behind Justice and popped the latches on one of the larger boxes. He lifted the lid and stood back. Inside the waterproof case, the money was vacuum packed in a single, tight block.

"Gets me every time," Justice said with a smile.

"It never gets old, does it?" John replied.

"I hope it never does."

The cases were made of hard, molded plastic and measured three feet long and two feet tall. In a different context, they might have looked like musical instrument cases, Justice thought. His old man had been a session drummer, at least when he was sober. A saxophone case or trombone or something. Something long and skinny. But there was no brass inside. No, sir. Just cold cash. Way more than his old man had ever made drumming.

The jewelry supplies were also in watertight shipping

boxes but smaller, square cases like old-fashioned hat boxes. There were almost three dozen boxes stacked in two tall columns. As Wimpy promised, it was going to be a good score. They hadn't counted, but that quick peek showed there were mixed denominations, nothing smaller than 20s, and the case was full. A very good score.

Justice carried two cash cases back toward the waiting van. Keres moved to the side and let him pass. Justice hadn't wanted this job. He'd left the motel and was on the verge of backing out when John had gotten in touch and asked him to stay in. He'd worked a few jobs with John and Lisa in the past. They'd always worked out okay, which meant he made money. He trusted them about as much as anyone in the game, so he'd agreed.

He passed the dummy door with the keypad and smirked. They'd marched Conder down the stairs and Keres had pulled the taped Woodman into the hall in his rolling chair. John had walked to the keypad, but Conder had waved him off and explained it did nothing. He walked to the next one. "It's like the fake security stickers people stick on their home windows. It's just there to slow down or confuse would-be robbers. I told them it would only make them mad and put any hostages at risk. The vault is in here." He'd opened the door marked six with a key attached to a ring on his belt and then entered a keypad code on the interior vault door.

"You're a smart man," John had said.

"Just want to see the sun rise."

Justice had pulled a chair from a storeroom across the hall and duct taped Conder to it, like he had Woodman. They'd left each man in a separate storeroom.

"Someone will come by and free you in the morning." John patted Conder on the shoulder. "You'll get to have breakfast with your kids."

. . .

Justice muscled two boxes into the van and adjusted the stacks.

"How many more?" Lisa asked.

"Two, then the cases with the jewels. Ten more minutes."

"Okay."

He walked back inside. He did the same dance in the hallway, this time in reverse, with Keres carrying the boxes.

He walked to the reception area. John was sitting behind the desk wearing Woodman's blazer. He was keeping watch and keeping things normal if anyone came through the front door. Unlikely, but not worth the risk. Justice had seen stranger things happen on jobs.

"Finishing up," Justice said. "Five minutes."

"Okay."

He hustled back to the vault room and moved to the jewelry boxes. He picked one up. They were lighter than the money, and he figured he could carry three at a time. He moved to grab two more and suddenly realized someone else was already in the room. He started to turn and felt the cold, sharp steel of a blade against his neck. The knife must have been very sharp because he never felt it cut into his skin.

Justice had pictured his death more than once. He dropped the box and looked down. Blood soaked the front of his shirt. He raised a hand to his neck and felt the wetness. It still didn't hurt. Not at all. He only felt very tired. He had to sit down. Just for a minute.

The room slid sideways. Or maybe he had. His cheek pressed against the cold concrete floor.

He didn't remember falling.

Then he remembered nothing at all.

Keres wiped the knife on Justice's pants and slid it back into his boot. He watched Justice's eyes jitter around, so he wasn't dead yet, but he would not be getting up.

"Superman, my ass," Keres muttered.

He stepped over the widening black puddle. To Keres, it resembled an oil slick more than a pool of blood. He dragged the remaining jewelry boxes a few feet away.

When Keres worked a job, he only saw things in black and white. Literally. It never affected him at other times, but when he was working? His life transformed into a black and white movie. Was it stress? A glitch in his brain chemistry? Some mental defect? He didn't know and didn't care. It wasn't as if he could go to a doctor and get it checked out. What would he say? How would he explain it? That wouldn't end well. No, he'd long ago just accepted it. It allowed him to push forward when others hesitated. Unlike the dying Justice, he had a personal superpower.

He picked up two of the square boxes and stacked them side-by-side on top of the longer cash box. Back in that Delaware motel room, he'd promised himself he'd shoot the woman first, but he was also a pragmatist. He realized tonight he needed to take care of Justice first. That was the smart play. Take out one man early. A man and a woman he could handle, especially if they were involved with each other, but two men might get the jump on him if he slipped up.

That didn't mean he'd thrown out the other plan. He'd still shoot the woman and make Sullivan watch. He hadn't forgotten the insults or disrespect they'd shown him. He walked out of the vault and smiled as he headed down the hall toward Lisa and the van. A few more minutes and he'd have Monty's money, with more than a little leftover.

Then the entire building lifted five feet off the ground and crashed back down. Keres stumbled, dropped the boxes, and went to his knees.

CHAPTER EIGHT

Lisa tapped the steering wheel with her ring finger. That was the one outlet she allowed herself. All the jobs were stressful, but she'd learned they were always the most stressful in the moments right before the end. There was a crescendo just as you were on the verge of getting away clean.

She checked the side mirrors. Nothing moved.

She willed John to come running out and jump in the van and tell her they were good. Tell her they had the cash and could start the rest of their lives. Nothing happened. The back door remained closed. Neither John, nor Justice, nor Keres came out. It all remained quiet. And that wasn't a bad thing, she reminded herself. She willed herself to believe it. A quiet, boring job was a perfect job.

She pulled her focus back to the front, out the windshield. This area of the wharf was away from the main cargo offloading near the water. It was in a darkened corner surrounded by weathered and discarded dock supplies. The Lir offices shared space inside a long, ribbed steel building, half of which was red, half blue. The security offices were in the blue half. Two other companies split the red one. Wimpy's research had noted their names, but nothing else. They weren't relevant to the job. Lisa studied the building. She couldn't find any reason the colors differed. The sun had bleached both sides. The dueling paint jobs had faded to a dull pastel. The entire structure looked used and tired, but not out of place. Time and salt had pocked and dented it like an old barnacle.

Lisa went back to the side mirrors. Tapped her finger. It had been almost three minutes since Keres had told her they were finishing up. She swapped back to the windshield. Both of the doors in the red section remained dark. Then something caught her eye. She looked out the driver's side window, across the wharf, and saw the tiny but unmistakable reflection of red and blue police lights approaching from the highway.

"Doesn't mean it's for us," she said to the empty van. She watched the lights inch closer. It was a single car. God forgive her, but she wished for an accident, or a fire, or some other terrible tragedy in some other place to be the reason for their approach. Let it be someone else's suffering.

The lights slowed and took the exit for the docks.

She reached for the door handle. The red half of the building exploded.

The reception area faced west toward the main cargo area, but stacks of supplies, dock storage boxes, and various other hardware that John couldn't identify blocked the view. He could see little beyond the narrow wedge of wharf visible through Lir's two glass entry doors. He could not see the access road that led off the highway. He was unaware of the approaching police cars. His view was dark, calm, quiet. He waited for Justice to come back and let him know they were good to go.

The door that led to the hallway was a standard fire door with a crash bar. It was heavy, by design, a core of steel, timber, and aluminum with the gap where the door met the wall filled with a fire-resistant sealant. It made the public-facing front room quiet. John couldn't hear Keres and Justice emptying the vault, but the clock in his head told him it had been almost five minutes since Justice had given him a heads up that the box transfer was almost complete.

He stood and pushed the chair in neatly. He refolded the newspaper that Woodman had been reading and left it next to the phone. He stood still and let his eyes roam over the desk. Saw nothing to cause him concern. He stayed in the same spot but expanded his field of vision farther out. He took his time. Stupid or careless mistakes had torpedoed many solid heists. He reached the glass doors and stopped. As far as he knew, no one on the team had approached the doors. No chance of inadvertent fingerprints. They were all wearing thin leather gloves, but you never knew. Sometimes it was second nature to take them off and wipe your face or your eyes and then you touch something else before you remembered the gloves. He took a small plastic bag out of his pocket and then took a bleach-soaked rag out of the bag. He wiped down the desk, chair, phone, even the pens, then he walked around the front of the desk and tried to remember where he stood and what he might have touched.

He was dropping the rag back in the bag when the world lurched sideways and he watched the large, crescent-shaped desk jump into the air. The force of the blast blew him off his feet, and he landed hard on his shoulder. He sat up. He saw bright bursts and thought he'd hit his head, then realized there were fire and debris raining down outside. What the hell had just happened?

He stood and the room swayed. Maybe he had hit his head. He went back to one knee until his equilibrium settled. He tried again, held his feet, and made it to the hallway door. A wall of heat greeted him as he pulled it open. The builders had invested in nice fire doors, but that expenditure had not extended to the dividing interior walls. Or maybe a subsequent landlord had subdivided the units on the cheap. John looked through a gaping hole in two walls to where the other non-Lir half of the storage warehouse burned fiercely.

The hallway was empty. There was smoke, but the fire hadn't jumped to their side of the building. Yet. It would soon. Small patches of embers were burning the cheap rug. The force of the blast had blown the door to the first room off its hinges. He could see the guard, Woodman, lying on his side, his eyes open wide, his chest heaving. He went across the hall. The door was still closed. He opened it.

Conder was upright, just the way they'd left him, but his expression was one of confusion and fear. J

John pulled a knife from his belt and Conder jerked back.

"Take it easy. The explosion wasn't us. It looks like it came from the other side of the warehouse. I'm cutting you most of the way loose. You should be able to work your way free in a few minutes and get Woodman out. Got it?"

Conder nodded. John slit the first few layers of tape and then backed out of the room.

Still no sign of the others. Maybe they had already gotten out and were waiting outside. He ran down to the vault room. The outer door was half ajar. The heavy interior door hadn't budged. John walked in and spotted Justice on the floor. Initially, he thought maybe the explosion had knocked him unconscious. Maybe Justice had hit his head when he fell, but as he came nearer, John saw the blood. Too much blood. He rolled Justice slightly to be sure and saw the deep cut on his neck. No explosion could cause that type of damage. That was a uniquely human wound.

He ran back down the hallway, toward Lisa and the van.

CHAPTER NINE

Lisa sat on the ground next to the van's open driver's side door. She wasn't sure how she'd gotten there. She reached up and wiped blood from one nostril. There was high-pitched ringing in her ears. She grabbed the door handle and pulled herself to her feet just as Keres burst out the back door.

"What happened?" she asked.

"No idea. I was walking down the hallway and then I was on the ground." He threw the boxes he'd been carrying in the back of the van.

"You didn't do anything? See anything?"

"No, but that's going to get a lot of attention. Blew a hole straight through the walls. Fire is going to spread. We gotta get out of here."

He was right. She climbed back into the van. Keres swung the back doors shut. As he came around the passenger side, the police car she'd seen approaching earlier came screaming around the corner and braked to a stop. She could see two officers inside. The one on the passenger side opened the door and got out. He stood and looked at the burning building as if he couldn't quite figure out what was going on, like seeing a giraffe in the middle of a baseball field.

The sound of Keres's gun made her flinch. Her foot came down on the gas and the van jumped forward. Keres jumped back. It probably saved the driver's life.

"Shit, what did you do that for?" Keres yelled.

"Why the hell did you shoot at them?"

"Why? Really? Why do you think? They're fucking cops."

She looked back at the cops. The driver was yelling into a radio mic. She could see the feet of the other one lying on the ground next to the door. Blue lights pulsed and mixed with the orange of the fire. She thought she saw his leg move. Prayed that she had. God, let him be alive. If they killed a cop, they would never stop searching for them.

Then John was in the passenger seat, cold and calm. But his reaction only made it worse.

"Time to go," he said.

"Keres shot a cop."

"Okay. Let's go."

"Okay? Okay? It's not okay. Not at all. What about Justice? Where is he?"

"He's on his own. This is too big. Cops will be swarming this place in minutes. We gotta go now. Justice knew the risks. We gotta get clear while we have the chance. Can't go back to Rockville now."

She forgot about everything else happening outside for a moment and snapped her head around to look at him. Rockville was their code. Their safe word. He was telling her that things were much worse than they appeared. And things were pretty bad as it was. Justice was likely dead. Someone was working against them or had set them up. Her eyes flicked to the mirror and Keres in the back.

"Time to go. Do your job."

. . .

Lisa had always loved speed. Ever since the summer day she'd beat Robbie Harmon on a dare and rode her skateboard all the way down Leaverman's Hill.

She dropped the van's gearshift into reverse and turned the lumbering old Dodge around on the narrow wharf. It felt like trying to get an elephant marching in the right direction. Each second felt like an eternity, and she kept expecting the second cop to fire on them. Or for reinforcements to show up. Finally, she got them pointed in the right direction and headed for the exit.

"Hold on," she said as she urged the van to pick up speed and aimed them at the employee gate. No use trying to be subtle now. The van went through the security gate like it was a toothpick. The big elephant was useful for something. But it wouldn't get them far. Not quickly. She spotted more flashing lights to the north, and her stomach sank.

She pressed the accelerator to the floor and heard the van's ancient V6 wind up and try to respond. It was agony, but slowly her speed crept up. She kept one eye on the mirrors. The blur of lights behind them resolved into four separate instances. Two cars went left toward the docks. Two kept coming straight. Coming after us, she thought. If she'd been local or had more time, she might have tried something more evasive. Tried to lose them in the old, winding streets of downtown Portland. But she'd only had time to study and practice the escape route. She'd looked over the map and various surface streets, but not enough to avoid a concentrated hunt by police. Not for long. Her best option was speed. Try to put enough distance between them until they could come up with a better plan. Even at this late hour, the police would need to slow down and be cautious through town. But she didn't need to be. She gripped the wheel tighter. The van inched above 80. The side panels vibrated, and she felt a grim smile crease her face. Even on a hopeless, last gasp attempt to avoid jail, she couldn't suppress it. If she was going to go down, she'd go down speeding.

The van topped out at 85 before the crappy tires and alignment threatened to shake them apart or toss them off the road. She held it there and concentrated on keeping the van pointed straight. As she predicted, the two squad cars chasing them fell away through the commercial district, but she knew they'd be back.

Lisa drove through the downtown shopping area and shot past the on-ramp for the freeway. She decided she would push the van as fast as she could on the smaller, more narrow surface roads. The big, open highway was tempting, but she knew it would be a mistake. It would give her fewer options and allow the authorities to close in and coordinate their capture more easily. She hoped the turns and cross streets and unpredictable traffic on the state roads would negate at least some of the speed advantage the more nimble police cruisers had on them.

"Take the bridge," John said.

They had been driving for 15 minutes, though it felt like hours. Her hands ached and knots tightened her shoulders. She glanced at him and then at the side mirrors. The flashing lights had fallen back but were closing again. There were now four cars in pursuit. It was like watching an anaconda slowly swallow its prey. She had driven off the map in her head. The turnoff for the vehicle switch was miles behind them. She felt a pang of regret that she'd never get to drive that yellow RS200. She would have blown the doors off the cops in that car. Now, she was driving in cement and did not know where they were going. She couldn't think beyond the next minute and just drove into the dark and tried to stay ahead of the chasing lights. To stay free a little longer. She concentrated on the road and fought hard to keep any images of Michael from entering her mind.

"What?" she said. The engine noise made it difficult to talk.

The trees and shrubbery alongside the road were thinning out. The pavement was broadening to include a shoulder. City roads becoming county roads. Wide country roads. The lights inched closer. Keres moved back to the last row of seats near the windows and was yelling something, but she couldn't hear him over the whining roar of the engine.

They passed a large, green road sign on the right. Big, reflective white letters in a clean font. Hard to miss. Tecumpscot River Bypass Bridge—2 miles. They had roughly 90 seconds.

"Take the bridge," John said again.

"What's the bridge going to do?" she asked.

"We're not going to outrun them, Lis. You know that better than I do. We need to do something they don't expect before they get organized. We need to go somewhere they can't follow."

"You're not—"

Sixty seconds.

He cut her off. "It's our only chance. The only one I can see. This time of night they will be happy to keep us in sight and set up some kind of takedown or just let us run out of gas."

"Or do something stupid."

"Do you have other ideas?"

"The money?"

Thirty seconds.

He looked over at her. "We can always hustle another job. If we're free. I will not let you or Michael see me grow old in jail. Plus," he cut his eyes to the back seat, "the cops aren't our only problem. Even if we get out of this, we can't go back to Rockville, remember? We need to end this soon."

Ten seconds.

She braked hard and then cut the wheel to the left. The van briefly went up on two wheels, the tires screaming, but this time the elephant's weight helped; it didn't tip but settled back on four wheels. She pinned the accelerator and drove onto the bridge.

The Tecumpscot River Bypass Bridge was a long, low brutalist concrete span with equally spaced concrete pillars running its length and anchoring it into the riverbed. There were no graceful arching steel supports, trusses, or cable supports. It was simple, efficient engineering to get the road over the river. Strong and durable. No doubt a good use of public funds.

They were now into a false dawn that cast the bridge in gray shadows. Lisa tried to glance down at the water below, but it was still too dark to make out any details. Maybe it was better to not know.

"Where?" she asked.

"Close to the apex as you can. The deepest water will give us the best chance," John replied.

A concussive noise and smoke suddenly filled the interior of the van. Lisa briefly took her hands off the wheel to cover her ears and the Dodge lurched sideways and came dangerously close to crashing. She regained control, but their speed dropped. She could see the driver of the lead pursuit car now. In her mirror, he looked young with thin dark eyebrows, a sharp nose, and a pointed chin. Later, she would learn his name was Gary Parker.

"What the hell, Keres?" John yelled. Lisa's ears were ringing, and she could barely hear her husband. She risked a glance over her shoulder. Keres had shot out one of the rear door's windows and was aiming a second shot. She jerked the wheel. Keres fell back into the seat and the shot missed. She could feel his eyes on her now, but she ignored it and went back to concentrating on the road.

"We don't need to kill a cop. Another one. That will get us all the needle," John said.

"We don't get out of this, I'm dead anyway."

"What does that mean?"

But Keres didn't answer, just turned around and started shooting again. Boom. Boom. Boom. Whatever he was carrying must have been large caliber. Even with the window shot out, the noise from the gun was like a physical blow to Lisa's chest.

John grabbed his seatbelt and latched it, then double-checked that Lisa's was secure. "Roll down your window now, otherwise it will be too hard in the water," John said and rolled his down. She did the same. He looked at her and then took her right hand. "Do it."

CHAPTER TEN

Lisa gripped John's hand, pushed the van up to 90, then jerked the wheel to the right.

They got lucky with the bridge design. The heavy concrete usage hadn't extended to the edges of the bridge. The safety barriers on each side were a five foot tall honeycomb of thin, crisscrossing steel. It might make it difficult for a jumper to climb over and it might slow a sedan down, maybe even keep it on the bridge, but Lisa suspected it would be no match for a speeding elephant.

"What the hell?" Keres screamed. The echo of the gunshots had faded. Now she could hear him. She flicked her eyes to the mirror. Keres had spun around, trying to keep his balance against the van's lurching turn. He knew right away what was happening. She could see it in his eyes. She watched as he brought the gun up. The end of the barrel looked impossibly big in the mirror's reflection.

She was right. The van had no problem with the slim bridge barricades. They hit the bridge at an angle, 20 feet from the apex. There was a jolt and then a high-pitched screeching as the broken barriers scraped against the van's side panels. Then there was a moment of complete silence before the van pitched forward and plunged down toward the black water.

Later, Lisa remembered only seeing the day's first slices of sunlight, early morning oranges and golds just peeking through the riverside branches.

She didn't remember the impact.

She didn't remember the shots.

After the rending of the barrier, the wisp of quiet, and then the blink of sun, it all went black.

She woke up to a nightmare. But she was alive. For the moment. Freezing river water rushed in the open windows. She could see the bottom of the river 15 feet below through the cracked windshield. She noticed a small hole in the windshield where the water spurted through like a fountain. A strong current pulled the sinking van downriver. Water filled the footwell and was already nearing her waist. They needed to get out. There wouldn't be much air soon. She reached down and unbuckled her belt. It took two tries with her numb fingers. She floated free. She turned to John in the passenger seat and met an empty stare.

"No. No. No. No."

She reached out and grabbed him and saw the gaping wound on his forehead. It creased through his hair and exited above his left eye.

Someone screamed and she twisted around to look for Keres before she realized the noise was coming out of her mouth.

The water rushed in higher.

She blinked back tears and looked away. Time for tears later.

She looked again toward the back of the van and this time

she saw him. Keres hung over the last row of seats. She could see a splotch of blood around the spiderweb-like cracks in the back window. The impact had thrown him against the back doors and knocked him unconscious. She left him there. She also left John. There was no choice. The current kept pushing. The van listed to one side. She'd have no way out soon. She kissed her fingertips and pressed them to John's cheek, then she turned her back, pulled herself through the window, and kicked for the surface.

Just as red spots bloomed in her vision and the urge to open her mouth became unbearable, she broke the surface with a gasp. She looked around. The bridge was already disappearing in the distance. She could just make out the tiny cars and small black dots that must be the police. She doubted they could see her, even if they were looking.

The black water rushed around her. Lisa had always been a strong swimmer, schooled in the riptides of the Southie beaches and the cold Atlantic. She didn't panic. She let the current carry her, using her arms and legs when necessary to avoid debris, until the bridge was out of sight and her legs were going numb. A dull ache began to spread up her neck. She got scared of hypothermia. When she spotted a sharp bend ahead, she slowly began working her way to the side.

She stroked hard as the turn approached, but the river appeared determined to keep her. It sucked at her arms, and legs, and chest. It held her in place and then dragged her back to the middle and pushed her under. She fought to keep her mouth shut and the river out. She couldn't let it win. It already had one of them. It couldn't have both. She could feel her strength fading. She didn't know this river. This could be her last best chance. She put her head down and kicked, even though she couldn't feel her legs.

The current picked up more speed as it whiplashed around the bend. She felt like a limp rag in a washing machine. She could see tufts of swirling white water along the shore. Her shoulders screamed. She gave one last effort, churning her arms and kicking her legs until her entire body vibrated with effort and then cramped in one painful spasm. She stopped. She was done. She let her arms and legs slump into the brackish water. And they scraped against gravel and sand. The river rolled her over and threatened to suck her back down its throat, but she reached out and grabbed some vines and weeds hanging over the bank's edge. A tree grew off the side, half in, half out of the water, providing a screen as its roots and branches reached into the water. She went hand over hand, using the weeds as grips until she rested her head against the thick, firm branches of the tree. She rested a moment, then pulled herself up onto the shore. With the absolute last ounce of her strength, she crawled 20 more yards until she was sure the foliage hid her from sight and collapsed in the moss and leaves. She lay there for a long time staring up at the dawn sky but thinking about John still down, forever down, in the dark water.

She woke up sometime later with her teeth chattering despite feeling the warmth of the sun on her skin. Cold and disoriented, she sat up and looked around. The sun was higher. It now cleared the tops of the nearby trees, but not by much. She estimated she'd been out for an hour, maybe more. She could hear animals skittering around in the woods. Birds were chirping. Somewhere off in the distance, she could hear the low thrumming of traffic. John was gone, but the world continued to spin.

She heard a heavy, clumping sound, almost like feet approaching, and she froze. Had the police recovered the van yet? Did they know she'd escaped? Had they already found her?

Thunk. Thunk. Thunk.

She shivered as her body fought to get warm and bit her tongue to stay quiet. But after five minutes, the sound didn't change. Didn't come closer. Didn't call out. She realized the rest of the forest on the edge of the river was not silent. The noise didn't spook the birds and squirrels. She stood and walked in a small circle. She paused and tried to pinpoint the location of the sound. It was coming from the water. She walked back to the tree she'd used to climb out of the water. She looked down into the angle between the bank and the extended branches and spotted the source of the noise.

She might have laughed if she hadn't been so goddam sad.

PART TWO: NOW

CHAPTER ELEVEN

Bradley Cobb sat in a leather chair on a small dais and tried not to fidget as the tech finished setting up the equipment. The man in the black suit sat in a matching chair to Cobb's right. Cobb would never admit to being nervous. Not even to himself. He'd trained himself to never betray an emotion unless there was an advantage or a reason to let the other person see it. He was confident his face betrayed nothing, but when he glanced over at the man in black, he had the feeling that the man saw right through his mask. It was an unfamiliar feeling for Cobb. He was used to being the apex predator in any room. For the past 25 years, this had rarely been in doubt.

Cobb studied the man. The man looked back without averting his eyes. His face was a mask of stone. Forget trying to read his thoughts or emotions, Cobb didn't know his name. He wasn't even completely clear about who the man worked for. Cobb had suspicions, but, despite his best efforts, he hadn't come up with any definitive answers, which was a kind of answer by itself. The only thing Cobb knew for certain was the man favored black suits and solid-colored ties.

This was their fifth meeting, his wardrobe had never varied. Today's tie was red and held in place with a plain silver tie clip. Cobb knew one other thing, he realized. When the man in black promised something, money or materials, he delivered. He then expected results in return.

Today's test was the first full simulation. Cobb and his team had proved the viability of the system before, but it had been within choreographed and controlled conditions. Today's test was still controlled, there was no way they could let this loose yet, but it was the closest they'd gotten to real-world conditions. Success today would be a big step. Cobb had felt like he'd been on this road for a long time, but now he could finally see the finish line. Then he could reap the rewards. Once they'd mastered the controlled simulations and moved the project out of the lab, the industrial and commercial applications would be huge. It would start with the military or intelligence, of course; most tech, whether or not the public knew it, started in the military, probably somewhere in counterterrorism these days, but Cobb knew it would quickly spread to law enforcement and then to the wider consumer market. The defense contracts alone would be worth hundreds of millions, but in five or 10 years, the consumer patents alone would be worth billions. Cobb was ready. But it wasn't just the money. He was already rich enough that he didn't have to think about money. Plenty of people were rich. He wanted to leave a mark on history. He wanted to be remembered for generations.

The man in black's mouth twitched, or maybe Cobb just imagined that, and he said, "Ready?"

Cobb looked down at the technician. He was a senior engineer, but even he didn't know the full scope of the project. Cobb kept all the individual departments in the dark. He'd shuffled departments to different parts of the country to further stifle leaks or curious employees from asking too many questions. Everything was siloed for security. Each department worked on a minor component of the design or implementation. The smarter ones might piece things together, but they were often intelligent enough to keep their mouths shut. If they didn't? Cobb gave them a generous severance and a severe nondisclosure agreement. If that didn't work, and this had only happened once, so far, he was willing to take more extreme measures to dissuade them.

The technician had heard the question and nodded. The technician left and Cobb stood and walked down to the controls. He sat and hit a series of buttons on a laptop that was hooked up to an array of monitors. The largest monitor sat in the center of the grid and gave a view of a city street. It could be any street, in any mid-sized city in the country. The view was crisp and precise. This was not grainy, washed-out surveillance video. It was all rendered in pixel-perfect high def.

There was a large office building with a revolving glass door in the center. To the right of the building was a storefront for mobile phones. A window decal proclaimed, 'Buy two phones, get a third line free!' in a loud pink font. To the left was a quick mart. A New Yorker might call it a bodega. Cobb could see a man behind the register, just inside a door that was propped open. People walked up and down the sidewalks. It wasn't crowded, but it was bustling. Two cars and a taxicab drove past.

It was all fake. Cobb had used the man in black's resources to hire a Hollywood set designer to build a very lifelike underground soundstage. Cobb hit a button, and the large glass panels beside the monitor array went from opaque to translucent. The man in black stood and walked to the glass. The street scene from the monitors played out far below him.

"Impressive," he said.

"Verisimilitude is important in these kinds of tests," Cobb replied.

"Who are the other people?"

"Actors. They believe they're shooting B-roll for an upcoming TV pilot."

The room lapsed into silence. All three men stared at the screens. Occasionally, Cobb hit a key or adjusted a knob on the panel in front of him. The air conditioner kicked on inside the room with a low hum. Cobb studied the monitors and tried to see the faces more clearly. He watched their posture and the way they walked. He saw nothing unusual and eventually sat back. The man in black had selected the test subject. Cobb didn't know who it was. It was a blind test.

Six smaller monitors, three on each side, surrounded the large central screen. The three on the left showed various charts and graphs of environmental data. These were super-fluous with the controlled conditions of the soundstage, but important to capture and test, especially if something went wrong. The three screens on the right were a blur of activity. The top screen showed lines of code scrolling past. Too fast for even Cobb to read. The second showed a changing view of the street scene from alternate cameras, and the third rotated between various headshots and other, more candid snapshots.

Five minutes passed. The man in black stood at his shoulder. The city scene continued. Cobb tried to remain calm and appear confident. People entered and exited the office building. Some used the revolving door, while others went through the standard set on the left. Cobb wondered if they'd been told which ones to use or were given some freedom to choose. He noticed the cars repeated. There were only three cabs. He spotted the same dented fender pass by. He was about to make a comment, just to break the silence, when the screens on the right changed. The code at the top sped up to a blur while the photos below stopped on a single headshot. The alternate camera zoomed in on one person.

"Potential target identified," Cobb said. "Proceeding to second-level scan."

The man in black shifted positions to better view the monitors.

It was a woman. Cobb watched the main monitor and saw her enter the scene from the left and pass the bodega. She was in her late 40s, maybe early 50s, and wore navy slacks with a matching blue and white patterned V-neck blouse. She had dirty blond hair, cut stylishly, so it fell across one eye. She wore dark Ray-Bans with gold rims and carried a large bag in one hand. She could be a bank executive heading for her office. Or in advertising, meeting a client for lunch. She didn't look suspicious or out of place.

"Second-level analysis complete. Confidence in potential target 99.14 percent," Cobb said. "Pre-cog percent is 94.32."

"How did it pick her out? What were the markers?" the man in black asked.

"It doesn't like the bag or the glasses. Clothes don't match expected socioeconomic data. The pulse rate is elevated. Eyes mildly dilated. Trace narcotics detected."

"You can check the pupils through the glasses?"

"Yes. Tertiary views can get behind sunglasses unless the subject is wearing goggles or a mask."

The man in black nodded.

Cobb continued, "Jean Statler, 51 years old. Served seven years, starting in 2012, on 10 for robbery and felony assault. Paroled in September '19. Two parking tickets since. No other arrests or interactions with law enforcement. Currently works as a cashier for Walmart in Benning, Texas. Parents are deceased. One sibling, a younger sister. No contact in the last eight weeks. One checking account with Wells Fargo. Balance of $528.45. Four active credit cards. Credit card debt of

$4382.34. A current credit score of 480. Active on Facebook and Instagram."

Cobb paused and looked over at the man in black, but he remained impassive. A stray thought floated through Cobb's brain that he should never play poker with the man. That was unlikely to happen. After today, he might never see him again. It all depended on the next two minutes. "Continue with deployment on potential target?" he asked.

"Any additional or other potentials?" the man in black replied.

There was a slight pause as Cobb scanned the data. "No, everyone else is below the threshold. The next possible is 1.32 confidence percent."

"Then by all means."

Cobb opened a new screen and keyed in the access code. Nothing happened for 30 seconds. Nothing visible to the naked eye. Then a new set of data flowed onto one monitor.

"Active tracking on."

The woman stopped briefly on the sidewalk and looked at something in her bag. She pulled out a mobile phone, flicked the screen, then put it away and continued to walk. She turned at the office building and used the revolving set of doors to enter. The view on the main monitor changed to one from inside the building lobby. The camera continued to change as it tracked the woman through the lobby. They watched her smile at the guard sitting at a reception desk and then walk to the elevator bank.

"Payload deployed and successful transmitting."

The screens on the left changed again, and biometric data replaced the environmental data.

Cobb hadn't seen it happen, even with the high-def screen, and he knew what to look for. He kept his eyes on the screen but felt the man in black lean forward. It was the equivalent of a shocked gasp. Cobb suppressed a smile. It was going better than he expected.

They watched a fish-eyed view from the elevator car as the woman ascended and exited on the fourth floor. The woman walked down a hallway to a door, double-checked the nameplate on the wall, then knocked. There was no sound, but she must have received a response because, after a moment, she turned the handle and entered. The view switched to a small room. To Cobb, it looked like any waiting room at a suburban dentist or doctor's office. A young woman sat behind a desk at one end. There were six matching chairs, three against each wall, with a low brown coffee table in the center with a spread of magazines on top. A large plant added a splotch of green in the corner. The young woman smiled and said something and indicated the chairs. The target nodded and sat in the middle chair. She ignored the magazines and took out her phone.

The laptop chimed. Cobb flicked his eyes to the monitor. A number was lit up in red.

"Body temperature rising," Cobb said.

It ticked higher as he watched. The woman wiped her brow. She looked around and shook her head like she had water in her ears. Her core body temperature continued to rise. It passed 100 degrees. The number flashed on the screen. They could see the woman perspiring freely. She stood up. She put her hands over her ears.

In the small control room, Cobb also stood, mirroring the woman on screen. The fake receptionist was no longer smiling. She'd pushed back her chair and was pressed against the back wall. The door opened and a third woman, this one wearing a white coat and pushing a crash cart, entered. The target took a step forward and caught her foot on the coffee table's leg. She fell to the ground and started convulsing. Her temperature hit 110 degrees according to the data on the screen. White foam bubbled from her mouth and mixed with a trickle of blood from one nostril. Cobb watched the heart rate line slow and then flatten.

It had all gone wrong so fast. Again.

He turned, ready to defend the test, and found the man in black smiling.

CHAPTER TWELVE

Martha Wells looked up from the cozy mystery she was reading and glanced at the prison gate. Still no movement near the doors. She flicked her eyes to the dashboard clock. 12:20. She'd been told all prisoner releases happened at noon, but she figured they did not hold these things to strict deadlines. In her experience with the justice system, everything ground along at its own pace. It usually got there in the end, but rarely on time. She could wait. She got paid either way.

Cobb had called yesterday afternoon with two names and a request to be outside Stanhope Penitentiary in Maine in two days. She was in the middle of tracking down another bail jumper, a typical Wednesday for her, and while she would have liked a little more of a heads up, she took the gig. It was something different, and Cobb always paid promptly and paid well. He was also the type of guy you didn't turn down when he called, not if you wanted to hear from him again, and she needed the juicy revenue boost that Cobb's semi-regular calls produced.

So, she'd put Earl Munroe's file aside and started

researching the names Cobb gave her. She could narrow down Munroe's location through the internet just as easily in Maine as she could from Jersey City. Martha had caught his brother Larry two years ago at their uncle's place down in Virginia. She smiled at the memory. Martha wasn't a petite woman, but she was still a woman and they had scoffed at her as she stood on the porch and announced her intention to bring Larry back to New Jersey for bail jumping. She'd made sure to get the tea extra hot, and she sipped it to make sure the 10-minute car ride hadn't cooled it off too much. It scalded her tongue. She tossed the tea in Larry's face, kneed him in the balls, and snapped the cuffs on before Larry's daddy could spit out his wad of Skoal. Dollars to doughnuts, Earl would head in the same direction. The entire clan was two sandwiches short of a picnic.

She'd parked across the street from the prison entrance in the visitor and employee lot. Posted signs reserved the first row for visitors. She didn't know if someone was coming to pick up Keres, and official visiting hours weren't until the afternoon. She didn't want to stand out. She parked toward the back, mixed in amongst the employee cars. She briefly heard her mother's hectoring voice complaining that standing out for Martha was the least of her problems. Sometimes she was glad her mother was dead. Then she felt guilty for having that thought, which set off another round of recriminations from her dead mother.

She let the old ghost prattle on in the background, much like their daily phone conversations used to go, as she gazed across the road at Maine's high-risk, high-security prison. If you only took in the blocky, white, one-story facade, you might think it was a medical center or dull office park. Maybe that was the point. To blend in with the neighbors. Or make the poor kids visiting Daddy feel a little better. She doubted it fooled any of the kids. Or the neighbors. Once you bothered to look left or right, you'd quickly notice the double line of fencing, the interior one topped with pointed razor wire. Stanhope was not an office park.

She shifted in the Buick's front seat. She'd left her personal car at home and rented this one from Hertz at the Newark airport. She didn't want to put the extra miles on her old Subaru driving to Maine, but right now she was missing the lumbar support and generously broken in seats. The rental was boring and nicely anonymous ('just like you, Martha,' her mom's ghost added), perfectly invisible in its blandness, and had a roomy interior, but after the long drive, she felt as if she were sitting on the jagged edge of a tin can.

She read for 15 more minutes and then put the book aside. The cat would eventually figure out the murderer. She wasn't sure why she read them. A type of comfort food, she supposed, without the pesky calories. She picked up the file that Cobb had sent yesterday via email. She had printed it out and placed it in a file folder along with her own research. Martha knew technology; she needed to in order to survive in her business, but she also liked to sift through paper when she could. Most of Cobb's paper was the prison file for inmate number 453928, George Keres. The file itself was a reminder of Cobb's reach and power. An unsubtle message not lost on Martha. George Keres had served his full hitch, 25 years, and generated a lot of paper. Transfer orders. Intake forms. Medical evals. Behavior and psych reports. Most of it was meaningless, Martha thought, but you never knew. Keres had largely been a model prisoner. A few dustups early on, but not a peep as he grew older. It even included a few achievement certificates for computer courses and letters of note from a couple of wardens. The most useful piece of information was the photo. Keres might have been a model prisoner, but he still looked like a con. His eyes were squinting and mean even in the bleached-out, black-and-white photo.

Cobb had sent her a second name. Lisa Sullivan. Unlike Keres, Cobb hadn't followed up with additional details and Martha had found little on her own. The file was disturbingly light. Lisa Sullivan had made a splash in the news 25 years ago as part of a robbery gone wrong in nearby Portland, Maine. The same robbery that had landed Keres in Stanhope. Lisa, on the other hand, had disappeared. Sullivan hadn't been seen or heard from since that night. It wasn't easy to disappear in the modern world, but she'd managed. Or she was dead. That was Martha's bet. Twenty-five years was a long time not to make a mark on the world.

She briefly thought back to what she'd been doing 25 years ago. She would have been a few years out of college, but not yet starting in the PI business. She thought of those times as the lost years now. Five years of aimless wandering after she quickly realized an English degree from Vassar was useless unless she wanted to teach. She'd given that a try for two years. One year of high school and one year of fifth grade. She enjoyed the summers off but realized she disliked kids, no matter the age. Ron and his thick mustache flitted through her mind, and she felt herself flush. Those lost years hadn't been without their fun.

A flash of sunlight across the Buick's windshield brought her back to the present. One of the glass doors had swung open and a solitary man carrying a plastic bag walked out. Martha picked up the camera with the telephoto lens from the passenger seat. The man paused on the sidewalk outside the doors and tilted his face up to the sun. Martha had watched this scene before. It wasn't the first con she'd picked up outside prison doors. It was the reaction to the first taste of free air. Free sun. Freedom itself.

Martha snapped off a few more photos, then watched the

man turn and raise his middle finger to the doors before he resumed walking. "Typical," she muttered. The sophomoric gesture told her more than anything in the official file about the type of man she was now tasked with tracking.

She took another series of photos as Keres walked down to the road and sat inside the small plastic bus shelter. One bus had already passed at 12:05. She'd checked the schedule. The next bus wasn't due until 2:05. She doubted the guards were unaware of that fact when out-processing an inmate. One last kick in the ass before they took off the leash. Keres settled in to wait. She took one last photo and put the camera back on the seat and picked up her book. Unlike Keres, she got paid to wait.

CHAPTER THIRTEEN

George Keres sipped his beer and watched the door to the bar. Fifteen minutes later, he smiled when Joyce Peters walked in. This was the third time he'd seen her in here in the last week. The first two times he'd simply stayed on his stool, drank his beer, and made sure she noticed him. Today would be different.

He watched her hang her purse from the little hook under the bar top and take her usual spot near the door, two stools down from the video poker machine. He sat at the opposite end of the bar, perpendicular to her, with a view of the door and the television mounted over the bar. Currently, the television was showing a sports-talking heads program, muted, with the closed captioning running. He feigned interest. Sports had never been his thing. He'd bet the occasional big game or threw some money at a Triple Crown race, but he mostly stuck to cards. His drug of choice had been baccarat and poker. The bartender, a thin, wiry woman with gray hair and a hatchet face, said hello to Joyce, poured a glass of white wine and topped it off with seltzer from the gun, and slid it in front of her without being asked.

George watched a second muted sports show, this one with more game highlights, while he finished his beer. He turned and looked at her occasionally. He took his time. No use rushing it. This was his best lead. If this didn't work out, he might have to give it up. So he sat. He ordered another beer. He watched Joyce drink a second glass of wine. Time and patience were two things he'd become familiar with in prison.

Prison didn't teach you much about women, but he thought he'd do okay with Joyce. The two previous nights, no one had approached her. Dark and down-at-the-heels, McLaren's was a place for drinking first, second, and third. Everything else fell far down the list. He knew from his research that Joyce was two years younger than her sister Lisa and was close to, but not over 60. The years of steady drinking and sitting inside smoky bars, however, had done her no favors. George didn't think he'd have a problem getting where he wanted. Finding what he wanted? He wasn't so sure. He could always kill her. That was an option.

He ordered another beer and waited until he was halfway done, then caught her eye again across the bar. He tipped his bottle at her in single drinker solidarity. She responded in kind and smiled back. The stool to her left was open. George slid off his seat, walked down, and sat next to her.

"Hi, I'm Cal. Can I buy you a drink?" he asked.

"I wouldn't say no, Cal."

He signaled to the bartender for another round.

"You took your time," Joyce said.

He smiled and rubbed a hand over the starfish-shaped scar on the back of his head. "I don't like to rush things."

He felt her eyes roam over him as the bartender put their drinks down. By the time the Maine penitentiary system had finished up with him, he was old enough to collect Social Security but the plain prison diet, no alcohol, plenty of sleep, and the exercise yard had given Keres the look of a man 10 years younger than his true age.

"Cal short for something?"

Cal had been Keres's longest cellmate. A Scottish guy with a halo of red hair over his entire body. He was a nasty prick who had murdered four people. He never figured out why he did it. "Callum. It means dove."

He bought her more wine and tried to get her talking about herself. She was happy to talk about her job as an administrative assistant. "Screw you if you think I'm just a phone call answering secretary. My boss couldn't find his dick without my help." She burped. "Not that I'd ever help him with that task. But I keep that place running. Without me, no one would ever get paid." He listened for well over an hour about all the ways she was keeping the credit union afloat. He had no idea if it was true or not, didn't particularly care, but he made sympathetic sounds and kept the white wine coming. She stubbornly refused to talk about her sister or any other family. She briefly mentioned a daughter who had passed away but just saying her name appeared to sober her up, so he steered the conversation away from children and she slipped back under.

"Parents are long gone. Kids are gone. Family... gone..."

She seemed on the verge of saying more, but the resistance or habit was so strong, so long ingrained, that she held her tongue.

"I've been alone since I was 13," Keres said. "No shame in that. You make your own way in the world."

The battle-ax behind the bar kept cutting him looks. He tried to project benign, old man horniness, but wasn't sure he was pulling it off. Bartenders were keen at reading people. It felt like she was looking right through his stiff new shirt to the jailhouse ink underneath. He didn't like it. While Joyce mumbled another useless story, he imagined brief fantasies of what he could do to the old, wrinkled bitch after the bar closed. It would be a distraction, a pleasant one, but one he couldn't afford. Not right now. Tonight was his best shot. He had to focus. He arranged his face into a smile, nodded along, and held Joyce's eyes.

By 9:30, she must have put away at least a full bottle of Sutter Home. Maybe more. He was a little concerned she might slide off the stool onto the floor. Given how sticky the floor felt under his feet, he wasn't sure he could stomach touching any part of her if that happened. He inched his stool closer. She closed her eyes and leaned into his shoulder.

Fifteen minutes later, when the bartender had her back turned filling a large order, he grabbed her purse, guided her off the stool, and out the door. He kept her upright on the short walk to her townhouse.

She was too far gone to ask how he knew the way.

CHAPTER FOURTEEN

Keres slipped off the bed and put his clothes back on. He'd done his best to appear interested and engaged in the bedroom. He'd seen enough movies to know the roles, expectations, and sounds he was supposed to make. He wasn't sure if it made a difference or not to Joyce. He didn't care. He knew many men in prison who needed the release of sex. It was like breathing to them and they would take what was available. George had never felt any arousal around other men, locked up or not. The urge for intercourse had never been that strong in him. In prison, it withered and died. He remained celibate and was big and mean enough that no one bothered him. He had other passions.

The glowing alarm clock on the bedside table said it was just after 3:00 a.m. He'd dozed lightly for a few hours. He never fell into a deep sleep. The constant hum of prison had cured him of that. Joyce lay twisted in the sheets on the opposite side of the bed. She snored with a faint whistle, like a tea kettle approaching a boil. She would be out for hours. If they were both lucky, she wouldn't remember anything at all about this night. After witnessing her prowess at the bar, George thought waking up with blank spots in her memory might not be unusual for her.

She'd perked up when they stumbled inside, momentarily shaking off the inebriation, and insisted they have one more drink. Maybe it had been a long time for her, too. While she went into the bathroom, he took the zolpidem pill, street Ambien he scored from his efficiency neighbor, from his pocket and crushed it with the beer bottle she'd handed him and dumped it into her wineglass.

Joyce's bedroom was on the second floor. He went back downstairs to the kitchen. He bent and drank water from the tap until it sloshed in his stomach. He'd nursed his beers, drinking one to Joyce's two or three, but it was still more alcohol than he'd had in years. He needed a clear head for the next part. He opened the refrigerator but found it almost empty save for cans of Slim-Fast high-protein shakes, a plastic clamshell of wilting salad mix, and various Styrofoam takeout containers. Joyce was not a cook. He settled for a half-empty container of fried rice. He finished the container, tossed it in the trash, and started to search.

Joyce's townhouse was a classic Boston three-decker layer cake. Three slim stories, made of wood, each story with a set of windows facing the street. The front facade's blue paint and white trim had faded. There was a small porch on the second floor, but it didn't extend up to the third like some designs. He knew some owners lived on one floor and rented out the others, but Joyce hadn't done that. Her unit was whole and undivided. It was another reason Keres thought she had likely maintained some contact, or gained some money, from her long-lost sister. How was a glorified secretary affording this place by herself?

The first floor included the kitchen at the back, then a living room, a full bathroom, and the front room with the street-facing windows. An old wooden hutch and round dining room table filled the front room. Keres didn't need to run a finger over the table to know it was dusty and rarely used. He gave the room a cursory check but didn't believe it hid any of the secrets he was looking for. He was guessing Joyce's bedroom or the third floor. People kept secrets in two places: their bedrooms or as high as they could reach.

He climbed back up the stairs. The second floor mirrored the first floor. Joyce used the largest room as her bedroom. He peeked in on her. She hadn't moved. He spotted her phone on the nightstand and then stepped inside. He picked it up. Password protected, but she'd also set up the biometrics. He took her hand and pressed her thumb against the screen. It opened. He dropped her hand. She stirred, mumbled something that sounded like 'Danny,' then rolled away.

He scrolled through the phone's apps. It was heavy on mindless games and social media. Could they communicate securely through those? He doubted it. Those companies would hoover up that information. He felt certain Lisa wouldn't trust them. He checked anyway, but found nothing interesting. He scrolled through her texts. She wasn't a heavy user. They appeared to be mostly password reset prompts, spam, or a few friends asking about getting together for drinks. Nothing that smelled remotely sisterly. The email app had even less personal correspondence and more spam. He had the thought that sending emails disguised as spam might work well but dismissed it as too risky. You'd never know what the automatic filters would trap and what they might let through. Still, he filed the thought away. Not a bad idea. He replaced the phone on the nightstand.

He riffled through both nightstands, her dresser, closet, and even under the bed, but found nothing.

The other two rooms farther down the hall were also bedrooms, one for a boy, one for a girl, though Keres wondered about the last time anyone had slept in the beds. Each remained frozen in time. Old, fading posters hung on the walls. Ray Borque on the Bruins in one. Mid-'90s boy bands in the other. He could see clothes hanging in the half-open closet in the girl's room. Each room had a small window with the shade drawn. Both rooms smelled of creeping mold and rotting paper.

He went up to the third floor. The first room was another bedroom. This one had the bland decorations of a guest room. Then a bathroom. He wondered if he'd need to check the basement when he found the back room converted into a home office. There was a corner desk with a laptop, separate keyboard, and monitor on the desk. There was nothing hanging on the walls, but there was matching all-white furniture filling out the room. A short, stubby file cabinet was to the right of the desk, then a throw rug, and a low couch with thin cushions that looked uncomfortable. Keres saw Joyce, excited to transform the house, starting on the top floor. She had picked out all the furnishings in a rush, maybe from a catalog or online, getting it delivered, and then... running out of steam. She got this one room done. That was it. But maybe it would be enough for him.

He sat at the desk and opened the laptop. It beeped softly, came out of hibernation, and asked for a password. He tried the obvious ones without success. He couldn't decide if Joyce was more a physical records person or digital. She was old enough that he'd say she probably preferred paper, but she was comfortable with technology from her work, so it was a toss-up. He'd come back to the laptop if he needed to. He swiveled in the chair and pulled out the first drawer of the filing cabinet. Pens, rubber bands, a notebook, Post-it notes. All the various junk that fills up any office drawer. He moved to the lower drawer. Hanging file folders, labeled, in alphabetical order, from front to back: bank, cell phone, credit card, life insurance, medical, miscellaneous, mortgage, taxes, utilities, and warranties. Bingo. It was a lot of paper, but it was neat and organized and it might allow him to bypass trying to break the laptop security. Whatever her problems or demons, at least Joyce's workplace organizational skills applied to her home office, too.

He started with the bank statements. He doubted they would be of any use. He guessed the sisters were both smart enough to avoid a straight transfer or deposit, but he had to rule it out. There were seven years of statements. He went methodically through one year and found nothing suspicious. No regular, unexplained deposits. No single large deposit. Nothing that caught his eye. He flipped more quickly through the remaining six years but also came up empty.

Next, he moved to the credit cards. He'd heard about people moving money through credits and balance transfers but found nothing like that in Joyce's statements. They were remarkably predictable. Regular charges for a gym membership, Netflix, Fifth Avenue Liquor, McLaren's, a few restaurants. It looked like once a year she went back to the same resort in Jamaica. He pulled out the mortgage. There was no mortgage on the triple-decker. She'd paid off the house two years ago.

He grabbed the most recent cell phone statement. Not a lot of calls. He grabbed the previous two months. Not a lot of repeat calls, either. No regular Sunday night check-ins. He took out his phone and took pictures of all three months, then considered it, and snapped photos of three more. If Lisa didn't call her sister within six months, she wasn't calling. But he couldn't run the numbers here. He'd have to do it later. He moved to the taxes, but his enthusiasm was dimming. Taxes were summary-level documents. If he found anything, it would be in the details, difficult to spot, or someone else would have found it earlier.

He spent 10 minutes reading 1040 forms and discovered nothing of interest. Joyce had some mutual funds with Fidelity and a 401(k) through her work, but the balances were modest and showed regular contributions. Keres didn't know if she would have enough to last her through retirement, but he did know that it was unlikely she was funneling any of his money into those brokerage accounts.

He put the taxes back and kicked the drawer closed, trying to keep a lid on his frustration. He spun in the chair and tried to think of what to do next. Joyce was his best shot at getting a line on Lisa and his money. It was the reason he'd started his search in Boston. People run but they always come back to family. Or at least keep in touch. That's what all the statistics said. Most bail bondsmen looking for jumpers didn't chase after them, they just went and sat outside mama's house. Or the girlfriend. Or the sister. But there were always outliers. Maybe Lisa really had just walked away completely, from everyone. It was rare, and it was hard, but it was not impossible.

Keres's eyes fell on a stack of thick hardcover books piled up next to the radiator under the window. There were 30 books, maybe more, in two towers. He'd just spent almost three hours talking to Joyce. She never once mentioned books. TV, movies, wine, work. Yes. Reading? No. She didn't even have a bookcase in the room for the hardcovers. He thought back to the bedroom and didn't recall any books on her nightstand, just a remote for the TV. The only books he'd seen in the house were in the girl's room.

He walked over and picked the top one off the pile. It appeared to be a thriller or a mystery, judging by the cover.

He opened it. It was stiff. The binding cracked as if Joyce had never read it. There was a sticker on the front: Book of the Month Club. Maybe someone gave it to her as a gift, he thought. Something didn't feel right, but people gave terrible gifts all the time.

He dropped the book back on the pile and returned to the desk. He took a thumb drive out of his pocket and plugged it into the laptop's USB port. A program he'd gotten off the dark web started running in the background to break Joyce's password. He leaned back and let it work. It could take anywhere from a couple of minutes to an hour, depending on how strong she'd made it.

It surprised Keres as much as anyone that he had an aptitude for computers. And it wasn't just computers. No one ever told him his exact intake IQ scores, but he could tell they impressed Goldsmith, the group shrink at Stanhope. He'd never done well in school in the past. He'd only made it to the 11th grade, but maybe he'd lacked the proper motivation.

The prison system did not have great computers, but they were still useful tools. He taught himself SQL, PERL, C, C++, then Java. He devoured programming books as the wave of technology built throughout the '90s and 2000s. Inmates got heavily monitored internet and email in 2010. No one wrote to him, but he didn't mind. The internet let him escape his cell even in a limited manner. With his new skills, it didn't take long for Keres to sidestep the monitors and exploit that access.

The laptop refreshed and the password prompt disappeared and then the desktop loaded with a snapshot of a beach at sunset, maybe from that annual Jamaican resort. He was in. He checked his watch. He had another hour. Joyce would be out until noon, but he wanted to be out of the house before first light. He pulled the USB drive and inserted another. This one was empty. He started copying the hard drive.

After an hour, it was clear to Keres she wasn't communicating with her sister. Not through the email on her laptop or her Gmail account. He'd been thorough. He checked the drafts folder and spam. They weren't being tricky. That faint tickle of doubt grew a little stronger in the back of his mind. Maybe Lisa really was gone. Maybe the money was gone, too. And the chance for revenge. A hot flicker of anger replaced the doubt, and he itched to find something sharp in the kitchen and take his frustration out on Joyce, but he pushed it back. He couldn't do that, not yet; it would bring too many questions and too much attention. He put the chair back the way he found it, gave the room one last glance, and then went back down the stairs. Time to go.

On the first floor, he checked the windows for any traffic, but the street was quiet. He was about to slip out the door when he spotted the pile of mail on the kitchen counter. There was a stack of white envelopes, likely bills or credit card offers, along with a supermarket circular and a larger, white rectangular box on the bottom. A stylized circular logo covered the front. He recognized it from the stack upstairs. Book of the Month Club. Another wasted book, thought Keres. He walked down the hall into the living room. There was a large couch, a large flat-screen TV, a coffee table, two end tables, an armchair, and a couple of houseplants, along with a few generic framed prints. A *People* magazine and a *US Weekly* sat on the coffee table next to the remote. No books. No bookshelves.

He went back to the kitchen and picked up the box. He turned it over in his hand. It was Joyce's name and address. He shook it and it shifted slightly. It certainly felt like a book inside. He went to the butcher's block and pulled out a thin knife. He carefully slit the packing tape along the bottom. A thick hardcover slid out into his hand along with a packaging slip. *Since We Fell* by Dennis Lehane. It smelled like cut wood pulp and the briny tang of ink. He flipped through the pages and then stopped.

Clever, Lisa. Very clever.

CHAPTER FIFTEEN

George Keres paced around the tiny room. The caffeine from the to-go coffee he'd picked up on his walk back might have been a mistake. He felt anxious. The acid in his stomach burbled. He checked the time again. Thirty more minutes. He could hear the guy next door watching an early-morning game show. His efficiency apartment was a one-room square on the second floor of a bland building in East Boston. Planes descended regularly overhead to land at Logan. It had thin walls, a thin mattress, and a shared bathroom at the end of the hall. It was the cheapest place he could find, and it still put a severe dent in his bankroll.

He'd served his full sentence by choice. No early parole even though he'd been eligible and might have gotten it. When he walked out of Stanhope, he didn't want to be on any paper. He didn't want a tether around his neck. No parole officer. No check-ins. No mandatory group home. He wanted to be free to come and go as he pleased. He wanted to find Lisa Sullivan.

But that also meant he was on his own when he finally

walked out Stanhope's front gate. After his room and board fees, plus his tab at the prison commissary, his jobs inside, first in the laundry, then in the cafeteria, had netted him just under $2300. An almost laughable amount, even considering, by the end, with his longevity and good behavior record, he was up to a first-grade pay level. And he knew he was lucky, so to speak, to be charged and sentenced in Maine, so at least he got paid. Some states gave inmates nothing for their labor.

He'd used most of that nest egg to purchase parts to assemble his laptop and buy a cheap phone. He might have walked out of prison alone, but he wasn't empty-handed. He had new skills, and he planned to use them. Prison had trained his body to live on very little food, but he needed a computer and a phone. He was confident with his laptop and his brain he could find anyone. And he was going to prove it. Lisa Sullivan had officially been missing for 25 years. Many assumed she was dead and had been since the bridge crash. Keres knew they were wrong. He'd seen her swim away. He knew she was alive and out there somewhere with his money.

He'd put the rest of his meager cash toward the crappy apartment. He was paid up through the end of the month. He hoped he wouldn't need to go an extra month. He hoped his investment in white wine at McLaren's would pay off. He didn't want to get overconfident or get ahead of himself. He had a lead, a good one, he thought, but he didn't have Lisa yet.

He sat on the bed and checked that the software he needed was set up on the laptop. Then he checked the battery on the phone and its connection to the laptop. He tested the small speaker and double-checked the Wi-Fi signal. He was piggybacking off the car rental place across the street. Satisfied, he went back to pacing and waiting. He just needed the billing department out in bumfuck Iowa to open for business.

He forced himself to wait until 10:05 then dialed.

"Thank you for calling Book of the Month Club. This is Steve in the billing department. How can I help you?"

Keres hung up. Steve wouldn't work. He waited two minutes and tried again.

"Thank you for calling Book of the Month Club. This is Melissa in the billing department. How can I help you?"

"Good morning, Melissa. I'm calling about my mother's subscription." Keres's voice came out of the small speaker sounding like a chipper Midwest housewife. Keres pictured a short, slim blond in activewear who had just finished a spin class and was starting her to-do list for the day. "She's getting older and, I'm afraid to say, a little forgetful. She's missed a few payments on other accounts. I just got off the phone with the bank. That was a nightmare I didn't need. I'm just checking if everything is okay with her account with you. She loves her books."

"I'm happy to help and sorry to hear about your mother. I hope she's just getting older and not... something worse."

Keres smiled. Bullseye. Melissa would work just fine. "Me too, Melissa."

"Let's start with the account number."

"Sure." Keres read off the information from the photo he'd taken from the box's packing slip.

"Okay, let's see. No, no problems on our side. The account is up to date. Everything looks good."

"That's great. It's a relief that I might not have to go through this with all her services. Listen, I'm going to take over the payments for her, but I'm still old school and like to send checks. If I send a payment to you guys, is there someone I can add to mark it for attention?"

"You can just put for Billing and Invoice."

"You know, I can do that, but I'd prefer to put a name on there, too. How about a manager or director?"

There was a pause. Keres forced himself to stay silent. He didn't know if he'd lost her, or she was just checking a database of canned answers. He wasn't sure if she went off script or not, but Melissa came through in the end. "You can mark it, David Smith, if that makes you more comfortable. He's a billing manager."

David Smith. Was there a more perfect example of a boring, corn-fed, anonymous name for a midlevel manager in some Midwest cubicle farm? Keres made himself smile so it came through in his voice. "Thank you, Melissa. That makes me feel more comfortable. As I said, I'm old school. I prefer sending money to a person, not just a department, even if David Smith never actually sees it."

Melissa gave a polite chuckle. "I understand. Is there anything else I can help you with today?"

"No, you've been very helpful."

"Wonderful. Have a great day."

He hung up and switched the voice modulation program over to the male voice he'd selected. It was an English voice, light accent, clipped, officious. He tested it. Perfect. He sounded like a pompous prick. He waited a minute, then redialed.

"Thank you for calling Book of the Month Club. This is Denise. How can I help you?"

"Good morning, Denise. May I speak to David Smith in Billing, please?"

"Certainly. One moment, please."

There was a click and then silence before the plastic rattle of someone picking up a handset.

"David Smith."

"Good morning, Mr. Smith. My name is Clark Goodall and I'm calling from the fraud team at National Bank. We've had multiple calls recently about fraudulent charges to our customers' accounts coming from your business."

"Really? I don't think that's true. I've heard nothing about that."

"That's why I'm calling, sir. We don't like to publicize these things. We understand the business and systems involved are complex and sometimes mistakes happen. Could we start with one of the affected accounts and see if you can spot anything on your end?"

"Sure."

"Great." Keres read off Joyce's account number and heard Smith punching it into the computer on his end.

"Let me see," Smith said. "I'm not seeing anything incorrect on that account. Are you sure?"

"That's what we hope to figure out today. Like I mentioned, we've had customer calls. In addition, our systems have flagged a few transactions as suspicious."

"Well, I see nothing suspicious in this account, just regular subscription billing for a basic membership."

"Mr. Smith, do you see a charge for $45.50 in April of this year?"

"No. I don't see that."

"Okay, how about $110.75 in June?"

"No, that's much higher than anything here."

"Okay, Mr. Smith, this is helpful. Can I get you to verify the address you have on file for that account?"

"Uh. I think maybe I should call you back."

"Mr. Smith, I will not ask you to disclose any payment or credit card information. Your relationship manager asked me to call you. We are hoping to resolve this quickly and speed is of the essence. If you can confirm the address, we can start sorting this out."

"Okay. I guess that's alright. It's 500 West Mammoth Road, Box 74, West Adams, MA 01244."

"And this account has been active for how long?"

"The membership has been active for over 15 years. That's as far back as this system goes."

"Thank you, Mr. Smith. That address matches what we have on file. Okay, you've been very helpful. I'll tell our systems people the charges are not originating with Book of the Month Club."

Keres hung up and disconnected the mobile phone from the laptop. He plugged the address into Google maps and knew what he'd likely find. He was right. Mailboxes USA. According to their website, it was a third-party commercial shipping and fulfillment center that also offered postal boxes for rent. He'd never heard of West Adams. He zoomed out on the map. It was on the far northwestern edge of Massachusetts, nearer to Albany, in neighboring New York, than Boston.

He didn't let himself feel disappointed. He was getting closer, peeling back each layer.

CHAPTER SIXTEEN

Max woke up from a light doze. The woman next to him was asleep on her stomach, her long legs tangled up in the sheets. He watched a bead of sweat run out of her hairline and down the divot of her spine until it hit the edge of the sheet. He ran a finger lightly along her ribs until it met her hips. She was beautiful, no one would deny that, but he'd also noticed a sadness that jutted out ahead of her and nudged people aside. No, not sadness. That wasn't quite right, Max thought. It was melancholy. Beauty and melancholy. He wondered which side of that coin had attracted him more? And what that might say about him? He looked up at the room's cheap popcorn ceiling and shook his head. He couldn't get out of his own head. Not even now.

Her name was Theodora. No last name. He'd had dinner at the diner and then began the two-mile walk back to The Cliffside. Even though the calendar said March, once the sun went down, it felt like January. He'd hunched his shoulders and stuffed his hands deep into the pockets of his coat. He was three steps past The Night Owl's door when he stopped. He looked up the road. It was only two miles. He made the walk multiple times a week, but tonight the road looked dark and empty and cold. He turned around and went inside.

The bar wasn't crowded. There were maybe 15 people inside. Even on a Friday night, things never got too busy at The Night Owl. Max had been in a few times in the past couple of months. Not often enough that he knew the thin old guy's name behind the bar, but enough to get a nod of recognition. He spotted Vic sitting in the back with Gil and another guy he didn't recognize. He gave a wave but didn't head in their direction.

She sat at the bar drinking something dark from a rocks glass. There were two empty seats on either side of her. A man named Lenny, whom Max knew because he worked for a local sanitation company and picked up The Cliffside's trash, sat at the far end of the bar underneath the television. He gave Max a look that said, 'Good luck with that one,' and gripped his pint glass tighter. Max ordered a beer with a bourbon sidecar from the old man. The woman turned and looked at him. They noticed each other. After that, neither of them needed much luck.

She rolled over onto her back and pulled the sheet up a little higher. "What was your name again?"

Max said, "Michael." It wasn't a lie. Not exactly.

"Are you going to call me?"

"No."

They both knew it was a one-night thing, more nature than nurture, so it didn't surprise him when she replied, "Good."

He found his jeans laying at the foot of the bed. He pulled them on, then found his socks. He could hear her moving behind him, doing the same. Where was his T-shirt? He glanced at the phones on the bedside table. His personal showed a missed call. He didn't recognize the number. He realized she'd asked him a question.

"Sorry, I missed that," he said.

"I asked what you do here. Are you the super?"

She looked around the room. He tried to see it through her eyes. It wasn't much. Not very different from a thousand other cheap rooms across the country.

"Something like that."

He found his shirt hanging off the back of the chair near the window that fronted the parking lot. The shades were only half-closed. He rarely bothered to close them anymore. There were few customers or passing traffic at this time of year and he'd grown accustomed to waking up to the view of the snow-capped mountains. Suddenly, a bright light filled the small room. He shielded his eyes with a raised forearm and squinted but couldn't see anything. Outside, a vehicle's high beams pointed directly into the room. Or directly at him. This was no accident or lost driver turning around in the lot. This was deliberate. They'd been waiting. Maybe watching. His brain finally caught up and he stepped to the side, up against the door.

Theodora stood by the bed in charcoal slacks and a white lacy bra. She held a high heel in one hand and held the other hand, palm out, toward the light.

He heard the vehicle's door open and then muffled voices. The headlights stayed on.

Max crouched low. "Get down," Max said.

"What?" she replied.

She was a simple target if they started shooting. His gun was in a locked carry case in the closet. The key was... he felt his pockets. Shit. Where was his keyring? "Get down," he whispered again and scanned the room, trying to spot his keys. There, by the leg of the bed.

He crawled over and snatched them off the floor, then

pulled at her pant leg. "Get out of the light." Her face was half amused, half concerned, but she took two steps to the right. He immediately felt better. The bathtubs in this place were solid metal under the cheap veneer. If he could get her in the tub, she might survive if they decided the best approach to take him was to hose the place down with bullets. He was about to pull her into the bathroom and dump her in the tub when a voice called out.

"Thea!"

Her, not him. He glanced up. "Ex?"

"Something like that."

He almost laughed with relief. He stood, pulled his pants on, and went to the window.

"It's definitely over. We separated more than a year ago. At least, I did. I moved out, got my own place, but he won't sign the papers. I've taken to carrying the damn documents around in my bag just so I'm ready when he finally accepts reality."

"Thea!"

He'd moved closer to the unit's door. He hadn't turned off the headlights. The vehicle's door was open. The other voices he'd heard were just talk radio.

"You sure he's going to ever do that?"

"Yes."

But he could see the question in her face. Maybe she'd started out sure, she just had to stay strong and weather the storm, but a year later, her confidence was showing cracks. This was not the first time, nor probably the second or third time, she'd witnessed this performance.

"It gets old," she mumbled.

"He does this regularly?"

"No."

Another lie. He didn't know if she was trying to protect

him or just didn't want to get into the sordid business with a virtual stranger. Either way, he liked her a little more for it.

"What's his name?"

"Ted."

Max stepped to the door and opened it. It was cold, and he wished he'd taken the time to put on a coat or sweatshirt. His bare arms prickled with goosebumps. At least he'd put on shoes. Ted was a dark silhouette in the headlights, 10 feet from the door. Max could make out the shape of a pickup truck behind the lights. He also noted the dark shadow of a beer bottle dangling from Ted's right hand. Thea pushed past him. She'd dressed, but in her haste had misbuttoned her shirt.

"Goddammit, Ted, you can't keep doing this?"

"Doing what? Finding my wife in random hotel rooms with other men? You're goddam right I can't keep doing this."

"I'm sorry," Thea said to Max.

"What the fuck are you apologizing to him for, you whore? You should apologize to me."

Max winced.

"Ted, you're drunk. Again. Go sleep it off and we'll talk in the morning," Thea said.

Max heard Ted let out a long breath as he decided. "You know what? That's a good idea, Thea. You always knew what to say. You always thought you knew the right answer." Ted turned and walked back toward the truck. Max watched him toss the beer bottle, and he heard it bounce twice before it broke somewhere in the dark. Ted shoved the driver's side door closed. "But you know what, Thea? Sometimes words aren't enough."

They heard Ted open a latch in the back of the pickup and then a heavy clunk as he moved something aside.

"What does Ted do?" Max asked.

"He's a mason. Mostly builds retaining walls and walkways for rich people he resents."

"Does he have a gun in that truck?"

"No," Thea said. Then a moment later, "I don't think so."

Ted turned and Max kept his eyes on the man's hands. As he passed the edge of the headlights, Max glimpsed a wicked-looking silver-tipped hammer. Ted turned with a smile and hit the low rock wall that surrounded The Cliffside's roadside sign. The rock on the end split neatly in the middle and tumbled to the pavement.

"Ted, seriously, what are you going to do? Beat up some guy I picked up in a bar? What's that going to prove?" Thea asked.

Ted didn't answer her. "Did you enjoy your time with my wife?" he asked Max instead.

"Not sure you want me to answer that, Ted."

That put a hitch in Ted's step. Now that he was closer, Max caught the glint of a watch face on Ted's left wrist. He carried the hammer in the same hand. Ted was a righty. Max stepped out of the doorway, off the small walkway, and down onto the cracked asphalt of the parking lot. He wondered how drunk Ted was. How much damage he'd have to do before Ted gave it up?

"You think you're a funny guy?" Ted said.

Max didn't bother to answer. Ted spit. "Fuck it." He came at Max in two shuffling steps and feinted a swing with the hammer, as Max thought he might, before trying a haymaker with his right. Max ducked and stepped to the left and Ted's punch missed by three feet. Max set his feet and waited until Ted recovered and turned to face him. Max shifted his hips and hit Ted in the nose with a straight right. He pulled it a little, but he still felt the crunch of the cartilage beneath his knuckles. Back in Philly, probably sitting near the ring in his gym even at this late hour, Max thought Ronnie Shelton would have approved of his technique. Ted's nose released a gush of blood that covered his Makita power tools sweatshirt. It was truth in advertising. Ted was a tool. He dropped the hammer and put both hands to his face.

Max had tunnel vision, not losing focus on Ted, but was vaguely aware of additional headlights pulling into the parking lot. He hoped Ted's friends hadn't been waiting in the wings to jump into the fray. He could handle Ted, but not Ted and two or three of his friends.

Max thought the busted nose might be enough to bring Ted to his senses, but it appeared he'd maybe polished off at least a six-pack in his truck. The alcohol was still fogging his brain. He ran at Max with a scream. Maybe he'd seen it in the movies. A war cry. Ted was a big man. He stood at least a few inches over six feet and had the neck, shoulders, and gnarled hands of someone who did physical work for a living. If he got those hands on some soft part of Max, he could do some damage. But he was also stinking drunk. Max could smell the beer wafting off him. Max sidestepped again and grabbed Ted's wrist as he blundered past. He used the man's momentum to follow along behind him as he cranked an elbow lock behind Ted's back and guided him directly into one of the walkway's old iron support poles. There was a hollow dung and then Ted took two staggering steps back and sat on his ass. Ted's mouth dropped open. His eyes watered and mixed with the blood still streaming from his broken nose.

Max looked around. He didn't want Ted's friends getting a cheap shot in with his back turned. He put a forearm up to his eyes. But there were no friends. Vic's truck sat perpendicular to Ted's in the lot.

"Vic, that you? What are you doing here?"

"Saw you at the bar. Just checking in. But it looks like you have it under control."

The truck's tires spit gravel as it backed up and left the lot. Max didn't know what to make of that, but he'd figure it out later.

He looked over his other shoulder. Thea still stood in the walkway, a hand up to her mouth.

"You still have those papers in your bag?" She nodded. "Why don't you grab them. I think he's ready to sign."

Thea disappeared and returned holding a sheaf of white papers and a pen.

Ted signed the papers without comment. The run-in with the pole appeared to have knocked some sense into him. He started to cry as he handed the pen back to his soon-to-be ex-wife.

CHAPTER SEVENTEEN

Bradley Cobb listened to the two men bicker over the speakerphone. They were like children arguing over Christmas presents. They did little to deserve the gifts yet couldn't help but complain and dicker and angle for more. Cobb reminded himself that letting them argue was the primary point of the call, even if it irritated him. A large part of his job as CEO of Cerberus was to assuage egos in Washington with calls or dinners like this. He knew it was necessary, but it was the part of his job he liked the least. He was still most at home doing the coding and engineering. He liked the tactical day-to-day decision-making. He looked at his watch. Ten more minutes and he could end this torture.

The second line on his secure phone lit up. He pushed the button to take himself off mute.

"Senators, I apologize, but I'm going to have to cut this short to take another call."

It was always good to remind these two that they were not his most important callers. They had a certain amount of power but limited. "I'll have our assistants set up another call in a week to finalize the details for the demonstration. Thank you." He disconnected without waiting for an answer and hit the button for line two.

"Martha. It's been two days."

If she heard the rebuke in his voice, she didn't react. "If you want a report on how long he's sat in his crappy apartment, I'm happy to oblige, but it feels like that would be a waste of your time. I'll call when there is something you need to know."

Martha Wells, the 50-something freelance private investigator from Jersey, was just about the only person who spoke to him this way. Some days, he admired it. Some days, he hated it, but Martha had proved herself very useful, so he let her get away with it. Up to a point. He felt like he rarely had actual conversations anymore. Most interactions, like with the senators, felt wholly scripted.

"And that's why you're calling now?" he asked.

"Yes. He's holed up in that apartment, only coming out to walk across the street for convenience store food. Seriously, Cobb, if you wait another week, your problem might solve itself. He'll likely die of dysentery from eating all that crap."

There was a pause that stretched past 10 seconds before he finally responded. "Let me be clear. I do not want him dead."

"I was joking."

"Right." But it was true. Cobb didn't want Keres dead. Not yet. "Why are you calling?" Cobb asked, letting some annoyance creep into his voice.

This time, she reacted. She dropped the jocularity. "He's on the move. He picked up a rental car this afternoon and we're headed west on Route 90."

"Any sign of Sullivan?"

"No, but Keres appears motivated. This isn't an aimless trip. He has a destination in mind. He took his computer and a plastic bag of clothes with him."

"Okay, stay with him for as long as it takes. And Martha?"

"Yes?"

"Don't play games with him. Or me."

He hung up. The timing was going to be close, but things were finally moving. If Sullivan was out there, with Keres chumming the waters, he was confident Martha would find her. Then, after 25 years of looking over his shoulder, he could finally correct his past mistakes.

Cobb maintained a small apartment inside the D.C. compound on the top floor of one of the secondary administration buildings. It allowed him to keep a close eye on things, especially now, so close to the end. Tonight, he was using a workstation connected to the lab's high-performance computers to model changes to how the bots transmitted wireless data through different plasma and bone densities. He tweaked the frequency and strength and hit enter. The internal temperature readings remained stable at first, then climbed. He stopped the sim. It wouldn't work. He sent emails to the different engineering teams with notes and ideas and then closed the software.

The call with Martha nagged at him. He was having second thoughts. It was an unusual feeling for Cobb, but this bit of ancient history was the exception in his life. Was Keres enough? Was using an outsider like Martha the right call? Could he do more? He was determined not to miss this opportunity and deal with it decisively this time. He needed to be all in. He was tired of having this sword hanging over his head.

He signed off his official lab account and then brought up some of the specialized software he'd installed. He navigated the folder directory to his notes on Lisa Sullivan. He'd read it all before, practically had it memorized, but he read it again.

He tried to find her in the past, thought he'd come close a few times, but the trail had been stone cold for years now. She was a ghost. He tapped the keys. Her sister was still alive, but that had always been a dead end. But her sister wasn't her only family. She also had a son.

CHAPTER EIGHTEEN

George Keres stared at the red dot marking the Mailboxes USA location in the far corner of the state. He knew he was still a few steps away, but this was as close as he'd been to her since the bridge. He was inching closer. A predator tracking his unsuspecting prey. Or maybe not unsuspecting. Did she know he was out? He thought she might. A woman as clever and careful as Lisa would likely track his progress through the system. Good. He smiled. He liked the thought of her knowing he was out there and still being unable to stop him.

He had known for a long time what he was going to do when he got out of prison. Find Lisa Sullivan and find his money. He'd known since the first day he went inside, and his focus hadn't changed. For 25 years, he'd dedicated himself to honing his skills for when he got out.

He stayed a safe five miles per hour over the speed limit and stuck to the major roads. West on Route 90 through Springfield, then north on 112 and 143. He didn't want to risk speeding or catching the eye of some bored backroads cop. It had taken less than three minutes to get into the rental car's system and set himself up with a prepaid reservation. The rental was a white Chevy Cruze. He hoped it was anonymous and as forgettable as it looked.

He stopped once for gas and to take a leak at a turnpike rest stop and arrived in West Adams three hours after he left Boston. He drove through the spartan downtown built around the spillway where the Houghton River split into smaller tributaries. Hulking brick warehouses dominated the town and once must have provided the reason and economic engine for the town. That boom time was long past. The town or optimistic developers had converted a few of the warehouses into apartments and smaller businesses, but far more remained boarded up and disintegrating. He spotted a few new businesses, a cafe, a wine bar, as he drove through, but the town felt mostly gray, tired, and down-at-the-heels.

He found the Mailboxes USA in an L-shaped shopping center on West Main, a secondary street off the town's central commercial strip. There were four businesses in the plaza. An urgent care center was the largest and took up the bottom of the L. A takeout pizza parlor, a Dollar Tree store, and the Mailboxes USA unit filled out the longer side with the shipping center tucked into the corner.

Keres pulled in and found a parking spot in the lot's second row that allowed him to see the front door. It was close to 5:00 p.m., but there was a steady flow of traffic through the parking lot. Most headed to either end, the pizza parlor or the clinic. He cracked the window and sat and watched for a half hour. No one entered or exited Mailboxes USA. At ten of six, a thin man wearing jeans and a baggy Celtics jersey hustled up the sidewalk carrying a large box and rushed through the door. He left again five minutes later with a piece of paper in his hand and no box. At 6:00, a UPS van pulled up outside and the driver spent five minutes shuttling in and out, loading and unloading packages and padded envelopes into the back before driving away.

Ten minutes after that, the lights went off inside and a man came out. He was potbellied with thick glasses and unstylish dishwater gray hair, parted and drooping over his ears. He wore wrinkled khakis and a red knit polo shirt that was untucked in the back. He locked the door, then pushed up on his toes to reach the top security lock. Manager or owner, Keres thought. Keres could tell just by watching the guy lock the door and pocket the keys that he was a humor-less asshole. He'd need to target someone else to try his next gambit. The guy walked to a silver Camry in the last row, climbed in, and drove off. Keres hoped the place generated enough business to require additional employees.

He continued to watch. Cars came and went, but more slowly. By 7:30, traffic had tailed off to the pizza parlor. Anyone looking for a takeout pie for dinner had come and gone. The Dollar Store closed at 7:00 p.m. The clinic was still open. Looking through the window, Keres didn't see anyone sitting in the waiting area. By 8:00, he decided he wouldn't learn any more tonight. There were less than 10 cars in the lot and he would soon become conspicuous just sitting there.

He started the car, backed out of the space, and drove around the end of the plaza by the pizza parlor. The space behind the shopping center was wide enough to accommo-date delivery trucks and backed up on a thin strip of forest before giving way to one of the smaller rivers. A chain link fence ran along the border of the property. In some places, the support poles were missing or bent, and the fence dipped and sagged along its length. The fence line held scattered trash and clumps of leaves. He drove slowly down the stretch of pitted and potholed pavement. He didn't envy the delivery drivers forced to come this way. There were three dumpsters placed roughly opposite the three doors leading, he presumed, to each retail shop. A lone light pole stood halfway along the fence. Its light wouldn't reach far. This wasn't a place people would choose to spend one second longer than necessary.

He steered closer to the building and braked to a stop outside the last door before the road cut to the right. He leaned over and looked through the window at the door's lock. There was a deadbolt above the handle. It didn't look like anything special. He wasn't a lock guru. He'd have to drill it, but he thought he could probably get through if he needed to. Did Mailboxes have an alarm? That was something to consider. He wouldn't be inside long, but he'd have to make it look convincing.

He started driving again before hitting the brakes abruptly at the right turn. A security camera sat high on the cornice of the building, pointing toward the clinic's back door. He edged the car forward a few more feet and spotted a matching camera on the opposite end of the building. They each looked new and relatively modern, at least from this distance. Likely mandated for insurance, he thought, in case of a break-in, given the drugs they probably had inside.

He took his foot off the brake and kept going. They had already caught him on camera. It would be more suspicious, if anyone ever looked, to stop and back the car up. If questioned now, he could just say he hadn't been paying attention and took a wrong turn. Or was simply curious about what was behind the building. No law against that.

He doubled back around the front and checked the pizza parlor end again to make sure he hadn't missed a camera there, but he hadn't. He could still go in through the back, but he'd have to think hard about it. He did not want to end up on video and, where there were two cameras he could see, there might be another that he couldn't. He thought about his next steps as he drove out of the lot and went to find a cheap place to sleep.

CHAPTER NINETEEN

Martha dropped her phone into the cupholder and shifted her weight more onto her right cheek. Seriously, who designed these seats? She let another car slide between her and Keres's white Chevy. He appeared to have the cruise control pegged at 70 and was content to sit in the middle lane. She had the sense that wherever they were going, the exit wasn't coming up soon. She adjusted her position again and flipped on the radio but only found commercials or bubble gum top 40 pop songs. She didn't mind that music but wasn't in the mood at the moment. She searched for an NPR station on the low end of the dial but came up with only static. She turned the radio off and thought more about the last conversation she'd had with Cobb.

She'd worked for Cobb occasionally in the past, mostly doing deep research on people or companies. Quietly digging past the obvious sources of information was one of her specialties. In her 20-plus years in the business, she'd gained many useful contacts and access to many databases. Some were more legal than others, but all of them were helpful. She did most of her work from behind a desk but going out into the field wasn't uncommon. She often had to verify locations before submitting a final report.

This was the first time for Cobb, however. He usually sent a terse message with an individual's or corporation's name and a request for as much background information as she could find and compile. Typically, she could see how Cobb might use the dossier she assembled in his business or political dealings, but this time was different. She couldn't yet discern what Cobb's ultimate aim was with Keres or Lisa Sullivan. She'd done more than just read Keres's prison file. She'd researched both of them. Keres was an open book and easy to peg, even without the prison file. He was a petty thug and grifter who likely had caused a lot more damage than the crime that ultimately landed him in prison.

Sullivan, on the other hand, she had found very little on, even in her special databases. Martha had looked hard, too. There weren't many people who could hide from her, but Sullivan had managed it. Martha had read all the accounts and retrospectives on the Lin Security robbery, the unsolved crime websites, and the internet rumors, but ultimately came up empty. Sullivan had disappeared the night of the robbery and hadn't poked her head up since.

Why did Bradley Cobb care so much 25 years later? During the chase, someone had shot and killed Gary Parker, a Maine state trooper. Martha had chased Parker down but didn't find any link or connection to Cobb.

When motives were murky, she liked to play it slow. Information was her only defense if this thing, whatever it was, went sideways. She'd told Cobb that Keres was on the move, but she didn't tell him everything. She didn't tell him she'd watched him pick up Sullivan's sister, Joyce, at a local bar and go back to her place. She'd needed two large Dunkin' regulars to stay awake long enough to witness Keres slinking out her door before dawn that morning. Now, less than 12 hours later, he was on the move. It wasn't a tremendous leap to figure he'd gotten something useful from Joyce. She'd keep the Joyce connection to herself for now.

In total, it all made her wary. She felt like she was walking on ice that was covered in snow. One false step could send her plunging into dark, frigid waters. She'd been useful to Cobb in the past, she knew that, but she also knew she was very replaceable. She had the sense that her work for him was off the books and as a sole proprietor with few stable relationships in her life... how long would it take for someone to notice if she went missing?

CHAPTER TWENTY

He veered off the game trail at the small brook, hopped over the water, slid between two trees, and then sprinted up the rock-strewn hill as far as his burning legs would allow before slowing to a walk. He clambered up the remaining scree to the flat rock that sat unexpectedly balanced on the top. He looked back down the way he'd come. Yesterday, he'd stopped at the maple sapling. Today, he'd made it five yards farther. That was progress.

His lungs still seared in complaint when he ramped up his heart rate and he could occasionally taste blood in the back of his throat, but he didn't think those were injuries. Not anymore. He'd have to live with some damage to his lungs, but the cost had been worth it. His head no longer ached with each running footstep and the spells of dizziness and vertigo appeared to be done.

He took in the view as he caught his breath. A carpet of thick trees covered the valley floor until they gave way to the rugged peaks of the Green Mountains in the distance. He'd started running parts of the Long Trail in the nearby national park to heal, mind and body, and burn off some energy. There was only so much he could do at the motel to distract himself.

"You're looking restless." Vic's words from yesterday echoed in his head. Vic had found him staring into the cracked and empty swimming pool in the motel's courtyard. He couldn't remember how long he'd been standing there. His hands had been stiff with cold, so probably longer than he realized. But was he feeling restless?

He shifted his gaze off the snow-topped ridge and looked down into the hardwood forest of yellow birch, sugar maple, American beech, and hemlock. There was no trail. On one run a month ago, he'd taken a wrong turn and spent most of the afternoon misplaced in the wilderness. Through the small pass, the valley was flat, forested, and mostly featureless save for the low rock outcropping he sat on. It was easy to get turned around and lose your bearings. He could see the mountain peaks through the forest canopy but wasn't familiar enough with them to sight his way back to the trail. You were unlikely to encounter another hiker, especially in the winter and spring months, when even the maintained trails were snow-packed or muddy and difficult to hike.

He'd gotten lucky that day and stumbled back onto a blazed section of the official trail and made his way back to the parking lot and his car. But the quiet valley called to him, and he had started running and hiking more in the uncharted sections of the park. He was more familiar with the area after a few months, but it was still wild and potentially dangerous. That only made it more seductive to Max. He liked the quiet stillness, maybe craved it as an antidote to other urges, the ones he kept locked up but occasionally escaped. Wild, feral feelings that drove him into the blackness. Stillness wasn't his natural state. He envied it. He was a man built to move through the world in constant motion. But maybe he could learn. Maybe that's why he kept returning.

He slid off the front of the rock and slid down the other side until he reached the tree line. It was time to go to work.

The heater in the corner rattled, shook, and then leaked out a stream of lukewarm air. The cheap faux wood paneling on the wall behind the unit vibrated. Max glanced up from the book he was reading, 5:00. Over the past four months, Max thought of the cacophony of 5:00 a.m. sounds as quitting time at The Cliffside Motor Lodge. He got up and checked the metal pan that sat under the heater. He took it outside and dumped it, careful to do it where no one was likely to slip on the frozen puddle that would inevitably form overnight. Not that the chance of a paying customer showing up was high. It was more for Vic's benefit. He went back inside. A weird vacuum effect made the loose panes of glass in the second door, the one that led to an interior courtyard, rattle. It happened to either door if you opened the opposite. He made a mental note to see if he could fix it. He walked to the corner of the small room and returned the tray to its place on the rug under the heater. Old stains, years, maybe decades old, already dotted the brown rug. He wasn't sure what he was trying to save with the pan, but he kept doing it.

Technically, as the live-in super, he was never off duty, but Vic said after 5:00 he could just post the sign in the office's window and carry the motel's phone in case anyone showed up late or needed something. The phone had yet to ring. Max himself was probably the last person to call the motor lodge. He'd been driving aimlessly west and north after leaving Lawrence's place in Boston. He stayed off the highways, took the rural routes, following some internal, perhaps irrational, compass, driving through the farming communities and small towns that dotted western Massachusetts. Max had been raised in the city, but he found he liked these places. Maybe it was nostalgia or not growing up with similar memories, but he liked the diners, the ma and pop hardware stores, the VFW halls, and Little League fields. Or maybe it was because the towns were small enough that he could keep an eye on everything. Discount chain hotels near the highway might keep him safer, but what kind of life was that?

He'd crossed the border into Vermont and ended up at Green Mountain National Forest, not realizing that trying to explore the area in December was a fool's errand. He'd quickly retreated to his car and followed a faded blue sign that promised lodging. He'd ended up at The Cliffside's parking lot and dialed the number in the office window.

"Yeah?" A whiskey-soaked voice answered.

"I'm looking for a room?"

There was a pause and Max thought that perhaps the connection had dropped, but the voice came back a moment later. "Just the one night?"

"That a problem?" Max's car was the only one in the lot.

"Nope. It's 50 for the night. That a problem?"

"Nope."

The Cliffside was a classic motor lodge motel. It had 12 rooms, shaped in an L, with each room's door opening directly onto the parking lot. A small office occupied the corner. There was an empty pool surrounded by a concrete patio in the interior courtyard along with two rusting charcoal grills guests could use. At least that was the theory. Each room had a pair of double beds, an old blocky television bolted to a dresser, but offering cable Vic was quick to point out, a mini-fridge, and a microwave. Two units, the so-called suites, also included a small kitchenette and mini stove, and cost an extra $25 per night.

Other than the low vacancy during the winter months,

the heaters sputtering to life three times a day was one of the more predictable things about the place. The Cliffside Motor Lodge was on a quiet state road in Chepstow, Vermont. Chepstow was a speck on the map. If it even appeared. The borders of New York, Massachusetts, and New Hampshire weren't far away. To Max, it felt like a good place to recover and regroup after his time in Philly. The ability to get into three different states quickly didn't hurt, either. If he found himself in a really tight spot, the border was less than four hours away. He was a man who liked to have options. He'd realized in the past few years that a man in his circumstances had to live in the background. As his friend Lawrence was fond of telling him, there were still many people trying to find him or simply kill him. Despite his efforts, trouble seemed to find him. Or, as he sometimes thought, he eventually went looking for it.

Chepstow and The Cliffside provided quiet and more. During the cold months, a blanket of silence hung over the place. If Max didn't venture the few miles into town for food, books, and other sundries, he might go weeks without seeing or talking to another person. He wasn't just living in the background. He'd become the background. Vic told him the summer and fall bookings paid for the rest of the year, but it was sometimes hard to believe in the winter isolation.

He'd ended up with a room for the night, stayed another, and then, a week later, got a job offer. Room and board, if you counted the office coffeemaker, plus 300 bucks a week to sit at the desk and handle any hassles that came up. Vic considered paying guests mostly a hassle. It was less than minimum wage, but Max didn't need the cash thanks to past adventures and Lawrence's business savvy. He also just liked to keep busy. Plus, he'd quickly grown fond of the ramshackle old motel. If he was going to encounter some of his old ghosts, there were plenty of rooms to go around.

CHAPTER TWENTY-ONE

Keres was back in the parking lot at 8:00 the next morning. The clinic was already open. Maybe they operated 24 hours a day. He watched a mother carrying a baby, a large bulging bag, and holding the hand of another young child struggle across the parking lot. He could hear both children crying before they disappeared inside the clinic.

At five to nine, he watched the same guy who had locked up the previous night park his old Camry in a spot at the back of the lot. He wore the same outfit as the previous day. Keres imagined he probably had a closet filled with no-iron khakis and red logoed polo shirts. His hair was slightly damp, and he carried a large travel mug of coffee in one hand as he dug the keys out of his pocket with the other and unlocked Mailboxes USA's front door. It looked like a well-rehearsed dance, minus any joy. Keres had a flash of the man carrying his coffee and opening the door every day for the last decade. Maybe he'd been ready to open an entire chain of Mailboxes USA when he started. A small business owner with energy and moxie to change his fortune. First, West Adams, then the world! Now, he just looked like a man hanging on, trying to get to the next pair of khakis and polos. Keres watched the lights flicker on inside as the guy disappeared behind a door into the back.

Keres sat and watched. He didn't feel bored or impatient. He'd waited so long already. What was another hour? The outside air was still novel. The freedom of movement still felt raw and fresh. The speed of the world still caught him off guard. Everything in prison was on a schedule. Usually, a very slow schedule, driven by the impulses of the guards. Out here, everything happened all at once. Or seemed to.

The manager of the Dollar Tree arrived at five to ten. At 10:30, a dented Civic with magnetic signs attached to the doors pulled in next to the pizza parlor. Two short guys with dark hair, thick shoulders, and the same rolling walk climbed out and went inside. A minute later, the neon green open sign glowed to life in the window.

The late morning was quiet. It surprised Keres the center could support four viable businesses. No other employees showed up. Not many customers either. Just the sad man with his limp hair. It occurred to him that he might have to figure out a way to time the next book's arrival and come back then to watch for Lisa. But the most recent book had only just arrived at Joyce's this past week. The next one wouldn't arrive for almost a month. Much too long to sit in the parking lot. He wouldn't go unnoticed that long. Nor could he afford even the cheapest hotel room that long.

He thought about grabbing a slice from the pizza parlor and starting the drive back to Boston when he noticed a lanky guy, early 20s, with blond hair to his shoulders and huge headphones over his ears walking across the parking lot. He was wearing wrinkled khakis and a red polo.

The guy flicked a cigarette away before he went inside Mailboxes. Keres had a clear view through the front glass.

There was no love lost between the two men. The manager pointed a finger at the guy's face and then waved his arm around. The guy shrugged and went through the door to the back. A moment later, the manager came out and picked up the cigarette butt with a small dustpan and broom. Keres smiled. No reason to go back to Boston just yet.

Keres pulled the door open and glanced around. The pizza parlor's kitchen took up the back half of the store. The customer counter bisected the space neatly in two. The register and soda fountain machine were off to the left. A short menu board hung from the ceiling. A couple of heat lamps warmed leftover pies behind a plastic sneeze guard. The dining area consisted of three red, molded laminate booths bolted to the left wall. A trash bin and a short stubby counter with four mismatched bar stools for singles were on the right. It smelled of grease, cheese, and sugar. America's perfume. Or was that gunpowder?

The young Mailboxes guy had taken a late lunch. He was sitting in the back booth, closest to the door, with his headphones on, halfway through a slice of mushroom. He didn't look up when Keres walked in.

Keres went to the counter. After a moment, one of the brothers he'd seen earlier came out from behind the oven. He wiped his hands on a stained apron.

"What can I get you?"

"Can I still get the lunch special?"

"Sure."

"I'll take that then."

"What kind of slice?"

"What's ready?"

The guy waved a hand toward the single slices under the lamps.

None of them looked appetizing to Keres. He'd never understood New England Greek-style pizza. Even when it's bad, pizza should be pretty good, but he'd never had good Greek-style pizza. This slice didn't look like it would change his mind. "I'll take the pepperoni."

"Warm it?"

"Sure."

The guy slid the slice onto a metal peel and flicked it into the conveyor belt oven. He adjusted a dial and then grabbed a paper cup and placed it on the counter. "$3.50."

Keres handed him a $5, took his change, and then filled up the cup with Coke from the dispenser. A minute later, his slice of pizza, the thick slab of cheese and circles of meat now glistening under the ceiling fluorescents, inched its way out the other side of the oven. The counterman snatched it off with his fingers and placed it on a double stack of paper plates and slid it across the counter to Keres.

Keres took his lunch and walked to the Mailboxes guy's booth and dropped into the seat opposite.

The guy looked up with a puzzled look on his face. Up close, he was less man and more boy. Keres doubted he could drink legally. Maybe he'd dropped out of high school. Patchy facial hair dotted his chin and jawline. Red acne dotted his forehead. He pulled the headphones off his ears. Keres could hear the bass thump of rap music.

"I know you?" the kid asked.

There was a name badge pinned to the left side of the red polo, opposite the Mailboxes logo.

"Nope. You do not, Brendan. But we might be able to help each other."

"I doubt it."

Keres picked up his soda and took a long sip, then inclined the cup toward the kid's shirt. "You work at Mailboxes USA, right? With that asshole of a manager?" Brendan's pizza was gone and his time for lunch was probably almost gone, too. He appeared to be getting ready to slide out of the booth and leave, but Keres's last statement made him hesitate.

"You know Dwayne?"

"No, not really, but I know the type. Always right, always pointing out flaws, always making things difficult. Just a walking headache. Am I right?"

"Yeah. Pretty much."

"So, I have a proposal." He looked over his shoulder as if checking to see if anyone was within earshot, but then wondered if he was selling it too hard. "I'm a private investigator and my client needs some information. And he needs it quickly."

Brendan hesitated, but then said, "Who's your client?"

The kid had taken the hook. Now, Keres just had to reel him in.

"That's confidential. But I can tell you it's an ex-husband trying to track down his old lady... ex-old lady, I guess, who ran out on him and his two kids and the alimony she owes the family."

"That sucks, but how can I help with that?"

"I traced her to box 74 at your store. You know it?"

Brendan shook his head. "No way. There are 300 boxes in there. About half rented out. Owners come in and out all the time. I rarely interact with them. I can't even see most of the boxes from the counter."

"Each box has a rental agreement, right? With a name, address, and payment method?"

"I guess."

"I need it for box 74."

Brendan leaned back, his eyes narrowing. "Don't you need like a court order or a warrant or something?"

"I'm not a cop."

"No, you said that."

"There is a certain time element here. My client is afraid if we go through... proper channels, the ex will get wind of it and split again. It's taken us a year just to get this far. I'll give you 20 bucks to make a copy and bring it to me."

Brendan tapped a finger on the laminate tabletop. The music from the headphones paused, then started up again with a new song. "Fifty," he said and leaned forward.

"Forty."

"Fifty."

"What if I just go to your boss and get him to do it?"

"Yeah, right. Good luck then. That prick jerks off to rules and regulations. Dwayne would never give you the info, no matter what sob story you told him."

Keres knew the kid was right and sharper than he looked.

"Fine, 50."

"Money upfront."

Keres reached into his right pocket and pulled out the money and held it out. Brendan reached for it and Keres snatched it back. "I'll wait here. Don't take too long."

Brendan shook his head. "No need. Dwayne always leaves at 4:00 to eat dinner at home before he comes back to close. He's too cheap to eat out. Wait until he leaves, you can come in and pick it up."

Keres glanced at his watch. Almost 3:00. "Fine." He held the money out. The kid took it and slid out of the booth. "4:00."

Keres had 100 bucks stashed in his left pocket. He'd gotten off light. Maybe 50 equaled 100 out here in the sticks. He'd have to remember that. And, if Brendan came through, he figured he was already 50 bucks in the black. He glanced down at his plate, then stood, dumped the congealed slice in the trash along with the half-empty cup. If he was in the black, he didn't need to settle for crappy Greek pizza.

.   .   .

Brendan came through with the agreement. At five after four, Keres watched from his car as Dwayne, the manager, gave Brendan some last-minute admonitions, which were greeted by a hand gesture that HR would not approve of after Dwayne turned his back and left. Keres gave it 10 minutes in case Dwayne forgot something and came back, then he walked across the lot to the store. Keres half expected Brendan to pump him for more money. It's what he would have done, but he didn't. It was pure commerce. Goods and services, in this case information, for a price. Brendan glanced up when Keres entered, then simply slid the single sheet of paper across the counter. Keres took it and left.

He read the information while sitting in the car. The name at the top of the agreement was Jill Williams. The entries for company or business phone were blank, but there was a home telephone listed. Keres figured they required some way to get in touch with customers. No email, but there was an address. The address was not in West Adams, 884 Mason Street, Clarkston, MA. Keres had expected that. She'd want to put a little distance between herself and anyplace she'd be risking exposure.

He continued reading. Fees and dense legalese filled the lower portion of the page. Jill Williams's signature was at the bottom along with a date, plus Dwayne Dreyer's signature as the authorized store rep. No wonder Dwayne looked beaten down by life. He'd been slinging rental boxes for over 12 years.

Keres plugged the address into the map app on his phone. The network access was spotty and slow but after 20 seconds, the screen redrew. By the most direct route, 884 Mason Street was 5.4 miles away, a 10-minute drive due east on Route 2. That surprised Keres. It was closer than he expected. He started the car and felt a flutter in his chest. So close now.

CHAPTER TWENTY-TWO

Keres's initial hope soon flatlined back to frustration. Eleven minutes after he left the Mailboxes parking lot, he pulled the car to the side of a quaint tree-lined avenue in front of 884 Mason Street in Clarkston. He looked out the window at Thomas Memorial Chapel on the campus of Clarkston College, home of the fightin' Cardinals.

He looked at the sandstone-colored Gothic cathedral. She hadn't picked a vacant lot or even a fake address. She'd picked this church. Why? Was it the first address to come to mind? That seemed unlikely. How many people knew the address of a church? Maybe she was worried the store would check if it was a valid address? That seemed more plausible but didn't solve the oddity of using the church's address on the agreement.

He picked up the agreement from the passenger seat and looked it over again. If the address was a dead end, he needed another way to crack this open. The spot for a credit card number for recurring monthly charges was blank. Keres assumed she'd paid in cash in advance or worked out some other ongoing deal with Dwayne Dreyer. Nowhere to go there.

Keres went back to the name and wondered if the store checked any ID before renting. Even if Jill Williams wasn't the name Lisa was using every day, it might still lead to some interesting places. He pulled his laptop out and scanned for Wi-Fi. He found a strong signal and didn't even have to hack anything to get online. Thank you, Clarkston College. But his good vibes didn't last. Jill Williams was a good name to use as an alias because it was so generic and common. A quick search found thousands of results across social media and the internet. He clicked through the first couple links, but quickly dismissed them. Too young, too old, too far away. He tried adding a few parameters. Jill Williams plus Clarkston. Jill Williams plus West Adams. Jill Williams plus Massachusetts. The first two brought back nothing. Including Massachusetts as a parameter brought back too much. It would take weeks to troll through everything, even filtering some results out automatically.

He had to give her some credit. Through luck, ingenuity, or experience, Lisa Sullivan had become very good at staying hidden. He closed the laptop and looked back at the church. Two women exited the main chapel doors and walked down the wide steps. They each carried a leather bag over their shoulder and were talking as they walked. Styled hair, conservative yet feminine clothes. Even from across the lawn, they gave off an air of education. It made him uneasy. Not scared, but uncomfortable. They were the type of women he'd instinctively shy away from. As he watched them walk across the gravel path and disappear behind another academic building, an idea formed in Keres's mind. A reason Lisa might have chosen that address.

.   .   .

One of the few moments from Keres's childhood that he cared about, or even wanted to remember, was Mule's Ice Cream Shoppe. An old Scottish man with a thick accent ran the shop. Or maybe he was Irish. Either way, he and his accent were foreign to young Keres's ears. Accent or not, terrible shop name or not, the place made wonderfully decadent ice cream and milkshakes. The handful of good memories Keres had of his father were never at home, but always in a window booth at Mule's with a thick black and white milkshake on the table between them.

It started a lifelong addiction to shakes for Keres. Prison may have cured Keres of any sexual urges, but it did little to curb his desire for dairy treats. Prison served milk in the morning and water for the rest of the day. So it might have saved him from diabetes, but for 25 long years, Keres only had milkshakes in his dreams. In the time he'd been out, he'd made up for the lost time, often forgoing meals in favor of a shake.

His dairy craving was the reason he was sitting in the Bates building by the window overlooking the quad in the second-floor cafeteria. He'd discovered the shakes on his second day of walking the campus. The cafeteria served a good shake: cold, sweet, malty with just a pinch of salt to make everything work together.

He'd spent the past three nights on his laptop on the motel's pitifully slow internet trolling through Clarkston College's website looking for Lisa Sullivan as Jill Williams. He thought she might have used the cathedral's address because she worked at the college in some capacity. Faculty seemed like a stretch given her background, but it took a lot of different staff to run a university, even one the modest size of Clarkston. So far, he'd come up empty. Each department had its own webpage and, while there looked to be some templates, there was enough differentiation to make doing anything other than clicking through one by one the only option. And while the sites listed most faculty members, they rarely included support staff. It might be a waste of time, but something told him to keep going. Maybe it was his lack of other ideas, but he stuck with it.

Around noon each day, he'd make the short drive over to the campus and just walk around. Lunch appeared to be the time when most of the campus went outside, either to get lunch, change classes, or just get some air. It was barely beyond the needle in a haystack approach, but it was the only thing Keres could think to do after the website.

His eyes would flick relentlessly across the heads and faces that walked the crisscrossing paths. He dismissed any men and any young women. He zeroed in on older women who looked anywhere from 40 to 60. He didn't know how time might have treated her.

Today, he sat in the cafeteria and stared out the window, having already completed three circuits of the quad on foot. He sipped his shake. His eyes moved across the thinning crowd, assessing and dismissing. Lunchtime was waning and his mind was wandering. He'd paid for the motel room in advance with cash and got a slight break on the rate in return, but now he found himself with only one day left. He'd need to decide his next steps soon. Maybe he'd been wrong. Maybe she'd chosen the cathedral address at random. Just plucked it off the map, legit, but a surefire dead end if someone ever became curious.

He was about to stand and toss the now empty cup when something in his brain pinged and brought him back to the present. He quickly focused on a group of women walking just below the wide windows. No, not them. His eyes went forward and back, racing along the path. Something had grabbed his attention. What was it? What? He knew the mind was the ultimate computer, the fastest microprocessor. If it threw off a signal, it meant something. He felt sweat bead along his hairline. His fists clenched. He pushed the chair back and stood. Looking. Scanning. There. A woman, riding a bike, her back now to him, on an outer path, weaving slowly between a few people. The biker turned at the corner and Keres saw her profile.

Gotcha, he thought.

CHAPTER TWENTY-THREE

Eddie stared at the screen. It was like a smudge or a very faint fingerprint marring a newly cleaned mirror. He took his hands off the keyboard. His brow furrowed. He glanced away and then back at the screen. Three large monitors encircled him at his desk. He looked at the middle one now. The smudge was still there. He blew out a breath, still not quite believing it. He brought up a new terminal window on the left-hand monitor. He pulled a Red Vine from the package near his elbow and popped it in his mouth. He chewed as his fingers danced over the keyboard. He compiled the lines of code. Still there.

He didn't spend that much time on this part of the database. It was boring. Tables and rows related to Lawrence and his various businesses. It held no interest for Eddie, but something in the larger log files had caught his eye and led him here. To this smudge in his clean code.

He took a moment to tidy up Lawrence's code. Eddie couldn't help himself. If he didn't do it, he knew he'd be thinking about it all day, so he just did it, like cleaning up after a toddler. It wasn't Lawrence's fault. Most people wouldn't see anything wrong with Lawrence's code. It was functional, but it wasn't elegant. To Eddie, it was like listening to a piano that was slightly out of tune.

But he didn't touch the smudge. He worked around it. When he had cleaned up, he sat back and took another Red Vine from the package and tried to decide what to do. He didn't recognize the smudge. It had no signature tics or tells. It used loops and expressions that were old. They worked, but there were other, newer functions that were better. Old or not, they worked. The proof was right there on his screen. He sat and studied the smudge but couldn't come up with any answers. He had no experience with this kind of thing. No one had ever done it before. He picked up the phone and called his brother.

Lawrence lived downstairs and two minutes later he was standing behind the chair, looking at the screen.

"Are you sure?" he asked. He was shirtless and wearing pale blue cotton pajama bottoms. It was 3:30 in the morning. Lawrence was used to Eddie's calls, but still groggy and annoyed when he answered. He was alert now. "I don't see anything."

"Remember how we always could tell when Ma had been snooping in our room?"

"Floor wax and poultry seasoning. That particular combination did linger."

Their mother had spent her career as a school cafeteria worker. Lawrence still believed the asbestos in the walls of the old Roxbury High contributed to the lung cancer that killed her at 52.

"It's like that. I can't see it, but I can smell it. Someone was in our files."

"What did they want? What did they look at? They looking for money?"

"No. You know I keep that walled off like you asked. They

didn't get near that. But they looked at just about everything else in this partition. They spent a lot of time on your cars."

"My cars? Why?"

Eddie shrugged and chewed more licorice. "Beats me. You know how you log all the miles and usage on that spreadsheet?"

"Sure. Good tax write-offs."

"Well, that's what caught their interest."

Lawrence grabbed a chair from the kitchen and placed it next to his brother. He was careful not to sit too close or touch him. Lawrence was the only person Eddie would let sit with him at his desk, but even that had limits. Eddie didn't like being this close to other people. It made his skin itchy. He took a breath and counted to 10 as Dr. Ashworth had taught him. It helped a little. He grabbed another Red Vine. The wax, sugar, and artificial coloring helped, too. He brought up the program that his brother used for book-keeping and then the database tables that were behind the front-end UI. He moved the screens over to the monitor on Lawrence's side so he wouldn't lean over any farther. Lawrence studied the numbers.

Finally, he pointed and asked, "What's this?"

It was a small table that didn't display on the front end.

"GPS coordinates. For these Cadillac models, when the car's on and in motion, the internal chip pings a satellite every 15 minutes and records the car's location."

"Huh. I didn't know that."

"It's an antitheft device. A low-key LoJack. Remember those things?"

"Sure, sure. I remember. You liked those commercials when you were a kid. I see the benefit for most employers, but I'm not sure it would always be good business for us. Can you disable it?"

Eddie looked at the screen then took a long sip from a

can of Dr. Pepper then typed for two minutes before he sat back. "All set."

"Can you figure out who was in the system?"

Eddie looked at him. "Why?"

Lawrence smiled. "You don't want to know who got around your security?"

Eddie thought about it. It hadn't occurred to him. It might be nice to talk to this person. Not face to face, of course, but through a chat program. They must be good to get around Eddie's firewalls. It might be interesting to compare notes. "I could try."

Lawrence put the chair back and walked toward the door. Eddie let out a small breath. He loved his brother, but he loved his solitude too. He couldn't help it. But then Lawrence paused by the door.

"Shit." He turned around. "Eddie, does Max have one of the SUVs that records the GPS coordinates?"

Eddie clicked a few keys. "Yes."

"Did the person access those?"

Eddie clicked again. "Yes, they accessed all of them, including the one Max is borrowing."

"Damn. I sometimes wonder if that white boy is more trouble than he's worth."

CHAPTER TWENTY-FOUR

Keres re-upped his motel room for another week. The bored clerk seemed mildly surprised anyone would voluntarily stay that long, but he was happy enough to take the cash. Keres had seen only two other cars in the lot all week and one woman briefly walking to the office. It was a shit hole, only a notch or two above his Stanhope accommodations, but it was perfect for his needs. After paying for the second week, he then rarely saw the inside of the room. He followed Lisa and watched her as much as he could for the next three days. He returned to the rented room only to shower and catch a few hours of sleep.

As he sat in his car and ate yet another gas station meal, he thought it might have been better to save the motel money and just bag out in his car, but he didn't want to risk running into a vagrancy charge. He also had credit cards but was leery of using them until he had to. He'd bought them off the dark web. Cash was safer while he had it. Which wouldn't be much longer unless Lisa gave it up soon.

It was a quarter to five now. Most classes had finished for the day. The sidewalks and dirt paths were no longer flush with students. He watched the door, and she came through a moment later. Right on schedule. Lisa Sullivan no longer looked like a perky 1980s lead in a teenage rom-com, but she hadn't aged poorly either. From afar, she might pass for a grad student. She was still trim, probably from riding that damn bike everywhere, with a short bob cut that framed her jaw. The color, no longer a vibrant blond but an ashy gray, was the only thing that betrayed her age. Unless you got closer and saw her face. She was careful to hide it. She looked relaxed and, if not happy, then satisfied most of the time, but he'd watched her long enough now and had seen her in unguarded moments when the mask slipped. It was then that the lines from her eyes and mouth showed the years, the hard years, and maybe the pain that she'd endured. Good, Keres thought. She might have gotten the money, but she had at least paid a price. Nowhere near the price he had paid, but it warmed his chest to witness her torment in those private moments. She wasn't completely undamaged.

She walked around to the side of the brick administration building and unlocked her bike as another woman stopped and spoke to her. Keres could see Lisa nodding. The pair continued their conversation as Lisa stowed the chain in the panier mounted over the rear wheel, then pushed the bike along one of the gravel paths toward one of the campus's side entrances. The other woman was younger than Lisa, but also too old to be a student. They appeared friendly and Keres put her down as a co-worker.

In the past three days, he had learned that Lisa did indeed work for Clarkston College. She was in the employment and payroll department. He wasn't sure why, but it mildly disappointed him. It sounded so banal after all the things he'd imagined she'd be doing. Then he realized, like much of the rest of her cover, it was a smart choice. It would give her access to all the employee records, including her own. If a change or two needed to be made, or conveniently left out, she was in a perfect position to protect herself. Likewise, she'd know, or be alerted, if anyone came snooping around.

He watched the women go through the side gate and split up. Lisa checked the traffic, mounted the bike, and rode off. Keres lost sight of her after 50 yards when the wrought iron fence merged into a thick stone wall, but he didn't panic. He knew now that Lisa was a creature of habit. Every weekday after work, she pedaled her way down to Clarkston's modest downtown to a small yoga studio above a frozen yogurt shop for a 75-minute Vinyasa class.

Habits could give someone structure and maybe the veneer of safety, always doing the same thing, always seeing the same people, easily being able to spot anything new or amiss, but they could also be a weak point. They made you predictable. And easy to follow.

It's a few ticks past midnight and he's parked half a block down from her building. It's a quiet street, but he's not worried about being seen or reported. There's a Speedy's convenience store at one end of the street and Trico, a bar/restaurant combo, on the other. There was street parking and foot traffic, even at this late hour. Sitting in his car wouldn't cause suspicion. Not right away.

He'd walked past the building once, the first day, after she had pedaled off to work. It was a recent construction, or a fairly new rehab, with modern aesthetics. Glass and struts and steel. Eight floors. The apartments that fronted the street each had a small balcony. He could see sporadic grills, patio furniture, and overgrown houseplants. A uniformed attendant sat behind a desk in the lobby opposite a wall of resident mailboxes. A concierge? Security? He didn't know, but it wasn't 24/7. He could see through the glass now and the desk was empty. The building was close to campus, not near the student apartments, but an easy commute.

That first day, another bit of social engineering got him Lisa's apartment number.

He dialed the building's main number. "Good morning, I'm calling from Express Delivery. I'm following up on a returned package to one of your residents?" He didn't bother using the software to disguise his voice this time.

"And who's that?"

"The mailing label says, let me see, a Miss Jill Williams. Apartment seven?"

"Ah, Miss Williams lives here but in apartment 42."

"I see. I'll adjust that and send it back out. Thank you so much."

"You're welcome. Have a pleasant day."

The building was big and anonymous enough that not every resident knew everyone else. The mild anonymity would be important to Lisa, but in this case, it might bite her in the ass. He slipped in the back entrance behind a woman struggling with grocery bags. He'd taken the stairs to the fourth floor. Unit 42 was the second one down on the right, facing the street. He could hear a television on loudly in number 44 across the hall. He walked past without slowing. He'd seen the cameras. He went back down the stairs and exited the way he came in.

He had a clear view of her balcony through his windshield. She'd drawn the blinds, but he could see a light on and the blue flicker of a television through the cracks. She was in there, alone, on her couch. He wondered how many nights she'd spent like that. He felt himself getting sleepy and cracked the window to let in some fresh air. The occasional car passed, but the foot traffic had died out. The blue light clicked off at 1:00. The blinds parted and he watched a shadow peer out at the street. He instinctively slid lower in his seat, but she couldn't possibly see him. The blinds slipped back into place. A moment later, the apartment went dark.

Still, he sat. Now that he was so close to the end, so close to her, he felt a strange reticence. The last 25 years had been building to this moment. Finding her. Getting his vengeance. Getting his money. But now his mind skipped ahead and he wondered what would come after? His plans had always been about her. Now, when he tried to see past her, he couldn't. It was just a wall of static, like when the broadcast networks would sign off at the end of the day.

"Fuck it," he mumbled out loud and shook off the malaise. "Gonna be rich." Whatever comes next, he'd have money in his pocket and a drink in his hand. With any luck, the view would include some sand and sun. What more did he need to know?

CHAPTER TWENTY-FIVE

Keres watched for another hour, but nothing changed. The street remained quiet. A little after 2:00 a.m., the last apartment light went dark. It was time to go to work.

He couldn't grab her in her building. Or on campus. It would be too messy. There were too many potential complications. The odds of him getting her and getting away clean were too small. He needed another way. He needed to grab her and get her someplace to talk. It did him no good to snatch her only to be cornered by the cops 10 minutes later. He needed the details on the money before he got rid of her.

He drove out of town, past the highway, to the older two-lane state road that had likely been the sole way into Clarkston before the bigger, faster interstate superseded it. Now, low-rent businesses, cheap apartments, and abandoned buildings cluttered each side. He drove the strip twice before he pulled into the cracked and weedy parking lot of a defunct fast-food restaurant. The signage was gone and plywood covered the windows, but the building retained a distinct bubbly shape that even Keres recognized. The front door was secured with a padlock and chain, a peeling 'For Rent' notice on the glass.

He drove around back and got out. There was only plywood over the back door. He gripped the top of the board and tugged. The wood was still strong, but time and nature had rotted the building's frame. He tested the edges. The upper left corner was the weakest. He got a grip with both hands and pried that corner up. After that, the rest of the sheet almost fell off on its own.

He set the wood aside, then walked to the edge of the parking lot and found a fist-sized rock, prepared to break the glass on the door, but first tugged the handle. Never discount the obvious. It was open and he walked right in. He could smell the fry oil under the damp scent of dust and mildew. He did a quick circuit. It didn't look like anyone had been inside for years. It was dusty and one corner had water damage from a leak in the roof, but otherwise, it was remarkably clean. The junkies and homeless hadn't discovered it yet. It might be too far out of the way. He found an old newspaper from 2013 splayed open on a plastic table.

He went back out the way he came in and propped the plywood back into place. It would work. He wouldn't need it for long. With any luck, they wouldn't find the body until he was in another state. Or better yet, another country. He drove back to town.

He moved onto the next problem. He didn't want to grab her by using his rental. First, it was small. He needed something with more space. Second, he needed to return the rental car. He was confident that they could not trace the car back to him, the reservation and payment were not in his name, but if they somehow managed it, he didn't want any chance of DNA putting them together. He knew the companies cleaned the returned rentals, but he doubted it was thorough enough to erase all traces. Why take the chance? A stolen vehicle brought its own risks, of course, but if he did it right, he rated those lower than leaving DNA behind.

He drove back to Clarkston College and parked the Chevy Cruze in the student lot. He walked across the campus. There were a few people out, even at that hour, returning from parties or bars, others laden with heavy backpacks from all-night study sessions. He kept his distance and kept his head down and shuffled along. He made a mental note to pick up a cheap knapsack. If he ever needed to come back to campus, it would make a perfect piece of camouflage. It was the equivalent of walking around a building site with a clipboard.

After 10 minutes, he reached the northwest corner of the campus and the facilities building. He walked past without slowing. No lights were on other than a single bulb mounted over the entry door. He cut down the side of the building and walked around the back. Another door, this one without a light. He kept walking. Unlike the academic buildings, they built this one for function, not form. It was a square, two-story box with a Quonset hut grafted onto the left side. Next to the Quonset hut was a fenced-in lot with various maintenance vehicles. There was no lock.

He slipped inside and walked the lot. There were various makes and models bought over the years with various budget allocations. Each had the college's name and logo. He thought it fitting that he would use something from her hiding place to pry her out of it.

He examined the choices until he found an old van that he knew he could hotwire easily. He peeked through the back window and spotted bins bolted to either side, filled with various wires, clamps, connectors, and other supplies. An electrician or plumbing truck. He didn't care particularly.

There was an aisle in the middle that was wide enough for a body, and he could secure her to the struts that supported the supply bins. He'd prefer darkened or tinted windows, but none of the trucks appeared to have those and he didn't want to look elsewhere. This would get the job done.

The van's door was locked, but he could handle that. He took off his belt and threaded it between the door and the window's weather stripping. It took four tries, but eventually he got the buckle hooked around the lock pin. He pulled it back and disengaged the lock. Inside the van, he searched the bins until he found a pair of pliers. He smiled. His luck was coming back. Then he had a thought. Don't discount the obvious. He flipped down the visors on each side then lifted the floor mat on the driver's side. No van keys.

He used the pliers to pry off the plastic around the steering column and then braided the wires together until the van's engine kicked to life. He kept the lights off and backed out. He jumped out, opened the gate, and drove through before reversing the process. He felt his heart rate kick up and the world went a little gray. It had been years since he'd felt this rush. He forgot how much he missed it. The next two minutes were the most dangerous. If campus security or some do-gooder spotted him and called it in before he could get out on the main road, it could be trouble. But his luck held. He kept the lights off as he drove around the front of the building, took a left on a service road, and exited the campus.

He flipped the stem on the left side of the steering wheel and the lights came on. He drove east, staying on the edge of the campus, and then looped north, avoiding the center of town. Ten minutes later, he was back at the abandoned restaurant. He pulled the van around back and parked close to the building. There was no development to the rear, just overgrown woods and swamp. No one would see the van from that direction. He walked around to the front of the restaurant and then out to the road. The building was in the center of the lot to provide parking on both sides and the rear. He couldn't see the van. He walked 50 yards in either direction and still couldn't see anything. Someone would need to pull in and around the back to spot it. Satisfied, a quiet calmness spread through his shoulders and down to his fingertips. He would bring her here and finish it. Soon. He nodded to himself, turned on his heel, and started the long walk back to the campus.

CHAPTER TWENTY-SIX

Martha woke up with a start and the paperback fell from her lap onto the floor. She had a moment of panic, but then spotted Keres's white Chevy in the parking lot. She hadn't lost him. He was still trolling the nearby college campus during the day and returning at night to do whatever he did in room 21. She didn't like to imagine what that might be. She picked up the book and set it next to the half-empty water glass on the nearby table.

The urgency with which he'd left his apartment in Boston had cooled. He appeared convinced that Lisa Sullivan was on or near the Clarkston campus, but he didn't know more than that. She'd watched him from afar the first two days. He walked around the campus. He went in and out of the buildings. He got a milkshake from one of the school cafeterias and then stared out the window. Then he returned to the motel.

She stood up slowly and groaned. She'd fallen asleep in the chair. She put her hands on the small of her back and tried to loosen up. She couldn't keep this up. It was taking too much of a physical toll. She wasn't a spring chicken. Next year, she'd hit 55 and officially be closer to 70 than 40. Aches and pains lingered longer. She'd been on Keres 24/7 for more than a week. She was running on fumes. She needed to call in some help or get some additional electronic surveillance. Neither would be cheap, but she didn't think Cobb would bat an eye. He could more than afford it.

She rubbed at her eyes and glanced at her watch. Almost 5:00. The sky was a light gray in the east. What had awakened her?

She had set the chair six feet deep in the room, back from the window, so that she could see out, but it would be difficult for someone else to see in. She peered out through the slit in the curtains. No passing traffic. The parking lot was quiet, almost empty. Besides Keres's Chevy and her rental, she counted three other cars. Five occupants in a building with 24 units. There was a central office in the middle, with a dozen units strung out on each side, a drained pool at one end. She was in 14, close to the office. Keres was farther along, in 21, near the pool.

She shifted her weight and an electric pain zipped down her leg. She let out a little yelp of surprise. Getting old was full of surprises. She briefly thought about getting a hot shower and then remembered the water temperature and pressure barely rose above a warm spring rain.

She put her head right up against the window and tried to look back toward the office. Maybe someone had pulled in late and banged on the office door for the manager. She couldn't see. The angle was too tight. This was bothering her now. She should be thankful something woke her up and got her out of the chair. Another hour and she might not have been able to walk upright today. But what? Now she had to know.

She put a hand on the curtain to pull it wider when she

saw a shadow approaching. Keres. She didn't need to see him. She knew the way he moved. She stepped back. Her heart jumped to her throat. He passed the window. The cheap soles of his sneakers barely made a noise on the cracked pavement. There was just a soft shush as his left heel dragged along slightly, then a pause, nothing wrong with his right side, then the shush again. She glanced at her purse on the bedside table. Her Glock G42 was inside. She took a sliding step to her left and reached out. The water glass fell to the floor with a thump. She winced. The soft shush stopped. She grabbed the gun and waited. She heard nothing. She slowly took three steps to the door and looked through the peephole. Keres was standing a few feet away. He had a can of soda in one hand. That was what had done it. The rattle and thunk of the can falling from the machine had woken her up.

Keres stood still. He looked like a hunting dog catching the whiff of a fox. As she watched, he turned his head and looked in her direction. She felt like he was looking straight through the peephole at her. She retreated a step, raised the gun, and leveled it at the door. She stood rooted to the spot and tried to remember to breathe. She watched the knob, convinced it was about to turn. Her mind went blank. She'd fired thousands of rounds at the range but now couldn't remember if the gun even had a safety. Had she loaded one in the chamber? She stared at the tarnished brass knob. She felt sweat bead at her neck and run down her back. Her arm shook with the effort of holding the one-pound gun. She lowered it to her side and stepped back up to the door. The sidewalk was empty.

CHAPTER TWENTY-SEVEN

Later, Lisa would realize she'd missed two things. Or, almost missed them. Not that the outcome would have been much different in the end. But she was upset with herself for not having caught on sooner. He must have been watching her for a while. He knew her movements, her habits, her routine. He had planned. Thinking back on it gave her a chill. She tried to blame her age or the start of the new semester, but the truth was she'd gotten comfortable. The long, quiet years had dulled her edge and made her complacent. It takes a lot of effort to suspect everyone and everything all the time. It will warp your mind.

But she didn't cut herself too much slack. She'd known George Keres was out of prison. She hadn't let things slide that much. She had no trouble recollecting how it felt to be in the man's presence in that hotel room in Delaware. Or how John and Justice had talked about Keres's past. And they'd been right. Keres was a weasel, and Lisa doubted prison had changed that. It had likely only sharpened his teeth.

She'd kept tabs on his case over the years as anniversaries passed and they held parole hearings. She'd been tempted to travel to Stanhope and attend his final hearing and get eyes on him and remind herself of the old but still potent danger. Maybe that would have helped. Maybe it would have shocked her system and recharged her vigilance. But it was a game of chicken and the egg. She couldn't keep close ties on him without potentially exposing herself. In the end, she decided not to go. The risks were too high. She was happy not to poke the weasel's nest. Maybe now that he was a free man, he would have other things on his mind besides Lisa Sullivan.

That, it turned out, had been a mistake. Almost a deadly one.

She tried to empty her mind as she lay on her back during the final shavasana but outside thoughts kept sneaking in like drips of water through a leaking roof, slowly building until it was a constant patter of distraction. Eventually, she stopped trying to fight it. She probably should have started with that strategy. She lay on her mat a few extra minutes and listened to the others pack up. Whatever was nagging at her faded to low background static.

She rolled up her mat and walked into the small reception room and took her bag off a hook.

"You okay, Jill?" Naomi asked.

"That obvious, huh?"

Lisa kept mostly to herself. She was polite and smiled and made idle small talk with some regulars, but didn't have anyone she'd consider a friend at the yoga studio. The closest person was Naomi. They'd been out for coffee a few times. Picked up some frozen yogurt from the place downstairs. Lisa never talked much. She hated the lying, but she'd become an excellent listener over the years.

"Plenty of people come in looking like you." Naomi scrunched up her shoulders and made a face approximating a troll doll. Jill laughed. "But few look like that when they leave. I feel like I let you down."

"No, it wasn't you or the class. Just the start of the semester, I think. Our busiest time, and one person in the department is out on maternity leave. Double the work. Orientation, onboarding, background checks, explaining benefits." Lisa waved a hand. "You don't want to hear it. You opened this place to get away from the nine-to-five grind."

It was the last class of the day. Naomi closed the laptop she used to check-in members and locked it in a drawer. "Doesn't mean I still don't remember that feeling. Happy to listen if you want to vent. Grab a drink at Sip?"

Sip was the new wine and tapas place on Sycamore. Anything less than a decade old would always be new in slow-moving West Adams. It was close to campus, but its prices and lack of beer taps kept most of the students at bay. Lisa thought about it. She could use a glass of wine and a good vent. Gary, her boss at Clarkston, though everyone recognized it was Lisa who kept the department running, had been driving her crazy all week with requests. A couple of glasses of Merlot or rosé might loosen the knot between her shoulders that yoga didn't.

"Sure. That sounds good."

She drank too much wine, but it had felt good to talk, even if it was just about work and not what she really wanted to say. She'd never go that far. It was too risky. It would put the other person in too much danger. Lisa couldn't deal with hurting anyone else she cared about, even just an acquaintance like Naomi. Not in this lifetime. The loneliness might get tough sometimes, she could feel a depression slipping over her now, but better she kept her true past to herself.

Turning down another glass, she'd left Sip and began the

short ride back to her building. But the respite provided by the wine and chat was short-lived. She felt the nagging tension nestle back between her shoulder blades as she pedaled. Then the physical sensation bled into the mental. She felt someone watching her. The hairs on her neck rose. She made a couple of abrupt turns, almost getting clipped by a car at an intersection, but had to admit to herself she spotted nothing suspicious. Wine and stress, maybe not the best combination for her at the moment.

The wine made her sleepy and she fell asleep on the couch with the television playing a Lifetime movie. She woke up after midnight to an infomercial. She felt tired all the time these days but rarely slept through the night. She'd been dreaming about John again but couldn't recall the details. She stayed still and tried to call them back, but they drifted away like smoke. She stood, turned off the living room lights and television, and went to the sliding door by the balcony. She peeked out from between the blinds at the dark surrounding streets.

She'd learned that grief was like hiking a mountain where the peak is just out of sight. Some days were pleasant, hiking through a field or glade, and for long periods she was okay, maybe not happy, definitely not happy, but numb, and able to get through the day. Then it would turn on her. A storm would lash out without warning. A phrase, a smell, even a sound brought it all crashing back. For a long time, those triggers were an addiction. She would seek them out like a prospector. She liked the pain. She would pick the scab, probe the wound, desperate to feel bad because it was better than feeling nothing.

She let the blinds fall back and turned away from the darkness outside.

. . .

Ultimately, it was the smile that saved her. And her chain derailing. Lisa owned a car, a small Jetta Gulf, that she parked in the spot that came with the apartment, but she found her bike to be a far more efficient way to get to most places in West Adams. Plus, she spent much of her job sitting on her butt all day, so the biking to and from work, along with the regular weeknight yoga at Naomi's, was her only chance at exercise.

Her apartment was just under five miles from campus and typically the ride took her 20 minutes, 25 if she was feeling frisky and took on Nog's Hill. She was just turning off Prospect Avenue onto the larger Cole Street when the cuff of her pants got caught in the ring and threw off her chain. She looked down to see the links draped on the frame and dragging along the road.

"Shit," she muttered. Gary had called an early meeting at 8:30 a.m. and now, if she wanted to be on time, she'd have to show up sweating and with grease on her fingers. Traffic had been light on Prospect but heavier on Cole, where the street acted as a feeder to Route 2 and the east side of campus. She braked and checked the small mirror that was clipped to the handlebars. A Jeep was approaching on Cole and a Clarkston maintenance van was pulling out of Prospect and coming up behind her.

She steered out of the designated bike lane and pulled the hobbled bike up onto the sidewalk. She knelt and examined the chain. She was lucky it hadn't jammed and only came loose. She glanced at her pant leg. Just a small smudge that blended with the light herringbone pattern. It was a minor inconvenience. She'd gotten off easy. She adjusted the shifter to the smallest gear and then guided the chain back onto the teeth before lifting the back wheel and using her other hand to crank the pedal until the chain righted itself. Sixty seconds and she was back on her way. The Clarkston van hadn't even made the right turn onto Route 2 yet.

On Cole, the bike lane split the lanes with vehicle traffic going straight or turning left on one side and those making the right toward campus on the other. The intent was to keep the bikes away from the parked cars on either side of Route 2, but it put the rider, who also wanted to go right, in a tricky spot. She didn't like being in the middle of such a busy road. Drivers were often too distracted or too aggressive, not wanting to wait another light cycle to make a turn. More than once she'd had to dodge a driver not being aware of the bike lane or simply not caring. She could go up on the sidewalk, but at this time of day it was crowded with students heading to class or morning dog walkers. She stayed in the bike lane and kept her eyes moving on the vehicles waiting in line. She slowed and checked the mirror, looking to see who was paying attention and who might run her down because they were sending a text message. The man driving the van kept his head facing forward, watching the traffic light, as she neared. She noticed the small smile on his face as she glided past. Just a flash and then it was gone. A horn sounded. She scanned ahead. Not for her. The light switched to green. She made the turn without incident and pedaled onward toward campus.

Two hours later, as Gary droned on about new employee identification standards, she suddenly gasped and jerked her arm, spilling coffee all over the conference room table. Gary looked annoyed. Everyone else looked relieved by the interruption in the tedium. Lisa had been thinking about her ride into work that morning. The man in the van popped into her mind. Maybe her subconscious was frantically hitting the panic button. She knew that smile. She knew those teeth. He hadn't gotten them fixed in prison.

George Keres had found her.

CHAPTER TWENTY-EIGHT

Lisa's hands shook as she tried to tear a paper towel from the dispenser. After two tries, she managed to grab one and blot her face dry. Keres was here. Not just out in the world, but here, in Clarkston. He had found her. She thought she had burrowed deep, but it had taken him less than a month since his release to find her. How did he do it? Then she decided it didn't matter. But then she thought about Joyce. She took out her phone and dialed. It went straight to voicemail. She sent a text and then felt a tremendous sense of relief when she saw the bouncing bubbles of a reply: *In a meeting, will call later.*

She tried to think through her options. Her mind drew an absolute blank. Think, Lisa. She wadded up the paper towel and clenched her fists until they stopped shaking. She slowly let out her breath and counted to 10. She felt herself slowly coming back. This was not a complete surprise. She had known this was a possibility. It was just the speed of it. She thought she had more time.

Could she call the police? Was that insane? Her Jill Williams alias was almost 20 years old. It was strong. It would stand up to a lot of scrutiny, at least initially. How much and how deep did the police check on the victim of a crime? But what would she report? What had Keres done? Nothing that she knew of right now. He'd driven past her. He wasn't on parole. There were no restrictions on his release. She dismissed the idea. Yes, it was crazy. Going to the police wouldn't solve her problems. It might help get Keres off her back in the short-term, but inviting any sort of law enforcement into her life was a recipe for disaster. The truth would come out. There was no way it couldn't. Either the authorities would find out or, more likely, Keres would simply tell them. What more would he have to lose at that point? Revealing her identity and her past sins would be his best bargaining chip.

She had opened several accounts at different big national banks. She had diligently kept the accounts active, and the ATM cards were in a locked drawer in her apartment. There wasn't a lot of money in the accounts, but there might be enough to get away and make a new start. The bigger problem was identification. She had a full set of papers, legitimate ID, cultivated slowly over the years, stored locally, but they were out-of-date. Another lapse on her part. She could run, but she'd have to stay in the country until she could safely get them updated.

Kierra poked her head in the door. "You alright, Jill? Meeting wrapped up. You want to grab a coffee?"

She gave the younger woman a wan smile. "Yes, I mean no. I'm okay but feel a little off. Maybe something I ate this morning." She usually walked with Kierra over to the cafeteria for a mid-morning caffeine hit. "I think I'm going to have to pass on the coffee this morning. Could you tell Gary I'm going to head home? Hoping it's just a 24-hour thing. Actually, do you mind calling a cab for me? Have it pick me up around back."

Lisa felt a pang of guilt. She knew Kierra was a bit of a germaphobe. True to form, the younger woman suddenly looked like she was having trouble swallowing herself and retreated quickly. "Sure. I'll let Gary know and call the cab right away. I hope you feel better."

Lisa double-checked her reflection in the mirror. Her face was pale and the circles under her eyes were more pronounced. She hadn't had to fake much for Kierra's benefit. That little white lie to Kierra would at least save her from having to look at Gary's face any more today. She doubted it would be the last lie she'd tell in the next few days.

She carried her purse and bike helmet with her as she walked down the back staircase to wait for her ride. She decided speed was the key. John's voice popped into her head, "Never miss a chance to make them make a stupid mistake." Them, in John's case, were usually the cops or other authorities keeping him from what he wanted, but she thought it would apply equally well to Keres. She'd been a soft target so far, slow and predictable, and easy to follow. She was going to change that, starting now.

She waited inside, peering out the back door, until she saw the old cab swing around on the access road, the worn-out struts bouncing and sagging, and slow near the steps. She stepped out and waved. The driver braked to a stop. She hustled down the steps and gave him the address of a bank in town. She scanned the nearby area as the cab made a ponderous U-turn. Even inside the cab, she felt very exposed. She kept expecting the door to jerk open and Keres to leer down at her. She pushed the locks manually closed on the two rear doors.

She had the cab take a circuitous route, doubling back, and going around the block a few times. If he found her behavior odd, he didn't comment, just followed her instructions. She kept watch for the Clarkston van but never saw it. After 15 minutes, she directed him to pull into the small shopping center with the bank branch on one end.

"Do you mind waiting? I should only be a few minutes."

The driver smiled at her. "Sure, lady. It's your time. Meter is running."

Inside, the bank was cool and quiet. There was a short, roped-off queue inside the door, but she was the only customer. A lone employee standing at a teller window smiled at her in anticipation. Lisa settled her nerves, no one was going to attack her in a bank, and, with an effort, smiled back.

"I need to open my safe deposit box?"

"Of course. I'll get Mr. Simons, the manager, to help you. He has the keys."

The woman disappeared through an opening behind the row of teller windows. She reappeared a moment later with a young man trailing behind her. Lisa hadn't visited this branch since she rented the box almost 15 years ago. She wondered if Mr. Simons had been in sixth or seventh grade then. Lisa still often thought of herself as 30 years old and was now always surprised to find her doctors, co-workers, and acquaintances were a decade or two younger. She added bank branch managers to that list.

The manager was wearing an off-the-rack black suit with a nametag pinned to the lapel. His cheeks were slightly red, and his neck showed bumps from razor burn. He put out a hand to go along with a smile that showed off very white, very square teeth.

"David Simons, branch manager."

Lisa had the feeling that he practiced in front of the mirror.

"Jill Williams."

"A pleasure to meet you, Jill. How can I help you today?"

"I'd like to examine something in my box."

"Of course." He took a set of keys from his pocket. "If you'll follow me."

He led her past two empty offices to a door with a keypad and card reader mounted on the wall. He blitzed her with another smile. She took a step back and looked away as he entered a code and then slid a card through the reader and opened the door. There was a second door, more of a barred gate, just inside the narrow room.

"If you'll just step inside. This door needs to be closed before I can unlock the security gate."

She stepped in and to the left. Simons pulled the first door shut and then used a separate key to open the security gate. The strong room was only 10 feet wide, but double or triple that in depth. Deposit boxes of various sizes lined all three walls. There was a small computer just inside the security gate on a small table jutting out from the wall. Simons walked to it and entered a passcode then looked at her.

"This computer isn't networked. No way for it to be hacked or compromised. What box number, Ms. Williams?"

"704."

He punched it in, and the screen refreshed with additional information. "Could I just see some identification to verify ownership?"

"Of course." She unsnapped her wallet and handed him her license. He glanced at it then at the screen before he handed it back with another glossy smile.

"Thank you. That matches up. Please follow me."

He led her over to a row of small boxes halfway along the right wall and inserted his key. She was ready and inserted her key, and he opened the door. "If you need to sit or have additional privacy, there is a small space through that door at the end." He indicated a space in the far corner.

"Thank you, but no, this should be quick."

"Okay then, just press the buzzer when you're done and I'll let you out."

"It should only take a minute or two if you just want to wait outside."

"Of course, Ms. Williams."

He left. The security gate clanged shut and something in Lisa's chest fluttered. She tried not to feel trapped, but the bars made it hard. She turned her back to the bars and concentrated on the box. She pulled it out and flipped open the top. A New York driver's license in the name of Molly Cahan, passport, two credit cards, plus a couple of random club cards to fill out a wallet. Everything had expired, but it could be helpful. There was also an envelope of cash. That would likely be more helpful. She scooped out the cards and the cash and stuffed it all in her purse.

That left only the small microcassette. She picked it up and looked at it. She studied the small, crimped handwriting on the label. He'd always been a meticulous man. It was safer in the box, but she didn't know if she'd ever be back. She put it in her bag and pushed it to the bottom.

CHAPTER TWENTY-NINE

She sat at an inside window table at Trico's, the restaurant down the street from her apartment building. It was early for lunch and the place was almost empty except for the staff. She ordered a salad and an iced tea. When the food arrived, she tried to eat, knew she needed the calories, but the lettuce tasted like chalk and her stomach rolled over. She didn't have much of an appetite even before Keres showed up. Maybe her body had known something her mind didn't. She put her fork down and took out her cell phone instead.

She found the number and waited for the phone to connect. Lisa recognized Emelyn's soft southern accent.

"125 Chiswick Arms. How can I help you?"

"Hi, Emelyn. It's Jill Williams from unit 42."

"Of course. Hello, Ms. Williams. What can I do for you?"

"I was wondering if my uncle had arrived yet? Older guy. Short gray hair. I was supposed to meet him there, but I'm stuck at work."

"No, I haven't seen him, at least not since I've been on, but that was only a few hours ago. Let me check the log."

Lisa knew the building had solid security. It was one of the reasons she'd picked it. There were cameras on all the entrances and resident floors. Plus, her neighbor, Mr. Wheatley, was a lonely, older man. He often came out to chat when he heard her opening her own door. If Keres was around, it was unlikely that he would be in the building without being spotted by someone.

Emelyn came back on the line. "There's just one note here about a call yesterday regarding a misdirected delivery. The shipper had your unit number wrong."

"Okay. Thank you, Emelyn."

"Of course, Ms. Williams. I'll keep an eye out for your uncle and if he arrives before you, I'll have him wait in the lounge."

"Thank you. I appreciate it."

There'd been no package. She never sent shipments to her apartment. She used the drop mailbox in West Adams. The call to the concierge had to have been Keres. So he knew her apartment, but was he watching it? Lying in wait for her? She needed to get up there. Was it worth the risk? Yes, she thought so, if she ever wanted to be clear of this mess. She made another call. There was one thing she could do.

"Hello?" The voice sounded hesitant and phlegmy. Lisa knew Terrence Wheatley suffered from seasonal allergies. He reminded her often.

"Hello, Terry. It's Jill from across the hall."

"Oh, hello, dear. Are you okay?"

"Yes, I'm fine. I wanted to let you know that I'm expecting a visitor but got delayed at work. Have you seen or heard anything this morning?"

"No, it's been all quiet in our little corner of the Arms since you left." His voice got stronger and deeper the more he talked. "Rodrigo ran the vacuum at half past eight. And Judy

Russell took Oliver for a walk. But that's it. Just the usual stuff. I was just thinking about the time Willard Scott—"

"Okay. Thank you, Terry. I'm sorry, but I'm getting another call."

She had a sudden vision of Terry opening his door and surprising Keres and then Keres's hands around the frail old man's neck.

"Oh, Terry. One more thing before I run."

"Yes?"

"My uncle, the guy that's coming, he's a bit agoraphobic. If you hear him or see him, best to leave him be. He's a little ornery until you get to know him. I can introduce you later."

She disconnected and briefly thought about a world where both Keres and the benign Terrence Wheatley co-existed. What did that say about any sort of higher power? Probably that He was too busy to concern himself with the minor affairs of men. That thought didn't lift her mood.

She put her phone back in her purse and sat, sipping at her water, pushing the greens around on her plate. Her feet itched to move, but she didn't know what to do. Speed could work both ways. It could force an adversary into a mistake, but it could also force her right out into the open. Her apartment was the logical place to pick her up again. He knew, or would soon find out, that she was no longer at work. He would come to the apartment, he had to. Should she risk going in now or wait to see if he showed up?

Keres decided for her. The stolen Clarkston van inched down the other end of the street, turned into the Speedy's lot, and backed into a parking spot. She knew from that vantage point that he could see both the apartment's front door and the rear parking lot.

She wasn't sure if he knew about her car or not but had to

assume that if he knew the Jill Williams name, he had the Jetta's registration. He had proven to be very adept at tracking her. Her plan had been to get the car and get some space in order to regroup. Clearly, prison had not distracted Keres's interest in her. It appeared to have had the opposite effect. She knew he would never stop looking, but if she could get some distance, she felt like she could be better prepared for when he found her next. But a car in the Jill Williams name was a clear link in the chain to her. She couldn't make it that easy.

What were her options? There were no car rental places nearby. And she knew a rental was also simple to trace. And a new car purchase would require a serious credit check. She could get an Uber or a Lyft but that would also require an account and a credit card, easy to hack, and would just strand her somewhere else. Trying to move and hide and stay ahead of Keres that way wasn't sustainable. She needed to avoid all of that. The safest option would be to buy a cheap car as a private transaction, but that would take time and a good chunk of her bankroll. Was it worth it? She needed to think about that. Keres couldn't sit there forever. Someone would eventually notice the van was missing. But she couldn't remain stationary either. She always felt better on the move. She decided she needed a car. It would give her more options. But first, she needed to change her appearance.

She paid the bill and left the restaurant. She waited until a group of women passed, going the opposite direction, then she walked south, away from her apartment building. She went down three blocks, past Jenkins Avenue, a busy thoroughfare, before she cut east and then north again, looping all the way around and approaching her building from the opposite side. She stopped in the small park down the street. From this perspective, she couldn't see Trico's or the Speedy's convenience store. Or Keres's van. She scanned the people out on the sidewalks and, satisfied that he wasn't lurking on the street, she started forward again.

There was a third entrance on this side of the building. It was an emergency exit. With its wide double doors and nearby freight elevator, it was most often used by people or moving companies to get furniture in and out of the building. It was also the way to access the basement storage units. It was less glamorous than the front and rear entrances, but her key worked just as well. She jogged to the door and slipped inside.

She blinked in the sudden dimness. The space smelled of concrete and moisture. She took the freight elevator up to her floor. She heard Mr. Wheatley. He was watching television and Judge Judy masked her arrival. Inside her apartment, she felt a pang of regret. She'd lived here now for almost a decade. The place was familiar and comfortable. Inside these walls was the one place she could let her guard down. Now it was gone. Even if she dealt with Keres, she'd need to find someplace new.

She avoided going near the windows. Her coffee cup from that morning rested on the counter. Warm midday light filled the kitchen and she suddenly felt drowsy. She went into the bedroom and fought back an urge to crawl under the duvet. She couldn't hide from this. Not anymore.

She changed out of her work clothes into jeans, a T-shirt, and a Clarkston sweatshirt. She pulled a small bag from her closet and filled it with a week's worth of clothes and toiletries. She could always buy anything else she needed. She went to the small second bedroom that she used as an office. She had no guests. She unlocked the bottom drawer of the desk and took out the file wrapped in rubber bands. In her mind, the information and the implications in the file were dangerous and world changing. In reality, the tattered folder looked ordinary and pedestrian. So many years of careful digging and it all added up to a couple of inches of thin paper. She stuffed it into her bag on top of the clothes. She grabbed her winter coat and gloves from the closet and took one last look around. She went back to the bedroom and picked up a single, small, framed photo of her and John and Michael and added it to her bag before she locked the door and left.

She took the freight elevator to the ground floor and then went down to the basement using a staircase to the left. The basement was divided into extra storage sections, slim rectangles of concrete separated from the next by chicken wire and wood planks bolted to the floor and ceiling. She walked down the aisle and glanced at the junk accumulated by her neighbors. Cardboard boxes, old appliances, furniture, and seasonal decorations stuffed each unit. Her unit was spartan in comparison. Two boxes, still taped from the last move, and her second bike. This bike was older than the one she'd left on campus, but it was still in good shape. It didn't have the thicker tires for biking in the Clarkston winters, but she thought it would be okay. It hadn't snowed in the last three weeks. The bike had a rack on the back with yellow panniers attached to each side. She stuffed her bag with her clothes, research, and picture on one side and then checked the contents of the other side. A woman biking alone near a college campus wasn't unusual, but she still liked to be prepared. Satisfied, she pulled her helmet out, clipped the pack closed, and wheeled the bike out of the unit.

CHAPTER THIRTY

Keres could feel the clock ticking. He would have to get rid of the van soon. This had to happen today, but something was wrong. Lisa hadn't come out for her mid-morning coffee with the other chick. Each day so far, Lisa and another woman got a mid-morning coffee and then Lisa returned alone. He wasn't sure where the other woman went, and he didn't care. He thought that the sliver of time when Lisa walked the narrow, little-traveled path between the administration building and the church was the best time to grab her. He tried not to panic. Maybe she was just delayed. Maybe her boss scheduled a last-minute meeting. He shook it off and went back to watching. Five minutes later, some intuition told him it didn't hurt to check. He jumped out of the van and jogged up the steps of the building.

Inside the set of double doors, he dodged left, opened a second door, and started climbing. On the third floor, he went right and walked toward the end of the hall. There was a low hum of activity but few voices. There were no classrooms in this building. It was all offices and departments devoted to college bureaucratic functions. Housing, tuition, records. The last group of offices on the left was Payroll and Employment. Lisa's desk was part of a four-cubicle set. Her cube could be viewed through the two panels of glass near the department's entry doors. He'd walked past twice previously and gotten a secret thrill of watching her as she worked.

This morning, her desk was empty. He searched the office, but he didn't see her blond hair poking up over any walls and she wasn't sitting inside any of the three offices lining the opposite side. He continued past and went into the men's room. He stood by the sink and waited five minutes before he walked back in the opposite direction. There was still no sign of her. He went back outside. Her bike was still locked and chained to the rack. Was he overreacting? Some animal part of his brain said no. He'd lost the scent. His prey had escaped. He walked the short distance to the cafeteria with the coffee shop in the lobby. Maybe he'd simply missed them. No sign of her there, either. He ran back to the van.

If she'd bolted and gone to ground, he was back to square one. Maybe even further back now that she knew he was actively hunting her. It would be very difficult to pry her out a second time. He didn't let his mind go there, not just yet. Lisa Sullivan had 20 good years invested in Jill Williams and her small-town life in Clarkston. It would be hard to just walk away. He thought it would take longer to convince herself than a couple of harried hours. He continued to wait.

He threw the empty cup in the passenger footwell. He was working on two hours of sleep, plus two large, and mostly bad, Speedy's coffees. His bladder was going to win out soon. He shifted in his seat. He looked up and down the street for a nearby place that might have a bathroom. He already knew Speedy's was one of those employee-only places. He didn't spot any other good options. The street was primarily residential and quiet at noon. He hopped out of the van and jogged across the street to the alley that cut behind Lisa's apartment building. He found a secluded spot between two stinking dumpsters. A bored cop nailing him for public urination was the last thing he needed right now. He took care of his business with great relief, zipped up, and was about to return to the van when he spotted a flash of neon pink and green go past the opposite end of the alley. He knew those colors. He'd been trailing Lisa on her bike for days and that helmet was like a beacon on crowded streets. He ran to the alley opening and watched as she pedaled away. He had no doubt it was her. She'd changed clothes and somehow changed bikes, but he knew that helmet and upright riding style, sort of like the wicked witch in the *Wizard of Oz*.

He hustled back to the van. He jumped in. His chest heaved from the effort. He couldn't remember the last time he ran like that. They did not encourage running in prison. He got the van going and pulled up the map app on his phone. It was slow and laggy. Goddam, he hated this sleepy burg in the middle of nowhere. He turned left and then a quick right and stayed on that street until it intersected with the road where he'd seen Lisa riding. She was already gone. He turned left again to follow. He slowed at the first two lighted intersections, drawing a few horns, but didn't spot her down any side streets. On the third try, he spotted her. She was furiously pedaling up a steep hill. He felt his whole body relax.

"Ready or not, here I come."

.   .   .

Lisa had been commuting on her bike for years. Her ears were well attuned to the sounds of approaching cars and trucks. She knew the truck or van following her up the steep incline of Nog's Hill was going too fast. She took a quick peek and saw the maroon and gold colors of Clarkston. She didn't panic. Keres had stolen an older model. He probably hoped it was little-used and its theft wouldn't be noticed right away. He was probably right, but he was also paying for that choice now. She could hear the cylinders grinding as the grade increased and the old Econoline struggled to shift into a higher gear and maintain speed on the hill.

She stood up and kept pedaling.

She felt the weight of the pepper spray she always carried in her jacket pocket, but if Keres simply ran her down or forced her off the road and had a gun, the pepper spray would be useless. She kept her eyes on the crest of the hill and pumped her legs. She needed to make it to the top to have a chance.

Keres hunched over the wheel and urged the van to go faster. He smiled as Lisa glanced over her shoulder and saw the van. Keres punched the accelerator to the floor. It was almost too perfect. She'd turned off the busy commercial strip for a quieter side street. Once he caught up, he could force her off the bike and get her in the back. He didn't have a gun, but he'd found a mallet, a wire stripper, and a box cutter in the van's supply bins. He thought any of those would be enough to convince her to play along. If not? She didn't need all her fingers or both ears to tell him where the money was.

He watched her disappear over the top of the hill. He wasn't worried. He was gaining and, going downhill, the bike would be no match for the van's speed, even an old warhorse like this. Gravity was a bitch.

He made the top of the hill and hit the brakes. She wasn't on the other side. She was gone. He eased the van forward to the next cross street and saw her pedaling away down an even smaller street lined with overhanging trees and tall fences on either side. She was like a rat trapped in an increasingly tight maze.

"Nowhere to run now."

He made the tight turn onto the street and continued the chase.

Ten seconds later it was over. There was a double pop and the van lurched hard to the left. Keres fought the wheel to keep from careening up on the sidewalk and through the fence. He jammed a foot on the brakes and the van skittered to a crunching stop against the curb. He banged a fist against the steering wheel, then jumped out and confirmed what he expected. Something had shredded both tires on the left. He walked back 20 yards and found a collection of tacks and nails spread across the road. He looked up the street just in time to see Lisa and her bike disappear around a corner.

Lisa heard the tires go with an audible squoosh, like two fat water balloons popping, but she didn't relax. The handful of loose nails was something she'd carried since she was a teenage waitress back in Boston. Sometimes customers, especially when she worked at bars, took her friendliness for more than what it was. The nails were a good deterrent if they didn't get the message and tried to follow her at the end of her shift. She knew two flat tires were only a temporary roadblock. And he likely wouldn't be fooled so easily again.

She didn't look back. She pushed harder and took a series of random lefts and rights as quickly as she could. When she tasted blood in the back of her throat, she knew she couldn't keep going. Her legs were cinder blocks. She spotted an empty driveway with a detached garage. She steered the bike up the drive and behind a stand of overgrown arborvitaes. She slumped to the ground and let her back rest against the dirty siding. She allowed herself five minutes to recover. Her chest stopped heaving and her heart rate came back down. She stood, her legs were still jittery, but her hands had stopped shaking.

"Shut up legs," she muttered as she wheeled the bike down the short drive and climbed back on.

But where to go? By design and necessity, she didn't have many friends. She had colleagues and acquaintances. There was no one she could call with a fake story about burst pipes or fumigation in her building to buy a couple of sympathy nights on a couch or guest room. Plus, she didn't want to put even vague acquaintances in that sort of jeopardy. That left hotels. Luckily, a college town, even one as small as Clarkston, had more than a few options for visiting parents.

But first, she needed new hair.

Keres left the keys in the van and walked away. He was sure he'd left some DNA behind, but he didn't think it mattered. Would they really try to pull prints? Or DNA? He doubted it. He guessed the cops would chalk it up to bored kids and a harmless joyride. He dropped the mallet and wire stripper down a nearby storm drain, he couldn't walk around with those without drawing some eyes, but slipped the box cutter into his back pocket. That might come in handy.

He looked at the map on his phone, but the neighborhood at the top of the hill was a warren of intersecting streets and dead ends. There was no point in going after her right now. It would be a waste of time and energy. He tapped the phone against his leg. What would she do now? He doubted she'd go back to the apartment again. She knew work and home were contact points that were now off limits. Where would she go? Would she keep on running? Put Clarkston at her back and try to find somewhere new or would she turn and fight?

He thought he knew the answer, and he had an idea how to make sure he was right.

CHAPTER THIRTY-ONE

The heater rattled and Max stood, stretched out the kinks in his back, and blew on his hands. It was March according to the calendar, but no one had told the state of Vermont. The surrounding wilderness seemed content to hold onto its quilt of ice and snow. The heat worked, but it was miserly. He looked around the office, trying to think of anything else he needed to do. If he was moving, he'd be warmer. The office was a simple square. A counter was to the right of the door with a computer, still using dial-up access, and a television stacked on top. A door behind the counter led to a bathroom that doubled as a supply closet. The heater sat on the opposite wall along with a secondhand orange couch and a rack of dusty tourist brochures and free trail maps. A last door led to the court-yard out back.

He picked the sign up from the shelf under the desk and wedged it in the window next to the front door, then reached over and flicked the switch to turn on the outdoor sign. Finally, he turned on the exterior parking lot lights before he walked out and locked the door. His room was to the left, about 15 feet, directly beside the office. Not a bad commute.

He turned right instead and walked the length of the building. He aired out the guest rooms every couple of days. As he walked, he checked each window and pulled on each door to check the lock. He glanced at the split rock that still lay untouched out near the road and under the sign from last night. He picked up a shard of broken bottle from the asphalt. A last, lingering piece of Ted. Max smiled, remembering that night. He didn't think about his time with Thea, though that was certainly pleasant. He remembered how it felt as Ted walked toward him and he knew Ted was going to take a swing. The tang of adrenaline in the back of his throat. The way all his senses sharpened and slowed down. The way his body felt in sync as his hips twisted and his arm extended toward Ted's face.

"Jesus, what is wrong with me?" he said, a puff of breath misting in front of him.

The only response came from the neon sign, honestly the best feature of The Cliffside, as it buzzed and crackled to life.

"I do not miss it. I do not need it." He said it like a mantra as he walked back to his room.

The motel sign sat atop an I-beam 30 feet in the air. The red neon cast a hazy pink glow over the parking lot that leaked into the rooms, even with the curtains closed.

He'd asked Vic about it once when they were sitting in the office sharing a beer.

"Why'd you put it up there so high?"

"Me? Do you think I'm dumb enough to buy this place? I inherited this place. My uncle was a cheap fuck. The scrapyard wanted to charge him extra to cut the signpost to size. He told them to forget it." Vic smiled a thin slash that was as close as Max had seen to actual humor and warmed to the story. "Uncle Ross got some return on his investment in the end."

Max bit. "How's that?"

Vic nodded toward the back door. "It might blend in closer to a city." Max had learned that city was a four-letter epitaph for Vic. "But out here? That sign is visible for miles. It comes in real handy when they're searching for some schmuck who's lost out there."

Max had followed Vic's gaze. It had been dark and cold that night with pebbles of snow pinging off the window glass. It was impossible to see beyond the cracked concrete circling the pool, but Max knew Vic was referring to the vast tract, over 400,000 acres, of the Green Mountain National Forest, that butted up against the Chepstow town limits. Getting lost out there even in the more benign summer conditions would be dangerous for all but the most experienced hikers.

"That happen often?"

"Often enough. Uncle Ross made a deal with the county that anytime they requested he turn on his sign, he could bill it as part of the search and rescue op. That sign has paid for itself 50 times over by now."

"You still got the deal?"

"Hell, yes. Uncle Ross wasn't very good with real estate or property management, but he was good with contracts."

Max let himself into his room and gave his own wall heater a little kick. It remained off. He aimed a second one a few inches to the left. This time, the heater kicked on obediently. He dropped his book and the motel's cell phone on the table next to the bed and turned on the little alarm clock radio. He liked to catch the news at least once a day, partly out of self-preservation, he was still a wanted fugitive, but mostly because it grounded him in reality. Those piped-in voices reminded him he wasn't actually alone at the end of the world. He sometimes worried, after long solitary stretches, that he'd become a ghost himself.

He walked to the closet where he'd stacked canned goods and other sundry items. He often went into town for his meals, but if a storm blew in, he didn't want to survive on the vending machine offerings. He was pretty sure Vic hadn't replaced them in the last five years. He was debating heating up lentil soup on the hotplate he kept in his room or driving to town when a phone rang. It wasn't the room's phone. The landline was loud and jangly. No, this was the fake, tinny ring tone of a mobile phone. He hadn't heard anyone pull into the lot. He stepped to the window. The lot remained empty. The ringing followed him. He pulled his personal phone out of his pocket. This was the default ring tone associated with an unknown number. Very few people had this number. He contemplated answering, but figured it was likely a spam call. He wasn't sure how the caller had gotten the number, maybe it was an auto-dialer, or maybe his carrier had sold him out, but he was sure it wasn't anyone he was eager to talk to. He swiped to decline the call and put the phone down next to the motel phone.

He picked up the can of soup and plugged in the hotplate when the phone lit up again. Same number. Spammers and auto-dialers rarely called right back. Maybe something had happened to Lawrence or Eddie or Kyle. It wasn't international, so unlikely to involve Mose, but he felt his stomach tighten.

He picked up the phone. "Hello?" he said.

"Michael?"

Ice moved through his guts. Few people knew his phone number and even fewer knew that name.

"I know that's not what you go by now."

"Who is this?"

It was a female voice. She sounded older. He could hear the faintest bit of gravel in her voice. She continued like he hadn't spoken. "I'd resigned myself to never calling. Never hearing your voice again, but... I need help."

"Who are you?"

"I'm your mother."

Max hung up.

CHAPTER THIRTY-TWO

Max pulled open the heavy door of The Chepstow General Store and walked into the aroma of roasted nuts, penny candy, and chicory. Maybe that was what heaven would smell like? A pleasant confection of legumes, sugar, and caffeine. Max didn't think that would be so bad.

Jim slouched, half-hidden, behind the big cash register with the pull arm. After a few visits, Max had realized that most of the things in the store were props. Sometimes even old Jim himself.

The Chepstow General Store was in a converted church. An old-fashioned peanut roaster sat in what once was the knave. Five bucks for a pound of warm roasted peanuts. Max had never tried them, but Jim said they sold alright, especially with the skiers in the winter.

"People eat so much crap these days that a plain salted peanut is a novelty. And they taste damn good. They'd probably pay eight or nine bucks, but I'm too lazy to change the sign and the locals would get on me about it. They'd think I was putting on airs if I tried to charge that much."

"Make two signs. Put one up during the season and then lower the price back down the rest of the year," Max had said.

Jim had rubbed the perpetual white stubble on his chin while he leaned against the counter. The man had the posture of a damp dishrag. "Aye. Suppose I could do that but doesn't seem right. Charging one person one thing and another person something different."

"Sounds like commerce to me," Max said.

"A thing's worth what it's worth."

Max had left it at that. No reason to antagonize the man. He had learned you needed all the friends you could get up here in winter.

Max went to the second to last aisle and sorted through the bin of loose screws until he found a few that matched the one he'd taken from room 12. The heater's cover was warping and missing two corner screws. He only needed the two now, but figured it was a harbinger of how the rest of the units might age and it couldn't hurt to have more on hand, even if he wasn't the one to eventually use them.

He added a purple and pink striped hard candy stick from the jar next to the register. Seven screws and a candy stick. He was a big spender. Jim didn't comment, just rung it up and stuck the screws in a small plastic pouch, then he pulled a wrapped brown paper package from beneath the counter.

"Angela dropped this off for you."

"Oh, yeah. Where'd she get this stash?"

Angela was a cleaning woman and off-season caretaker for some of the ski properties nearby. Like Dickens's charwoman, she was often the first on the scene when a property was up for sale or being renovated. She supplemented her income by reselling various items the owners were more than willing to let her scavenge. She was happy to find out about Max's predilection for books.

"I usually just toss 'em. I've donated so many to the library over in Oxbow that they rarely take them anymore." Now she left interesting finds with Jim or occasionally dropped them off at the motel if her travels brought her close. Max tried to give her money a few times, but she wouldn't accept it even though she sold other items. "Most of these are more beaten up and tattered than I am. Wouldn't feel right taking your money for them. And besides, I like to think of myself as the Johnny Appleseed of books. I'm spreading the literary love. A room without a book is a room without a soul, right?" He'd found out where she lived, out on the edge of town in a trailer, and done a few light repairs or just visited. She had plenty of books, but not a lot of visitors.

"The old Cranmore place is going to probate and having an estate sale. She's spending a week cleaning. They gave her first crack at a few things," Jim said.

Angela usually passed on worn paperbacks, but this package was bigger and more substantial. Max carefully ripped the paper and slid out three hardcover novels. All John D. MacDonald first editions. There was the first Travis McGee, *The Deep Blue Good-By*, and two more that Max thought were from the latter part of the series. *The Dreadful Lemon Sky* and *Cinnamon Skin*. All in very good or excellent condition. Each was probably worth 150 or 200 bucks, maybe more, to the right collector. He'd read the first one, but not the other two.

"This is too much," Max said.

Jim peered over the counter at the books. He shrugged. "They look old." He pointed at *Good-By*. "I remember those types of painted covers from the pulps my dad would read back in the '40s and '50s."

Max nodded. "This one is from the early '60s. You know if she's still up at the Cranmore place? I want to thank her in person."

"Aye, she's still cleaning. Said it would likely take until

Saturday to finish up. The sale is on Sunday, but I doubt she's up there this late. She starts early but doesn't like to drive after dark. Eyes aren't what they used to be."

Max nodded. "She can still spot buried treasure."

"Aye."

Max turned to leave. Jim called out. "You planning on heading to the diner for dinner?"

He had been thinking about a Reuben, maybe some fries. "The thought had crossed my mind."

"Don't bother. Billy's grill is on the fritz again. He closed after lunch."

The downtown area of Chepstow was a simple crossroads, with the commercial buildings clustered near the center and the residences farther back. Vic's hotel was two miles north. Max exited the General Store and looked right, due south. The Countryside Diner was dark. The silver aluminum sides caught the yellow light from the streetlamp, but the pink and aqua sign was dark and the lot was empty. There was a coffee shop, Hopper's, that also sold pastries and simple soups for lunch, but that was long since closed. There was a steakhouse out by the interstate ramp, but that was another two miles in the wrong direction. He had food. He could make himself dinner. He turned north and started walking.

But the idea of a hot, greasy sandwich had lodged in his brain like a musical earworm. Normally, he was relatively indifferent to food. He could eat the same meal for a week and not flinch, but the idea of lukewarm Dinty Moore or Campbell's soup from the hotplate turned his stomach at the moment. That only left one choice.

The brush snare and slide guitar of Willie Nelson's *Bloody*

Mary Morning greeted Max as he stepped inside The Night Owl. The 1970 version, not the remake. Unlike Willie, Max wasn't running to forget a woman. Vic was at the corner table with two men he didn't recognize. He tipped an imaginary cap in their direction and headed for the bar.

The music might change, depending on who controlled the juke, but the bartender remained the same. The old guy stood at his station behind the taps. There were two other men at the bar, and Max took a seat equally spaced from each to keep the barroom equilibrium.

The Night Owl's kitchen was comprised of a microwave, a griddle, and a fry basket. It was good enough for tonight.

"Beer and a burger."

The bartender took a frosted glass from a small refrigerator below the bar and pulled the beer. He slid it across to Max and then disappeared through a swinging door in the back. He emerged five minutes later with a plated burger and fries. He put it in front of Max and inclined his head to the left. Salt and pepper and a bottle of ketchup sat next to the napkin dispenser.

"Thanks."

While Max ate, the bar settled back into its regular rhythm. An undercurrent of low talking, the occasional clink of a glass or bottle, and the scrape of a chair. It stayed that way for 15 minutes. Willie gave way to Waylon and then Johnny, but either someone ran out of quarters or didn't like Kristofferson, because next up was Journey. Or maybe someone just had eclectic taste.

The door opened again, and he stopped thinking about music.

Two men walked in. In the shadows of the doorway, Max first pegged them as early season hikers. Both men were on the shorter side of average, maybe five eight, and thin. As they moved into the bar, Max recalibrated his opinion. There was a predatory quality to their faces, lean and carved with watchful eyes. The one in front had the dark stubble of a five-day beard. The trailing one was slightly younger and kept his hands in his coat pockets. A trucker hat sat low on his brow and partially covered his face. Max now thought military or ex-military. It was something about the way they walked or shifted as they moved: discreet, careful, watchful. Maybe they were out here just to hike or bivouac. Maybe. But Max kept his antennae tuned to the usual or unexpected. He had to. And he was picking up a vibration from the pair. The nearest military base was halfway back to Boston. No one stumbled on Chepstow or The Night Owl by accident. Not at this time of year. Not unless they were bringing trouble. Or looking for it. He thought about what Lawrence had told him about someone looking at the SUV's GPS data.

Beard veered over to the bar while Trucker Hat took one of the tables and put his back to the wall.

"Two beers," the man said.

The old bartender pulled the draughts and made change from the 10 the beard slipped across the bar. The beard left two singles, looked in Max's direction and nodded, then carried the frosted glasses back to their table.

Max contemplated the last few swallows of his beer. Was he being paranoid? Jumping at shadows? He used the bar mirror to keep tabs on the pair. They were drinking and engaged in a conversation. They were not paying the slightest bit of attention to Max or anyone else in the bar. He drank the rest of his beer and waved to the old man to settle up. He'd use the bathroom and then make the walk home forti-fied with fat, fry oil, and alcohol. Maybe he'd start reading one of the John D. MacDonalds.

The restrooms at The Night Owl were down a back hallway behind the kitchen. Just past the jukebox and dart-board, the hallway jogged to the left. There were three doors. The single door on the right led out to the back lot and the dumpster. The two on the left were for the restrooms. First the women's and then the men's. There was a payphone, still well used with the spotty cell coverage around Chepstow, in the back corner just after the men's room. He recalled Vic telling him that the one outside the office at The Cliffside brought in an extra 50 bucks a week during tourist season.

There was a man hunched over the phone now. His back to Max. The conversation was low and whispered. Max reached out a hand and shifted his weight to push through the men's room door. Maybe it was the beer and fries, but his mind was a second slow, which made his body two seconds slow, which meant he didn't dodge the heavy plastic phone receiver completely. He twisted, but it clipped him over his right eye. He jerked back, but the hallway was narrow and he hit his head on the men's doorframe. He stumbled forward, momentarily stunned. He fell to his knees on the dirty tile. The man brought the phone down on the back of his neck. Max swung a wild, desperate punch and connected with something. The man grunted. Then his knee came up. Max moved to block it but was still a beat slow. There was a jarring pain through his shoulder and down his back. He grabbed the man's leg and tried to twist his knee. Then he felt a sharp pain, the unmistakable point of a blade, at the base of his neck.

"Stop," a soft voice said. "Let him go."

Max let go of the leg.

"Stand up."

Max stood and the blade slid from his neck down to his back. It stopped between his lower ribs where it could slide in and lacerate his liver. The knife holder knew what he was doing.

"Hands together, behind you."

Max had little choice. The restraints bit tightly into his wrists.

"Get the door."

The guy who had pretended to be on the phone moved around Max and opened the door that led out back. Max twisted slightly and wasn't all that surprised to see Beard and Trucker Hat follow him outside.

They weren't cops, that much was clear, but that didn't narrow it down all that much. Max had a lot of ghosts chasing him. Whoever these guys were and whatever they had planned, Max was sure it would not be pleasant. He'd prefer to head back to The Cliffside and read his books. He glanced around, looking for an opportunity or a weapon. But there was nothing but the dumpster and a moldering pile of cardboard liquor boxes.

Beard jabbed him in the back with the knife. "Around the corner." He tossed a set of car keys to Phone Guy. "Get the trunk open. Ryan, go around and watch the front. Make sure none of the yokels get curious."

Trucker Hat jogged around Max and turned the corner, headed for The Night Owl's front door. He didn't make it. There was a meaty thwack followed by a scuffling grunt, and then Trucker Hat's body dropped to the pavement. His upper body just visible to Max. Vic stepped around the corner holding a baseball bat.

"Too late. The yokels got curious," she said.

He felt Beard step closer and the knife pressure increase. "Nothing to do with you. We just want a few words with this guy. Go back inside and no one gets hurt."

Vic kicked Trucker's Hat's leg. "You mean no one else gets hurt?"

Phone Guy was circling slowly around to get the angle on Vic.

Max took a breath, about to warn Vic, but felt the knife cut into his side, the message clear.

"I can let that one go," Beard said. "I respect you sticking up for your friend, but you really don't want to push this."

"You don't know me, but let me tell you I used to drive my mother crazy on the regular. She would tell me not to go somewhere or not do something and I just couldn't help it. Vic, don't go near the old railroad tracks. Vic, don't go near the quarry. Vic, stay away from that Segal boy. I mean, can you imagine? It just grew in my mind until it was all I could think about. I had to do it. So, you telling me not to push it is the wrong thing to say. You understand?"

Phone Guy hadn't stopped moving and Vic now had to turn her head in both directions to keep each of them in view. They could both move at once and pinch her in-between them and disarm her. He'd be unable to help.

"Have it your way." Beard must have made some sort of signal. Max watched Phone Guy come forward.

Vic smiled. "Tommy."

There was the heavy cha-chunk of a shotgun being racked and the old bartender stepped around the corner.

CHAPTER THIRTY-THREE

"What the hell was that?" Vic asked. Her voice had lost the steel from the confrontation. Now she sounded nervous and more than a little scared. That made Max feel a bit better. She was human.

"No idea."

"No idea? Really?"

Max didn't want to lie to her but wasn't sure how much he could or should tell her. He hadn't known her for long, but he trusted her. She'd just proved she would step into the thick of it to help him, but that was when he was just a guy, an acquaintance, maybe a friend, who worked at her motel. The more she knew about his past, the more precarious her position would become. Would she do the same thing if she knew everything about his past? Or would she pick up the phone and call the cops? He wouldn't blame her for that reaction, either.

"Really. I don't know," Max said. "There are people... who might be looking for me, but I didn't recognize those guys."

No lie there. They had smelled like hired muscle, but Max really couldn't pin down the scent. He'd snapped a quick photo on his phone of Beard before they jumped in the truck. He'd pass it along to Lawrence. He was confident Eddie would have a name by morning. That might give him a clue as to who had the means and resources to find him and go after him.

Vic took her eyes off the road for a moment and looked at him across the truck's cab but didn't say anything. Max felt guilty for putting her in this position.

"How did you know to come looking for me?" he asked to fill the silence.

She tapped the stack of books on the bench seat between them. "I thought you forgot these. I was running them out to you. Didn't realize I was walking into whatever that was. I ducked back inside and grabbed Tommy."

"He okay with that? Not afraid of it coming back on him?"

She barked a short laugh. "Life has whittled Tommy down to bone and gristle. There's nothing left for fear. Plus, he's always looking for an excuse to let off that shotgun."

Max believed it. He flashed back to the parking lot and the old man pumping two rounds into the engine block of the men's SUV. He'd been smiling as he did it. If Beard or his pals came back looking for payback, Tommy probably wouldn't complain. Max didn't think Beard would be that stupid. He knew they'd blown their shot. It was hard to sneak up on someone twice in a town the size of Chepstow.

"But it wasn't random, was it?" Vic continued. "They didn't just happen into The Night Owl and pick you out."

"No, I don't think so."

She braked to a stop at one of Chepstow's few intersections. A single yellow blinked overhead.

"But it's not a stretch to think that if they found you at The Owl they might know about The Cliffside."

Max shrugged. "Yes, that's possible. Probably likely." He'd

been thinking much the same thing and wondering what to do.

Vic decided for him. She turned left, east, onto SR124, away from The Cliffside.

"Okay. It's unlikely they know who I am. Not yet, at least. You can crash at my place for the night, and we can figure out what to do in the morning."

He didn't like how quick she was to throw in with him. He felt the point of the knife on his neck again. She didn't know the stakes. But, short of getting in his car and driving out of town, and maybe never finding out what those guys wanted, he couldn't think of a better alternative.

Vic's place was... frillier than he expected. Vic wore barn coats and an old seed catalog hat. She drove a 15-year-old pickup and probably changed the oil herself. He might have guessed they were in the wrong house except that Vic's dog, Bailey, a mixed black and tan coonhound, bounded around their legs, looking for attention.

Despite not saying anything, she appeared to pick up on his thoughts as they entered and walked around the center staircase to the kitchen at the back. "I inherited the place from my mom. Never really got around to redecorating."

The house was a standard Cape with a square living room and dining room on either side of the stairs. The kitchen had an eat-in nook and a half bath in the corner. Vic dropped her coat on a kitchen chair and grabbed two beers from the fridge. "You owe me a beer. I left a half pint back at the bar."

"Owe you more than that. I never properly said thank you for stepping in. Not everyone would have done that."

Vic seemed embarrassed by the compliment and searched for a long time in a drawer. Max took a bottle opener that was stuck to the fridge by a magnet and handed it to her.

"Thanks," she mumbled. She popped both tops, handed him a bottle, and finally looked back at him. "And you're welcome. You've done good work on the motel and I've never properly said thanks for that. Consider us square."

"You're paying me for that, so I don't think it's quite the same. Besides, I'm not risking my life trying to patch up the roof."

"I wasn't risking my life. Maybe a few cuts and scrapes."

Max wasn't so sure about that. Those were serious men hired for a serious job. He didn't know what they had in mind, but cuts and scrapes likely would have only been the start. Vic and Max had gotten lucky. The men had been too confident and surprised by the unexpected resistance. It wouldn't happen again.

He was about to say as much, but Vic turned and walked out of the kitchen.

There was an additional room tacked onto the side of the house, next to the kitchen. There was a long leather couch against one wall and a recliner at the far end with a big dog bed on the floor as a sidecar. A low coffee table was in the middle of the room and a large flat-screen TV dominated the other wall. Two built-in bookshelves framed either side of the TV. It was clear this was the room Vic spent the most time in. He could almost see the shape of her body in the recliner. She dropped into the chair now and turned on the television. The Bruins were playing the Islanders.

"Who roots for the Islanders? You ever met an Islanders fan?"

Max sat on the couch. "They were good in the early '80s."

"Ancient history. You ever play hockey?"

"I played some."

"Yeah, you got the look."

"What's that mean?"

Vic shrugged. "I don't know. Just a sense. A forward, right?"

"Center. You play?"

"Sure, my dad loved hockey. He grew up with Orr and Esposito and the big, bad Bruins of the '70s. Hockey was a religion around here back then. He always wanted a boy. That never happened, so I was on skates early. Pond hockey, pee-wees, midgets, juniors. Thought I might have a shot at the Olympic team but," she paused, staring at the screen, then continued, "I sort of outgrew the competition around here. We couldn't afford a club team and most of those were far off, closer to Boston. Then my dad got sick." She took a long swallow. "And then hockey didn't matter that much."

"I'm sorry."

Vic just shrugged.

They finished a couple more beers and watched the rest of the game in silence. There was a brief awkward moment after Vic switched off the television.

"There's, ah, a guest room upstairs, but the sheets might be from the '90s."

"Couch is fine."

And it was. She set him up with a pillow and a thick quilt. He tried to read a few pages but couldn't concentrate. He took out his phone and sent a text message with the photo of Beard to Lawrence and asked him to dig up any information he could find. He listened to Vic as she moved around upstairs. Water ran through the pipes, boards creaked, then the house fell silent. He lay in the dark on the couch and thought about fate and circumstance. Was it luck or choices that led Vic to walk outside with those books? He didn't come up with an answer before he drifted off.

CHAPTER THIRTY-FOUR

At the end of each day, Cobb received various reports from different labs and manufacturing plants around the country. He was the only one to see all the reports. Many of his engineers complained about being unable to do their job effectively when they could only see a single piece of the puzzle. He ignored them. He paid them very well to live with the problem or they could find a different job. Most learned to live with it. Engineers couldn't resist a challenge.

He re-read the latest reports on the wireless biosensing again. The lead engineer was hedging. He kept referring to hard-wired solutions. Cobb knew that was a dead end. They'd taken that as far as they could. It was good. It was even groundbreaking, but it didn't do what Cobb knew it needed to do. If he was going to make his mark and change the world, groundbreaking wasn't good enough. Cobb knew the department head was a brilliant scientist, but also, perhaps, too conservative. Cobb thought he might have to replace the man to get that piece of the project where it needed to be.

If true modulation of the body's peripheral nervous

system was going to be workable, then the long-term mechanism for communicating with the spinal cord and other organs needed to be precise, wireless, and stable. Cobb believed they'd solved two of the three. The latest test proved that stability wasn't there yet. He was damned if he was also going to revisit hard-wired solutions, too.

He knew comfort would eventually be another thing he needed to consider, but he didn't think the man in black, the senators, or the Defense Department were going to judge his success or failure on that variable. Soldiers, foreign or domestic, were used to dealing with some level of hardship.

The phone rang. It wasn't his personal or business phone that each sat on the desk. He put the reports aside and opened the lower drawer. He'd been waiting for this call. The phone in the drawer was not a smartphone. Not on the surface. It appeared to be an older model with a small monochrome display and a number pad below. It looked like something you might pick up off the rack at a pharmacy or convenience store 15 years ago. Cobb had made it himself. The case was deceiving. The guts of the phone were state-of-the art to deter tracking and potential hacking.

He pressed the button to answer. There was no preamble or apology.

"There was a problem," Captain Bradley said.

That was the last thing Cobb expected to hear. He considered Bradley one of his best men. It wasn't the first time he'd asked the man to do something a little... unorthodox for him, and he'd never had a problem in the past.

"What happened?"

"We located Sullivan, or Strong, as requested. Got eyes on him. The intel provided was good. It was him."

Cobb didn't tell Captain Bradley that the intel had come from him personally. He'd spent two nights slowly, painstakingly tracking Lisa Sullivan's son Michael as he morphed from Michael Sullivan to Max Strong to a missing and wanted fugitive. But he couldn't hide from Cobb. Maybe he was old news to the authorities. Leadership changed. Agendas changed. Maybe they'd given up on finding him. But Cobb didn't lack motivation. He'd tiptoed into different systems and databases until he caught a scent. A very faint scent that was really more of a hunch. Now Captain Bradley, ex-Special Ops and current military contractor, was telling him that his hunch was correct. And that he had screwed it up.

"He was still in that small town in the southwest corner of Vermont," Bradley continued. "The team went for speed. We underestimated the locals."

"A bunch of hicks in the sticks got the best of your men, Captain?"

"Plans are always unpredictable. They tried to go in quick and dirty and grab him at a bar."

"They?"

"We. It was a mistake. A couple of locals responded with more force than expected. We did not want to escalate things further and create a bigger situation."

Cobb could tell the man was trying to spin the situation, and it was probably the right call after a blatant fuckup, when you are in a hole, stop digging, but Cobb was still trying to wrap his head around the fact that some townies got the drop on what he had assumed were professional soldiers.

"So Strong is still out there?"

"Yes."

"Do we know where?"

"Approximately."

"Of course, you know approximately. I know approximately that he's in the state of Vermont. I meant, specifically."

"Not at the moment, but we can locate him. Do you want us to try again?"

Cobb weighed the pros and cons of creating more waves. "No, Strong is on alert now. Stand down and standby. That location is so small and insular that anything else might cause some uncomfortable questions to be asked or people getting involved that I cannot control."

"Yes, sir."

Cobb hung up and dropped the phone back in the drawer. That felt like a missed chance, but he didn't dwell on it. He had another idea of how he might get Strong and still accomplish his larger goal.

CHAPTER THIRTY-FIVE

Keres double-checked the supplies in his laptop bag and then zipped it up. Duct tape, trash bags, plastic zip ties, rolling pin, box cutter. He smiled. He loved America. Guns were harder to come by, at least in places you didn't know, but a homemade mayhem kit was always just a hardware store away. He exited the car and went into Manchie's yogurt shop.

There were no other customers inside. March appeared to still be too cold for ice cream or frozen yogurt. A single employee was behind the counter, a young woman, probably still in high school, working an after-school job. The shop closed in five minutes. She wiped the counter and then moved to the two small round tables near the shop's single window. "Let me know when you're ready," she said and drifted back behind the counter, knowingly or not, putting a barrier between herself and Keres. Smart girl, Keres thought. He glanced out the shop's window. Manchie's was on a small side street, close to the center of town, but traffic, both pedestrian and car, right now was low. Through the window, he could only see a narrow strip of sidewalk and part of the funeral home across the street. The funeral home was dark and deserted. No one had died tonight.

He took a small cup off a teetering stack and used the self-service machine along the wall to get himself a chocolate/vanilla twist. He would have preferred a thick shake, but he had work to do first and this was just a prop. He'd get his sugar and dairy fix later. He took the cup to the register. The woman weighed it and he paid. She handed him a white plastic spoon, which he took with a smile, and then left. There was a short bench to the right of the door, just at the bottom of a set of stairs. He sat on the bench. The light in the window on the second floor remained on. He hadn't missed her.

Ten minutes later, a green minivan with a dent in the front quarter panel pulled up and parked. The lights went off in Manchie's. A middle-aged man with a gray brush cut and matching mustache was behind the wheel. Keres could feel the man's eyes take him in as he sat on the bench. A single, older man, eating yogurt on a bench after dark. Keres didn't look back up a second time. He did his best to look bored. He took a bite of the melting yogurt and tapped randomly on the phone perched on his knee. A moment later, he heard the small bell over Manchie's door jingle. A lock turned with a squeak and then one of the van's doors opened and closed. The sound of talk radio leaked out. The minivan backed up and drove off.

He looked up again. The last class had ended more than half an hour ago. What was she doing up there? If he had to wait out here much longer, he'd need to adjust his plan. The yogurt was supposed to put her at ease, but now the shop was closed and it might only put her on guard. He didn't know the layout upstairs, and he didn't know what she might have for self-defense. It was a new-age place, so maybe nothing, maybe she didn't believe in weapons or force, but it was also a small business run by a woman. He'd wager she was prag-matic, hippie or not. He didn't want to walk into a cloud of pepper spray or eat a bullet. He was about to toss the cup and see if the building had a back entrance when the light clicked off and the door on the second story opened. He looked back down and continued his act with the phone.

He heard her lock the door, no squeaky lock for her, just a satisfying, secure thunk, and then start down the stairs. Her steps paused halfway down as she noticed him sitting there. Time to make a decision, honey. Are you going to trust that warning bell in the back of your brain or are you going to play the odds and walk on by? He kept his eyes on his phone and didn't look in her direction.

She continued down the stairs. He let her walk past. He could smell the sweat mixed with some sort of scented lotion or deodorant. She turned her back on him and walked toward the small SUV parked in the last spot of the row. He let her get a few steps clear, let the hackles on the back of her neck relax, let her think she was safe, then he went after her.

He checked the tape on the woman's wrists and ankles. She made a mewling sound through the strip over her mouth but didn't open her eyes. The restaurant had no power, but he'd bought a camp lantern at the store along with his kidnapping kit. He'd turned it on full power and then went outside and checked the view. No light leaked out from the boarded-up windows.

He pushed the woman's head to the side and looked at the gash on her scalp. He only had the lantern at half power now. He held it close to the woman's hair. The wound had stopped bleeding. The blood trickling from her ear and nose had also stopped. She'd survive at least a little while longer. That was all he needed.

He didn't feel any remorse, just relief that he hadn't killed her. He'd never been good at judging how hard to hit some-one. It wasn't a skill he particularly ever needed to cultivate. If it came to it, his credo was to always hit first and hit as hard as he could. This job was a little different. He'd come up behind her just as she turned. He could see she had some-thing in both hands, but she didn't get to use it. He'd cracked her on the side of the head with the rolling pin. She'd grunted and fallen flat.

The something in her hands turned out to be some sort of small electrical self-defense whip and her iPhone. He picked both items up. He'd put the phone in his pocket and consid-ered the little whip. There was a molded plastic handle with a braided 16-inch cord at the end. The tip gave off a slight hum. It crackled and snapped in the night air. It was a wicked-looking thing. He found the off switch and stuffed it into the pocket with her phone. Then he'd quickly grabbed her around the waist, threw her over his shoulder, and carried her the 15 yards to his car. He dug his keys out and unlatched the trunk. He dumped her in and bound her wrists and hands with the plastic ties. He shut the lid and looked around. Everything remained dark and quiet on the small side street. Start to finish, the kidnapping had taken less than a minute.

Next, he'd driven carefully, coming to a complete stop at every intersection and never going above the speed limit, back to the abandoned fast-food restaurant. Halfway back, when he cleared the town center and campus, he dug the woman's phone out of his pocket.

"Stupid," he said to himself out loud. He'd briefly consid-ered keeping it. It was a newer and better model than his phone and it wouldn't take much to wipe it clean and swap out the SIM card, but it was too much of a risk. He didn't have the time. When he had the money, his money, he could buy as many phones as he wanted. He powered it down and tossed it out the window into the weeds on the side of the road.

Ten minutes later, he safely reached the restaurant. He didn't like tying his rental car to the location, even for a short time, but he didn't have another choice. Lisa had seen to that. He didn't want to risk stealing another car and he needed to move fast. Still, he made a mental note to ditch this car soon. Even if the reservation was under a false name, he didn't like leaving footprints behind.

Keres sat down across from the unconscious woman. He put the lantern in the middle of the table, then took out his laptop and connected to the hot spot on his phone. The dusty plastic booths and the scent of fry oil remained, but the Wi-Fi, if it ever existed, was long gone. He waited as his secure VPN connected and then he brought up a browser for the dark web and went digging. It didn't take long. If people knew how much of their personal information was easily available, they might finally kick their online habit.

He realized it was a problem of perspective. He'd been chasing Lisa Sullivan and the money since they all took a high dive off that bridge in Maine 25 years ago. Even while he was in prison, he was following in her footsteps, or trying to. After the stunt with the nails and the van's flat tires this afternoon, he decided that he'd had enough. He was going to change the rules.

He looked away from the screen at the woman. "You are my lure. I don't need to chase her." He looked back at the screen, which now showed Lisa's, as Jill Williams, mobile phone account. He took out a burner phone, another big box purchase, and turned it on. After five minutes of tapping through the registration process, he held it up and took a picture of the woman. He examined it. The phone was cheap with a crappy camera, but it got the job done. He thought it made her clear. He attached the photo to a text message, added the burner's number, and then sent it to Lisa/Jill's mobile number.

Less than a minute later, the phone rang.

"What did you do? Is she alive?"

He could hear the fear and stress in her voice. This had been the right decision. She'd been so calm and collected even when he was bearing down on her in the van. He smiled. It felt good to rattle her cage. He drew out the silence and let her wait.

Finally, he said, "I only did what I had to do, Lisa, to get what is mine."

"Is she alive?"

"For now. She's going to have a nasty headache when she wakes up. Not sure how much help yoga is going to be. Still, it could have been worse. Being friends with you, being married to you, is turning out to be quite dangerous."

"What do you want?" Now her voice had gone cold.

"I want my part of the score. I've waited long enough, don't you think? In fact, I think I've earned a little interest as well. Why don't you just bring all the money and we'll call it square?"

"There is no money, Keres."

"Bullshit!" he yelled, then in a calmer voice, "Those boxes were gone, maybe not all of them, but a lot of them, when I woke up drowning in that van."

"You really think, in that situation, my dead husband strapped in next to me, that my first thought was how to get the score?"

"Yes, I think that's exactly what you did. You are an outlaw. You would have cried for John, but not right then. Hell, no. You would have thought about surviving. And you did. Very well. For a long time. You made yourself disappear.

And to do that, you needed cash. I don't think you have it. I *know* you have it."

"Wrong. That river up in Maine has your cash. Not me."

"You've got 24 hours to come up with a better answer or your yoga friend's going to start losing fingers."

CHAPTER THIRTY-SIX

Lisa sat on the hotel bed with her head wrapped in a towel. She'd used cheap drugstore dye to change her natural gray to black. She stared at the muted floral wallpaper without really seeing it. Keres had kidnapped Naomi. Despite her efforts to isolate herself and keep everyone at arm's length, she'd failed. Again. She was friendly with Naomi, but they were hardly best friends. Keres must have seen them the night they'd had a drink and assumed there was more to the relationship than there really was. Either way, someone else was paying a price for her decisions. Again.

She stood and paced back and forth between the windows and the room's thin door. The room was a simple square with two double beds, each covered with a brown checkered bedspread. There was a rust-colored rug to clash with the yellow walls and heavy beige drapes over the windows.

After she'd ridden away from Keres and the broken-down van, she'd ended up on Roebuck Street, south and east of West Adams' modest downtown, a half-mile west of the highway interchange. Off-brand lodging, fast-food restaurants, gas stations, and auto repair shops filled the street. There were two lower-end chain hotels closer to the Clarkston campus that sucked up visiting parents, but otherwise, West Adams didn't have the geography or attractions to support much more.

Lisa chose the Jackson Inn and Suites at random and handed over $60, the weeknight rate, for a room with a double bed and free Wi-Fi. It was cheap and functional and a step up from anything along old Route 1. That was a wasteland slowly being colonized by dirt, weeds, and addicts. She hoped she never got low enough or desperate enough to seek out those places.

She tried to come up with a plan, but her mind was frozen. Anytime she closed her eyes, she saw Naomi's face in the small cell phone photo. Without the twin trickles of blood, stark red lines that ran along her jawline, she might have been sleeping. But she wasn't. Keres had kidnapped her and taken her hostage. Because of her. She stood and looked around the room for a notepad, but the Jackson Inn wasn't that type of place. She opened the bedside table drawer and found a King James version of the Bible. She tore out the front few pages and dug out a pen from her purse.

She made a list. It had always helped calm and organize her mind in the face of stress before, and it worked now. It was how she kept Gary's department running in the face of his incompetence. Oh, what she would give right now to only have to deal with Gary's piss-poor management and funky chinchilla teeth. She put pen to paper and slowly felt her mind shift from blind panic to coherent thought. First, she would need a car. Whatever Keres had planned, and wherever he planned to do it, she would need a car. She couldn't load Naomi onto the handlebars of her bike.

Next, she would need a gun. She didn't like it. She'd sworn off handling any firearm since that night. She debated with herself, but ultimately decided it would be necessary. Keres needed to be dealt with and half measures would not get her there. Throwing out another handful of nails and hoping for the best wouldn't cut it.

She quickly jotted down a number of other things that filtered into her head: first aid kit, aspirin, clothes, food, a safe place to stay, flashlight, gloves. Finally, she added one last thing to the list. She needed help. She sat back on the bed and stared at the last scribbled word. Her hand had appeared to write it without her input. Maybe it was John. Maybe it was her subconscious telling her what she didn't want to hear, but there it was in blue ink at the bottom of the King James copyright page. Help. Who could and would help her? She couldn't ask Joyce. That would only get her sister hurt, or worse. She had no friends. And no one else she felt comfortable asking to take this type of risk. It would drastically increase her odds of success if it was two versus one. She felt cornered and out of options. And yet... there was still one person.

There was no answer. She redialed. Same result. He'd picked up once. He'd pick up again, she told herself. She put the phone down and felt a wave of feelings surging toward her. She knew if it hit, it might overwhelm her. She couldn't afford to curl up in a ball right now. She'd try again in the morning.

She looked back down at the list on the torn sheets of paper. She needed something to occupy her mind. Stores were closed but maybe she could work on the car. She had seen the free Autotrader papers in a plastic kiosk in the office. She stood and checked the window. The street was deserted except for two women standing under the 24-hour gas station sign across the street. One had red hair, one blond. Both were artificially tall, swaying slightly on pointed heels, and skinny in a wrung-out way. They had not zipped their coats. Lisa could see one wore a red sequin top while the other had chosen white. Despite their coats, they must be cold. Their black skirts didn't cover much of their thighs.

A pickup truck with high struts and mud splattered on the side panels pulled into the station and up to a pump. A man got out and started pumping gas. He was not Keres. He was young and short, with long hair that trailed out from under a red and white ballcap. Lisa was too far away to read the logo on the hat. The blond wandered over and struck up a conversation with the man. Lisa opened the door and walked toward the office at the end of the row.

The Jackson Inn and Suites office had the same footprint as her room, but the bed had been replaced by a counter and a computer and the floor was laminate tile instead of hide-the-stains low-pile carpet. An overweight woman with stringy yellow hair and sallow skin looked up from the desk when Lisa walked in and raised her eyebrows.

"I just need..." Lisa trailed off and waved an arm at the racks of brochures and dusty postcards crowded into the corner next to the vending machine.

The woman looked relieved that she didn't have to get up. She appeared not to be surprised or curious why Lisa might need these things at 2:00 in the morning. Maybe it made her good at her job. She'd probably seen stranger things on the overnight shift. Lisa stepped to the left and opened the small, scratched plastic door that held the free Autotrader papers. She grabbed a similar classified one from the neighboring kiosk, this one red to the Autotrader green, and then returned to her room.

The redhead was now standing alone under the broken glow of the Citgo station sign.

. . .

Back in her room, she spent a half hour reading through the ads and circling the potential options, but when that was done, there was nothing more she could do until morning. She felt tired but knew she wouldn't be able to sleep. Or maybe she was afraid to sleep. She knew when she closed her eyes, she would find Naomi and maybe others waiting for her. She went back to her list and thought about the gun. Then she thought about Naomi. And then the gun again. She realized her friend might still be part of the solution.

She checked her watch. She would go now. She wheeled her bike outside. She gave a polite nod to the redhead as she rode past, but the woman didn't return the greeting. Her eyes skipped over Lisa and continued to scan east and west along the road.

Lisa had driven Naomi home once when Naomi's car wouldn't start. It had been over five years ago, but Clarkston wasn't a big town and Lisa was confident she could find the house again. She pushed hard and was sweating lightly when she made the turn onto Franklin Street 30 minutes later. She was sure this was the right street, but in the dark, her confidence in picking the right house waned. She'd hoped she'd recognize it, but now all the small two-story detached houses looked very similar. She really couldn't afford to pick the wrong house.

There were nine choices. Four on each side of the street and one on the dead end lot. She did a slow circuit and tried to recall the time she'd dropped Naomi off. They'd been chatting and Lisa hadn't been paying too much attention. Lisa narrowed the choices to the two nearest houses on the left. Then she realized she was overlooking the obvious solution. She pulled her phone out and googled Naomi, but all the addresses that came back were for the yoga studio. Then she almost slapped herself on the forehead. She had become so accustomed to her phone giving her answers that she forgot to think for herself. She rolled up and checked the first potential mailbox. It was empty. She went to the second. Two pieces of junk mail addressed to 'Current Resident' and one electric bill for Naomi Sinclair.

She checked her watch. It was creeping past 4:30. She needed to be in and out while the street was still quiet. She carefully scanned the houses one last time, looking for twitching curtains or lights in upstairs windows. She didn't need a neighbor with insomnia or suffering from prostate problems to see her lingering. What she had done so far was curious, but not illegal. Her next step was not so innocent.

CHAPTER THIRTY-SEVEN

Spotting nothing to make her change her mind, Lisa wheeled the bike up the short driveway, trying to make it look natural, and leaned it against the side of the house. She followed a small flagstone path around to the rear yard. The back yard was a small square divided into four plots of raised beds. The beds had been recently turned and Lisa caught a smell of damp, rich soil. Only one bed looked to be active, with tiny leafy seedlings peeking out in neat rows. She turned her back to the garden and faced the rear of the house. Standing on the short concrete steps that led to the door, the neighbors on the right could see her, but a tall evergreen hedge blocked the view from the ranch house on the left.

The door was a simple exterior door. A slab of rust-resistant galvanized steel painted flat white with hinges on the left and a latch and a deadbolt on the right. There were decorative rectangle panels, but no panes of glass. There was a double casement window five feet to the right of the door. She could see the top of a stove, a microwave, and part of the refrigerator. There were no other windows on the first floor.

She tried the knob. Locked. She checked under the knotted burlap welcome mat. Nope. Okay, she hadn't expected it to be that easy. She stepped back down and examined the short beds that abutted the house. A single woman living alone was likely to have a spare key available outside the house. Would she hide it on her property or give it to a neighbor? It likely depended on how well and how much she liked, or trusted, her neighbor. Lisa hoped the answer was not much, or she was shit out of luck.

She bent down and turned over a few rocks, but they were just that, rocks. She looked around. The tilled beds offered little in the way of hiding places, unless Naomi simply buried it. Lisa would never find it if that were the case. There was a small upright shed, not much bigger than an old phone booth in the back right corner of the yard. It likely held fertilizer, gardening tools, and other bric-a-brac. Even a tiny outdoor lock-up would have plenty of places to hide a spare key.

She started in that direction when a voice in the dark asked, "Who are you?"

Lisa almost jumped out of her skin and put a hand to her mouth to stifle a scream. She turned in the voice's direction but saw only darkness. A moment later, the red cherry end of a cigarette sparked off the neighbor's porch.

"You scared me," Lisa said. She took a few steps in the voice's direction and tried to catch her breath and settle her nerves.

"Imagine what you did to me then," the voice responded. "Not every night I find someone walking through Naomi's garden in the middle of the night."

"I wouldn't say it's the middle of the night." Lisa turned and made a show of looking at the thin band of light expanding on the horizon.

"Seems like semantics to me. When you get to be my age, night, day, awake, asleep, time becomes a bit more relative.

So, I'll ask again before I call the police. Who are you, and what are you doing over there?"

Lisa walked to the waist-high picket fence, more decorative than functional, and opened the gate. She walked across the driveway and put a hand on the porch rail.

"That's far enough. I'm old, but I'm not deaf."

The woman was sitting in an old-fashioned metal porch glider. She wore a puffy down coat and had a patterned afghan over her legs. As Lisa watched, the woman raised her smoke and took a long pull. It was a thin cigarillo, not a cigarette, and Lisa caught the heady aroma of tobacco, honey, and cognac. The woman's skin was dark and creased. She might not yet have hit her centennial, but she likely wasn't far off. Lisa also saw that whatever her age, her eyes remained lively and focused directly on her.

"You don't look like no burglar. Least not a normal one."

"I'm not."

"Naomi in some kind of trouble?"

"Why would you ask that?"

"We've been neighbors for four years now, since my daughter made me move in with her because she thought I couldn't live by myself anymore, pssht to that idea, by the way, and I've watched her build that garden. She checks it every night, even in the middle of January. What can you possibly do with a garden up here in the middle of January? But she's always poking and prodding at it. Didn't see her tonight."

"Maybe you missed her?"

"Did I?"

Lisa doubted this woman missed very much. "Maybe she took a trip?"

"No, she didn't do that."

"How do you know?"

"She wouldn't have left Rizzo without telling me."

"Rizzo?"

"The only thing she loves more than her garden is that cat. My daughter feeds it when Naomi visits her brother or goes on vacation. Rizzo is an impudent and insolent beast, but we try to be neighborly when we can."

Lisa smiled. She wanted to sit on the glider and talk with this woman but could feel time slipping past. The band of light on the horizon was growing thicker. "I need to get inside."

"Why?"

Honesty, to a point, seemed like the best strategy. "Naomi needs help."

To Lisa's surprise, that's all it took. "Okay."

"Okay?" Lisa asked.

"Yes, are you the deaf one? I said we try to be neighborly. If our neighbor needs help, then I'll try to help."

She stubbed out her smoke in a large clay ashtray next to the glider and then slowly stood up. She folded the afghan before placing it back on the seat, then moved to the back door, opened it, reached inside, and came back with a key.

"I consider myself a righteous judge of character. I know you're not telling me all of it, but I do believe you when you say Naomi is in trouble and I can see that you want to help. I'll let you in and wait while you do whatever you're here to do."

"Thank you," Lisa said. It was a better outcome than Lisa could have hoped for 10 minutes ago.

Lisa waited while the woman carefully stepped down off her porch and walked alongside her as they crossed the space to Naomi's back door. She unlocked the door and stepped inside. A brown shorthair cat materialized by the woman's legs. "Hello, Rizzo," she said, then turned to Lisa. "Go do your business and I'll get the cat some food and water."

Lisa headed for the stairs that bisected the house and

opened into the kitchen. She'd start upstairs. The second floor had two bedrooms. One immediately to the left at the top of the stairs and the other at the end of the hall. There was a bathroom and a closet in the middle. Lisa glanced in the first bedroom, but it had the distinct feel of an infrequently used guest room. She walked the length of the hall. While approximately the same size as the guest room, Naomi had picked this one as the master bedroom. Maybe for the east-facing window or maybe for the view of her garden.

Back in her younger and wilder days, she and John had pulled a few home robberies before finding their natural talents and skills suited them more toward planned heists. Still, Lisa found she had a knack for quickly assessing a room for hiding places. In her experience, people kept secrets and valuables close to where they slept. She went to the bedside tables first but found nothing before she moved on to the double-wide closet. There was a portable free-standing safe on the floor. She gave the handle a tug, locked. Lisa didn't give up. She didn't think it was in the safe. No point. She moved to the dresser and found it, not in the top drawer, but at the bottom, under a pile of folded sweatshirts.

People kept secrets, valuables, and guns close at hand.

They'd had a conversation about self-defense options during one of their wine chats. Naomi had told her she kept a gun at home but not at the studio.

She examined the gun in the light. It was a Smith and Wesson .38 revolver. It was black and modern and very light. Maybe it was designed specifically for women. Lisa had never been a gun person and avoided them on jobs when she could. Still, John had made her practice and she could handle herself, but it had been a long time. The gun smelled slightly of oil. Naomi had taken care of it. She pressed the cylinder release and checked the rounds. It was loaded. She didn't look for more bullets. If she needed to reload with Keres, she had already lost. She put the gun in her jacket pocket and went back downstairs.

The old woman leaned against the kitchen counter and watched Rizzo eat his food.

"Find what you were looking for?" she asked.

"Yes, thank you."

The woman reached out a hand and pulled open a drawer. "You didn't have to go all the way upstairs."

Lisa glanced down and saw a second, identical .38 special and a box of cartridges sitting next to the tinfoil and plastic wrap.

"In my experience, two guns are always better than one."

CHAPTER THIRTY-EIGHT

Martha woke up and immediately wanted to close her eyes again. Every inch of the place smelled of nicotine, desperation, and loneliness. She wondered how many cigarettes and bottles of liquor had been consumed in this room.

She swung her feet over the side of the bed and picked up her phone from the side table. No alerts had gone off. According to the locator app, Keres, or at least Keres's Chevy, was outside in the lot. She stifled a yawn and moved to the window, parting the curtains with a finger. Yup, still there. She didn't always fully trust technology. It sometimes felt a little too close to magic for her taste.

But it sure had its uses. She'd slept for 16 straight hours. Her back remained sore and achy, but that wasn't going to change until she got back to her clawfoot tub, bath salts, and red wine. The sleep had cleaned the cotton out of her head. That was almost worth the cost of reconnecting with Myers.

She'd called him yesterday and asked for a favor. Could you still call it a favor when the guy asked for 500 bucks on top of the cost of the tracker? Martha thought he still held a grudge from the two dates they'd gone on after working a fugitive job in the Finger Lakes a decade ago.

She stewed on it, getting more annoyed about the cash, while she waited the four hours, plus an additional half hour in a coffee shop because Myers got lost, as he drove up from Staten Island. When he finally walked in, she remembered why they'd gone on the two dates in the first place. He was gorgeous and, while age had gifted her fine lines and sore feet, it had only burnished his looks. Life never stopped taking potshots at middle-aged women. But despite feeling like three-day-old meatloaf, she thought she detected a spark of similar interest in his eyes, too. Maybe she was being too hard on herself. She thought about asking him back for a ride on the lumpy mattress, but then he opened his mouth and she remembered why there hadn't been a third date. The intervening years hadn't dulled his fervor for talking about his mother or the Mets. She doubted his taste in bourbon had improved, either. She'd taken the bag with the magnetic GPS tracker, paid him, and went back to the motel alone.

The next step had been to get it in place on Keres's car. She couldn't just slap it on the bumper. She didn't need Keres to stumble on it or hit a pothole and have the thing pop off. Then where would she be? Out 700 bucks and up shit's creek. She could still pass along the cost to Cobb. Even so, it was the principal. She'd feel bad and still be dog-tired trying to track Keres on her own.

It wasn't just a matter of security. She also needed to consider a power supply. The tracker had a decent battery but the way this job was going, long and hard, if she could hook it into the car's power supply, she would be in better shape. It would be one less thing to stress about. Getting it hooked into the car's battery would likely also keep it out of the elements and better protected. Rain or snow could just as easily fry the tracker as a dead battery. She didn't want to have to swap it out and do this song and dance twice. No, better to take her time and do it right. But she couldn't do all of that with Keres sitting in his room. Not awake, at least. She needed time and a second pair of eyes.

She had considered the front desk clerks, but then dismissed the idea. The night guy would definitely take her money, but she had the feeling he would then immediately call and sell it to Keres. The day guy was a rule follower. When she'd checked in, he had earnestly run her through a laundry list of rules and regulations as if she was boarding the Queen Mary and not a third-rate roadside bed barn. And third-rate was being generous.

She had settled on the cleaning woman. There appeared to be only one. A squat woman with broad shoulders and dark-complected features who wore faded jeans and a navy Clarkston sweatshirt. Martha had seen the woman at various points during the day pushing a maid's cart, turning the rooms, as well as hauling garbage bags and changing out an exterior light panel. She gave off a vibe of being tough and capable.

Martha approached the woman as she was finishing up room seven on the far side of the hotel. A stringy guy with a full beard and no luggage had pulled in yesterday evening as Martha watched the lot through her window. He had apparently moved on again.

"Hello," Martha said, stopping a few feet away, trying to appear open and harmless. Martha was on the tall side for a woman, a shade under five ten, and had been told more than once she could come off as cold and overbearing. Martha preferred to think of herself as calm and professional, but if she was honest, she preferred books to most people. Did that make her cold?

The woman looked at her but didn't speak. Martha's initial impression didn't change with proximity. The woman wouldn't have been out of place on the frontier. She looked like a migrant woman from Dorothea Lange's photos, a woman whittled down by life and the landscape, eyes on the horizon, always looking for something better but knowing it wasn't coming over the horizon.

Martha tried to smile wider. "Hola."

"I speak English."

"Of course."

The woman squinted. "Room 14."

"That's right."

"Do you need something? A towel? More soap?"

"No, nothing like that."

Martha had a story ready. She knew from experience that people responded better to requests for help, especially help that skirted into a moral gray area, if it was part of a story. The sadder the better when the person replayed the narrative later to reassure themselves.

But it didn't work on everyone. Martha sized the woman up again. She stood slightly hunched, maybe in some pain from being on her feet all day, but there was a shrewdness around her eyes. Life had ridden her hard, but she'd learned some lessons. One thing Martha liked about working in these parts of town? The parts with old motels, cracked pavement, back alleys, and bars where the neon signs were always missing a letter. The parts she called the low down. It stripped away the artifice. Most of the time, it just came down to commerce.

"You know the guy staying in 21?" she asked.

The woman nodded. "I know it's a guy. Keeps his room neat. Doesn't tip. Don't know no more about him. Been here about as long as you."

"He in there now?"

The woman shrugged. "Don't know. He wasn't this morning when I replaced the towels."

"He's not a good guy."

No response to that.

"I need you to check if he's in there now," Martha continued.

"How much?"

Martha smiled to herself. Commerce.

"Fifty to knock on his door. If he's not there, I've got another 50 if you keep an eye out for him. Without his car, he's probably on foot. I need a few minutes. I need to get into his car."

"Another 50 to keep my mouth shut?"

She'd definitely learned to seize an opportunity. Martha pretended to think about it but didn't really have a second option. "Alright."

Martha had been married four times, though the third one had only lasted two months and she didn't really count it. Martha's fourth and final husband, Daryl, had been a mechanic, a good one, a better mechanic than husband, actually. Daryl liked three things in life: beer, cars, and dancing. It was the last one that had hooked Martha one night in the Tin Lounge down in Asbury. That man could move. You didn't find that many men who really enjoyed dancing. You found plenty that would tolerate it to get you in bed, but Daryl really did like to bust a move. Unfortunately, Martha learned, he didn't discriminate in his partners, and he didn't stop when the music ended. He boogied his way into quite a few unfamiliar beds during their three-year marriage. Probably more than she knew. Still, he'd been an excellent mechanic and he liked to tinker and talk out in the garage. Martha didn't mind the occasional beer and after she kicked Daryl out, she realized she'd learned quite a bit about cars while drinking and chatting in the garage. Over the years, once the sting of the cheating faded, she didn't think it was all that bad of a trade. She often used Daryl's knowledge on the job. And some of the tools he left behind in the garage. Martha's rule when kicking out a cheating spouse is they could keep what they could carry.

Martha stood around the corner, out of sight. She heard the woman, whose name was Valeria, knock on Keres's door. Valeria said something. Martha couldn't make it out, but a moment later, Valeria came around the corner.

"He's there. He was asleep. He was not happy I woke him up."

"Shit. That will make things more challenging."

She handed Valeria a 50.

Keres had parked the Chevy directly in front of his motel room door. She'd need to get the tracker on with Keres less than 20 feet away.

"Okay, you still want to make some money?"

"Yes."

"Meet me back here in 30 minutes. I want to give him time to fall back to sleep."

Martha placed the tracker, along with a bag she'd taken from her trunk, next to the driver's side door of the Chevy. The bag was what Martha considered her work bag. It was an old gym bag that had never seen the inside of a gym. It had helped her get inside many places when she didn't have a key but did have a pressing need to get through a locked door.

She glanced at Valeria who stood with her maid's cart directly in front of Keres's door. Valeria nodded. The room was quiet. Keres was asleep. She hoped.

She took out an air pump wedge and worked it between

the doorframe and the weather stripping. A friend of repo men everywhere, the wedge was a simple but ingenious contraption. She got the deflated bag in position and then used the hand pump to inflate the bag and create a crack in the door. Next, she used a simple coat hanger with a wad of tape balled at the end to reach through and disengage the lock. It unlocked up with a painfully audible crunching pop. Martha froze and waited for Valeria. After a tense minute, the woman shook her head. No noise from inside.

Martha put the tools back in her bag and picked up the tracker. After a little internet research on the Chevy Cruze, she'd decided that the OBDII port was the best place to stash the tracker. It was a little more visible than she would have liked, just below the dashboard and to the left of the steering column, but the upside of it being inside the car, protected from the elements and plugged directly into the car's power supply, convinced her it was the best option.

She eased up the door handle slowly, by degrees, and then carefully opened it wider. She quickly knelt and attached one end of the adapter to the car's port for power and connected the other end to the GPS tracker. Then she used a few drops of Super Glue to attach it to the underside of the dash, as far out of sight as possible. She would not be coming back to get this one after the job was done. She stepped back and looked at it. It wasn't overtly visible and looked a little like it belonged there. She had to hope that Keres wasn't the paranoid sort.

Now, as she stepped out of the shower and tried to dry her hair with the limp towel, her phone, sitting on the bathroom counter, pinged with a message. Keres was on the move.

CHAPTER THIRTY-NINE

Max lay on Vic's couch and looked down at the phone screen as his finger hovered over the red decline button. The phone vibrated again. Max felt his pulse kick up. Despite himself, he found his curiosity piqued. Many people and organizations would like to find Max and have a quiet word. Some would like more than just a chat. But which one would be bold and creative enough to use his dead mother as a lure? What was going on? How did they know his name? His real name. How did they get his number? He continued to argue with himself as the phone vibrated, then he shifted his finger and hit the green button.

He waited and said nothing and neither did the other person, not at first, but he could hear breathing on the other end. Someone was there.

"I need help."

"Who are you?" he said.

"I've already told you that."

It was the same voice as before. He didn't recognize it, not exactly, but there was something about it, something familiar like walking into a new place but catching a smell, a hint, or a whiff, of home. Only that couldn't be right. Max had no home. He hadn't had one for a long time. The voice sounded older, not frail, but worn and experienced, almost patrician. There was no accent that he could detect, but there was an almost careful formality and enunciation. Like maybe she was trying to hide an accent.

"I don't believe that. My mother is dead. She's been dead for over 20 years. She le—" He stopped himself. He could feel the heat rising to his cheeks. He relaxed his grip on the phone. That is what they wanted. They wanted to provoke an emotional response. They wanted to force him into making a mistake. Then they would pounce. Again, he questioned who it was. Max had to admit they'd chosen an effective strategy. The appeal to his lost family was a direct thrust at his underbelly. And he could feel it working. He pulled himself back. "She's gone."

"You were never forgotten, Michael. Not by me. I thought about you every day."

"Who are you?"

There was a pause and the connection crackled with static. He was aware of the time passing. If they wanted to track his location, it would be difficult. Lawrence had set up the phone with layers of security and each call, incoming or outgoing, bounced through several virtual private networks then routed through multiple cell towers on different continents, plus a satellite or two. Not impossible, but not easy. He had some time.

"I never intended to leave you," the woman continued. "Believe that. I left you with my sister, your Aunt Joyce. You had your cousins, Danny and Mary, at least for a time. You played hockey. You were great at it. I even saw a few games at that old rink in Southie. God, I can still smell that place."

He almost smiled at that. She was right. The old Murph had decades of sweat, blood, and other fluids caked into both the stands and the ice. It slapped you in the face when you walked in. Max loved it. He could still smell it if he tried.

"You could have looked any of that information up."

There was another pause, longer this time, before she spoke again. "When you were small, we lived in an apartment that was just a few blocks from a park. We went there almost every day. And each time, as I was packing you into the stroller, you would ask how far it was. You were three or four and had no concept of time." Max felt something shift in his chest. He closed his eyes. Something dark and dangerous was bearing down on him. "You had a favorite song and that was our unit of measurement. You'd ask how far away the park was and I would say—"

"Three *Teddy Bear Picnics*." He didn't recognize his own voice.

He heard a sob from the other end.

"I never wanted to leave you. I always wanted to come back. You were—"

He disconnected and dropped the phone like it was scalding.

But she hadn't come back.

He felt a stiff knot between his shoulder blades. His mother. Alive. He tried to will himself to relax. This was not happening. He didn't need to be wanted. He stood and tried to get himself under control. He could not make this personal. It could only lead to rash decisions and mistakes.

"Don't be stupid," he said to the empty room. "Someone is deep, deep inside your head but don't let them play you." He bounced a fist off the side of his head for emphasis. But who? Not his mother. It couldn't be. It just wasn't possible.

The phone vibrated and jittered across the carpet. He

walked over and this time didn't hesitate. "Tell me you got it," he said when he answered.

"I told Eddie I had to call right away because you'd be all hot and bothered. White people don't know how to relax." Lawrence laughed and Max had to smile. He felt his shoulders drop a few inches, a little of the tension leaked out at the sound of his friend's voice. When Lawrence spoke again, his voice was more serious. "Eddie's on it. He captured the caller's," Max appreciated Lawrence didn't say mother, "SIM signature and he's querying cell phone towers now to get a location."

"Any idea how long that will take?" Max asked.

"Hold on." He heard Lawrence relaying the question to Eddie. After the initial calls a few days ago, Max had reached out to Lawrence, explained the situation, and asked him to put a bug on his phone and figure out who was calling him and where they were.

"He says the location triangulation should be simple once he can get the towers. The actual identity might be harder. It depends on the network and SIM card."

"Okay."

Max found he had nothing else to say and remained silent. Lawrence didn't fill the gap. Max sat back down on the couch. Bailey padded in and nudged his leg with a cool nose. He scratched the dog's ears as he listened to Eddie tapping away furiously at his keyboard. Max tapped a foot on the floor and then made himself stop. He thought of himself as a patient man, even viewed it as a strength, but not today. They were in deep and messing with his head.

"Okay. The caller is in West Adams, Massachusetts. Do you know it?"

"No, never heard of it."

"Hold on, we're bringing up a map. Okay, no wonder. It's

way, way west of Boston, practically in New York. It's a speck in the upper northwest corner. I'll send you a pin."

A moment later, his phone beeped. Max put the call on speaker and pulled up the map program. Lawrence wasn't lying. You could spit in West Adams and it might land in New York or Vermont, depending on which way the wind was blowing. There was a college nearby, Clarkston, and a river, plus large swaths of state-preserved land. A couple of minor state roads ran the compass points, but other than that, there was nothing Google figured was worth noting on the map.

"Bad news on the ID. The SIM is a prepaid Ultra Mobile. That's a dead end. You can pick them up in any 7-Eleven or CVS."

He hadn't expected a simple answer on that one. Whoever was doing this would not broadcast their name or the organization they worked for. Which made the ease with which they'd gotten the location a little suspicious. Maybe they didn't know about Max and his access to Eddie?

"How sure is Eddie on the location?" Max asked.

"That's solid. He said it was moving during the call but not jumping towers. The caller might have been in a car or bus or just between towers or something. They sometimes load balance, but every ping came through three towers. They made the call from West Adams."

"Anything on the other thing? The photo?"

Lawrence hesitated a fraction, then said, "No, still working on that."

Max wondered what that meant, but let it go for now. He had other problems. "Okay, thanks Lawrence. And thank Eddie for me."

"No problem, brother. Be careful and call if you need me."

"Will do."

Lawrence didn't know where Max was. He could easily find

out, but he didn't. Safer for both of them. Max looked down at the small primary-colored map on his phone and tapped the screen. Lawrence and Eddie might not know, but Max wondered if the caller might. West Adams was about an hour, 57 minutes according to Google, south of where Max currently sat.

CHAPTER FORTY

Max pressed the button on the phone and a moment later, Lawrence's voice boomed out of the car's speakers. "Really? You just called 10 minutes ago. You're as antsy as a whore in a confessional."

Max winced and turned down the volume before responding. "No change?"

"No change," Lawrence mimicked in a flat voice. "Now you're all business, huh? I think I might start putting my money on this woman being the real deal. She has certainly messed up your head as only a mother can. To answer your question, just like I did 10 minutes ago. No, Eddie will tell me if something changes. He's got a tag on it. If it moves, I will let you know, posthaste."

"No chance she just left it behind?"

"There's a chance. But why call you multiple times and then abandon the phone?"

"To get me here."

"I don't think it's bait. How do they know where you are? I can't figure how that would work unless they have much better toys than Eddie. Possible, but not likely. I think whoever called you is right there with the phone on the bedside table."

"And you can't tell me which room?"

"No."

"But you're sure it's the hotel."

"Yes, she's smart enough to turn off the phone's GPS, which could get us within five to 10 feet, but she's hitting the hotel office's Wi-Fi, so she must be close by. The previous call data also helps and puts her at the hotel, but Eddie says he can't get more precise. Hold on." Max heard shuffling and low whispering. "He says he has coordinates, but they are plus or minus 50 feet in each direction. That's still gotta be a bunch of rooms. Not sure you want to take that risk."

Max checked his side mirror and looked down the street. It was late morning, seven hours after the early morning wake-up call from the woman pretending to be his mother. Max had driven down and, aided by some quick data hacking from Eddie, narrowed the caller's location to this end of Roebuck Street and, more specifically, a room in the Jackson Inn and Suites Hotel. But that was as close as technology could get him.

Roebuck was busy, but not bustling. He'd have to move soon or risk being noticed. And Max didn't like to be noticed. A gas station and a competing hotel sat across the street. Max could spot another rival gas station farther down the street. Other lower-rent businesses filled in the street, a commercial dry cleaner; two takeout joints, one Chinese, one wings; a quick change oil shop; a metal machinist. The Jackson Inn's parking lot was less than a quarter full. Eddie's 50 feet were close but not close enough. He couldn't make a move until he knew more. If he started knocking on doors, if the calls were a lure, he might just walk himself right into a trap.

"No, not worth the risk. Not yet," Max said.

"Not ever, brother. Be cool. Don't do anything stupid. We'll figure this out."

"I know." Max disconnected the call and went back to chewing his nails and watching the mirror. He wasn't even sure who he was looking for. If his mother were alive, would he recognize her? He thought he'd grown out of asking himself that question a long time ago.

His phone rang.

"She's got an incoming call," Lawrence said.

"Who?"

"Don't know. We can see the number. That's it. We can't hear. We don't have a tap. But the incoming is another prepaid and likely a dead end but Eddie's checking."

"Okay."

"Keep an eye out. Every other time she's used the phone, she's been on the move. She must know or suspect that her location can be traced when she's on the phone."

"Good point." As he talked, he kept his eyes on his mirror and watched a woman exit a room at the Jackson Suites and wheel a bike across the parking lot. "She on the move now?"

"Eddie says no. Wait. There's a little lag. Yes, she's on the move. Heading north, away from the motel. You see her?"

"I've got her."

"Can you follow?"

Max knew what he meant was, can you follow safely?

"She's on a bike. Can you track her?"

"As long as she's on the phone."

"Okay, I'm going to give her a long leash."

"I'll feed you updates. Be careful."

Max knew what he meant was, don't be an idiot.

Max pulled out of his parking spot, made a U-turn in the gas station, and followed.

. . .

"She's turning left onto Overbrook."

Max was two blocks back, with a traffic light between them. The highway interchange was ahead and slowed up traffic as four crossroads converged. He briefly caught her profile as she turned. She was still on the phone. Max couldn't figure out why. It seemed dangerous and difficult to hold a conversation while riding on these crowded streets. He was in the middle lane but put his blinker on and forced his way left. A white sedan two cars ahead was also trying to make the same move. Max watched it inch over. Had it been there long? What about the Dodge Ram pickup that was also making a left? He'd been concentrating on her and not enough on the surroundings. He could see the back of the sedan driver's head, but that was all. He checked his mirror. There were a couple of cars behind him, too. A large Suburban with two men in front and a smaller Toyota with an older woman behind the wheel. Should he monitor them, as well? Often it was what you couldn't see that was the most dangerous. He swatted the thoughts away. Being alert and aware was one thing but seeing enemies on every corner didn't help.

The pickup and the white car, a Chevy Cruze, made it through the next light, but Max had to wait. By the time he made the turn, the woman on the bike, the pickup, and the Chevy were gone. Overbrook ran down toward the river and was less crowded away from the highway artery. It would be more difficult to follow without being seen.

"Lawrence? Talk to me. I got held up at a light. She still on Overbrook?"

There was no response. Max glanced at the phone. The call had dropped. He was in a dead zone with no reception. The abandoned mills, once so vital to this town's growth and history, were now just empty shells, blocking out sunlight and cell phone service. He sped up. The road appeared to be a cut-through to other places and wasn't maintained as well as some of the surrounding roads. Another New England winter hadn't helped. Cracks and potholes covered the road like landmines. At one time, a train must have run along the route to gather up the raw materials that the mills produced, but it too was long gone. The town had ripped up the tracks and converted the rail bed to a bike path along the river. It was also empty, but more likely because of the cold March temperatures than a lack of popularity.

He followed the abrupt twists and turns as fast as he dared, without risking putting the vehicle off the side and into the water. He had to balance trying to catch up if she was still ahead and driving too fast with the risk of missing her if she went off one of the side streets. Better to be cautious. He wouldn't be able to help anyone if he sunk the car in the river. He kept one hand on the wheel and tried to redial Lawrence. No luck. Still no reception. Still no sign of the biker.

He was about to turn around and double back to check the smaller streets when he spotted her. She was a half mile ahead, going down a small hill and pumping hard. She turned her head and, even from this distance, Max could see the fear on her face. That was strange. The road was empty in both directions. The nearby bike path, too. Up ahead there was an old trestle bridge, maybe too expensive to tear down when they removed the tracks, but nothing else that Max could see. She had the road to herself. What was she scared of?

And then he had his answer. It wasn't what she saw. It must have been what she heard.

CHAPTER FORTY-ONE

Back at the hotel, Lisa showered. She needed it physically and mentally. Despite the cold temperature, she had worked up a sweat riding back from Naomi's house. Then she'd tried Michael again. It hadn't gone well. Or maybe it had. She was tired and twisted up. She'd tried to call once before. She didn't know what to expect when she called this time. She didn't know what she wanted.

She dressed and went back to the ads she'd circled earlier in the Autotrader paper. It was still before 8:00 a.m., but Lisa didn't want any potential sellers to disappear into their workdays. She needed to find a car. She had circled a 2014 Acura, a slightly more compact but more modern 2018 Ford Focus, and a 2015 silver Nissan Maxima. She'd prefer something with a little more muscle, but each would suit her purposes and were within her budget. She picked up the phone and dialed. She ended up with appointments to check out the Acura and Focus at 10:00 and 11:00 and left a message for the Maxima seller.

She lay back on the bed. She rubbed her palms over her eyes and grimaced. They were dry and felt spackled with grit.

She was exhausted and weary, but her body stubbornly wouldn't let her rest. She rolled over. What would John do? She had to admit that she didn't know. He'd been gone so long. It was all she could do to picture his face. She'd lost the thread of his thoughts. She felt a lump in her throat and swallowed it back. That wouldn't help. She would work her list. She would go look at the used cars. She would go out to Dyson's Hardware and get the rest of the supplies she'd need. And then? It depended on Keres. She repeated the short list like a mantra as she counted the yellowed ceiling tiles. At some point, she stopped counting and biology took over.

Her ringing phone woke her up sometime later.

"Did I wake you, sweetie?"

Lisa sat up like she'd been hit with a cattle prod. She'd answered, expecting it to be the Maxima owner returning her call. It wasn't.

"Imagine what your friend, Naomi, would think if you were sleeping on the job."

"Just let her go, Keres. She knows nothing."

"She knows you. Right now, that's enough for me."

She glanced at the digital clock on the nightstand, 9:45. She'd slept for a little less than two hours. "Why are you calling? You said 24 hours."

"I changed my mind. Banks are open. I'm betting you've got the money close by. Start collecting it. You have until noon."

"That's not enough time."

There was a pause, Lisa glanced at the phone. The call was still connected.

"Funny you bring up time," Keres continued. "I spent 25 years of my life in various stinking prison cells in the shitty state of Maine. I've had a lot of time to do nothing but think about time. Did you know that Einstein's original paper on the theory of relativity included a math error?"

The abrupt change of subject caught Lisa off guard. "What?"

"He was wrong. Einstein. I don't know all the details, but he was wrong. The math wasn't quite right. The good news is Einstein later corrected the error, and his theory on the elasticity of time was later proved correct. I'm giving you the same opportunity. The chance to correct past mistakes. Get me my money and you get your friend back. But I want to make sure you are properly inspired, Lisa." She heard a thunk and then the echo of a speakerphone as Keres spoke again. "Last time, we talked about Naomi's fingers. I'll let you pick which one I start with."

Lisa could hear frantic grunts and moans under Keres's voice, and she tried hard not to picture Naomi. "No," she whispered. "I can't."

"You can't or won't?"

"Can't."

"I don't believe you."

"Please. Let her be."

"Too late for that. Pick a finger, Lisa."

"No."

"Oh yes, and if you don't, I'll take a whole hand off at the wrist. And I gotta tell you, this is a sharp little knife, but I'm not sure it's up for bone and gristle. Could take me quite a bit of time to saw through all that. I imagine it would be quite painful. Not to mention bloody. Not sure I'm equipped to deal with that kind of wound. I guess we'll see."

"Pinky," Lisa whispered again.

"Pinky. A wise choice. She can still teach all those yoga classes with just nine fingers." There was the sound of tape being ripped off. "There, I wanted to make sure you had the full experience, even if you can't join us in person. Don't hang up. If you hang up, I'll take another finger."

Lisa shut her eyes, but it did nothing to soften Naomi's screams.

Nothing to do but wait. She forgot about the used cars. She needed one, but there was no time. One owner tried calling, but she ignored it.

Keres called back two hours later. "Ready? Or should we pick another finger?"

Lisa hesitated. What would Keres believe? She knew he wanted the money, but he wasn't stupid. Gathering that kind of cash takes time. Time he hadn't given her. Was this a test? Did it matter? This whole back and forth was a charade. Maybe he believed in the money, but he would never let either of them go. "I have most of it."

"Most of it?"

"You didn't give me enough time. I spread the money out. I made it to three banks so far. There are two left. Despite what Einstein thinks, I can't bend time. You give me more time or you take what I have now."

"How much?"

"Enough for you to disappear somewhere warm and sunny."

"How much?"

She'd be on her bike. He'd probably be watching at some point. A million bucks was about 20 pounds. Not light, but not heavy, either. It could conceivably fit in the bike's pannier bags. "A little over a million."

"That's it?"

"It was 25 years ago, Keres. I wasn't swimming around in that river trying to grab all the boxes. I took what I could get and then I had to make it last while avoiding the FBI. That ain't cheap. I'd say a million isn't too fuckin' bad given the circumstances. You can live a long time in whatever cheap banana republic you want with that much cash."

"Alright. Take it easy, sweet cheeks. A million is a good start. You bring it to me and I'll let Naomi go."

"That simple, huh?"

"For Naomi, it is. You and I have a more complicated history."

"Where?"

He gave her an address. She knew vaguely where it was. Someplace down in the old mill and warehouse district by the river.

"When?"

"Now. I think I've waited long enough. Don't you?"

CHAPTER FORTY-TWO

Lisa made the turn onto Overbrook. She looked down at her arm where she'd written the address. Her skin was stark white in the cold air and the blue ink stood out, 170 Overbrook. She pushed her sleeve down and glanced up at the crumbling textile mills.

The old buildings along Stone River once housed wool and cotton looms, cabinet builders, hat makers, bricklayers, and iron forgers. They were the reason the town existed. At the nexus of three different states, and with a strong river current, the early conditions were excellent and a lot of settlers accumulated vast wealth. The railroads only spurred that growth and opened up more gateways to New York and Canada. Business was very good for West Adams for a long time. It even shielded much of the region from the worst of the Great Depression. It hit new heights during World War II. But then things changed. Labor unions weakened and jobs moved south, then overseas. West Adams and its wealth slowly eroded. The old mill buildings followed suit, just at a slower rate. There were occasional efforts to convert blocks to housing or use the cheap space to spur an art scene, but nothing had taken hold.

She pedaled past another hulking structure. Thick chains padlocked the wide doors on the river-fronting side. Dust, grime, and soot covered many of the large glass windows. A mix of multicolored graffiti tags adorned the lower portion of the facade. Had Keres found a way inside? Was Naomi close by? She tried to think back to the photo he'd sent. Had there been details in the background? Maybe. It was a closeup shot, so there wasn't much visible in the margins. She'd been so shocked at first, and then focused solely on Naomi and the blood, that she hadn't noticed anything. The phone was in her pocket, and she itched to take it out and check again but didn't. She kept pedaling.

Keres was sitting in a Dunkin' parking lot two blocks from the highway interchange and the intersection with Over-brook. He'd given Naomi a zolpidem pill, like he'd used on Joyce, and left her gagged and duct taped to the chair. He'd gone back to his room to get some sleep. He needed to be sharp for this next part. He didn't intend to let Lisa slip away again.

He'd studied a map of West Adams before picking which address to give her. Based on the surrounding area, he was confident that she'd come from either the west or the south. North was the acreage containing the old mills and beyond that, the degrading, low-rent business district where he'd stashed Naomi. He didn't think Lisa had decamped there. There were few options in that direction that didn't involve squatting or dealing with potentially dangerous junkies or the mentally ill. To the east was the Clarkston campus and surrounding town proper. Lisa's apartment building was there and, he admitted to himself, she could still be in that area, could have returned to the apartment itself, but he was betting she wanted more physical distance from the previous place where he'd found her. No, she'd be coming from the south or west and he'd parked with clear sightlines in both directions.

And he was right. She rode past on that damn bike 10 minutes later. He smiled. He'd been thinking about the best way to get her out of a car, but a bike would be much easier. A bit of a nudge and she'd just be lying there waiting. Maybe a little bloody and broken, but that was okay. More than okay, really.

He watched as she approached and took a spot in the turning lane. He guessed she was staying in the string of small motor court and roadhouse places to the south of town that catered to the less affluent college parents. He put his coffee down and pulled out into a gap in the light morning traffic. Most cars were going straight through the light to the highway onramp and he had to force his way across the three lanes to follow.

The light turned, and she pedaled through the intersection. He had to push a yellow, but he made it too, along with two other cars. The other cars quickly peeled off into the mill district. Despite looking like decomposing badlands, there were still a few viable businesses in there. Or the cars, one a pickup laden with assorted junk in the bed, were going to dump trash in a vacant lot. Maybe he'd use the spot to dump some trash later, too. He checked his mirror. Nothing behind him on the road. He slowed and let her pull farther ahead. He could do it now but coming up from behind might give her too much time to react. He wanted to give her no chance this time. He wanted her blindsided. He tapped his phone and brought up the map. He'd downloaded a local map so he wouldn't have to wait for a slow connection. He looked at the surrounding roads and then made the next left.

.   .   .

She pedaled past the last of the old mill buildings. There was no 170 Overbrook. It didn't exist. She slowed, unsure of what to do next or what game Keres was playing, when she heard a high-pitched sound like a scream. It cut through the wind in her ears as she rode. She turned and looked behind her, but the road was empty, save for a dark car way back in the distance. That was not the source of the noise. There was a pause, then everything fell silent. Had she imagined it? No, it suddenly ramped up again. She looked to the left and could see a car speeding down the side street and coming right at her.

She knew who was behind the wheel. The address was fake, but Keres's intent was real. She thought he would trade Naomi for her and the chance for more cash. She'd underestimated his greed. He would kill her and take what he could get. She stood and started pedaling. The leftover sand in the gutter from the winter storm prep made her tires slip and slide. It was difficult to get any speed. She didn't look back but could feel the car coming like a tornado sweeping over the horizon, hungry and destructive. She pushed harder. Lactic acid flooded her legs. She felt like she had a piano on her back. She concentrated only on the next second, the next half-second. Keep pushing, she told herself, as her lungs heaved with the effort.

She was just fast enough. For now.

She felt the car miss her by inches, maybe less. Her back tire slid out from the turbulent air pressure as the car went past. She thought she might go down, but she'd hit patches of black ice before and this was similar. She steered into the skid and recovered her balance. She heard a crunch, followed by a bang behind her. For a brief moment, she thought maybe the impact had disabled the car, but then she heard it shift and knew she hadn't been so lucky. The near miss had given her a shot of adrenaline, but she knew it wouldn't last. She looked ahead. There was an old railroad bridge 50 yards ahead. A grim thought flashed through her mind: another bridge would decide her fate. Was it one last stand or a second chance?

Wait. Wait. Go!

Keres pressed the pedal to the floor. The 1.4 liter 150-horsepower engine in the Chevrolet was sluggish. It had a fuel-efficient six-speed transmission, fine in most situations. It was probably preferred by the rental companies. It was not designed for fast acceleration or nimble handling.

The engine whined in response. Keres urged it forward as he watched Lisa pedal into the intersection. She looked at him and for a moment they locked eyes and he could almost smell her fear. He smiled. The color bled from his vision. The car finally got the message and gained speed. It shot past 40 miles per hour, then 50. He saw it all in his mind. The car striking the bike, Lisa flailing through the air, then falling and hitting the pavement. It would hurt. She would be in pain. A lot of pain. She would be desperate for help, to make the pain stop. She would give up the rest of the money. Or she'd die, and he'd settle for the million she had. He was okay with that, too. She was right. He could live easily for a long time on that. He deserved that.

Fifty-five. Sixty. The intersection was coming up. Lisa no longer looked at him. She was pedaling frantically, but she was no match for him. He had her pinned like a bug under glass. The Chevy was finding its stride. The engine hummed. So close. He could see the sweat dripping off Lisa's face. He touched the wheel slightly to adjust his aim. The car entered the intersection and...

Keres blinked in surprise. He'd missed her. How was that

possible? He suddenly realized he was going to drive straight into the river if he didn't do something. He hit the brakes and spun the wheel. The car bucked against the maneuver, the antilock brakes shuddering as the car slid into a spin and then hit the curb and slammed into the metal barrier dividing the road and bike path. Keres's head banged against the window, and he yelped in surprise. Bright white stars popped in his field of vision. Then everything started to go dark.

"No, no, no," he growled.

He brought up a hand and slapped himself back to full consciousness.

The car was still running. Good. Keres took his foot off the brake and touched the gas. The car's body shuddered, probably knocked out of alignment, but it responded.

The road was still empty. Except for Lisa. She was still right there on her bike.

The old trestle bridge was not getting closer. She pedaled and fought to get the cold air into her lungs and go faster. The barrier running along the road next to her shook from the car's impact. Then everything went quiet and still. She only heard the blood pumping and her ragged breath in her ears. Then she heard the car again. She looked up. The bridge still hung there, just out of reach. She didn't look back. She didn't look up. She just put her head down and pushed the pedals.

Pushed down with her right leg.

Her life had come down to single seconds.

Pushed down with her left leg.

She survived for another revolution of the pedals.

Up. Down. She pushed on.

The engine revved closer. Up. Down.

The bridge was old and rusting. A forgotten rusting spine spanning the river, rarely considered, but always there in the background. The bridge was thin, just the length of the railroad ties bound by the old steel rails. She had no idea of its integrity or safety. There were signs posted, but she couldn't stop to read them. Would they change her mind? She doubted it. She had a better chance of surviving if she went into the water. She'd done it before. She heard Keres coming closer. No choice. She steered the bike onto the bridge.

Keres slammed on the brakes and watched Lisa pedal onto the bridge. The railroad ties across the bridge were set close. She could pedal across, not without difficulty, but she was making progress. He studied the bridge and made a decision. She wasn't getting away with his money that easily. Good enough for a train, it would be good enough for a crappy rental.

There were two heavy concrete planters, empty now in the March chill, set along the path at the bridge's opening and likely meant as some sort of security deterrent. Lisa and her bike had no trouble slipping past, but the Chevy would be a tighter fit. But Keres was motivated. The right planter took out the passenger side mirror and ground off the paint from bumper to bumper, but he made it and steered out onto the bridge in pursuit.

He could see Lisa, more than halfway across now but slowing. He soon learned why. Some ties in the middle were missing, leaving wider gaps, like rotted teeth. The car shook and jumped across the bridge and Keres fought the wheel to keep the car on the bridge. But he was gaining.

He pushed down on the gas and gripped the wheel tighter. He saw Lisa glance back and reveled in the fear he saw on her face. She would see him coming. He needed to time this right. He couldn't push her off into the water. Not if he wanted the money. He needed to let her get across and then do it.

There was a loud crack and he looked in his side mirror. He saw a tie fall away behind him and splash into the water. The entire bridge felt like it was shaking. He looked ahead again. She was across the bridge. He was 20 yards behind. That was the blink of an eye with a car. He needed just a little more speed to close the gap. Another tie snapped, this time as his front wheels passed over it. The car lurched left, and the back tires caught in the gap. Keres wrenched the steering wheel in the opposite direction but kept his foot on the gas. The car fought the skid and the back end of the car fishtailed out into open space. Everything seemed to come to a stop. He saw Lisa watching, just a few yards away. The Chevy's engine whined as the rear wheel drive searched for purchase. He was so close. He thought he could almost reach out and touch her.

Then momentum saved him. The car's front wheels rolled forward, off the bridge, onto the asphalt, and pulled the back wheels out of thin air and back onto the bridge. Keres breathed out. He was safe. Then the car shot forward and slammed into the concrete planters on the opposite side.

CHAPTER FORTY-THREE

Max gripped the steering wheel and hunched forward. Was she really who she said she was?

He could still help. If he chose to. Did it matter who she was? She needed help and here he was. Why not him? He knew what he would do. It was like trying to fight gravity. No matter that this situation had not started with Max. It might not even involve him. Maybe that was better. It wasn't a conflict that he'd started. It let him commit with a clean conscience. The dark thing that lived in him woke up and stretched. His fingers prickled with electricity. He felt that humming wire in his blood.

He turned the car around. He got lucky and caught the light. He took a left and then another quick left. Now he was on the opposite side of the river.

Max went past the wrecked car, which was venting gray and white smoke from its crumpled front, and stopped next to the woman on the bike. She stood still, maybe in shock. Her arms and legs were shaking, and her eyes were small pinpricks. She would likely faint if she didn't sit down soon. Max noticed another car pull up behind him and stop. Then he saw two more on the opposite side of the river. He climbed out of the car. In the distance, he could hear a siren. Small town, fast response. Or they were unlucky and one was nearby. He stepped closer to the woman.

"We have to go. Now." He took her elbow. She turned slowly and looked at him. Then smiled. Then her eyes rolled back. He caught her and guided her quickly to his car. The other Good Samaritan pulled on the driver's side door of the wrecked car. Max could see the airbags had deployed. The interior of the car was a chalky haze of white. He could just make out the slumped head and shoulders of a man but nothing else. It didn't matter. Not right now. She was half-conscious, on the edge of passing out, but she was confused and fighting against him as he tried to get her in the back seat and close the door.

"We have to go. Right now."

"Need my bag. Get the bag."

"What bag?"

"The bike. Check the bike."

That was all she got out before she sagged sideways. He got her feet inside, then shut the door and jogged back to the bike. He quickly riffled through the traveling packs attached to the back frame. One bag held assorted bike gear: two plastic water bottles, both empty, a small mechanic's kit, a spare inner tube, and a couple of energy bars. Nothing worth saving. He left it alone. The other side held a small duffel bag, the woman's purse, and two guns. The guns made him pause. He looked over his shoulder. The Good Samaritan had managed to get the car's door halfway open and was pushing the airbags aside. He looked across at the bridge. He could see two people jogging across. More help. He also saw a police cruiser pass on the opposite side. It wouldn't be long before they arrived on this side. He pocketed the guns and carried the bag and the purse back to the car. He pulled away from the curb and accelerated away up the hill.

"No." The woman in the back was trying to sit up, but still looked pale and clammy. She looked out the back window. "Need him. Naomi."

Max kept his eyes on the mirror. The other driver looked up as he left, but he wasn't worried. Eyewitness testimony was unreliable. He didn't think the driver had gotten a good look at either of them.

"Michael, go back. Please. We need him." Her voice was hoarse and unsteady.

The woman struggled up to a sitting position.

"That's not my name." He saw her wince, but she said nothing. "We can't go back. Maybe you can, but I can't. The cops were 30 seconds away. I can let you off here and you can walk back if you want." He took his foot off the gas, but she closed her eyes and shook her head.

He drove on. They didn't speak. The woman reached up and unclipped the bike helmet she was still wearing and then stared out the window. After he'd put five miles between themselves and the river, he pulled into a bank parking lot and parked around back, between two other cars where they couldn't be seen by passing traffic.

He half turned in his seat. "Who are you?"

"You know who I am, Michael."

He didn't comment this time. He knew she was trying to use it for effect. He shut his emotional side off. It was something he used to do when a job was getting close. He'd gradually turn down any sentiments or feelings, like lowering the volume on the radio. By the time the job arrived, he was as coldly rational as he could be.

"It says here that you're Jill Williams," he said, holding up the slim beige handbag. "Not my mother. Or wait, maybe it's

Molly Cahan," he said, taking an Illinois driver's license from the side pocket. "Still not my mother."

"You wouldn't be here if you didn't know who I am. You might not want to admit it, but some part of you recognizes me. I know it. Because I feel it, too."

She was very good. Very convincing. He turned the knob further. "Bullshit. Who are you and how did you find me?"

She waved away the questions. "My name is Lisa, but we really don't have time for this back and forth. Not right now. I know you deserve answers. A lot of them. And I'll give them to you, as best I can, but right now we need to find my friend Naomi."

The irritation, or the anger, or just the distance from the man in the car, was putting a little color back in her cheeks. Max couldn't help but notice her eyes and the shape of her nose and mentally compare it to his own.

"Who's Naomi?"

"A friend of mine that Keres, the fucker back there who tried to run me down, kidnapped to lure me out after I escaped his last attempt."

"Where is she?"

The woman ran a hand through her matted hair. "That's why I wanted to go back. I don't know. I was willing to trade myself for Naomi. But Keres had other ideas."

"Who is he? What does he want with you?"

She turned and looked at him and he could suddenly see how tired she was, and he didn't think it was just the recent near escape by the river. She looked wrung out and weary. "It's a long story, and it includes a lot of the answers you want, but I need to make sure Naomi is safe first. She's innocent. We need to find her."

"She might already be dead."

"Maybe."

"You ready for that?"

"No. I'm not going to believe it until I see her body."

"And then what?"

"Keres and I already have unfinished business. I'll just add that to his tab."

"Easy to say, but hard to do."

"You know that for a fact?" she asked.

"Yes."

"Your own long story?"

"Yes."

CHAPTER FORTY-FOUR

When Martha watched the car drive onto the bridge, she knew she had a problem.

She was on a parallel street trying to watch the GPS tracker showing Keres's location and not plow her own car into the side of a building. She'd watched as he drove around the warehouse district for a few minutes, then stopped on a busy avenue. She drove past and saw him heading back to his car carrying a coffee. He'd then just sat there, forcing her to pull into a neighboring competing coffee chain to wait. Twenty minutes later, he'd pulled out into traffic and bullied his way into the turning lane. She followed. Small side streets and alleys crisscrossed the warehouse district and allowed her to stay close without being visible. But now, she needed to see what the hell was happening. She wondered if the GPS had glitched. She drove to the end of the street where there was a view of the river.

No glitch. She tried to make sense of the scene in front of her. She watched as a woman, presumably Lisa Sullivan, on a bike made it across the old railroad bridge and then Keres lost control of the Chevy as he attempted to follow and plowed into some concrete planters. Keres's stunt had totaled the car. The impact had crumpled the front end like an accordion. She couldn't see clearly from this distance, but nothing was moving inside. The woman on the bike stood 15 yards away with a hand to her mouth. Then a second car arrived, and things got even more interesting.

She took her foot off the brake and coasted down the hill and stopped with a few other cars on the opposite side of the river. She watched as the man from the second car bundled the woman into his car, went back for her bag, and then drove away. Who was he? It was hard to get an accurate description from where she stood. How had he gotten involved? She shifted focus. Still no movement from Keres's car. A third man had stopped and was trying to pry open the door, which appeared to be jammed shut from the impact. Was Keres dead?

Now she could hear the distant wail of a siren. Time to decide. She hadn't gotten much of a return on her investment in the tracker. It had lasted barely a day. She wondered if anyone would find the tracker or if the crash had destroyed it. She watched a police car, followed by an ambulance, pull up to the scene. She didn't want to stick around and be a witness... though the things she could tell them.

She drove off, away from Keres and the accident scene, and followed the winding river in the same direction as the car that had whisked Lisa Sullivan away. She could just make out the rear end of the car in the far distance. Traffic was light so she hung back. She took out her phone and dialed.

"I think you might have a problem," she said after Cobb picked up.

"My life is a series of prioritized problems. I got to where I am by figuring out how to efficiently mitigate those problems, sometimes even capitalize on them. I often hire people to deal with them. People like you."

She understood the insinuation but didn't rise to the bait. His bad mood wasn't her problem. "The job was to follow Keres. That's what I'm doing."

"Then what's the problem?"

She told him about the accident and Keres likely heading back to jail. Cobb was silent on the other end of the line, then said, "The woman on the bike. You think that was Sullivan?"

"Stands to reason."

"And you're following her now?"

"I'm following the car that picked her up, yes."

"Alright. Stay on Sullivan."

Martha disconnected. She noted Cobb hadn't asked about the man driving the car. Maybe he'd come to the same conclusion she had.

CHAPTER FORTY-FIVE

Max rubbed his hands on his jeans. Whoever the woman in the back seat was, she was clearly concerned for her missing friend. She did not appear to be an imminent threat to him. He'd spotted no one following them. He sensed nothing other than the worry and stress rolling off her in waves. He could help her with this situation and then, when she was calmer, get answers to his questions.

He asked, "How do you know Keres kidnapped your friend?"

"He called me and told me, then he sent a text with a photo of her."

"You have her number?"

"Sure. In my phone." She dug an iPhone out of her purse.

"Try her."

"I have."

"Just try her again. Let's eliminate the obvious."

She nodded and tapped at the phone then put it on speaker and held it away from her slightly. It never connected and rolled straight to Naomi's voicemail.

"Now what?"

"Did he call you on her phone or his?"

"It was a different number. Probably his. Probably a burner."

"Try it anyway."

She tapped and scrolled through her call history and eventually held the phone out again. Same result, but this time instead of a welcoming voicemail message, they just heard a pre-recorded company message informing them that the user had not set up voicemail.

"Send me the numbers," Max said and grabbed his own phone from the dashboard cradle and called Lawrence. He did not put it on speaker.

"Hey, it's me," he said when Lawrence picked up. Max could hear the barbershop guys bullshitting in their chairs in the background.

"Gimme one second," Lawrence said. A minute later, he was back and it was much quieter. Max pictured him sitting at the desk in the shop's basement. The basement that would never show up on city plans or blueprints.

"You okay? I lost you."

"I'm good."

Lawrence picked up on his tone or mood. "You with her now?"

"Yes."

"And?"

"We have a more pressing problem than discussing our family tree. I've got two cell phone numbers. Can you get me more info on them?"

"What do you need?"

"Anything Eddie can find would be helpful, but we are really looking for location data."

"When do you need it?"

"ASAP. It's very time-sensitive."

"Send me the numbers. I'll head over to the apartment and wake his ass up."

It was closing in on noon, but Max knew Eddie preferred to work after dark and sleep most of the day. Better to avoid people.

"Thanks. I owe you."

"Eddie and I have stopped keeping a tab. We do it for the cocktail party stories."

"When was the last time you went to a cocktail party?"

"When I do, I'll have plenty of interesting stories to share. Don't worry, I'll change your name."

They hung up, and Max texted the two cell numbers to Lawrence's phone.

"Who was that?"

"A friend."

"Will he be able to help?"

"I don't know. I'm not good with tech myself, but if there is any information to be found, he'll get it. Trust me."

"So we wait?" She didn't seem happy with that option.

"Getting geo-location data from the phone is the easiest way, but not the only way."

"So what? West Adams isn't a major city, but it has to be at least 20 square miles and 10,000 people. Maybe 15 with all the students in town. You can't think we're going to just drive around and stumble onto her."

"Not aimlessly. No. We need to first think like him."

"Not a pleasant thought."

"But necessary to find your friend. You know about my past, right?" She nodded. "That was a key part of how I prepped for a job. I learned to think like a cop or a security guard. What would they do? What would they expect?"

"And it worked?"

"I didn't go to jail. Not for robbery."

"Alright. So how do we do it?"

"Normally, I'd spend weeks researching and casing a job and figuring out how I'd both do it and prevent it. The prevention part was my way of thinking like law enforcement. Asking how I would improve security or what I would change. That was my way of finding the weak points."

"But in this case, we don't have weeks."

"No, but we do have you. You know him."

"A little."

"More than me. You've interacted with him. To me, he's just a guy who was chasing you in a car. It tells me a few things, but maybe not enough to find Naomi. You talked to him. He's told you things about himself, whether you know it or not. Let me see the photo you mentioned."

She did the phone tapping thing again and then held it out. He took it and looked at the image on the screen.

It was a head-and-shoulders view, shot from slightly above, of an Asian woman, somewhere in her 40s with dark brown shoulder-length hair. Her face was turned slightly to the left. Max could see a line of blood running out of her hair and down along her cheek. There was black duct tape wrapped around her head, covering her mouth. The one eye that was visible was opened wide. It was easy to read her expression. The woman was terrified. He looked beyond her face to the edges of the frame. The flash had washed out a lot of the detail. He could make out the molded plastic of a bench seat. The floor appeared to be tile or plastic in different shades of gray or black. He could make out the legs and other molded parts from additional seating behind and to the woman's left. There was a bright glow from the right, outside of the frame.

"Not much to see," Lisa said.

"No," Max agreed. "But every bit helps."

He reached over and unlatched the glove box and took out a road atlas. He was getting better with technology, thanks to Lawrence and Eddie, but he still enjoyed having a backup. He'd learned he was most comfortable in places with little to no internet. It kept things simpler.

He flipped through the pages until he came to the section showing the far western edge of Massachusetts and the first slivers of the surrounding states. The map gave him a general sense of the town's layout around the river and the Clarkston campus, but not a lot of detail. He laid the atlas on the armrest between the seats. He put her phone with the photo next to it so they could see both at once.

"Any idea what or where this is?" She was about to speak, and he held up a hand. "Take another look. Don't get distracted by her. Try to look at everything else."

She pulled the phone closer and took her time. She pinched and zoomed to see into the corners of the frame, but eventually shook her head. "No. I can't see much and nothing looks familiar."

"I think we can we assume she's inside, right?"

"Yes," Lisa agreed.

"This glow here," Max pointed to the light streaks pushing into the frame from the right, "looks like a flashlight or some type of other light. I don't think the building has power."

"Okay."

"What about these?" He pointed to the rounded edges of the plastic.

"Booths or restaurant seating?"

"That was my thought, too. Definitely not an office building. It's some type of commercial establishment. Probably a restaurant. Maybe a bank lobby. See anything else?"

"No."

"Okay." He put the phone aside and gave her the atlas. "He's probably close by. Probably within the city limits. So, think about it. Where in West Adams would there be a closed or abandoned restaurant?"

She stared down at the atlas and then put a finger down. "I think we can eliminate the area around campus. There's just too much activity. Too many people around. Too many chances to be seen unexpectedly. He'd want something quieter."

"Agreed."

She moved her finger to the mill district. "The mills were my first thought. Plenty of space. Plenty of easy ways in and out. Some people, but not a lot. He wouldn't attract a lot of attention, but I can't think of any spot in there that might look like this." She shifted the atlas. "This spot here to the west is a little on the lower socioeconomic ladder than other parts of West Adams, but it still catches a decent amount of traffic off the highway. There are definitely fast-food spots there, but also hotels, gas, and auto body places. It's hanging on. He might stay there himself with the cheap, anonymous hotels, but I doubt he's keeping her there. Again, too many people. Too many uncontrollable variables. We should check, but if I had to choose a place to start, I'd say here." She moved her finger to a thin stretch of road leading north, out of town. "This was the primary commercial district 50 years ago but was bypassed and cutoff by the highway. The town shifted south. It's still a viable road. A lot of locals use it to skirt the turnpike congestion, but it doesn't get a fraction of the traffic that the turnpike does. Half the businesses along that strip are abandoned or on life support."

CHAPTER FORTY-SIX

It was only a 15-minute drive from the bank parking lot to the two-mile strip Lisa had pointed out on the map, but it was a lifetime away from the bars, restaurants, and coffee places near the Clarkston campus. This was the slow urban rot that hit many small- to mid-sized cities at some point. A bad business decision, a poorly timed expansion, a wrong bet on the next trend. Any of them could sink a retail business and, in many strips like this, the stores swim or sink together. Image is everything. One might be a cell phone store and another a liquor store and another a bookstore, but if one goes bankrupt it can become an anchor on all of them. Some areas could weather the storm, revitalize, and recover. Others could not.

If Max had to bet, he'd say this section of West Adams was in dire straits. Maybe beyond saving. As they drove up one side, he witnessed two drug deals in less than five minutes. Poor perception, low-priced real estate, and an open-air drug market were putting a thumb on the scale. Better to raze the entire block and start over.

There were still a few places giving it a go, mostly cheap,

off-brand, fast-food restaurants with drive-throughs, but Max counted far more 'For Rent' signs and boarded-up windows than open businesses. When the buildings had receded and the trees closed up on the side of the road again, Max pulled over and turned around.

"Christ," Lisa said. She'd climbed into the passenger seat before they'd set off. She scratched at a patch of dry skin on her arm. "I didn't know it had gotten so bad."

Max nodded. "A lot of places to search."

"A lot of places to hide," Lisa agreed.

"No police presence. I can't imagine they don't know."

"They know. They're happy to cede this strip. It's an unspoken agreement: you stay here and we won't harass you too much. It's a quarantine zone far from the college and any visiting parents."

"Would Keres know that?"

"It's a constant source of friction with the locals and the police. If he spent any amount of time here, he might pick up on it. But a guy like Keres probably wouldn't even need that. This is hardly unique to West Adams. Keres is smart in a cunning, self-serving way. He could probably sniff this out with just a few questions at any local bar."

Max took his foot off the brake, and they rolled back toward the first of the buildings. This time from the south.

They eliminated any building that still had an open and viable business as too risky and focused on standalone buildings that were closed and boarded up. Based on the photograph, they gave priority and extra attention to ones that looked like they had once been restaurants. Even cutting down the search grid that way, it took over two hours to cover one side of the street. Three times they thought they might have found the right place. The back entrances were open, but when they entered, they only found trash, used needles, and junkies with one foot in the grave.

Max reached the rotary at the end of the road and went around. He turned into the first potential target and pulled around back and braked to a stop. Their routine had been for Lisa to jump out and test the boards or locks if they weren't obviously open.

This time, she paused and didn't move from her seat. Max looked over at her.

"I don't know if I can go in again."

The last one had included a group of skinny, dirty kids that couldn't have been older than 16 or 17. Lisa had tried to get them to come out. She'd offered them a ride to a shelter or to buy food. They'd only stared back at her as if she was speaking a foreign language. Finally, one of them had asked for money or Percs or Oxy. When she'd refused, they told her to get the fuck out and leave them alone.

"I'll check." He put the car in park, got out, and went to the building's back door. The building was a plain cinder block square painted a now faded yellow but was relatively unmarked with graffiti. There was a molded plastic roof that may have once evoked straw or perhaps a tiki hut. Max couldn't think of anything more diametrically opposite of West Adams than a tropical thatched hut. He checked the plywood nailed over the door. Snug and tight. He examined the edges but didn't see any signs that someone had tampered with it recently. He returned to the car.

"This is taking too long," Lisa said.

Max shrugged. "It takes as long as it takes. We're making progress." He tried to keep his voice light, but he could see the toll the chase, then the search, and maybe other things were taking on Lisa. Any adrenaline rush from surviving the bridge crossing was gone. Her skin looked gray, and he'd noticed she was coughing more.

"You okay?"

"Fine," she replied. "Just the tail end of a winter cold that won't quit."

Max let it go and they watched an addict, it was impossible to tell if it was a man or woman, slowly step into the street, heedless of any approaching traffic, and cross the four-lane road and then disappear behind a square building with a blue roof that to Max's eye looked like an old IHOP restaurant but now was nothing more than a shell with 'Space Available' signs plastered everywhere.

"If we're acting like cops then it's first-year rookies on patrol," Lisa said. "We're just going door-to-door. It's not enough. It's too slow. She's hurt. Bleeding. Or worse, dying. You said you could think like him. So, think like him. Find her."

She was frustrated and angry, but she wasn't wrong, Max realized. He could do better. He pulled the car around to the front of the building, looked left, and considered the strip laid out in front of them and tried to see it like Keres might.

"Alright. He'd come at night, right?"

"Yes. He's broken no laws yet, but a guy like Keres is more comfortable in the dark."

Max glanced back to the right and envisioned driving through the rotary at night and taking the first right. "He wouldn't take the first one. He probably wouldn't even check. It's too obvious. He would probably go by the second and maybe even the third, depending on how close together those two were."

"Okay."

"He wants something by itself. He wants something he can keep secure. Free standing but empty. He doesn't want to waste time clearing people out or risking getting stuck with a needle. And he doesn't want people getting in."

He waited for a break in traffic and then turned out of the lot and cruised at the speed limit in the right-hand lane and studied the buildings. They drove past a discount liquor store that was still in business then an auto repair shop in a low cinderblock building with stacks of tires piled out front. He kept driving.

Next was a long, single-story, brick building with a vape shop, a massage parlor, two empty stores with soap-scrubbed windows, and a final shop with a yellow and red sign that just said CAP. Max couldn't tell what it did or sold. Then an abandoned lot with only a rubble foundation, fenced off, but clearly inhabited as a sort of drug camp or shelter. There was a mass of tents and boxes with rough lanes dividing up the space. There was a stretch of woods and then a bunker-like building with a cracked Anheuser-Busch sign bolted off the side and Smitty's in green script painted onto the side of the building. Smitty's had a wide parking lot to the right and then a strip of unpaved gravel that was maybe an overflow lot that included two dented dumpsters. He kept driving.

After Smitty's came a narrow, rectangular building with the bland shape and facade that said it had changed hands many times over the years. The realtor or holding company had boarded up the windows, but the plywood looked fresh. It wasn't tagged or marked. Something pinged in the back of Max's brain. It was empty, but maybe hadn't been for long. He braked and pulled in. The change in direction roused Lisa.

"What?"

"This one."

"Are you sure?"

"No, you're never 100 percent but this checks all the boxes. Abandoned but not colonized by the addicts. By itself. Down a bit, but not too far from the start of the road." He pulled around back and stopped near the door. This time, they both got out. There was another piece of plywood hammered over the back door. It matched the boards covering the windows. Max studied the edges where the board met the building.

"Look at this." He pointed at the wood facade along the top edge. Someone had nailed rough cut two-by-fours to the building and then re-nailed the plywood to the fresh wood. "Someone's been here recently. You can still smell the sawdust from the cuts. Hold on."

He stepped around to the trunk of the car and used the key fob to pop it open. There was both a first aid kit and a small toolbox secured next to the wheel well because that's the type of person Lawrence was. Max could appreciate that. Hope for the best, prepare for the worst was an ethos they both believed in. He freed the emergency kit from the Velcro strap and unzipped it. For such a small kit, it packed an impressive array of gear. There was a pair of pliers, a flat-blade screwdriver, a Phillips blade, an adjustable wrench, a vise-grip, a set of wire cutters, a Swiss Army knife, and a small ball-peen hammer. You couldn't rebuild an engine on the side of the road, but you could fix just about anything else.

Max took the hammer and the flat-blade screwdriver and stepped back to the door. He poked at the weathered wood a foot from the nailed plywood. The screwdriver sank in. "Rotted or termites. Someone repaired it to make it harder to get in." He paused and said what they were both thinking. "Or out."

He worked his way around the plywood frame and used the screwdriver and hammer to loosen the nails from the fresh wood. By the time he freed the board and placed it aside, they could hear someone moving inside.

Naomi was alive. Max retrieved the pocketknife from the kit and cut the tape that bound her ankles and arms to the chair. Keres had also wrapped tape around her head and forced her to breathe through her nose. He gently tried to cut that away, but she became anxious and skittish, jerking away from Max and the small blade. He didn't feel it was safe to keep trying. She also kept anyone from looking at her left hand. She cradled it gently in the other arm and almost shielded it against her body. It had been unsubtly bandaged with a wad of dirty cloth torn from her shirt and more heavy tape.

"Let's get her out of here for now," he said. Lisa led Naomi outside and sat with her in the back seat of the car.

She kept her eyes closed against the sunlight. Naomi was in rough shape. Her skin was pale and clammy, and her breathing remained shallow. She was likely dehydrated and certainly in shock from the experience.

"She needs a doctor or a hospital," Lisa said.

Max nodded but said, "That could be a problem."

Lisa looked at him. "Why?"

"We can drop her off, but do you want to stay and explain what happened?"

"We can come up with a story. Something plausible. This isn't Boston or New York or some big city. People do their own repairs. She could have had an accident. Hell, she could have a hobby. Metal sculpting or woodworking. Lost focus for a second."

"That might explain the finger, but what about the other symptoms? Dehydration? Shock?"

"Confusion and disorientation are symptoms of shock, right? The doctors can just chalk it up to that."

"What about you?"

"What about me?"

"We can come up with a plausible story. But with this kind of injury, I bet the hospital has to report it. That will bring the cops and, even if the story is plausible, the cops are likely to check. Even if we do nothing more than drop her at the ER doors, we are going to be on video. That could be checked, too."

He looked at her and watched her face change as it ran through the gamut of emotions from denial, to guilt, to fear, and finally to acceptance. Then it shifted one more time.

"I might know someone who can help."

"You again."

"Like a bad penny," Lisa replied.

The old woman sat in the same spot on the glider where Lisa had first met her, wrapped up in the afghan with a mismatched hat and muffler adding bulk to her tiny frame. A pair of pink slippers poked out from beneath the blanket. The ashtray held a few more dead soldiers and was now balanced on the arm of the glider. She sipped from a coffee mug as Lisa stepped up on the porch. Max remained a few yards back in the yard. He felt her eyes jump from Lisa to himself. It felt best to remain still during the inspection. Eventually, she shifted her gaze back to Lisa.

"You find her?"

"Yes, ma'am."

"You need the second gun?"

"Didn't even need the first."

The woman paused at that, but then nodded her head. "Probably for the best." She adjusted the blanket to cover up the slippers. "Naomi's okay then?"

"We need some neighborly help."

"She alive?"

"Yes, of course."

"Good. I'm too old to bury any more bodies. At my age, it's far better to just tell the truth."

"Probably at any age."

The woman laughed at that, a deep resonant sound that

belied her tiny stature. Max wondered what she had been like 50 years ago. "Oh, honey, lying has its uses."

Lisa sidestepped that one and instead asked, "Is your daughter around?"

"No. She's off at work. She's got the morning shift as a cashier at the Stop & Shop over in Ashford."

Lisa looked back at Max. He just nodded.

"Can you drive?"

"Sure, I can drive. I still go to First Baptist each Sunday. Drive myself. My daughter never took much to church. I don't get there fast, but I get there."

Max wouldn't have pegged this woman as a church goer, not based on just the few comments he'd heard while standing in her yard, but human beings were full of surprising contradictions.

"Naomi needs to get to a hospital, or at least a doctor. Can you drive her?"

The woman looked them both over again. "I could do that. The medical center is not more than two miles from here. But I'm sure you know that. So why can't you drive her?"

"Do you still stand by your prior judgment?"

"What was that?"

"That you were a righteous judge of character and could tell I truly wanted to help Naomi?"

"Yes, I don't think that's changed."

"It hasn't. Naomi will be okay, but she needs help. Only it can't be the two of us."

The old woman nodded and stood up. "Okay, I'll do it."

CHAPTER FORTY-SEVEN

Keres woke up slowly and then all at once. He remembered a long-ago trip, one of the times his dad reappeared, flush and sober, to an amusement park. They'd ridden an old wooden roller coaster. It had been thrilling and terrifying. As the cars came around the last bend, they started to slow as the station approached, then they jerked to a sudden stop as the air brakes caught. That was a similar feeling now. He had been drifting along in a gray haze, not dreaming of anything, just floating, and then it was like the brakes grabbed the rails and jerked him awake. He sat up. Or tried to. Both arms were handcuffed to bedrails.

He settled back down and looked around. The room was dim. A low light illuminated an area near the floor at the foot of the bed. The room was small and felt vaguely industrial, with light green tiles on the walls and milky white and gray squares on the floor. There was a smell of disinfectant, bleach, and a pungent flowery perfume. A hospital, not a jail. No warden would bother with air freshener. There was medical monitoring equipment to his left. Two drips were attached to his arm, and he could feel something attached to his chest underneath the cotton hospital gown. A man in a black suit was sitting in a chair to his right.

"Good morning, George."

The man was slim with short black hair flecked with subtle gray near the temples. His nose was slightly hooked and sharp, but otherwise, the rest of his face was symmetrically bland. His suit was solid black, with no pinstripes or patterns. He wore a red tie, also plain, with a solid silver pin keeping it neatly in place. He didn't give off a cop vibe, but there was something officious about him that put Keres on edge.

Keres looked down at the man's shoes. His mother always used to say you could tell a man's financial standing in life by looking at his shoes. The man's were shined black leather with a slight heel and stitching over the mid-sole. At least Keres thought it was leather. He'd spent the last two decades wearing flip-flops and cheap canvas sneakers. He didn't know shit about shoes. His mother probably hadn't either. Certainly not based on his old man or the parade of other men she brought home.

"Who are you?" Keres asked.

The man stood and walked to the window. He poked his fingers between the blinds and let in a shaft of bright sunlight. Keres wondered if it was still the same day. He remembered driving the car over the bridge and Lisa right there, and then... that was it. A wall of fuzzy static until those air brakes yanked him back into the world.

"Not a bad question, George. Maybe you're smarter than we thought."

"Who are you?" Keres repeated. His throat was dry, and his jaw ached. It hurt to talk. Maybe it wasn't the same day.

"I'm no one, George. I'm just the lubricant in the system. I'm the oil in the gears." He turned around and looked at Keres. His face was now in shadows except for small points of reflected light in the corners of his eyes. If Keres was expecting more, he didn't get it.

"A bureaucrat."

The man in black appeared to weigh the word before sitting down again. He poured water from a pink plastic pitcher on the bedside table into a paper cup and then left it there. "The term bureaucrat derives from 'bureaucracy,' of course, which in turn derives from the French 'bureaucratie,' first used sometime in the 18th century. But I have to think it's been around far longer than that. Another profession always tries to stake a claim to the world's oldest, but humans have done bureaucratic work for centuries. Am I a bureaucrat? I've been called many things, but never that. You might be onto something. However, you won't find me in any corporate directory or attending any weekly staff meetings."

The man's wall of words made Keres's head throb. He heard them, but he didn't hear an answer. He tried again. "Why are you here?"

"I'm here because things are stuck. Or they are slowing down and potentially might become an impediment. At the very least, a distraction. So, I'm here to do my job. To be the oil, another French word, or Anglo-French, I think. I'm here to make the gears turn."

Keres closed his eyes. If the man preferred to talk in riddles, that was up to him. Keres didn't have to listen. If the man in black noticed a change, he didn't care, just continued.

"You are in some trouble, George. Can't sugarcoat that. The handcuffs are there for a reason. They got your sheet. There are a couple of officers outside. The only reason they aren't busting down the door and dragging you back to prison for the rest of your life is the doc told them you rattled your brain when you hit those planters. She wants to watch you one more day and the local police chief is too cowardly to force the issue. What is one more day to him? After she discharges you, well, you've just got me standing between you and a return to that cozy cell."

Now they were getting down to it. "The bureaucrat. Not much of a shield."

"Oh, you might be surprised."

"I did my time. There's no parole violation. I get a trial."

"Sure. And they've got plenty of witnesses that saw you trying to run Lisa Sullivan down with that Chevy."

Her name, her real name, made Keres open his eyes. "What do you know about her?"

"Probably more than you. She's disappeared again, by the way. The locals might have your sheet, but they have nothing on Lisa. She's in the wind. But I know what you want. And I can help you get it."

"Yeah? Tell me, what do I want?"

"You want the money she stole from you when the dock job went awry. You probably would like it with some interest too, right? Back pay for past pain and suffering. Of course, you shot her husband. She might consider you square."

"Does she have it?" This was the question that Keres rarely let himself think about. Of course, she had it. She'd been able to hide and avoid the cops for 25 years. The only way you could do that was with cold, hard cash. And he knew, knew for a fact, that she was sending money to her sister. Yeah, she still had it.

But the man in black just shrugged. "I don't know. I've never spoken to her. One way to find out."

"What's that?"

"Find her and ask her." He gave Keres a look that said he might be reevaluating his earlier comment about Keres's intelligence.

"She could just lie."

"Yes, but I'm guessing you have ways of being persuasive." He paused. "Just like I do."

"Where is she?"

"I said she disappeared. I didn't say I knew where she was."

Keres tried to keep the disappointment out of his face. He'd have to start over. If she still had the cash, she could run a long way and burrow deep. If she cut off Joyce, he might never get another sniff.

"But I might have some ideas. I think our mutual goals might intersect and we could help each other out. Are you interested?"

Keres noted that they'd never discussed what the man's intentions or interests actually were. He also knew that deals with the devil rarely worked out well for both parties. The man's offer might resemble a carrot, but Keres knew it was a stick. And guys like him always had sharp sticks. But he also didn't see that he had much choice except to walk away. And where would he walk? Back to that crappy SRO apartment in Boston? Hustling or scamming enough to cover food and rent? No thank you.

"What do I have to do?"

"Nothing you weren't already planning on doing. Find Lisa and... ask her your questions."

"That's it? What do you get?"

"I get the system moving again."

CHAPTER FORTY-EIGHT

The next time Keres woke up, the blinds were open and the sky outside was black. The room was empty, and the handcuffs were gone. He thought he'd dreamed the whole thing in a drug-induced stupor, but he could still see the red, irritated skin around his wrists. He pulled out the IVs from the crook of his arm and sat up. The only consistent thing from earlier was the drumbeat of his headache.

The cup of water was still on the bedside table. The ice had melted. He drank it down in three long swallows, then poured another and drank that just as quickly. He sat back and the water sloshed in his empty stomach. He thought it might come gushing back up but didn't. When it settled, he leaned over and looked at the monitor mounted on the wall near the bed and monitoring equipment, but he couldn't make any sense of the numbers, graphs, and other data pulsing and flashing across the screen. It was some sort of medical code to keep people like him from understanding and to keep places like this in business. He gave up and lay back.

Messing with the IV lines or the change in his vital signs from moving around must have set off an alarm somewhere. A heavyset nurse in pink scrubs and white clogs bustled through the door. The hallway appeared empty behind her. No one waiting.

"Did something happen with your IV?" She leaned over and put the chart back in its place.

"Pulled it out. Don't need it."

She tsked at that but didn't try to re-insert the needles. She hit some buttons on the machine, presumably to stop the pump, and then adjusted a few other knobs. "Let's see how you feel in a few hours without the juice." She gave a thin smile. Keres just looked at the wall.

"What time is it?" he asked.

She checked the watch on her wrist. "2:15."

"Can I leave?"

"Now?"

"Yes."

She stepped back and considered him before speaking again. "We typically discharge patients in the morning after the doctors do their morning rounds."

"What about un-typically?"

"Huh?"

"You said typically. What if I want to leave now? You can't keep me here, right?"

"That's right."

"Well, I want to go. Now. I'll sign whatever you want."

She tsked again and pursed her lips. The grooves around her mouth showed this might be her usual expression. "Alright. I'll send the doctor in."

"Tell him to hustle."

"Her. Dr. Ashwan."

"Whatever."

The nurse left with one last tsk.

He could just walk out. No one was going to stop him, but he needed to know if there was anything seriously wrong with him. He didn't want to walk out and then keel over before sunrise. He also couldn't walk out in the hospital johnny. He slowly shifted his legs over the side of the bed and put his feet on the floor. He stood and held onto the rolling medical cart, but after a moment of dizziness, he felt fine. The headache still pounded away, but he'd had worse.

The room was spartan. A bed and necessary equipment. A guest chair. A television bolted to the wall in a corner. There was a door to the right of the bed. He walked over and opened it. It wasn't a closet with his clothes, but a bathroom. He shut the door again. He thought he might have to buzz the nurse again and ask her what they'd done with his clothes when he pulled open the drawer on the bedside table that held the water pitcher. There were clothes folded inside. Stiff blue jeans, a tan canvas work shirt, white boxer briefs, wool socks. Boots and a light brown quilted work coat were on the bottom. He checked the shirt and jeans. Everything was the right size. The bureaucrat. He changed into the clothes and draped the coat over the chair.

There was also a manila envelope in the drawer. He undid the clasp and emptied the contents onto the bed. His wallet, nothing appeared to be missing, a set of keys, his cell phone, and a separate smaller white envelope. He put the wallet and the keys into his pockets. He picked up the white envelope. There were crisp 50-dollar bills inside. A lot of them. He quickly counted, $2500. He assumed that this was his expense and walking around money. He transferred some to his wallet. He left the rest in the envelope and tucked it into a pocket of the coat. If Lisa came up short, maybe he'd go back to the man in black and ask about further payment for helping him get the system moving.

. . .

It took another 30 minutes before Dr. Ashwan appeared in a starched white coat and carrying a stack of files. Keres was sitting in the chair next to the bed and stood when she entered. She put the files on the side table and introduced herself. She was a small woman with light coffee-colored-skin and a lilting accent. Keres immediately didn't trust her. She opened then closed the file and looked at him for a moment before speaking.

"You have a head injury. My recommendation is that you stay at least one more day for observation."

"I feel fine. Unless I'm going to walk out that door and die before I get to the elevator, I don't need any more observation. I need to get out of here."

He lied. He didn't feel fine. His head hurt worse now that he was standing and talking.

She nodded, then continued. "We did a CT scan when they brought you in. You were still unconscious. CT stands for computed tomography. It's basically a series of x-ray images taken from a number of different angles and then combined. It gives us a very detailed internal picture of the body without being overly invasive."

He looked at her, unsure if there was a question, but liking her less for using that code again to keep him in the dark about his own health.

"The scan showed a brain contusion you suffered on the left side due to blunt trauma. I understand it was a car accident. There's a second contusion, what we call a contrecoup contusion; basically, your brain rattled around in your skull. Big bruise on one side, then a slightly smaller sibling on the other side when the brain rebounded off your skull."

"What are the symptoms? Because I really do feel fine."

"It's the brain, so it's hard to diagnose standing here, on the outside. The primary contusion is not the worst I've ever seen, but it's not trivial either. You should expect, to some degree, a headache, dizziness, more sleepiness than usual, potential nausea and vomiting, perhaps coordination and memory problems. Managing emotions. There are others, but those are the basics."

Those words he could understand. "That's a long list."

"There's a lot we still don't know about the brain and its reaction to trauma. Hence, the recommendation for observation. You don't want to run into those symptoms when you're driving out of the hospital parking lot. The people on the sidewalks wouldn't care for that either."

Her affect remained polite and placid, and Keres wasn't sure if she was making a joke. "So, you don't really know what will happen to me. You're guessing."

Her eyes narrowed slightly before she responded. "We know your brain has a bruise. We can see that on the scan. We're not guessing about that."

"But the rest of it?"

She eventually nodded. "Yes. I don't know for certain what might happen. I believe the scan results necessitate further observation, here, under medical care."

"Not going to happen. Bruises heal in a few days, right?"

"We are not talking about a bruised shin from running into the living room coffee table. This is your brain."

"I understand. You can write that in the file. It was a fine speech. I still want out."

She took his patient chart from the stand at the end of the bed and began writing. When she was done, she returned it and said, "Okay. I cannot keep you here against your will. You are an adult. Sign yourself out at the desk." She turned on her heel, picked up the stack of files, and left.

. . .

He exited through the front door and walked carefully down the sidewalk to the hospital parking garage. He pressed the key fob intermittently as he walked. The lights of a sedan responded on the third floor. It was a grayish silver and didn't look that much different from the Chevy he'd wrecked on the bridge, but this one was some version of a Nissan. He didn't like the idea of a Japanese car any more than dealing with that foreign doctor inside but, beggars, choosers. He opened the driver's door and sat down. He wasn't dizzy or nauseous, but he was sweating lightly from the short walk and the headache hadn't quit. He glanced in the back and saw a bag with the rest of his clothes and his laptop from the motel. There was another case in the footwell of the front passenger seat. He picked it up and opened it. He smiled. Two matching handguns and a knife. Persuasion tools.

The man in black appeared thorough in everything except the whereabouts of Lisa Sullivan. Keres had expected some sort of note or map. Some type of information to get him started. He didn't need to be spoon fed, but he needed to be pointed in the right direction. He had a thought. He pulled out his laptop. After it booted up, he hopped on the hospital's Wi-Fi and checked his usual message boards and accounts but found nothing that could remotely be from the man in black or about Lisa. He tossed the laptop in the passenger seat. Taking his things out of the motel indicated that Lisa was no longer in West Adams, but Keres could have guessed that. So where would she go? Back to Joyce? It was his only lead, however tenuous. He pressed the ignition button and the car started up.

"Please proceed to the highlighted route and the route guidance will begin."

He touched the screen and tried to figure out how to turn it off or cancel the destination. Then he paused. He smiled.

He'd found the note. He exited the garage and when he pulled out onto the street the navigation system kicked in with a route overview. He was headed to a place called Chepstow, Vermont.

CHAPTER FORTY-NINE

After leaving Naomi with the old woman, Max and Lisa had driven east out of West Adams. Five miles past the town line, Lisa started to shake and her teeth began to chatter. She tried to roll down the window, but her hands were shaking too badly.

"Pull over," she croaked in a hoarse whisper. Max pulled onto the shoulder and she just got the door open in time before she threw up a hot, liquid puddle. She stayed like that, head bowed, breathing through her nose for another minute, then spit once more, sat up, and closed the door.

"Sorry about that," Lisa said and wiped her mouth with her sleeve.

"Aftereffects of an adrenaline dump. Been there."

"Never happened to me before."

"You'll feel fine in an hour."

"If only that were true," she replied and put her head against the seat and closed her eyes.

Max pulled back onto the road and continued east, passing the occasional car, but mostly tracked by skeletal trees and dirty piles of snow built up along the guardrails. He eventually turned north onto 8A. Thirty minutes later, Lisa opened her eyes. She was no longer sweaty or shaking, but still looked pale. She looked over at him with a weak smile and he saw her pupils were small pricks.

"Let's stop and get some food."

"That bad, huh?"

"You're doing a good impression of a scarecrow."

Two miles later, he pulled into the parking lot of The Wagon Wheel Diner. It was a square box filled with dark, lacquered booths and matching chairs and looked more like a saloon than a diner. Maybe that was the point. There was only one other table occupied, a gray-haired man bent over a newspaper doing the crossword. They chose a booth in the opposite corner. Max put his back to the wall so he could watch the door. It was an old habit by this point. Lisa dropped her bag, the one that Max had pulled from the bike pannier, onto the seat and then slid into the booth after it.

A skinny, older waitress with dyed hair and creased skin dropped off two glasses of water and menus without a word. She returned a minute later, and they both ordered coffee and a slice of pie. She didn't write it down, just nodded, and went away again. She seemed happy enough to leave them alone.

"How did you find me?" Max asked.

"I thought that part would be obvious."

"Joyce."

"Who told you the *Teddy Bear Picnic* story? Joyce?"

Lisa looked across at him and he saw the flash of pain in her eyes. "Still don't believe me?"

"Would you?"

She looked away. "I don't know. Maybe not." She scratched at a raw patch of skin on her wrist and then pulled her sleeve down over it.

The waitress returned with two solid white mugs and a carafe of coffee, plus two plates with slices of pie, one sweet potato, one blueberry. Max poured the coffee. It was hot and strong and Max clutched the cup with both hands as if it might shield him from the conversation that was coming.

"Here," Lisa said after the waitress had gone. She dug in the bag she'd brought in and put a picture frame on the table, then pushed it toward him. "This is the last thing I have that might convince you if you still don't believe me. When Keres came after me, I risked going back to my apartment for two things. This was one of them."

Max picked up the frame and looked at it. It showed a man and a woman, obviously a younger Lisa, and a small child. Three or four years old. A boy. They were walking on a beach, the boy between the two adults, the wind tousling his hair, a seagull, forever frozen, circling overhead. The boy was smiling. It was the uninhibited ear-to-ear smile that only care-free kids can pull off. It was a smile that knew you were safe and loved. Max could never remember feeling that way. Not completely. Not like this. But there was no doubt it was him in the picture. He put a finger on the glass. The boy in the picture held his mother's hand, but the other was in a cast.

"You still have the scar," Lisa said and touched the ridged white tissue that ran from his pinky down to his wrist.

Her touch felt like an electric shock and he pulled his hand back, dropping the picture frame to the table.

She didn't react, only reached across the table and picked up the picture. "You'd only had the cast on for maybe a week at this point. I'd been so worried about you being out on the ice, skating, never mind playing hockey. You were small for your age, and then this happened on the second day. I almost killed John when he called from the ER. I swore we'd never go back to the rink, but you were crazy about it. Obsessed. We ended up getting the cast cut off a week early and you were back at it the next day. I was a wreck for the first few months, but the panic faded. You were so good."

He had been good. More natural on skates than without. More at home on the ice than almost anywhere else.

He felt something crack and relent inside him. His mother. Alive. Sitting across from him.

"What happened?"

Lisa sat back but kept her hands wrapped around the frame. She'd had this conversation so many times. Late at night staring at the ceiling. In the shower shampooing her hair. She'd had it on her bike riding through traffic. She'd rehearsed and she'd practiced hundreds, maybe thousands of times. She didn't want to make excuses or absolve herself. She just wanted to be clear. She wanted him to understand. But now? When she was finally seated across from her son? She could find none of those words. She looked down at the snapshot then at the grown man sitting across from her. The stranger. She'd missed so much. All those practiced words seemed woefully inadequate. How could they ever make him understand why he grew up without a mother?

The silence stretched out. Her jaw felt locked shut. He seemed to sense her discomfort and asked, "So you knew where I was this whole time? And Joyce knew about you?"

The question was enough to loosen her tongue. "Joyce knew I was alive, but she never knew where I was."

"The car crash story was a lie?"

His voice was steady, but Lisa could hear him fighting the anger and pain riding just below the surface. "No, that was true, or mostly true. There was a crash, a terrible crash, and John, your father, was killed and for some reason, I was not."

"But you never came back. You left me with Joyce. Why?"

"What did Joyce tell you we, your dad and I, did for a living?"

Max rubbed his eyelids and pinched his nose in an imitation so close to John that Lisa felt her heart break all over again.

"Joyce didn't talk about you much and to be honest, I was, at first, too young to ask that many questions. Later, I was too angry to listen. I think she said you were a waitress and Dad did odd handyman jobs."

"That's about right. But that's not really the whole truth."

"What is the truth then?"

"I did come back, you know. I tried to. A few times."

"I don't remember that."

"You wouldn't. I didn't come to the house on L Street, but I saw you play hockey at the Murph when I could."

He stared at her for a long time and then he surprised her. "Red scarf. Your hair was darker. You sat up high." She felt a tear run down her cheek. "You always moved behind the goal we were going toward."

"Whatever goal you were going toward."

"But you stopped coming after a time."

"I had to consider the alternatives."

"What?"

"It's the same reason I've stayed away all these years. Someone was looking for me and looking hard and they weren't afraid to bully, intimidate, and hurt people to find me. It was too big a risk to keep seeing you, even from afar. If they had ever gotten a whiff that you or Joyce had seen me or might know where I was, then they would have forced you to tell them. Even if you didn't actually know. I couldn't risk hurting my family like that."

"Better that it was a self-inflicted wound?"

She could only nod.

Max went quiet again. "What did you and Dad really do for a living?"

CHAPTER FIFTY

She had a hard time getting started, but once she started, she talked for almost 30 minutes straight. The waitress refilled their water glasses and brought another pot of coffee. The more Lisa recounted her earlier life, the more it forced him to consider nature versus nurture. His parents had been part of a heist crew. All those years, he hadn't been doing anything outlaw. He'd only gone into the family business.

She finally paused and took a drink from the perspiring water glass. She'd only picked at the pie.

It was a long and twisted tale, one he'd likely revisit in his mind many times, but it wasn't over. Not yet.

"You swam out of that river and pulled some of the money out. Then what?"

"You want to know about the money?"

He could see the anger flickering in her eyes. He waved a hand. "Yes and no. I'm not asking for me. I don't need money." Max didn't want any of the blood money associated with the story he'd just heard. "I need to hear about it because it's what Keres is chasing. He might want revenge, but his primary motivation appears to be the money."

"There is no more money."

"None? How much did you take out of the water?"

"A little less than a million. A lot of it went to help Joyce. I still send her a little every month. I'm not sure why, with you being grown and Danny and Mary both..." She didn't finish the sentence. She didn't have to. Max already knew what happened to his two cousins. The ones he shared a childhood with and still thinks of as siblings. They are both dead. "The rest of it went to Mary's treatment."

"She was in a study."

"Not the entire time. And it turns out dying is expensive. Really expensive."

He gripped his water glass tighter. He'd sold a piece of his soul to get Mary into that experimental study and now he realized that it all might not have been necessary. He'd thought they were broke. He'd gone to Carter because he'd believed Mary had no other options. Now he had to wonder what his life might have been like had he never met the man. Would his wife and child still be alive? Would he be a fugitive? Or would he have ended up in the same place? Nature versus nurture.

"I never thought it would go on this long. Never. I thought maybe a few years at most and they would lose interest," Lisa continued. "I started going to your hockey games, but I saw cars I didn't recognize and people giving me second looks." She raised a hand even though Max had said nothing. "I know. I know. I sound paranoid, but I was always careful, and I had every reason to be hypervigilant. I know what I saw."

"People see what they want to see."

That made her snap her gaze back to him. "You think I wanted to stay away? You think that was easier?"

Max didn't respond, but that was answer enough for her. She held his eyes for another moment, but then looked away. "Okay, I deserve that. And you deserve your anger." She turned in the booth and dug through her bag again. She pulled out a folder, tattered, old, and fuzzed at the edges, and placed it on the table. She laid her hands on top like it was a hymnal. "But I wasn't lying to myself. I wasn't being paranoid. This whole thing should have burned itself out. It was a big deal at the time, sure, but two guys were dead and another went to prison. People were punished." Max was going to say she hadn't been punished, but maybe that wasn't true. She'd likely punished herself plenty over the intervening years. The victim's family or law wouldn't accept that, but he could see it written in the lines on her face. "The appetite to chase me down shouldn't still be there. But it is. It's not front-page news, but it's still there. It's like a live wire running just under the surface. Anytime I tried to get close to anyone from my previous life, I could feel it spark to life. I told you I went back to my apartment for two things. This was the second thing." She pushed the folder into the center of the table.

Max slid it over the rest of the way and opened it. The top page was a recent article from a medical journal. *Wireless Recording in the Peripheral Nervous System with Ultrasonic Neural Dust*. He scanned the first paragraph and quickly lost the thread in the jargon. He flipped through the pages. More journal articles. Neuroscience and miniaturization. Then patent filings with complex CAD drawings. Then business incorporation documents. It appeared to be in reverse chronological order. Each time he turned a page, he was going deeper into the past. The documents getting older. The last item was a microfiche print of an article from *The Bangor News*. Max glanced at the date. Six months after Lisa told him the robbery had occurred. He shuffled the papers back in line and butted the ends together, closed the file, and looked at her.

"None of this makes any sense to me," he said.

"It's not supposed to. To anyone. Not yet."

"But you think this is the reason someone has continued to look for you all these years?"

He couldn't keep the skepticism from his voice. He was beginning to wonder if this woman who claimed to be his mother was sick. Maybe she believed all the talk from the last hour, but had it really happened? Was this folder, what she believed was proof of something, but what appeared to be random printouts, the delusions of a broken mind? He needed to talk to Joyce.

"Yes. I think it could be," Lisa said. "And I think it goes beyond just me. He wants to get me because I am a very old, very loose end, but he's after something much more."

"He? Who are you talking about? Keres?"

"No, Bradley Cobb."

The name rang a faint bell in Max's head, but he couldn't place him. "Who is Bradley Cobb?"

"A very wealthy, very dangerous man. He owns several companies, most of which deal with defense contracts."

Max had more vague recollections of half listened to news stories. Maybe a scandal.

"He keeps a low profile. Anytime he pokes his head up for some press, you can bet there's a reason for it. If you've heard of him at all, it's probably because of AlphaSigma."

Max now pictured an older, distinguished man with the tight, pinched features of a fox, testifying before a government panel.

"The military contractors?"

"Yes. One tentacle of his myriad businesses."

"And he sent Keres after you?"

Lisa shook her head. "No, I don't think so. Keres is another loose end, like me. Keres can't see beyond his own shadow. He just wants money and vengeance. Cobb probably wouldn't mind if Keres did his dirty work and saved him the trouble of getting rid of me himself. Keeps his hands clean. In fact, I think Keres was Cobb's fail-safe originally, but I'll get to that." She looked over her shoulder. The crossword guy was gone. A woman had taken his place, one table farther along in the row of banquettes near the window. The woman was drinking a cup of coffee and reading a book. What looked like a half-eaten Danish was near her elbow. The waitress was leaning against the counter by the BUNN machine and scrolling on her phone. There was the distant clank of dishware from somewhere out of sight in the kitchen. The rest of the place was quiet. She turned back around and faced Max. "How did the job at the pier go so wrong, so fast?"

"The fire."

"Yes. And what are the odds that something in that warehouse would catch on fire during the brief time that we were inside?"

Max felt as if they were back on terra firma now, talking about a job. "Minuscule. Not worth considering. You were set up. Why?"

Lisa nodded. "The robbery wasn't the point. The fire was. The robbery was a smokescreen. Me, John, Keres, Justice. We were all decoys. We were never supposed to get out of there. Or we weren't supposed to get far. We certainly weren't supposed to still be walking around 25 years later. The cops were there too fast. That fire was too convenient."

"Why?"

"Who benefits?"

"Follow the money. That's the rule. Who got paid?"

"Other than the money that I fished out of the river, the

only person to see a cent from that night was Cobb. He was the inside man."

"Cobb, the rich and powerful guy who testifies before Congress and shows up in the pages of *The Wall Street Journal* was the inside man on your heist?"

"He wasn't always rich and powerful." She pulled the folder back to her side of the table and flipped to the pages at the back then pushed a clipping from *The Bangor News* into the center of the table and tapped a finger toward the bottom of the story. Cobb's name was buried in the sixth paragraph. "Far from it. He was just about to go bankrupt. He was the owner of the other half of the warehouse at the port. It was a small tech shop trying to make better navigational systems for fishing boats. No defense contracts. No military. He was down to his last couple of employees and his last couple of bucks."

"And when the warehouse went up in smoke, he filed an insurance claim."

"Bingo. A policy he had adjusted a year earlier."

"A planner."

"Maybe he was supposed to get a cut through Wimpy too, but in the end, he took almost as much from the insurance company as we did out of the vault. He pivoted after that. Ditched the marine hardware and went after military applications. Got lucky or, more likely, used some of that insurance money to pay the right people and landed a contract for improving the early SCUD missile targeting systems. It was a small contract, he was the fifth or sixth subcontractor to the subcontractor, but Cobb had found his niche. He thrived."

"You know this for a fact? Or are you just guessing?"

"The business background is documented, if buried. You hear about his humble beginnings, but the original company down by the docks rarely gets mentioned. It was in a few early stories, but it's now been scrubbed from the official record. It would make a nice little origin story, but I don't think he wants anyone looking too closely. I had to dig deep for the original records."

"You think Cobb is still after you because you know about his role in the heist? Is that in here?" He pointed at the folder.

"No. But Wimpy was a careful and meticulous guy. We, your father and I, used a few different fronts to keep our everyday life shielded as much as we could from that side." Max nodded. He'd done much the same. Layers gave you protection and gave you a warning when someone was coming. "About six months after the job, I got word that there was a package waiting for me at one of the drops. It was from Wimpy. I hadn't seen or heard from him since that day in Delaware. I'd assumed he was dead. Keres had likely done it. Turns out I was right. The package was a dead man's switch of sorts. When Wimpy didn't turn up, or tell someone, or enter something into a computer, the package was mailed off to John and me as insurance."

"What was it?"

"A recording, audio and video, of a meet between Cobb and Wimpy. It's grainy and shot in a dark bar but it's clearly Cobb, and they talk enough details to be very clear about what's going down. No judge or jury would find any reasonable doubt."

"And you still have it?"

She took a USB drive out of her purse and held it up.

"And you think that's the reason he's been keeping the pressure up all these years?" Max asked. "He knows about the recording?"

"I think he knows or suspects. Maybe Wimpy threatened him. Or maybe he's just plain paranoid." She pulled another sheet out. This one from the top of the pile. One of the medical journal synopses about the neural dust that was mostly Greek to Max. "He's about to be given a very, very large defense contract. The largest ever awarded to a private company. And that might be just the tip of the iceberg. It's not hard to see the wider commercial applications."

"And you are the one loose end out there that could scuttle that plan."

"I think I have to."

CHAPTER FIFTY-ONE

Max directed Lisa through the increasingly small tributary roads of southern Vermont until they hit Chepstow's meager town center.

"Slow up," Max said at the town's crossroads.

Lisa braked and Max looked for Vic's truck but didn't see it parked along the road. They drove past The Night Owl, just two cars were in front, but it was still early for the usual crowd. He thought about stopping in and asking Tommy if he was alright but then decided against it. The man would take it as an insult. Max wondered about the men who had jumped him at the bar. Where had they gone? What had they wanted?

They drove past the diner. No sign of Vic's truck.

"Alright, keep going."

Five minutes later, Lisa pulled to a stop in front of Vic's house. No truck, but he hadn't expected her to be home. She was out doing whatever it was Vic did. Just like Lawrence, he'd never really been clear on her employment status other than owning the motel. She appeared to survive on a rotating array of odd jobs, from gutter cleaning and landscaping to junk removal and carpentry.

They parked in the driveway and got out.

"This yours?" Lisa asked. He could feel her taking it in. He stopped her before she drew any conclusions.

"No, a friend of mine."

"Good friend?" Lisa asked.

"Just a friend," Max responded, and started around toward the back of the house.

He didn't expect the door to be locked and it wasn't.

Year-round Chepstow residents rarely locked their doors. If there was a break-in, you'd know who it was before they got off the property.

Bailey started barking as they entered, but the familiar smell of Max and a few well-placed scratches behind his ears took care of that. He took out his phone. One thing he liked about Vic was that the phone was the last resort for them both.

"Where are you?" he asked when she picked up.

"At the motel doing your job. Where are you?"

"I'm back at your house."

"Seems like we've swapped places."

"I won't sit in your chair, but no promises about not drinking your beer."

"Your ass is too big to fit into that chair. I've got it imprinted after years of hard work."

That got him thinking about Vic's ass. Not something he'd really considered before. He'd only known her since November, and she always wore bulky clothes and thick jackets. Hmm. He changed the subject.

"I'm not alone."

"She's with you?"

Over coffee, scrambled eggs, and toast that morning, Max had filled Vic in on his past. Not all of it. Not even most of it, but a general sketch about his mother returning from the grave to call him.

"Yes." Max was in the kitchen but could see through into the added-on TV room where he'd slept last night. Lisa was looking at the books lining the shelves and scratching at her arm.

"Given what happened at The Owl, I thought you getting out of Chepstow was a good idea. But now you're back so soon."

"Can't turn away family."

"Can't you?"

He didn't have an answer to that. Not yet. He changed the subject again. "You hear anything today? You talk to Tommy?"

"I talked to Tommy. The guys left the car. Brian towed it this morning. But no one has seen those guys around since last night and you can't hide, not for long, in this place. I think they're gone."

"Coming back?"

"I put the word out but haven't heard anything. If they're coming back, it's not right away."

"Feels a little weird that they'd come on that strong and then walk away."

"I got the sense someone hired those guys. They do a job, they get paid. It's not personal," Vic said.

"But they didn't do the job. Thanks to you and Tommy. Something changed."

"Maybe. No way to know," Vic replied. "Look, why don't you stay for another day or two? See what happens."

Max couldn't think of anything better at the moment. They needed time and space to think, and here was as good a place as any. They spent the rest of the afternoon on the couch. Lisa alternated between dozing and being awake, flustered for a moment, her eyes wide and startled, before remembering where she was.

"Trouble sleeping?" Max asked at one point after she had jerked awake for the third time.

She stood and walked to the window. She rubbed at her leg.

"I get these muscle cramps. They wake me up."

"You get them a lot?"

"Not every night." She looked back at him. "You sleep alright?"

Max thought about the ghosts that liked to circle above his head as he lay in the dark. "Not every night."

Vic returned home at 5:30 with two large pizzas and more beer.

"Smells good," Max said. Other than a few mouthfuls of pie, he hadn't eaten anything since the quick breakfast he grabbed at a gas station over 12 hours ago. The smell of grease, cheese, and carbs made his stomach roll over.

"You're lucky I didn't have Bailey in the truck. He would have eaten at least one of these on the way. That dog is lactose intolerant, but he wouldn't hesitate to eat it. He loves to find ways to torture me." Bailey leaned his body against her legs, and she rubbed his ears with a smile.

"Anyone take a room?"

"Actually, yes. A woman called. I had to hustle and prep a room since my help is on vacation."

"I happen to know every room up there is ready and prepped."

"Alright, I had to pretend to be a five-star rated establishment."

"You got five stars?"

"Yelp and TripAdvisor. The views alone get me four stars. My winning personality pushes it to five."

He raised his hands in surrender. "Whatever you're doing, it's working."

"Exactly."

"So you left her up there by herself?"

"The odds of a hungry bear picking the right room are pretty low, right?"

They made a formal affair of dinner. Set out plates, sat at the table, and poured the canned beers into proper glasses. Lisa and Vic made small talk. Lisa asked about life in Chepstow and owning a motel. Vic steered clear of questions about Max's childhood and instead asked Lisa about Clarkston and her job. It was a conversation that likely happened around many family dinner tables. It gave Max a strange feeling that he couldn't quite identify as he sat and listened.

When they were done, Vic shooed Lisa out of the kitchen. It was obvious the long day had caught up to the woman. The food and alcohol had made her drowsy. Lisa didn't put up a fight and collapsed back onto the couch. As Max cleared the dishes, he could hear her already snoring softly. He took the pizza boxes from the table and placed them on the counter. Vic stood at the sink rinsing the glasses.

"Did you talk to her?" she asked.

He recounted what he'd learned from Lisa at the diner. Her history, now part of his history, Keres, and Cobb. He left nothing out. He didn't want to lie to Vic. Not after the risks she'd taken for him. He hadn't told her everything about himself, but he'd decided he would if she asked.

"Sounds like you definitely had a yammer, as my Grams used to say, but did you say what needed to be said?"

"Crazy as the story is, I believe she is who she says she is."

Max paused and looked across the kitchen toward the add-on room. Bailey had made the snoring into a duet in his own nearby bed. "All those years she knew right where I was, but she never came back."

"And she bore that burden."

"Did she? Or did I?"

Vic made a noise. "I'm not one to give advice." Max made a face and Vic smiled with an arched eyebrow. "Much. But one thing I've learned as I've gotten older is that you never get the answers. Things that looked obvious to me then look downright stupid now. I'm sure I'll feel the same way in another 10 years. Maybe growing up is just learning to make those gaps smaller until you finally realize you really don't know anything."

"So do you think I would have been better or worse off if I knew the truth?"

"That is not a question I'm old enough to answer yet. But maybe you should think about it." She dried the last plate and put it back on the shelf. "Let me go make up the guest room for Lisa."

Later, after Lisa and Vic went upstairs, he spread out the blanket he'd used the previous night on the couch. He reached down for the pillow and knocked over Lisa's purse where she'd left it that afternoon. Three orange pill bottles spilled out. He picked them up and looked at the labels. Vitamin D, calcium, and something called benazepril. The vitamin D and calcium made some sense, given Lisa's age. They would both help strengthen bones. He'd never heard of benazepril and felt a surge of panic in his guts. He'd been thinking of Lisa only as the mother who walked out on him, not as a human being. Something that was frail and could break when put under stress. Someone who might need these pills.

He heard footsteps on the stairs and put the pills back in her purse. Lisa walked in a moment later wearing sweatpants and an oversized sweatshirt. She plucked at the arm. "Vic's." Max nodded. "Ah, was looking for this." She leaned down and grabbed her purse.

"Mo—" Max started, but the word caught in his throat like a piece of barbed wire. "Goodnight," he finally managed.

He thought about Vic's question as he stared up at the ceiling for a second night. Would he be the man he was today if he'd known the truth? He had to think it would have changed him. Would he have made the same choices? Would he have been stronger or weaker? A more stark question followed that observation. Would that have been better or worse?

CHAPTER FIFTY-TWO

Max woke to a fly buzzing in his ear. He reached out to the coffee table and picked up his phone. He didn't recognize the number but had a good idea who it was. Lawrence loved phones with disposable numbers. And no self-respecting telemarketer or scam artist would call at 5:00 in the morning.

"Hello, Lawrence."

"I'd apologize for calling so early, an ugly mug like yours needs all the beauty sleep it can get, but once again you've got me poking around in shit that's probably best left alone."

Max sat up on the couch, fully awake now. The Beard. "You get a name to go with that photo I sent?"

"No, Eddie can't find anything, which is what has me worried. There should be something. Whoever this guy is, he's clean. Too clean."

"What does that mean?"

"It usually means some government agency I've never heard of and never will."

"Why would the government send some black ops guys after me?"

"Are you kidding?"

"If they sent anyone, it would be the traditional three-letter garden variety. Plenty of those to go around. I haven't stepped on enough toes to warrant some off-the-book black ops hit."

"You're probably right. And exactly what I thought. You aren't interesting or important enough. This facial recognition program Eddie wrote is excellent, but not foolproof. Which is why I also searched on the license plate of the truck in the background."

"And?"

"It's owned by a company called Cerberus International, incorporated in Delaware."

"Let me guess. Shell company?"

"Delaware's greatest export. There was a phone number. It was in service, but no one ever picked up."

"Okay, now I'm nervous too. That's a lot of effort to make it look like you're not hiding anything."

"What rock did you kick over now that has these guys after you?"

Good question, Max thought.

"What did you say?" Max asked.

It was two hours and a pot of coffee later. Vic stood in the doorway. Max had spread Lisa's file out on the table.

"I asked what you'd littered all over my kitchen table." She waved a hand, then walked to the coffee pot and poured a cup before coming back over to the table.

He'd listened to Lisa and flipped through the file at the diner, but he hadn't had the time to take it in. He'd been getting too much information at once. After Lawrence's call, he went looking for a distraction. He'd spent the last two hours reading through the pile. A lot of it was dense technical jargon. He had a long way to go before he finished. He sat back and rubbed at his eyes.

"This is what Lisa's been up to for the last 25 years and, if you believe her story, the reason someone is trying to kill her now."

They'd all been too tired last night to get into it. Max sketched out the basics for Vic now.

"Do you believe her?"

Max thought about it. "I don't think she fabricated all this," he indicated the various piles on the table, "and I'm sure she believes it to be true."

"But," Vic said.

"She saw her husband get shot. She survived a plunge off a bridge. She lef—walked away from her family. She's been on the run half her life. That has to affect a person."

Vic nodded. "No doubt."

"But," Max said.

"Doesn't mean it's not true."

"Hard to prove."

"Is that what you're after? Proof? Or something else?"

"What do you mean?"

"Whether it's true or not, you drove down there and got involved. Someone is threatening Lisa. Someone tried to run her down on her bike. Proof or not, you're involved."

"Okay, I admit, I'm involved. I don't need proof about Keres. I saw him. He's a lone psycho. But this," he waved a hand over the papers again, "is on a whole different level."

"John once called Keres a weasel." Wrapped up in their own conversation, neither had heard Lisa come down the stairs. "A weasel is a pain in the ass and hard to kill, but mostly a pest, when you get down to it. Bradley Cobb might have started out as a weasel, like Keres, but he's evolved into something much more dangerous."

"How?" Vic said.

"It's all right there in front of you. Read it and then I'll answer any questions you have."

That's what they did. Lisa made another pot of coffee and Vic and Max read through the pile of paper. Vic was a faster reader and had an acuity for the science stuff. She was also good at government documents.

"I've spent a lot of time in town halls around here pulling permits or checking zoning regs or plot surveys. You get a feel for it. It's like learning a foreign language."

After another two hours, they were nearing the end of the pile. The documents on top were more recent but also more opaque.

Lisa noted Max scrutinizing one document as if holding it closer to his face would make it easier to understand. "He got smarter at hiding his intent."

"I noticed," Max said.

"The early documents, even the patent filings, are relatively straightforward once you get your head around the science and engineering, but as the security classification increased, so did the obfuscation."

"And the money."

"Of course. It's always tied to the money. That's a given. A graph of the security clearance needed to look at those documents and the money involved would show a direct correlation."

"Basically straight up," Vic said.

"Over time, yes."

"How did you even get these?" Max asked. Many of the documents they were reading now were marked confidential and classified and heavily redacted.

"For a time, I was working with a reporter from *The Washington Post*. Gill Lessin. He had good government contacts."

"Really good. And brave, too. I'm pretty sure leaking these documents is a crime."

"Yes, but we thought it was worth it."

"What happened? You said for a time. You're not still working together?"

"No. He died."

Both Max and Vic sat forward. "What? How?" Max said.

"He was working so hard. Both of us were but because of my situation, a lot of the work fell to him. He was close to cracking. It was too much for one person. I could see it even if he didn't want to admit it. I told him to take a few days. We knew the DoD's rough approval timeline. A few days to preserve his sanity would not make or break the story. I needed him clearheaded. I finally convinced him to book a ticket and take a long weekend. He flew down to the Bahamas. I'm sure he took some work, but at least he'd be at a resort, maybe on the beach, have some rum nearby." Lisa paused. "I didn't get worried until Tuesday morning. I found the newspaper report on Wednesday. They said it was a diving accident. He drowned."

"But you don't think so?" Vic asked.

Lisa shrugged and kept her eyes on the table. "I don't know. He never mentioned diving. But that's what you do down there, right? We were being careful, but he was the front man on this. Could be a tragic coincidence. It's also possible Cobb got wind of his digging and didn't like it."

"And had him killed for it?" Vic said. The skepticism was apparent in her voice. "Did you have that kind of proof?"

"No, not yet. He was excited about this new source. The one that got us those internal documents. We were getting close."

"And now?"

She shook her head. "Gone. They were his source. They didn't know about me. I have no way of getting in touch. I don't know their name or how they communicated."

"So you just have these papers."

"And the video."

"Right."

"You still haven't stitched it all together."

Lisa let out a long breath. She was frustrated. "And that's Cobb's genius. The science is insane but his approach to getting it out there is brilliant. Dangerous, egotistical, immoral, maybe sociopathic, but still brilliant."

"How?" Max said.

"He's putting this all together and locking down all these patents piecemeal. It's as if he's using a Trojan horse but shipping it inside the castle walls one part at a time. He's breaking it all up, even within his own company. He has factories and labs around the country, but I guarantee you very few people know exactly what they are working on. They only see their own little corner. There is no larger context. And that's by design. I can't believe at least a few of the people smart enough to work in these places also don't have the intelligence to see how dangerous it all is. And he's getting the government to fund it all." She gave a bitter laugh. "Genius. Our tax dollars at work."

"You keep giving us these doomsday proclamations but, you're right, I don't see it. What's he building? What are you so afraid of that you'd risk your life to stop him?" Max asked.

"I'm afraid of losing my mind."

"Do you know what the biggest future threat to humanity is?" Lisa asked.

"Terrorists. Nukes. Climate change. Bioweapons. Take your pick. I don't think humanity is lacking for ways to kill each other off," Max said.

"All true. But what does that look like?"

Vic and Max shook their heads and Lisa held out her hand, palm up. "Like this."

"What's that?" Vic asked.

"Something so small that it's almost impossible to see." She dropped her hand. "Conventional death and destruction through 50-ton nukes or ICB missiles or even dirty bombs in suitcases isn't the future of war. The U.S., Russia, and China are investing billions in nanoweapons research. Nanoweapons that could unleash attacks using mini-nuclear bombs and insect-like lethal robots. If that happens, how long before that tech leaks to the black market?"

"Sounds like science fiction," Vic said.

"Of course it does. Fifty years ago, the internet sounded like science fiction. In 10 or 15 years, nanobots smaller than a human hair that can be programmed or, hell, even learn, to do certain tasks will be commonplace."

"It could have major benefits on the positive side, too, like medicine," Max said.

"Exactly," Lisa said, her eyes almost shining. "That's how they get you to swallow the bitter pill. Wrap it up in a sweet coating. They've already developed fascinating therapies for Parkinson's by using nanotech in a person's brain to simulate dying nerve endings."

"Doesn't sound all bad. My grandmother died of Parkinson's. Nasty disease," Vic said.

"I don't disagree. Used morally with ethical guardrails, it could be a boon to humanity." She paused. "When have you ever said those phrases in conjunction with the military? Or national interests? Or capitalism? Do you think it's more likely that any advances in nanotechnology will aid humanity or harm it? What happens when we can program inhalable microparticles to supersede someone's mind and take control of someone's spinal column? Will that be used to heal or to cripple?"

Max had no answer to that. He could see her point. "If

what you're saying is true, the train has already left the station. You can't stop progress."

"That's the same thing Oppenheimer said."

"He wasn't wrong."

"And look where it's led us. If we can make war appear more precise, less destructive, less costly, then it only makes it easier. The moral cost is reduced. But there is still a cost. It's just different than wars of the past. We're seeing that now with PTSD and mental illness in drone pilots who are killing people from thousands of miles away. What happens when we remove even that level of human intervention? The future of war will be small but never-ending. And how long will it take to move from distant places overseas to America's street corners?"

"What's your plan?"

Her shoulders sagged and she looked down at the table. The fervor was gone. "How many thermonuclear missiles have ever been used?"

"None. Yet." Max replied.

"You're right. The future is coming and the seeds of this are likely planted in too many places to contain it. The safest thing, I think, would be to give it away. To make sure everyone had it."

"Mutually assured destruction."

"Whatever keeps the world in balance."

CHAPTER FIFTY-THREE

"What's this?" Vic asked Lisa, holding up a sheaf of paper. Lisa leaned over the table and looked at the top sheet. She frowned, and Max recognized the crooked wrinkle that ran up the bridge of her nose and between her eyebrows.

"Not sure, to be honest," Lisa said. "Part of the puzzle. Sometimes I gather lint and don't know what it's for. If I recall, this came up in a records search. I set up alerts on various sites to flag anything related to the addresses that we'd put together for Cobb or his businesses. I run the searches once a month."

"Pretty sophisticated. For an old lady, I mean," Max said with a smile.

Lisa smiled. "I feel much older than I probably look, but when you're on the run, you pick up things quickly when your life is on the line. The college had a good computer lab and a lot of grad students willing to help a frail old lady."

"Oh, yeah? Did you show any of them just how frail or frisky an old lady could be?" Vic asked.

Lisa smiled. "Maybe one or two."

Vic whooped and Bailey jerked his head up from the floor. "I knew it. In the stacks or on your back?"

"I'm definitely too old for any library closet shenanigans."

"I don't know," Vic said. "Now I'm thinking maybe we should call you Mrs. Robinson."

"Maybe you should just keep reading."

They all fell silent again for a few minutes and plowed through more paper.

Then Vic spoke up again. "What does Cobb do at his lab in Virginia?"

"I don't know exactly what he does at any single facility. That's the point. We think we know where most of the labs and fabrication plants are based on past corporate filings and state registries. But the state documents are slim for private companies like Cobb's. He's bought out a few public companies in the past and those filings were available. Those helped fill in some blanks. Why are you asking?"

"This shipping manifest you flagged? From what I can tell, it's a bunch of computers. Maybe supercomputers. Souped-up hardware." She turned to the last page. It had a different header and font than the previous pages. "This is a permit and zoning exception from the town of McLean. I've seen more than my fair share of these. Whatever he's doing there, it needed a special exemption from the local board."

"I'm sure that wouldn't be a problem for Cobb," Lisa said. "When you've paid off senators and congressmen, a local zoning official must be pocket change."

"What did they need approval for?" Max asked.

She pointed to a section in the middle of the document. "Whatever they're doing with that souped-up hardware, it was going to put a serious dent in the electrical grid. Cerberus Innovation Labs needed to have two special transformers installed to even out the load and avoid causing rolling blackouts in suburban Virginia."

"Cerberus?" Max said.

Vic caught his tone and looked down at the permit again. "Yeah, that's the name listed. Mean something to you?"

"The guys that jumped me the other night at The Night Owl. My friend got back to me. He didn't get a name and that sort of surprised him. He's very good at finding what he wants. What he did find was the SUV Tommy scratched up with that buckshot was registered to a Cerberus International."

"Cerberus. It's a mythological thing, right?" Vic asked.

"The hound of Hades. It's the three-headed dog that guards the gates of the Underworld to prevent the dead from ever leaving," Lisa said. "Cobb likely thinks it would make a good pet."

"And you believe it's all connected?"

"Sort of strange to be a coincidence, don't you think? Too separate threads of this named after the same mythical pet?" Max said.

"Assuming you're right, why did Cobb send them after you?" Vic asked.

They both turned and looked at Lisa. She opened her mouth to reply, and Vic's phone rang. She looked at the display and then picked it up. "Hey, Georgie. Got something?"

Georgie Smilla ran the other motel in town, The Blue Sparrow. Technically, The Sparrow wasn't in Chepstow, but Craftwick. But Craftwick was unincorporated and, at last count, held a total population of 24. It existed mainly on maps. Most locals just referred to it as East Chepstow or Eastie. Georgie himself was only slightly smaller than Craftwick. He was a big, gregarious man whom Max had run into at The Owl a few times. You could usually tell he was in residence before you opened the door. His deep baritone easily creased through the loose mortar that made up The Night Owl's walls.

Max heard Vic say, "Uh-huh, uh-huh." With Georgie, Max knew, a simple drink order could last 20 minutes.

Cerberus. The Beard. Cobb. Why?

His mother's enemy had suddenly become his enemy. What did that mean?

What would he do about it?

Vic put down the phone and said, "We have a problem."

CHAPTER FIFTY-FOUR

"Georgie knew it wasn't the guys from the bar I'd asked about, but he thought he'd pass it on," Vic said.

"But we don't know that it's Keres," Max said.

"No, not for sure. But Georgie's got a good eye, and his description matches up pretty well with what you told me." Vic glanced over at Lisa. "Right down to his snaggleteeth. Georgie said that's what made him sit up and take notice when he checked in. The man looked like he chewed on rocks for breakfast."

Lisa nodded. "That's him. You don't forget that picket fence of a mouth."

"What time did he check-in?" Max asked.

"A little after 5:00," Vic replied. "Georgie had just put the coffee out."

"So he's been in town for at least three hours."

"Yes, though Georgie thought he might have driven all night. Or been up all night. He had that punch drunk look. As if a truck had hit him. Also, his car hasn't left the lot this morning."

"Alright, so he's not onto us yet."

"How would he even find us?"

"I think we have to assume Cobb is feeding him information. If Cobb knew I was here and sent those guys after me, he might have pointed Keres here, too," Max said.

"And he has a certain charm when he wants to. Doesn't work on everyone, curdles my milk, but if he asks around, spins the right story, he might find someone to tell him about you, Vic, or the motel."

Vic nodded. "This town watches its back, but fundamentally, they're decent people and believe others are the same. If he spins the right story, someone will spill. They'll probably call us too, but they'll tell him. They'll think they're helping."

"Then I don't think it will take him all that long to get to The Cliffside," Max said. He glanced at both women. "I'm sorry, coming back here, especially after what happened at The Night Owl, wasn't a good idea."

Lisa shook her head. "It's not your fault. You couldn't have anticipated Cobb going after you or pointing Keres here."

Max shook his head. "But I should have. It's not a secret that you had a son. It's in all those old news stories. From what you've said, Cobb is ruthless. Worse, he has deep pockets, connections, and the motivation to find me. He will try to get as much leverage as he can. In whatever way he can. This is exactly the type of move he would make."

"Better to take a stand on familiar ground then," Vic said. "Beat them once before."

"I hate playing defense."

"What are you thinking?" Lisa asked.

"Keres is already here, so we need to deal with him first. I don't want to be looking over my shoulder when we go after Cobb."

. . .

"You're talking about killing him," Vic said. She turned and looked at Lisa but found no ally there. Lisa's face remained impassive.

"No. I'm not executing him. I'm not ambushing him. I'm not shooting him in the back. I'm giving him a choice."

"He follows you out there, he's not coming back." She tapped her phone. "It's 16 degrees out right now. And that's with the sun shining and no wind. By sundown, it will drop close to zero. Or below. I wouldn't be surprised if we get some snow. You think he's prepared for that?"

Max knew he wasn't. He was counting on it.

"What would you and Tommy have done in that parking lot if those guys hadn't backed down?"

"But they did."

"Because you gave them a choice."

He didn't blame her for her reaction. The fact that the question got her moral hackles up was another reason to like her. For all her gruffness, she had a soft core of humanity inside. He didn't want to pull her any further into his family's black hole. But he needed one more thing.

"Will you do it?"

Keres was late. Maybe the good citizens of Chepstow were more guarded than they thought.

Vic's cell phone rang. It was Max.

"Let's give it another 30 minutes. This won't work in the dark."

Just as she ended the call, lights washed over the office windows. She watched a silver sedan pull into the lot, stop, then drive closer and park near the office. An older man got out of the sedan and looked around. She felt her heart rate give a quick kick. It was him. Not much to see, buddy. The only other guest, a woman, had asked to park around back.

He's being careful, Vic thought. She tapped out a quick message to Max and then did her best to look bored behind the desk. Her baseball bat rested out of sight but within reach against the desk's leg. The door opened a moment later and Vic got her first close-up look at George Keres.

"Help you? You look a little lost," she said.

"No, not lost. Just confused. In a pleasant way, I suppose. Back in town, they told me to expect a guy, not a pretty lady." He smiled as he closed the door and took a few steps into the middle of the room. His eyes bounced around, taking it all in, before pinballing back and landing on her. His teeth were worse than advertised, she thought. Rock biter, indeed. "I've been trying to find my friend. Single, older woman, name's Lisa? She staying here by any chance?"

Interesting, Vic thought. They assumed Keres was in Chepstow for Max, but he'd just asked about Lisa. Vic wasn't sure that mattered. The plan should still work.

She leaned her elbows on the desk. "Forgive me, but I don't know you."

"I'm a friend," Keres said.

Vic could see traces of what Lisa had mentioned. Keres had a certain magnetism that she knew appealed to some women. Not her, though. Even without Lisa's stories, she would have seen behind his mask.

"So you say, but I still don't know you."

He kept the smile pasted on, but she watched his eyes sharpen. She dropped her hand below the desk to the bat.

"So you do know her?"

"Didn't say that either."

"Sort of seems like you did. If you didn't know her or talk to her, you'd just say that. Nope, haven't seen anyone like that. Trust me, people have been telling me that all day. Like a reflex. Like when people ask how are you? And you say I'm good or I'm fine without really thinking about it. It just pops out. But you didn't do that."

"That right?"

"Yup. The fact that you're putting up this front tells me she's likely been here, or you at least know who I'm talking about."

"You think you're pretty smart, huh?"

She saw the anger flash across his face before he held up his hands. "Hey, I'm not sure how we got off on such a wrong foot. I'm just looking for my friend."

"Laura?"

"Lisa. Now you're just playing games. Look, it's clear you've seen her, but you have your policies or principles or whatever. I respect that. I'd probably want the same treatment if the shoe was on the other foot. I'll just try back later."

She looked at him and pretended to think it over some more. They'd talked about it for a solid 30 minutes over her kitchen table. What would be the best approach? How would they get him to take the bait without realizing it was a hook? They decided it would be best to make him work for it.

"My principles are not inviolate. If you're a smart guy, you know what that word means."

They looked at each other and then he smiled again and brought out his wallet. "What's the standard room rate here?"

"Forty-nine a night in the offseason."

"So $50 would cover it?"

"I was thinking of a two-night stay."

He glanced at her but then took the bills, all crisp 20-dollar bills, she could smell the papery sweetness as he stepped forward, and pushed them across the desk. She could smell something else, too. A rotting mustiness that she recalled intensely from the room where her mother spent her last days. The smell of death. She worked to keep her face neutral and picked the bills up, folded them over, and slid them into her pocket.

"She's here. You just missed her. She left with some guy."

"A guy? Where'd they go?"

"Local guide." She tilted her head. "I saw them turn left out of the lot. There's not a lot up there except the Green Mountain Park trails or a long drive to Canada. The trailhead is just a few miles that way. You'll see parking on the left."

That smell was filling her nostrils. She held her breath. She didn't want to breathe this man in. She wanted him gone.

He headed toward the door, but then stopped and turned back.

Go, just go, she pleaded.

"What's she driving?" he asked.

Vic took a breath and then paused, trying not to gag. The smell had filled the room.

"I think a two-night stay gets me that info," Keres said. He thought she was stalling or holding out for more money. He edged back, closer to the desk.

She forced herself not to step back and then nodded. "Black SUV of some kind. Not sure the make or model. Looked pretty new. Something higher end."

He smiled and she tried not to look at those gray, crooked teeth. "That wasn't so hard," he said and then walked out. She put her head down on the desk and let her shoulders relax. That had taken more out of her than she expected. It took an effort to raise her head back up. Despite the late afternoon sunshine streaming through the window, the room felt chilly and dark. Keres had left, but the rot lingered.

She picked up the phone to call Max when she realized she hadn't heard a car. She put the phone down, came around the desk, and went to the window. Her left hand reached out absently and flicked on the switch for the motel's outdoor sign. Keres's car was still sitting in the lot, just a few feet away. The driver's door was open, but she didn't see Keres anywhere. She tried to look down the row of rooms, but the angle was tight and she couldn't see more than a few feet. Where could he have gone? She reached for the office doorknob to step outside for a better look when the loose panes of glass in the door rattled in their frame. Max had mentioned wanting to fix that. She made a mental note to let him do it. He'd said it only happened when the door to the courtyard… she spun around. Keres was standing by the door with that ugly smile. Only this time, he was also holding a gun.

"Sorry."

Her legs were weak. She wished she had the bat that was sitting behind the desk, but really, what would that do against a gun? She did her best to keep her voice steady. "You're apologizing?"

He smiled and she forced herself not to look away. If this guy was going to shoot her, she'd make him do it to her face. She looked away from his mouth to his eyes, blank and cold, and she realized it wouldn't make a difference either way. He'd have no problem shooting her in the back. Whatever got the job done.

"Guess it's something people say."

"You have experience in it then? Or did you pick that up from the movies?"

"I like you. Sort of regret having to shoot you."

"Why would you?"

"If things go my way, you won't be the last person I shoot. Can't have you giving the cops a good description."

"You just told me you've been all over town asking after this woman. You don't think they'll remember you?"

"Oh, a couple might, but what they'll mostly remember is

an old man. Most of them won't even remember that much. Most people aren't looking and listening to other people. They're just thinking about themselves, waiting for you to stop so they can talk again. I'm not worried about them. But you? I think you're one of the few who is actually paying attention. We've been having a nice chat. Even did a bit of commerce. I think you could help the cops quite a bit." He shrugged. "So, you gotta go."

She glanced around. The office was 10-feet square. He stood a few feet inside the door, maybe eight feet away. The gun gleamed with oil under the office lights. It looked new and well maintained. He might miss, but it wasn't likely. Not at that range. Especially if she just stood there.

"Sure, I could give them a physical description, but how far is that going to get them? You plan on hanging around after you shoot the woman?" She tried to sound relaxed but tensed her legs. If she could get behind the desk and get to the bat, maybe...

"No, I won't be hanging around, but you could describe my car. You were just staring at it through the window. I'm going to need a running start. I need that car to stay anonymous for at least a few days."

He raised the gun.

She flung herself to the right.

The noise was incredibly loud in the small space. She felt a hot sting in her left arm. She ignored it and crawled along the floor. She heard another thunderclap and chips of wood flew around her head. She grabbed for the Louisville Slugger but missed. Her left arm wasn't working right. Then, through the smoke and the noise, she heard a growling bark. No. The sound made her heart freeze. She was so focused on Keres, she'd forgotten Bailey was asleep at her feet under the desk. He was no longer asleep. He was trying to protect her. There was another gunshot. She grabbed the bat with her right arm and stood up in one motion. Bailey was snapping and snarling at Keres's legs. He was trying to back up and shoot the dog. Her dog.

Vic came around the desk using her momentum to put some power into her one-armed swing. She heard another growl and realized it was coming from her. Keres was aiming down. She screamed and swung with everything she had. She saw the muzzle flash and heard the bat connect with Keres's arm. He grunted and dropped the gun. Vic tried to swing again, but Keres lashed out and kicked her in the stomach. She lost her grip on the bat as all the breath went out of her. Bailey was barking and lunging. Keres was trying to stomp on both of them now. She rolled away from another kick. She heard him yell as Bailey's teeth clamped onto his ankle. She crawled across the floor and picked up the bat. It took two tries. It was hard to get a grip. Blood covered her hands. She turned, ready to take his head off at the neck, but the room was empty. A moment later, she heard his car start and drive off. She let go of the bat. Bailey didn't come to her side. He was lying on the rug. He let out a whimpering cry.

CHAPTER FIFTY-FIVE

Max put the phone back in his pocket. "She's not picking up." He looked from the parking lot back toward the road that led to the motel.

"Don't assume the worst," Lisa responded.

"Plan for the worst is one of my basic rules. With Keres that seems like a safe bet."

"You want to go back?"

"Maybe. I don't like that she's not responding."

"She could have just ducked into the bathroom or had to deal with a guest."

As she finished, they both heard a car approaching.

"Goddam bitch. Goddam dog." Keres pounded the wheel with his right fist. His left arm was still numb from where the woman had clocked him with the bat. And where had that damn mutt come from? He took his foot off the gas and thought about going back and finishing the job, but who knew if the woman had her own gun. She might be ready and waiting this time. He glanced down at his leg. Once the dog had sunk his teeth into his calf, Keres's only thought had been to shoot the dog and get the hell out of there. He'd gotten a few shots off and thought he'd hit the dog, but then the woman and her bat had jumped back in and everything was moving too fast to be sure of anything. Keres got free of the melee and bailed.

Had it been the right decision? Yes, he thought so. Lisa was the primary aim. She was close. Deal with Lisa, get his money, and then if he had to come back and clean up this minor mess, he could do that. Shoot the dog and burn the whole place to the fuckin' ground. He felt the blood drip down his leg. Shit. He'd have to deal with that. That dog had gotten a real good taste. He put his foot back on the gas.

Keres had turned left out of the parking lot, as the woman had indicated, and driven north. As he went around a bend, and the motel disappeared, the trees loomed closer and crowded out the light. Tall and dark, Keres could barely see five feet into the forest on either side of the road. He'd grown up mostly in the south, mostly in small towns way out in the sticks. They were rural but it was a different kind. Swamps and glades. Flat and wet. These woods looked thick and menacing. Maybe a little hungry.

The road bent now in the opposite direction, maybe following some contour in the forest that he couldn't discern and then he saw the parking lot. It was a narrow dirt lot whittled out of the trees. There was a sign at the entrance that showed there was additional parking a half mile farther along, but that wouldn't be necessary today. There was a single car in the lot. A black Cadillac SUV with Massachusetts plates.

"Bingo," Keres said out loud.

Keres parked his car a few spots away. He got out and pulled his pant leg up to examine the bite. It wasn't good. The dog had gotten a mouthful and really gnawed on the muscle. There was a loose flap of skin around the teeth marks. The wound was angry and red, but the blood was clotting. He hoped the mutt had all his shots. He opened the back door and pulled a clean T-shirt out of his bag. He ripped it into long strips and bound it tightly around the wound. It was the best he could do right now. He took a few steps. His leg throbbed, but he could walk. He rotated his arm over his head and winced. He was going to have a hell of a bruise, but he didn't think she'd broken anything. He went back to the car and dug through the bag, wondering if the bureaucrat had put any aspirin in his bag. He hadn't. He quickly checked the rest of the car and the trunk for a first aid kit but came up empty.

He took the black tactical knife and the second gun from the hardcase and closed the lid. What else? The sun was still out, but not for too much longer. The day would not get any warmer. He grabbed his coat and wished he'd bought a hat and gloves at the general store when he was in town. He glanced at his cheap sneakers. Boots wouldn't have been a bad idea, either. Too late. He didn't want to miss this chance. It was too good to pass up.

If he could take Lisa out here, it would make things a lot easier. He didn't think the other guy, this guide, would be a problem. He'd make a judgment call when he saw him. Alive or dead. Another body wouldn't bother him. He looked around. It was quiet. Maybe he'd get his answers right here. No one was around to hear Lisa scream.

Something niggled at the back of his brain. Why was she out here? Why now? Did she think she'd run far enough? That maybe she could hide nearby and go back to her life when Keres moved on or lost interest?

"Honey," he said out loud, "you are vastly underestimating me."

After so long, the money was so close. He pushed any other doubts out of his mind.

There was a large map near the trail's entrance showing this portion of the network. He walked over and studied it. He doubted they were going for any long or arduous hikes. Not at this time of day. The other trails looked longer or steeper. Lisa was a 60-something-year-old woman. She was in shape from all that damn biking, but she wasn't doing any black diamond trails up a mountain. He traced a finger along the main trail. It was a five-mile loop. He tapped the map. That was the one.

He placed a palm on the hood of the Caddy as he passed. Still warm. They weren't far.

Vic had given him a pair of binoculars and Max took them out of the pack now.

"Let's stop here for a second."

"Is it him?"

When they'd heard the car, Max had quickly led Lisa down the trail and away from the parking lot. They'd pushed hard for 10 minutes.

"I don't know. I assume so. The odds of it being someone else at this time of year are small. This is a good place to make sure he sees us. He'll have a good view down into this valley when he walks past marker 11 near that big rock."

"You're sure he won't have a gun?"

"Oh, he'll have a gun or some type of weapon, but I doubt he'll try to pick us off like a sniper. First, the odds of hitting us are slim, even with a rifle, unless he has a skill we don't know about. Second, he needs, at least, you alive."

"Okay," Lisa responded. She sat on a fallen log. "Could use a break."

Max looked at her. He was worried. They hadn't been walking long, but she looked wrung out. He'd have to watch her. This was the easy section of the trail. Once they veered off into the unblazed section, it would become harder. Max put his attention back on the trail. He scanned the ridgeline with the binoculars.

The plan was simple. Lead Keres off the path into the flat, featureless forest at the base of the mountain. Max knew from experience that it was very easy to get turned around and lose your bearings. A few hundred yards in the wrong direction and you might never find the marked trail again. Max turned it over in his mind again and came up with the same moral calculus. The forest swallowing up George Keres, never to be seen again, would be a net positive for humanity. Max wouldn't lose any sleep over what he did here. Keres was following them for one reason. It was his choice.

Max took his eyes from the binoculars and glanced up at the slanting sun. Only a couple of hours of daylight left. Then this national park would show the sharp teeth hiding behind the groomed trails and pictorial lookouts. Even with no other weather, like rain or snow, the cold and wind alone would make life very difficult for an experienced outdoorsman. He didn't think a recently released con stood much of a chance.

He scanned back up the ridge with the binoculars and glimpsed tan canvas moving through the trees. "Here he comes," Max said, putting the binoculars back in the pack and hoisting it onto his shoulders. "Let's get moving. He should be able to see us soon. We continue dead straight on this trail for another half mile. He should have us in sight the entire time until we turn off. Don't look back."

The air was still cool, but Keres was walking briskly and could feel prickles of sweat running down his back. He was glad he hadn't wasted time going back into town for anything. A hat, gloves, or thicker coat would have been overkill. He slipped on a patch of fallen pine needles. The boots might have been an upgrade over his sneakers, however.

He came to a fork in the trail at the top of a gradual rise, the foothills of the surrounding mountains, he supposed. Despite spending the last 25 years in New England, he never got out much to see the local geography. He was on a few roadside litter crews, a plum outdoor gig for most guys, but he'd swapped that for the library and extra computer time as soon as he could. He'd once driven through the Smoky Mountains on the way to a job in Gatlinburg. Vermont? Tennessee? Mountains looked largely the same to Keres.

He looked left and saw nothing in that direction but trail and treetops. He looked right and spotted two shapes in the distance moving away from him. Lisa? Had to be. And not far. He checked the knife in one pocket and the gun in the other. Satisfied they were secure, he started after them.

The trail sloped gradually down into a valley, and he kept them in sight. It was easy to do with their bright jackets and hats standing out against the almost uniformly gray and green forest backdrop. He steadily closed the gap.

Then they disappeared.

CHAPTER FIFTY-SIX

Max pulled Lisa onto a small game trail. The entrance was easy to spot from the main trail and easy to confuse as a marked section. It was how Max had found himself accidentally on it the first time. He'd been running, lost in his thoughts, dodging branches and roots, letting his feet follow the trail, when he looked up and found himself standing in a vast patch of unmarked forest. The game trail petered out near a small, dried-out brook. He'd turned and looked back, catching his breath. The path through the trees and shrubs was not as obvious in the opposite direction. It was only later that he realized how lucky he'd been to find his way back out again.

"Quick," he said now, standing by the same dusty stream bed. "Flip your jacket around." He dropped his pack at his feet and pulled off his jacket. One side was bright blue, but the opposite was a black fleece lining. He tugged the coat back on inside out and pulled his hat off and put it in the backpack. Lisa did the same and dropped her hat into the bag. It wasn't hunter's camouflage, but they would no longer be quite so visible.

"Stay here."

"Where are you going?" Lisa asked.

"I need to make sure he followed us."

Max walked back toward the main trail but kept 20 yards to the left of the narrow game trail he hoped Keres would follow. He eventually spotted Keres at the fork. The guy looked confused, trying to figure out where Max and Lisa had gone.

"C'mon," Max whispered. He decided to help things along. He picked up a rock and threw it in the general direction he wanted Keres to follow. It did the trick. The man's head snapped toward the sound like a hound that's finally caught the scent. As Max watched, Keres touched each pocket of his thin coat and then stepped off the trail.

Max hustled back to Lisa.

"Okay, he's coming. Follow me."

Max led her deeper into the wooded valley. There was no defined path after the brook, but this section of forest was also no longer unfamiliar to Max. For the first 15 minutes, he made plenty of noise to keep Keres following. Then, at the big rock formation where he typically pushed himself upward and finished his run, he skirted around the base and looped back to the south.

"Now, step where I step, try to make as a little noise as possible."

Keres fixated on a gnarled tree where he'd last seen them. He walked forward and back 100 yards in each direction. The trail continued its gentle downslope. He could see a mile or more in that direction until the trees became fuzzy and indistinct. There was no one walking the trail.

He walked back to the old tree. Maybe they'd stepped off the trail to look at something. He stood still, then spun in a full circle. Nothing. They had been right here. He was sure of it. Two splotches of color in a forest of gray. Finally, holding his frustration back, he let his focus go soft and let his eyes roam over the path. Then he saw it. Or thought he did. It was the slightest gap. A hint of a trail going off to the right. He walked toward the gap and then stopped. Why go this way? There was a crash and the sound of something large moving through the undergrowth. Too loud for a squirrel or a bird. Keres marked the direction he'd heard the noise and then followed.

The going was easy at first. The trees were sparse and the trail, while faint, was clear. He heard the occasional branch snap or the hint of a voice that told him he was on the right track. He still hadn't seen them yet, but felt he was getting closer. He pushed harder, trying to close the gap. It was getting late. The low winter sun barely penetrated the valley canopy. It was dark in the woods and getting darker. He needed to finish this.

He was breathing hard and sweating when he reached a large outcropping of overlapping stones at the base of a hill covered with thin saplings and scrubby ground vegetation. He caught his breath and realized he'd heard no sounds ahead of him recently. He stood still for two minutes but heard nothing. Had they gone up and over this hillock? He didn't think he was that far behind them. He would have expected to see them still climbing if they had climbed up that way. Maybe they'd gone around. But which way? Left or right? He looked up to orient himself. The last bit of sun was just visible. Left was west. He felt that made more sense. That would take them back toward the original trail. A gust of wind swirled down and eddied around the rock formation. It cooled the sweat on Keres's brow, and he suppressed a shiver. He needed to keep moving. He went left.

· · ·

Lisa rubbed her hands together in front of the car's heater. "You said you got lost in there before?"

"The best way to learn a place is to get lost," Max said.

"A dangerous way, too."

"Yes, I'll admit it was not the original plan. But it's funny what you remember when you find yourself in those situations. I was never in the Scouts or really saw too much of the woods as a kid, but one summer, Joyce was dating a guy, Patrick, I think, who was really into camping. One weekend, he took all of us up to Acadia. Danny, Mary, me, and Joyce. I don't remember much except a leaky cabin roof, baked beans for three meals, and one piece of advice from Patrick. If you ever get lost in the woods, stay put. But if you can't do that, then walk downhill. Since most cities were originally built near water, you'll likely come across other humans within a day once you reach a stream or a river in a valley. Going downhill is also easier on your body and will save you energy."

"And that's what we just did?"

"Yes. It feels like you should go west at that rock, especially if you've studied the map. But west is essentially a dead end unless you want to climb over the mountains. I looked it up on some plat maps after I got lost the first time. There's a steep gorge on one side that narrows to the mountain's base. The official trail skirts that but it's on the opposite side. You won't get across without serious gear."

"So, this all works if he goes left?"

"That's the plan."

Keres tripped and fell to his knees. A sharp pain ran up his knee to his hip. There was a hot, steady throb from the bite in his leg. He couldn't see it in the dark and he was glad for that small mercy. There was a strange sound echoing off the rocks and he looked around, trying to spot the source. Were there coyotes or bobcats in Vermont? He patted his pockets. He still had the gun and knife. He'd be okay. But what was that noise? He slowly stood and wiped the mud off his hands on his jeans. His arm throbbed. It was drizzling now, occasionally turning to sleet or snow. Not hard, not accumulating on the ground, but just enough to make everything slippery. And Keres's clothes damp and cold. There was that sound again. He spun in a circle, but whatever it was stayed just out of sight. He clamped his jaw shut and held it there with some effort, but his arms and legs continued to shake.

After leaving the rocks, he'd walked 30 minutes in one direction, picking his way through trees and dense thickets of brambles that left small cuts across his arms and face, until he finally broke free and almost tumbled down into a canyon. Standing there, on the edge of nothing, he felt on the verge of madness. How had he gotten here? Lisa was gone. She'd evaded him again. She had a talent for it, and he almost laughed. He turned back, he had no choice, and faced a wall of trees. There was no path. It was full dark, and he was lost.

By primitive survival instinct, or blind luck, he made it back to the rocks. He looked up and then started to climb. He needed to get to higher ground to orient himself and figure out a way out of this hell. The strange sound continued to stalk him. A strange mix of chattering, clicking, and grunting. At one point, Keres thought he could smell it. He whipped around, desperate to confront whatever was stalking him, but found nothing. He'd slipped and fallen back precious yards. He screamed in pain and frustration. After that, the creature, or creatures, kept their distance. For a time.

It took almost an hour and almost all his remaining energy to scrabble and claw his way to the top of the short, rocky hill. He looked around and saw... nothing. The clouds and drizzle muffled the stars and moon. Everything was just shades of black. He dropped to his knees and this time he did laugh. The creatures came in close and circled him. They were him. His chattering teeth, his shivering exhaustion, the sour smell from his leg. He hung his head. There would be no money. There would be no revenge. To survive his father, to survive Monty Green, to survive all those years in Stanhope, and then die alone on a hill in the Vermont darkness was a weird middle finger from the universe.

He wasn't sure how long he stayed like that, but when he lifted his head, he realized it wasn't all blackness. He wiped his eyes. He knew he wasn't in good shape and the mind could play tricks on a person. But no, it was still there. A red glow to the south.

CHAPTER FIFTY-SEVEN

"Now what?" Lisa asked. The car heater was now running hot. Max unzipped his jacket.

"I want to check on Vic. I don't like that she didn't answer my last call while we waited for Keres. Once that's done, it's time to play some offense. I think we head to D.C. and track down Cobb."

"How? We don't have a home address. That seems to be a trade secret. Even Lessin never found that, and he was good at digging."

"We have a work address where that electrical work was done. That's a start."

"But not a guarantee."

"Nothing in life is. If he's thick with the Department of Defense, I bet he's nearby. McLean is close to the Pentagon. Do you have a better idea?"

"No, not really. I'm just trying to wrap my head around it. I've never been in a position to go after him. I was trying to do that, take him on, in a roundabout way, with Lessin and the press. Take him down through exposure. But that didn't work."

"He's got a lot to answer for."

"He won't see it that way."

"Maybe not. But he's also got to answer to me personally. I don't like bullies and I don't like the fact that this guy came after me." He looked over at her in the passenger seat. "Or my family."

Max pulled into The Cliffside parking lot. The big outdoor sign was lit up, but Vic's truck was gone. Max pulled close to the office and he and Lisa both jumped out.

"Vic," he called, as he opened the office door, even though he could see it was empty. He went to step around behind the desk and stopped. There were splotches of blood, enough to stand out even on the old, stained carpet. Enough that Max knew something violent had happened. This was no accident. He turned to say something to Lisa and found another woman standing with her in the doorway. She was younger than Lisa and wore jeans and a large Rutgers sweatshirt. She looked vaguely familiar, but Max couldn't place her. The sweatshirt showed smears of blood across the front. Something must have shown on Max's face. She held up her hands.

"She's okay," the woman said. She had a north Jersey accent. "It's not her blood."

Max felt a wave of relief but then realized it couldn't be Keres's blood, either. From what Max saw through the binoculars, Keres didn't appear injured or to have lost significant blood. "Whose? What happened?"

"The dog, I think. I'm not sure what happened. It was over by the time I found them. The woman was manic, not making sense. She was banged up, bleeding a little, but not heavily. Scraped up. I called 911. Ambulance took them both away."

"Thank you," Lisa said when Max didn't respond. "You're staying here?"

"Yes."

The relief Max felt at the blood not being Vic's boomeranged back at the mention of Bailey.

"Not sure I did all that much."

"From the looks of that sweatshirt, you did more than most might have."

"You friends of hers?"

Employee. Friend. Max wasn't sure where one started and the other began. He knew he was concerned. "Yes," he said. Let this woman draw her own conclusions.

"Was this a random thing? Did she have enemies or problems with a guest? Though it seems like an extreme reaction for a motel guest."

Max looked at the woman more closely now. She didn't give off a cop or law enforcement vibe, but that wasn't your usual citizen question.

"No. This was not random," he responded. "I don't think the guy is coming back. You should be safe staying here."

"That's a relief."

"Did the EMTs say where they were taking her and Bailey?"

"No, I'm sorry. I'm not from around here. The woman was yelling at them when they arrived, and they bundled her and the dog into the ambulance and took off. I think they forgot I was even here."

"Okay. Thanks again for helping them out."

Max took out his phone. He knew Chepstow didn't have a vet or a hospital. He googled the nearest animal hospital and found two. Each was almost an hour away in opposite directions. One to the north and one to the south, back over the border in Massachusetts. He called the one in Massachusetts and was told that no one had brought in a dog with a gunshot wound. He dialed the second one in Vermont but got a similar answer. He disconnected from the second call and tried to work out what to do next. He wouldn't be able to concentrate on Cobb until he knew what happened with Vic and Bailey. Lisa sat on the old orange couch against the wall. Drying puddles of blood were on the floor between them. He told Lisa that Vic and Bailey weren't at either of the nearest animal hospitals.

"Maybe they're still en route?" Lisa said.

"Maybe, but I'm betting this happened before Keres came after us and we led him around in the woods for an hour. If they were going to either of those hospitals, they'd be there by now. And it seems like a far run for a local ambulance company to make, at least with a dog, doesn't it?"

"Would a regular hospital work on a dog?"

"I have no idea. Never owned a dog."

"We must have passed a dozen farms on the way in before the ski resorts took over. I saw horse paddocks at most of them. There must be a large animal vet in the area."

"Good idea," Max said. He looked up the number for the Chepstow General Store. "Jim? It's Max out at The Cliffside. Listen, are there any large animal vets on-call in the area to help out the local farms if the livestock gets sick?" He had a lie prepared about a guest asking, but Jim didn't ask why Max wanted to know. Maybe he was used to out-of-the-blue questions as a general store proprietor.

"Sure, Lance Hicks over in Woodford handles that sort of thing. If he can't do it, he'll refer them to one of the places over in Brattleboro or Bennington."

"Thanks, Jim."

Max ended the call before Jim found any curiosity and googled Lance Hicks and quickly dialed the office number. It was after hours but a woman answered.

"Hicks Vet."

"Has someone brought in a dog recently with a gunshot wound?"

There was a pause. Max wasn't sure what the code of ethics was for vets and patient confidentiality. "I'm a friend of the owner, Vic. Is she there? Can I talk to her?"

"No, they took her over to St. Vincent's. She didn't want to go but she couldn't do anything here and she needed to get checked out. I thought she was going to fight the EMTs."

That brought a small smile to Max's face. That sounded like Vic.

"Is Bailey going to be okay?"

There was another pause and Max's smile fell away.

"Lance is very good, but we won't know for a while."

The lights in the room were on low and everything was cast in overlapping shadows. Vic was in the bed. She looked pale and exhausted. Her arms stuck out of the white cotton johnny and disappeared under the thin hospital blankets. But Max could still see a deep purple bruise blossoming down her left arm. He could also see scrapes and a contusion on her cheek that ran up into her hairline. The nurse told them that the doctor had given her a sedative. She had bruised ribs, a deep abrasion on her arm, and a mild concussion. A long list of maladies, but she would be okay. She just needed time to rest.

Max took a seat next to the bed. After they'd spoken with the charge nurse, Lisa had gone down to the cafeteria to get them coffee rather than crowd into the small room.

Vic was asleep, but her eyes were moving rapidly behind her lids. Max doubted she was dreaming about anything pleasant, but maybe the drugs helped with that, too. He had put her here. He reached out a hand and then withdrew it. Friend or just employee? A question to consider later. Right now, it was enough to know that Vic would be okay, at least physically. He sat back and watched her.

He woke with a start and found a skinny man in a suit leaning in the doorway. Max watched him glance at the bed and then make a motion toward the hallway. Max stood and followed. He didn't need to see the guy in better light to know he was a cop. He could smell him from across the room. He mentally kicked himself for not being more careful. Of course, the cops would follow up when Vic landed in the hospital. Any assault or gunshot wound was reported to the police.

The guy held up a badge but focused just over Max's head. "Snell. Sheriff's department. Bennington County. We handle the police support in Chepstow when needed." It sounded like the guy said the phrase at least 10 times a day. Now his eyes came down to Max's face. "Who are you?"

His suit was wrinkled and his tie was askew. There were dark circles under his eyes and the smell of nicotine wafted off him in waves. Max almost said Lindell. It was the name he'd been using in Philly, but he'd had to adopt a new one after how that all ended. An alarm went off somewhere down the hall, followed by an announcement over the PA system. Max used the time to recover.

"Max Hobbs."

"That Irish? You don't look Irish."

"English," he said.

"How do you know Ms. Rattan?"

It took a beat to figure out Snell was referring to Vic. He wasn't sure he'd ever heard her last name before now. Chepstow was so small that first names or old nicknames were enough to know who you were talking about.

"I work for her."

"Doing what?"

"This and that?"

He stopped scribbling on his pad and looked up. "And you drove all the way out here?"

"Friend and employee."

"You sure?" Snell's smile was full of small, yellow teeth. The grin wasn't overly friendly. It was calculated.

Max didn't answer, just stared back. Snell let it go and continued. "You found her?"

"No, I wasn't working. It was over when I showed up. A guest at the motel found her and called 911."

He flipped back a page. "Ms. Wells."

"If you say so. I didn't get her name."

"You going to stick around?"

"Need to check in on Bailey. Vic will want to know when she wakes up."

"Bailey is the dog, right?"

"Yes."

"You got a number if I need to reach you?"

Max gave him The Cliffside's number. He had no intention of sharing his cell phone number with a cop. The guy gave a final nod, slipped the notebook back into his pocket, and started down the hall toward the exit. Max heard the chime of Snell's phone as he returned to Vic's room. She didn't appear to have moved. He sat in the chair just as Snell reappeared in the doorway.

"Does this and that include the motel Ms. Rattan owns?"

"The Cliffside, yes. Why?"

"It's on fire."

By the time he found Lisa in the cafeteria and made it outside, Snell was long gone. They climbed into the SUV. Lisa drove. It wasn't a discussion anymore. Max liked that he didn't have to prod her to push it on the way back to Chepstow. She drove hard, but under control. Snell was climbing out of his car when they pulled into the far end of The Cliffside's lot. A deputy stepped in front of the SUV and came around to the driver's side. Lisa rolled down the window to explain, but Snell beat her to it.

"Johnson, it's okay. They can stay. I need to talk to them." He pointed to a space out of the way, near the base of the tall sign. "Put it over there. I'll be back once I check-in." Lisa backed up and put the SUV in the spot Snell had indicated. They each got out but stayed close to the car. Satisfied that they weren't going to charge into an active crime scene, Snell left them with the deputy, turned, and walked away.

The Cliffside was no longer on fire, but it was still smoking. The air stank of wood, rubber, insulation, and chemicals. The roof had collapsed on the office. There would be no salvaging that part of the motel, but the fire hadn't fully made the jump to the rest of the rooms. The outer walls of the first few rooms, including Max's own, were scorched. There was likely internal smoke and water damage, but the drizzle slowed the spread enough that the firefighters could get on top of it and save most of the building. He wouldn't miss that crappy old carpet.

"What do you think?" Lisa asked.

"The place was old. The wiring was spaghetti. I'm sure it wasn't up to code. But I think Vic got off easy. If she has insurance, she should get enough to repair the place. If she wants." What Vic wanted continued to be a mystery to Max.

"You think this was an accident?"

"You don't?"

"Just the one guest. Not a lot of activity. What would have caused it?"

Max looked around but didn't see the woman in the Rutgers sweatshirt. He hoped she was alright.

"I've been working on the place for the last three months.

I could name 10 things off the top of my head that might spark a fire."

"Alright. I'm just saying. Feels hinky to me. I don't like it."

"Here comes Snell. Maybe he can tell us."

The detective walked over. He had a cigarette hanging from his lips. It was unlit. Maybe he felt that lighting up at a fire was thumbing his nose a little too closely at the fates. "Do you know if Ms. Rattan kept any painting supplies around?"

"Sure. There were supplies in the maintenance closet. Probably old cans in the shed out back, too. I've been touching up the rooms over the winter. Why? What happened?"

"Someone dumped what looks like a can of paint thinner on the rug in the office and dropped a match."

"Arson?"

"The official arson investigator will be here in the morning, but it looks that way. Whoever did it, didn't try to hide it. There's an obvious point of ignition and some melted plastic. Guessing that's the paint thinner bottle. Whoever set it, did too good a job. The rain helped, but the fire mostly consumed itself. Burned itself out. You know anyone that might want to do this?" He looked at both of them.

"No," Max said.

"You aware of Ms. Rattan having any financial problems?"

"No," Max said again. "You think she did it? She was in the hospital when this happened."

"Yes, rock-solid alibi," Snell said it without inflection and Max couldn't tell what he might be implying.

"Who called it in?"

"Another bit of luck. Someone driving past."

Max knew all this luck wasn't going to help Vic look like the victim, at least to the cops and insurance people.

"Do you know which room the guest, Ms. Wells, was staying in?"

Max shook his head and glanced down the line of rooms. There were no cars parked out front. He suddenly felt a sinking feeling in his stomach. "No, Vic checked her in. I haven't worked since she took a room. Why?"

"And she was the only guest?"

"Yes. Why?"

"She's missing."

CHAPTER FIFTY-EIGHT

There was a knock at the door. Eddie waited until he heard the faint ding of the elevator down the hall. Then he stood and walked to the apartment door. He checked the peephole just to make sure the hallway was empty. It was. He opened the door and picked up the bag and carried it inside. Four packages of Red Vines, two bags of Flamin' Hot Cheetos, and two six-packs of Dr. Pepper. Eddie knelt down and put the food in the back of the cabinet where Lawrence wouldn't find it. He took one bag of Red Vines back to his desk.

To Eddie, sometimes it felt like the entire world was a play and he was the only one without the script. He understood what was happening because he knew how to watch, but he didn't understand his role or, many times, his expected reaction. He hated the way some movies portrayed people like him. It wasn't logical and it wasn't close to being accurate. He wasn't some unchanging, mumbling math freak. Okay, they got a lot of the math parts right. Still, it wasn't a disease. It was who he was. It was in his genetic code. And it didn't mean that he didn't learn or change. It just took him longer. And sometimes he had to go off-script.

Take, for instance, making friends. That was very difficult for Eddie, even through the ones and zeros of a computer screen. It could be awkward and time-consuming and embarrassing, at least judging by his observations of others' reactions. Eddie couldn't immediately recall the last time he was embarrassed. Maybe once or twice in elementary school. He didn't go out much. The world was always so bright, loud, and shiny. And that was before he had to talk to people. It wore him out. He preferred to stay inside his apartment as much as possible.

But sometimes you had to go off-script. The last time Lawrence took him to the doctor, when he'd passed out at his desk, the doctor had talked about hypertension and diabetes. Since then, Lawrence had been on a crusade. He bought Eddie a treadmill. That wasn't too bad. With the Xbox hooked up to the TV, he didn't mind playing Minecraft and walking, but Lawrence had also taken his reforms to the kitchen. That was the last straw for Eddie. It had forced him out of the apartment and down to the small market at the end of the block. It smelled funny to Eddie, but he bought a soda and some candy. He'd noticed the boy sitting behind the cash register with the laptop. Eddie had gone home, hacked into the store's network, and introduced himself to the kid. Since then, Kamal had been bringing Eddie's stash up to the apartment in exchange for some hacking lessons and some bitcoin. Kamal was Eddie's friend.

Or take Max. He didn't treat Eddie differently. He treated him like an equal. Max was Eddie's friend. Friends were the family you chose. There was nothing Eddie wouldn't do to help a friend. Eddie didn't have many and he wanted to keep the ones he had. So if this person, the one who had left smudges and fingerprints all over his system, did all that in order to find his friend Max, like Lawrence believed, well, then Eddie was determined to return the favor. Whoever had been inside his system was good, but Eddie was too. He'd quietly been tracing the guy, tiptoeing along in his digital footprints. Eddie hadn't quite gotten there yet, but he was getting close.

"I see you," he whispered out loud as he got comfortable in his chair again. "But who are you?"

He would know the answer soon. And then? He didn't know. He'd have to think about that.

CHAPTER FIFTY-NINE

Keres kept his eyes on the sky and followed the red sign like the north star. His muscles were cramping. He stumbled and fell and might have passed out for a time, but when he awoke, he forced himself back to his feet. Follow the red sign. But even he knew he couldn't last much longer in his current state. He tried to grab a fallen branch to use as support but couldn't close his fingers around it. They were cold, numb claws. He kicked it away in frustration.

"I'm a stubborn asshole," he told the trees. "That's what my father always told me."

He continued to push his way through the forest.

"A hard man."

He was no longer cold or hot. He stripped off his jacket and tossed it aside.

"A hard man to kill."

He kept his eyes on the sky. That big red sign was a beacon. And it was getting closer.

· · ·

He fell one final time. He tried to push himself back up, got one knee up, but toppled sideways. A heavy weight pushed down on his back and spread to all his limbs. His cheek pressed against the dirt and leaves of the forest floor. It felt rough and warm. He closed his eyes and then stopped. His brain sent up one last, desperate flare. The ground felt wrong. He opened his eyes and rolled onto his side. It wasn't dirt, or pine needles, or damp leaves. It was cracked concrete. He forced his head up. The red sign was now a supernova and loomed almost directly overhead. Below it, there was a long, low building that looked vaguely familiar to Keres. His mind felt like shattered glass. There was a patch of yellow light coming from one end of the building. He decided that was his destination. It appeared impossibly far away. He tried to stand but fell back down again.

"A hard man," he whispered. He forced his battered body to listen.

He got to his hands and knees. His arms shook with the effort. He crawled into the red light.

He made it the last few yards by using his elbows and knees. He bumped his head against the bottom of the door frame. Once, twice. No one came to investigate the noise. He dragged himself up slowly to a sitting position against the building's outer wall. If the door was locked, this is where they would ultimately find his body. He could go no farther. He reached up and grasped the cold brass handle. He twisted and the door opened. He heard panes of glass rattle. He crawled through and kicked the door closed.

He lost track of time. When he opened his eyes, his fingers, ankles, knees, and toes were all screaming in pain. Someone had poured boiling oil into his joints. He flexed his hands, but that only increased the deep, throbbing ache. He gritted his teeth and focused on the ceiling. It was how he passed the time when he had bouts of claustrophobia in Stanhope. It happened to all the cons. At one point or another, the walls closed in. Some guys turned to drugs, others to extreme exercise. Some did their best to hurt themselves. Keres traced and counted the cracks in the ceiling. He did the same thing now with the pitted, sagging drop ceiling tiles.

The pain had one benefit. It sharpened his mind, cleared the cobwebs. He used the end of the couch to get to a standing position. His legs felt wobbly, but after a moment of vertigo, they held. He looked at the brown circular stain on the carpet and knew where he was. He went around behind the desk where the woman had stood talking to him. When was that? He looked around and spotted a small clock on a shelf. Over six hours ago. He went through the door behind the desk and found a water closet and small supply room. He pulled a box of candy bars off a shelf and ripped it open. There was a case of soda next to that and he grabbed two cans. He ate the first candy bar and almost threw it back up. Too much, too fast. He ate a second one more slowly. He couldn't get the can of soda open. His fingers were stiff and hot and clumsy. He threw it against the wall in frustration and instead bent his head under the tap and drank water until his stomach sloshed.

He could feel the sugar hit his bloodstream. It was like being hit by a cattle prod. He found a line of keys hanging on pegs just below the office computer. He grabbed the one marked 'Laundry.' He stuffed two more candy bars in his pocket and, after a moment's hesitation, another can of soda.

To the left, the guest rooms started immediately. He limped in the other direction. The bite on his leg was also now thawing out. It burned. He found the door for the laundry and maintenance room in a small alcove with a dusty vending machine. Inside, a line of two washing machines and two dryers divided the room in half. Next to the machines were shelves stacked with white sheets, towels, detergent, and bleach. The other half of the room was a small workshop with a long worktable and pegboard filled with hanging tools. Shelves at the far end held more cleaning and landscape supplies. A second door provided access to the courtyard behind the office.

He stripped and put all his clothes in the big industrial dryer and set it on high. He found a folding chair propped against a wall and sat down on it. He carefully unwound the wet and bloody T-shirt strips from the bite wound. He gently poked at it with a finger and jerked his hand back. It had stopped bleeding, but the flesh around the puncture marks from the dog's teeth was red and inflamed. He took a towel off a shelf and gently tried to wipe it. He'd check in the office for a first aid kit. For now, he took a bedsheet off another shelf and ripped it into more rough strips and tied them around his leg. Then he pulled down more sheets and towels and wrapped himself in them for warmth. He ate another candy bar and waited for his clothes to dry. This time he got the soda can open.

While he waited, he thought about Lisa and the motel woman and the mystery man. The more he thought about it, the angrier he became. It should have been a simple thing. Track her down and make her talk. He replayed their latest confrontation in his mind. Why had she stepped off the path? How had she escaped? The only answer to those questions, for Keres, was that Lisa knew he was coming. How had she known? It was a setup. The hotel woman had told her. Could that be right? Could the two of them have rigged up a plan on the fly if she called Lisa after Keres left? That would be some quick thinking. No, they must have known he was around before he hit the motel. How? He didn't know. Maybe bad luck. Maybe Lisa had spotted him in town. Maybe small-town gossip. Either way, she had set a trap and he had walked into it.

The dryer buzzed and he pulled his dry clothes out and dressed.

But he'd also walked back out of it.

"A hard man."

He might not see this motel woman again, she was probably in the hospital or burying that damn mutt, but he could still leave her something to remember him.

CHAPTER SIXTY

Martha twisted in the sheets. She was at a loss about what to do next. The injured woman and the bleeding dog were too much. It had pushed her over the edge. She was done. She would drive back to Jersey in the morning and bill Cobb for what she'd done. That would be a nice check. And if it disappointed him and ended her business? She was okay with that. She'd survived before Cobb came into her life and she could do it again.

She rolled over again. She missed her bed. These sheets were stiff and rough on her skin. She hated to leave work incomplete. It felt like giving up, and Martha prided herself on not being a quitter. Even if Cobb had never told her exactly what the job was. It had all been so vague, but she knew she'd come up short. She liked her job because it had very specific parameters. Find this person. Research this. Recover that. She did it and then she packaged it up and delivered it to the client. This time wasn't so cut and dried. And now she'd reached her breaking point. Physically and emotionally. She'd been pulling long solitary hours following a skeevy ex-con across multiple states for no discernible reason and it had led her to some podunk motel in the middle of the woods where she'd walked in on a bloody scene straight out of a Tarantino movie. No thank you.

With that decision made, she rolled over and finally fell asleep.

She woke up to the smell of smoke.

Keres knew he couldn't stay much longer. Someone would drive past and notice the fire. Still, he lingered. His lower leg felt hot, but the rest of his body still felt chilled. The heat of the fire felt good. He rubbed his hands together and held them out like it was a bonfire and not a motel office that was burning. He turned toward the road and considered his options. He could walk back to the trailhead parking lot. The keys were still in his pocket and, presumably, the car was still there. But his leg was aching and walking two or three miles wasn't going to help. Maybe the fire and smoke attracting attention could be a good thing. If anyone stopped, he could grab their car. He put one hand in his pocket. He'd lost the knife somewhere in the woods, but he still had the gun.

He walked across the parking lot and stood on the double yellow in the road. He looked in both directions. The road was empty. He waited a minute. Then another. No vibrations. No headlights. No sounds other than the snap and crackle of the burning motel. He realized that a car driving past after dark might be a rare occurrence at this time of year. Five cars a day might go by on average and none after the sun went down. He resigned himself to dragging his leg up the road to the trailhead. He turned and saw a woman standing in the parking lot. Her hair was mussed, she was wearing sweatpants and an oversized sweatshirt. She wasn't wearing any shoes. She just stood there in her socks. She'd obviously been sleeping, but where? Where the hell had she come from? The obvious answer was a room at the motel. Keres looked past her. Yup, a door, three from the end, was open. But the parking lot was empty. Where was her car?

"Hey!"

Martha turned away from the blaze and her jaw dropped. Keres stood in the middle of the road. Then he started walking toward her. No, not walking. Limping. He looked terrible. There were scrapes on his face and his clothes were ripped and dirty. She took a step back toward her room. She'd left her gun inside. She'd woken up groggy and disoriented and just walked out the door. Stupid, she chastised herself. But too late now.

"Hey," he said again. Maybe he realized the effect his appearance had or maybe he just read her face. He held his hands up and smiled. "Sorry, didn't mean to scare you. Hell of a thing, huh?"

"What?" Martha replied. He was carrying on like this was a normal conversation. A chance encounter on the street.

He waved at the fire and smiled again. "The fire. Hell of a thing, huh? Not something you see every day."

She looked over her shoulder at the office where she'd found the woman and her dog earlier that night. Had that only been a few hours ago? Sleep, when it finally came, had dragged her down deep. She couldn't seem to get her mind going. The fire was blazing bright but still contained to the office. If it made the jump to the guest rooms, she knew the entire structure would burn hot and fast. What was she doing just standing here? She needed to get her shit and get out of her room. Keres said something, but she didn't hear. She walked back to her room. She started throwing the few things she'd unpacked into her duffel. She went into the bathroom and scooped up the toiletries with both hands. When she walked back out, Keres stood in the doorway. He had a gun in his hand. Her own gun was still 10 feet away in the side pocket of her bag that was sitting on the bed.

She held the toiletries to her chest, the floral aroma of her favorite shampoo drifted up and briefly blotted out the smell of smoke. A few pieces tumbled into place. She didn't know how she knew them, but they felt solid when she turned them over in her mind. They had the weight of facts. Keres had hurt that woman and her dog. She didn't know why or how he'd even arrived in this town. Or how he was not back in prison. But he wasn't. He'd slipped his bonds somehow. Or had help. Either way, he was out and he was looking for Lisa. He'd also set that fire.

Finally, she realized, Keres was going to kill her.

Keres casually raised the gun and pointed it at the woman when she came out of the bathroom carrying the toiletries.

"Where is your—" He wanted her car keys before deciding whether to put a bullet in her, but then noticed something. Keres had a thing for faces, and now that he could see this woman in the light of the motel room, he recognized her. He took two steps into the room to get a better look. No, he didn't recognize her. That was too strong of a word.

"I've seen you before. Where?"

"What are you talking about? I just woke up."

Keres raised the gun. "Stop bullshitting me. I've seen you. You can wait for me to figure it out and then decide where to shoot you or you can start talking."

She didn't take long to decide. "I was hired to follow you. I've been on your tail, more or less, since you walked out of Stanhope."

"Who hired you? The man in black."

"Who?"

This time she looked genuinely confused. He thought back to his time in prison, but he'd kept mostly to himself, especially in the last few years. He didn't kick up any trouble. He couldn't think of anyone who might be interested in him. And then a name occurred to him. "Lisa?" But she shook her head. "Who then?"

"A man named Bradley Cobb."

"Maybe he works for the man in black."

"Cobb doesn't work for anyone but himself."

"You know this Cobb?"

"I've worked a few jobs for him before."

"Jobs? What are you?"

"A private investigator. Mostly do skip tracing, insurance work, some background checks."

"But here you are."

The woman shrugged. "Cobb pays."

"Who is he?"

"Started as an engineer. Now he mostly does work for the Department of Defense."

"Why does he have you following me?"

"No idea."

"You didn't ask."

"Sometimes asking too many questions as a PI will get you fired. Cobb told me to follow you. He signs the checks. So, that's what I did. At least until you pulled that stunt on the bridge."

Keres grinned. "You saw that, huh?"

"How are you not on your way back to Stanhope right now?"

Now it was Keres's turn to shrug. He didn't have time to recount his bedside chat with the man in black. "I don't really know. But maybe this Cobb guy does. Maybe I should ask him. He's got money then?"

"I don't think he has problems paying his bills."

Keres thought about it. He'd lost his chance at Lisa. The man in black had staked him and pointed him in the right direction, but who knew how long that would last if he didn't produce. And without another tip on her location, he wasn't sure where to start. He couldn't hang around here. The cops, even the slowest ones in a hick country town, would start sniffing around eventually. But every problem was an opportunity. If he was going to hide and regroup, he needed money. This woman clearly didn't have any, but maybe she could help. Maybe she could get him to Cobb, and he could shake down that guy for some cash. Keres didn't know why Cobb wanted him, but he could smell leverage and opportunity.

The woman broke into his thoughts. "Look, can I put this stuff down." She held up the toiletries in her hand and took a step toward the bag on the bed.

"Sure," Keres stepped forward and grabbed the bag. She hesitated and then dumped the soaps and creams inside. He zipped it up and then asked her, "You got a car?"

"Yes."

"Where is it?"

"Around back."

"You know where this Cobb is?"

"Right now? I have no idea. Probably asleep."

"You know where he lives?"

"In D.C."

"Can you get in touch with him?"

"I have a number."

"Okay then, let's go."

CHAPTER SIXTY-ONE

Max and Lisa left Snell and the firefighters to deal with The Cliffside. Max gave one last look in the side mirror and wondered if he'd ever be back. He wouldn't miss anything in his room, but he might miss the morning views of the mountains.

"Now what?" Lisa asked as they put the emergency lights and smoke behind them.

"That's a good question. If that was Keres, he's a wild card. I don't want to stick around here and give him another shot."

"I don't want to leave him at our backs either."

"No, that wouldn't be a good idea. We don't want to fight a battle on two fronts, so we need to pick. Cobb or Keres?"

"We don't know where Keres is, so I vote for Cobb. The address is at Vic's. Keres is a danger to me, but Cobb and his tech are a danger to far more."

"I agree. Keres will keep. Putting some distance between us might be a good thing. It might force him to reveal himself."

"But once we're done with Cobb, we find him. It would be dangerous to forget about Keres."

Max thought about Vic in the hospital bed and Bailey's blood on the floor. Then he thought about what Lisa had told him about Keres and his father. "I won't forget."

They drove back to Vic's house. Lisa found the work order with the address, folded it up, and put it in her pocket. She quickly gathered the remaining papers and put them back in the old file folder. Then she climbed the stairs to grab her duffel.

Max used the bathroom and splashed water on his face. He had nothing to pack. He didn't even have a toothbrush. He hadn't been back to his room since the guys jumped him in the bar. He looked down at the clothes he wore. They were no longer fresh and clean, but they might last another day. He could buy something on the road.

Lisa came back down after a few minutes, carrying her small bag. It hadn't taken her long to pack. She picked up the folder and looked at him.

"Ready?"

He was about to respond when headlights swept across the front of the house and through the windows.

"Who's that?" Lisa asked.

"No idea." He reached out, turned the light off in the hallway, and then approached the front door. A car, a small boxy sedan, sat idling in the driveway behind the SUV. He felt Lisa come up behind him and take a position at the other window. As he watched, the back door of the car opened, and Vic gingerly stepped out. Max was out the door before she'd taken two steps.

"What are you doing here? You should still be in the hospital."

"Bullshit. Doc said I'm fine. Bumps and bruises. No worse than a rough game of pond hockey. Plus," she held up a small plastic bag and shook it, "I got some magic pills." She wore the same clothes from that afternoon, now speckled with blood. Despite her bravado, her face remained pale. A red and purple bruise blossomed near her right ear and ran down along her cheek to her jaw. "I wasn't going to sit there feeling sorry for myself. Not my style."

"What about Bailey?"

She looked away and blinked rapidly. Max braced himself for the bad news.

"I talked to the vet before I called the Uber. He's going to be sedated for a few days, but he's going to be okay."

Max felt a flood of relief that was out of proportion for his relationship to the dog. Maybe it was realizing both of them would be okay.

"Where are you going?" Vic asked and nodded toward Lisa, who still held her bag. "Running out on me in my time of need?"

"Did Detective Snell talk to you?"

"Yes. I had the Uber guy drive by The Cliffside. Right now, I'm pretending it didn't happen. One thing at a time. So, you're taking off?"

"Going after Cobb."

"Cobb, not Keres? I assume it was Keres that started that little campfire."

"We think so. He survived the woods, but we don't know where he is. We have a decent idea about Cobb."

"You think Cobb knows where Keres is?"

"It's possible," Lisa said. "We're all tied together in this."

"Then I'm coming with you."

"No way. You need to rest."

"I just told you, not my style."

"Uh-uh. Not happening," Max said.

"It might be your car, but it's not your decision." She stepped closer. "That man shot my dog, tried to shoot me, and then burned down my business. I'm coming." She turned, walked to the car, and got in the back seat of the SUV. "I can rest in the car. It's a long drive to D.C."

Max dreamed of smoke and fire and scarred flesh. He woke to a hand on his arm.

"You were shaking and mumbling. Bad dream?"

He didn't answer. He looked over his shoulder. Vic lay sprawled in the back seat. He looked out into the dark. "Where are we?"

"Somewhere in Connecticut. Getting close to New York."

He closed his eyes again. There was nothing to see in Connecticut.

The next time he woke to the steady rhythmic slap of tires rolling over plates. He opened his eyes to find himself on a bridge, the Philadelphia skyline off to his right. He searched the waterfront but couldn't see his old building. He racked the seat back to an upright position. He was stiff but felt more rested. Vic snored steadily in the back seat. The radio murmured, almost too low to hear.

"Pull over, let's switch."

"I'm good. Old ladies don't need much sleep."

Max looked at her. Maybe she wasn't tired. Maybe her mind was racing, but her face betrayed her. Fatigue carved grooves around her eyes.

"Maybe they don't, but if you're going to help with this thing, whatever it ends up being, I need you sharp and ready to drive. I know it's painful for you, but let me drive while you get a little rest."

She tapped a finger on the wheel, but then relented. "Okay."

She pulled over at the next rest area and they switched spots. Vic didn't stir.

Three hours later, Max pulled the SUV into the parking lot of a roadside diner just off the Beltway, west of D.C. The car's navigation system said that the address on the work order was 10 miles farther south.

Lisa stirred as Max turned off the engine. It was just after 8:00 in the morning.

"Where are we?"

"In Virginia, near a town called Reston."

"So we're close?"

"Fifteen minutes."

"Why'd you stop?"

"Caffeine and calories. Eat when you can."

"Plus, I gotta piss like a racehorse," a voice said from the back seat.

CHAPTER SIXTY-TWO

"They're doing their best to make it all look innocent, aren't they?" Lisa said.

This was the second time they'd driven past, and Max didn't want to risk a third trip. He was sure they'd been captured on video at least once already. They drove past an orange electronic public works sign on the corner warning of road closures and detours in the area in the coming days.

"Notice the bushes?" Lisa asked. Max looked at her. "What? I guess it's like riding a bike."

"What about the bushes?" Vic asked. "Looks like a fancy English garden. I'm surprised none of them are shaped like a peacock or a prancing elephant."

Vic was right. The grounds were extremely well manicured. The lawn cut short like a putting green. The hedges and ivy along the surrounding brick neat and clipped. For anyone just driving by, the place might be a small private school, a museum, or even a wealthy private residence, but Max's trained eyes saw other things.

"That's the point. There are no signs. You see money and privilege and tidy landscaping and you move on. You don't think cutting-edge technology or black ops defense contractor."

They drove past the main gate. There was a guardhouse, a discreet gate, but Max suspected there were also other unseen deterrents that could be utilized. Spike strips or crash-resistant barriers. A 10-foot high brick wall with cameras along each cornice surrounded the property. They only caught a quick glimpse at the interior buildings as they drove past. The main entrance, with a sweeping drive, led to a large four-story building made of brick and limestone. Smaller, similar buildings surrounded it like satellites. There was a second entrance on the north side, the rear of the rough square compound. The same level of security was evident, but it didn't have the understated grandeur of the opposite entrance. It led to a sparsely occupied parking lot.

"Despite all the trees and shrubs, there is no easy way to approach the buildings without being seen," Max continued. "No place to hide. We try to go through the gate or over the wall and they'll spot us in less than 10 seconds."

"And that's only the stuff we can see," Lisa added.

"Yes, I'm sure they have motion sensors, maybe underground load sensors, and more."

"So, what do we do? Drive up and knock?" Vic said.

"That might be our best approach," Max said. "There's always a way in, but I'm not sure we have the time to find it. We could use Lisa's name and maybe the threat of exposure to get Cobb to see us. We know he's paranoid about it."

"It might get us in. But how do we get back out?"

"We use the same threat Wimpy did. A dead man's switch. He doesn't let us walk, we release it all. Also, we leave Vic outside. Just the two of us go in."

They were past the end of the compound now. Lisa made the next right into a leafy subdivision and pulled the car to the curb.

"Would Cobb buy it? That I would just show up and hand this over?"

"Sure, because you're also going to ask for $5,000,000."

"What?"

"He won't understand anything else, but I guarantee he will understand, and maybe even respect, the money. And $5,000,000 is life-changing for you, but he won't miss it. Especially if it clears the way for his nanotech. In a few years, $5,000,000 will be a rounding error for him. He'll pay."

"But I don't want to just confront the prick. Or exhort him. I want to stop him. This nanotechnology is seriously dangerous stuff. We need to neutralize both Cobb and the tech. Mutually assured destruction, remember?"

"I know. I remember. And I agree. I have an idea about that."

"Want to tell us?"

"Not yet. I need to make a call."

They drove back out to 495 and backtracked two exits to the diner they'd stopped at originally.

"Seriously? You want to eat again?" Lisa asked.

"Stress makes me hungry," Max said.

It was between the breakfast and lunch rush, or the diner just wasn't very good, and they had their pick of seats. Lisa led them toward the back corner. They remained quiet as they each ate their way through a round of cheeseburgers, fries, and milkshakes. Max noticed that while Lisa professed to be hungry, she mostly picked at the burger and pushed the fries around on her plate. Max ate her leftover fries. Vic had no leftovers. Max was worried he'd lose a finger if she tried to get near her fries. He took that as a sign she was feeling better.

She slid out of the booth after dredging the last fry

through a puddle of ketchup. Her face turned more somber. "I'm going to go outside and call the vet."

Max ordered more coffee and asked the waitress for the check before he turned back to Lisa. The closer they came to the end of this, the worse Lisa looked. With each passing day, she looked grayer and more washed out. The spark he'd glimpsed when she first got behind the wheel of the SUV and tore out of West Adams was gone. She looked like an empty husk with anything vibrant or alive drained away.

He'd stopped thinking about his mother a long time ago. He wasn't angry. She just wasn't there. Those first few minutes and hours after he learned she was indeed alive had lit a fuse that burned hot. Why had she hidden? What secrets had she kept? Why hadn't she come for him? It all hit him like a hammer. It had seemed selfish and cowardly. But now? Looking across at her, he saw the raw pain that had chipped away at her mind, body, and soul. He knew about a solitary life. But her life, as she described it, was almost ascetic. And for 25 years? He hadn't truly considered the monotonous, everyday routine of it all. Never considered the isolation and loneliness. The courage and discipline not to cave in and call.

He reached out a hand, then stopped. It was all too much, too fast. Maybe that's what she was feeling, too. He grabbed his coffee cup instead. "Are you up for this?"

She had been staring down into her own mug but looked up now. Max watched her make the effort to rally herself. She slid out of the booth and her knees popped. She scooped up the car keys and looked at him. She pulled back her shoulders and, while her smile looked brittle, her words were strong. "I've been ready for a long time."

Vic was still on the phone, walking on a thin strip of grass between the parking lot and the diner. She smiled and waved when she saw them exit.

"Hey, look at this," Lisa said, holding up her phone.

"What?"

"I think I know why they had those road closure signs up around the property."

"Trouble?

"Not exactly. But if we want to do anything about Cobb, our window might have just shrunk."

"Why?"

"I added Cerberus Industries, weapons, and McLean to my watch list of searches. Probably should have done it before, but after Lessin died, my interest waned. Seemed too risky. Anyway, I added them yesterday after we found the work order and it just flagged a news story from *The Washington Post*. Three senators from the Armed Services Committee and most of the Joint Chiefs of Staff will attend a demonstration of potential future weapons." She paused and skimmed the rest of the story. "It's a minor note. The larger story is about the look and logistics of future wars. No details and no names beyond a facility in McLean, but it has to be Cobb, right?"

"Makes sense. You said he was getting close to signing that big contract."

"If the military gets their hands on this, even a working prototype."

"You can't shut Pandora's box."

"Right. So, I hope this plan of yours works."

He glanced over at Vic. She was wrapping up. "Let me check in on the progress."

He took out his phone and called Lawrence. "Are we set?" he asked when Lawrence picked up.

"You called two hours ago."

"How long does he need?"

"I'm just playing. He finished an hour and a half ago and it only took that long because I had to walk up there and tell him what you wanted and then we got into an argument for 20 minutes."

"You find another Twizzlers stash?"

"Red Vines, but yeah. Boy won't listen. He's going to end up in a coma if he keeps eating that shit."

"Want me to talk to him?"

Lawrence let out a long breath. "Can't hurt. I'm clearly not getting through."

Max was about to say he'd do it when he got back, but realized he wasn't sure when or if he was going back. Instead, he went back to the original reason he called. "So, it's ready?"

"All set. I was waiting on you."

"It works?"

"No way to know. We can't exactly test it, can we? I don't think Eddie would make any guarantees, since he's going in blind, but he's confident. And he says you told him it didn't have to be subtle."

"But he built in a delay, right? It can't get right to work and leave us exposed."

"Relax. If you told him, he did it."

"Okay, I know. Sorry. You posted it?"

"Yup, sent you an email with the link. It's disguised as a .jpg file but be careful with it. It's radioactive."

CHAPTER SIXTY-THREE

Martha drove. Keres sat in the back seat, directly behind her. She could see his thin face and dark eyes anytime she looked in the mirror. She couldn't see his hands, but assumed he still had the gun pointed at her back. Keres had brought her bag. It sat on the seat next to him. She might as well have left her gun back in the motel room. He caught her looking and she dropped her gaze back to the road. Could he keep up his vigilance all the way to D.C.? It was a long ride. The road could be hypnotizing. If he drifted off? Or fell asleep? What would she do? She'd been in cars with plenty of cons before, but she'd always been the one in control. They'd been in cuffs, or she'd had help. Her mouth felt like she'd been chewing cotton. She tried to remain calm and think through a plan that didn't end up with her dead in a ditch. Nothing came to mind.

He had her drive a short distance to a state park entrance. He'd taken the key and zip tied her left arm to the door's armrest, then got out and transferred two bags from a parked car over to her car. He went back and wiped down the other car with the sleeve of his coat.

They'd now been driving for 20 minutes and had just left Chepstow's dark back roads for a wider state highway when he spoke up. "You got a license?"

Was he making small talk? She knew kidnapping victims should try to talk and establish a rapport with their captors, but she was finding it hard to think and keep the car on the road, let alone talk. "To be a PI?" she choked out.

"No, to drive."

"Oh, yeah. Of course, I have a license."

"Of course, she says. Funny, the things you take for granted when you're not in prison."

She had nothing to say to that. Maybe he was right.

"Where is it?"

"In my purse. In my bag there. Right on top. The main pocket." She didn't need him digging around and finding the gun. She wasn't sure how he'd react. But she knew she'd never get her hands on it if he found it. She heard him unzip the pocket of the bag. She glanced in the mirror. He held her small clutch purse. He unzipped it and took out her wallet. What was he up to? He flipped through her wallet until he was looking at her license. "This is your current address? Jersey City?"

"Yes."

He put her wallet down on the seat and then took something out of his own bag that was sitting in the footwell. She didn't know what it was at first, but after a silent minute, a soft glow lit up the back seat. A laptop. She heard him typing and clicking, making frustrated sounds under his breath. The signal must be weak out here. After five minutes, he looked up and met her eyes in the rearview mirror. She didn't like his smile.

"493 Cedar Lane. Jack and Eli."

She clenched the wheel tighter and felt her heart lurch into her throat. She opened her mouth, but no words came out. Her brother's address. Her nephews. Nine and 12 years old.

"New Mexico is a hike, but I could get there eventually. What's that, a two-, three-day drive? You behave yourself and we never find out. I found your brother's address in five minutes. Imagine what I could do if I tried. We good?"

She nodded.

He shut the laptop, sat back, and closed his eyes.

Eight hours later and her eyes felt like sandpaper, but she found Cobb's office again. She slowed as she approached the entrance.

"What do you want to do?"

They'd stopped when they crossed the line into Virginia, and Keres had gotten in the front seat. A strange odor of ammonia had grown in the car as they'd driven. He'd asked her to put the air conditioning on despite the temperature outside barely rising above 40. She'd watched as he heavily favored his left leg while he walked the three steps to the passenger door. She'd have no trouble outrunning him, but... the faces of her nephews floated in front of her. Running wasn't an option.

"Pull in and ask to see the man."

"He's not expecting me. He might not even be there."

"One step at a time."

She pulled in and stopped by the gate. A man in a pseudo-combat uniform, gray patterned top, black fatigue pants, and lace-up boots stepped out and she rolled the window down.

"Martha Wells to see Mr. Cobb."

He leaned farther down and looked in the window at Keres, then nodded and stepped back to the gate. She watched him pick up a clipboard, then put it down again. He picked up a phone mounted on the wall and spoke, listened, hung up. He stepped back out.

"Open the trunk and hood, please."

"Excuse me?"

"I need to check your vehicle."

She glanced at Keres, but he was just staring straight ahead.

"Okay." She reached down and popped the trunk and hood releases. The man went to the trunk first. She couldn't see what he was doing but heard a thunk as he moved something. A second later, the trunk lid came down. He went around the front and rubbed a square of cloth along the edge then stepped back into the gatehouse.

"What's he doing?" Keres asked. Martha realized Keres had been in prison for much of the Homeland Security post 9/11 era.

"Explosives check."

"Huh."

The guard came back out again.

"Drive around the main building, Ms. Wells. You'll see visitor parking around the back and to the right. Someone will meet you at the rear entrance."

"Thank you."

The man nodded. "Have a good day." He stepped back into the gatehouse. A moment later, the gate rose and Martha drove through. She followed the paved road around the main building and followed the discreet signs to visitor parking.

Keres suddenly stiffened and sat up straight. "Holy shit. I don't believe it."

She followed his gaze and her mouth dropped open as well.

CHAPTER SIXTY-FOUR

Cobb put down the phone and smiled. "Sorry about that. Today seems to be a day of surprises."

Max looked at Cobb across the desk. He was shorter than Max had expected, with neatly trimmed gray hair and clean-shaven, angular cheeks. He stapled his fingers on the desk and looked at them with pale blue eyes. The desk matched the bookcases and the wood frames of the abstract art prints on the wall. A laptop and two monitors sat on the desktop. The rest of it was clean. The entire office was modest and had a temporary feel as if Cobb had bought the place furnished and never bothered to update it. The parts of the complex they'd seen since parking and being escorted inside felt the same. Clean and sterile, less like a workplace and more like a catalog. They'd briefly walked through a large, open room with the standard cubicles, but Max hadn't seen one personal effect. He hadn't seen many workers, either. Maybe the labs, experiments, and engineering were on different floors, tucked away and out of sight from casual visitors.

"As you can imagine, Ms. Sullivan, you were about the last person I expected to walk into my office."

"Really? You haven't been looking for me?"

His smile widened, but his eyes narrowed. "Why would I be looking for you?"

Now it was Lisa's turn to smile. "Can we drop the bullshit? You had us searched on the way in. I'm sure this place is well equipped to jam anything it doesn't like. We're not trying to entrap you or record you. We're here to do some business. Business that doesn't need to go beyond the walls of this room. That's something you can understand, right?"

Cobb stared at her, then nodded. His voice lost its false cheer. "Okay. No bullshit. What do you want?"

"I want you to stop hunting me. I want a normal life. What's left of it. I leave you alone. You leave me alone."

"What assurances do I have that you will leave me alone, as you put it?"

"You're paranoid. I get it. Your entire empire, this place," she swept a hand up, "and the rest of the ones around the country are built on sand."

"How so?"

"It's all built on that one night back in Maine. Your big gamble. Your seed money. Your start-up capital. It's all a fraud based on a felony. I don't think you want to be answering questions about that in front of a Senate committee."

Max watched Cobb. He was leaning forward slightly, twin points of red had blossomed on both cheeks. A coiled intensity radiated off him. Yes, he wanted what they had.

Lisa continued. "I've brought the proof that's kept you up at night. The thing that has kept you chasing me for the last 25 years."

"And what's that? What's the proof?"

Lisa took a USB memory stick from her pocket and held it up. "My friend Wimpy was more paranoid than you. He recorded your meeting. Makes for a nice little movie. Maybe he did it with all his jobs, or maybe he just really didn't trust you. Turns out, he was right too. I don't know if it was you or Keres, but I don't think Wimpy survived to even see if the job got done, but he has a long reach. When he disappeared, the recording ended up with me."

She leaned forward and slid it across the desk. Cobb didn't move. The stick just sat there like an unlit piece of dynamite. How much did Cobb value his reputation? The video proved he didn't mind getting his hands dirty. Had time and success softened him? He could likely bury the video, even if Lisa released it somehow. Make it seem like a fringe conspiracy group or a convincing deep fake. Surely someone would poke and prod at the story, but would it catch fire and bring him down? Or quickly flame out?

Max knew that Cobb could have them detained and handed over to the authorities, or he could simply have them killed. But Max bet Cobb didn't want to risk any distractions or complications with the demonstration coming up.

Finally, Cobb leaned forward and picked up the memory stick. "And what do you get?"

"My life back."

"I don't control the FBI. I can't get you off any fugitive lists."

Lisa waved a hand. "I can handle that. I just want you to stop looking."

"That's it?"

"And I want $5,000,000."

Cobb raised his eyebrows.

"It's enough for me to live comfortably, I think," Lisa continued. "And more than worth it for you. Frankly, I think you're getting off cheap, but I've never been greedy."

"Says the thief."

"Life is full of contradictions. And I was just the driver."

Cobb tapped the stick on the desk and then said, "Let's see what $5,000,000 will buy me." And he plugged the memory stick into the laptop's port.

The video finished playing and Cobb sat back in his chair. He looked past them and stared at the wall, but Max realized it was a tell. The video wasn't great, but it was real and even a minor problem right now was not something that Cobb wanted to deal with. It was a variable he couldn't completely control. He would pay.

"Two million," he finally said.

"Five," Lisa responded.

"I don't think you understand how negotiations work."

"That's because this isn't a negotiation. It's a transaction. You pay us $5,000,000 and we give you the video."

"All copies?"

"Once we are outside and gone, we'll verify you transferred the money and then we'll send you the location and access codes for the site where we stashed the backup copy. You can keep the USB stick."

Cobb pulled the stick out of the laptop, snapped it in half, and tossed the pieces into a metal trashcan behind the desk. Then he stood up. "You called it a fraud, but do you know what that night has produced? Do you know what I created?"

Lisa looked at Max. They hadn't scripted anything out past the money. He wasn't sure where Cobb was going with this.

"Nanotech."

Cobb laughed. "I guess that's technically right, but it's also like saying Galileo contributed a few things to astronomy."

He stood and walked to a door next to the bookcase at the rear of the office. Not the door that they had entered. "Maybe it's best to give you a demonstration. I think it's only fair. You should also see what that $5,000,000 is buying." Cobb opened the door and Max could see a plain concrete stairwell, the walls and floor painted white, leading down. Cobb didn't wait. He was a man used to having people follow his orders, even when couched as suggestions.

Max and Lisa followed.

CHAPTER SIXTY-FIVE

Keres put his hand on the door handle, "Remember New Mexico, Martha." Then he opened the door and stepped out. A wave of dizziness almost made him fall. He pulled up his pant leg. Yellow pus leaked out from under the makeshift laundry bandage. Streaks of red also ran down toward his ankle. His arm and shoulder were stiff and sore from the bat. And he just felt so damn tired. Once they talked to Cobb, he'd make Martha drive to a pharmacy and get some meds to deal with his leg. He dropped the pant leg and stood up straight.

Martha was standing by the driver's door and staring at him. "What?"

She shook her head. "Nothing."

After the pharmacy, he'd need to get rid of her. But first things first. He didn't have any antibiotics or ibuprofen, but he knew what would make him feel better. He glanced around. The parking lot was empty except for the three of them. He thought there were likely discreet video cameras somewhere to keep an eye on employees, but he couldn't immediately spot any. He put his hand in his pocket and felt for the gun. He left it in his pocket. If he needed it, it was there. No dogs around this time. No distractions. Martha would behave. He wished he still had the knife. That might be more satisfying. He smiled and started across the parking lot toward the other car.

And he learned he was wrong. It was the bitch from the hotel, but she was not alone. She was leaning against the hood of the SUV and a man stood next to the driver's door, blocked from Keres's view by the height of the car. Martha was a step in front of him and stopped abruptly when she came around the SUV's hood. Keres, eager to get to the woman, stepped around her and saw the man. And his gun.

He was short, only an inch or two taller than the hotel woman, and wiry with a full beard and a short buzz cut. He wore the same gray and black uniform as the guy at the front gate. Even without the quasi-military clothes, the guy's bearing and intensity screamed ex-soldier. The gun was steady in his hand.

Keres's hand twitched toward his pocket and the guy took a step forward and to the left, keeping his angles and space right to cover all of them. "Easy now. Go slow. Take it out with two fingers and put it on the ground."

Keres didn't see an alternative. Not right now. This whole situation had just taken an unexpected left turn. He decided the best course was to wait it out and see what else might develop. He was good at surviving. He took the gun out and placed it on the ground.

"Now kick it over to me."

Keres did and the guy asked, "Anything else?"

Keres didn't move. Maybe the guy would move in closer to frisk him and he could get his hands on that gun.

He shifted the gun slightly toward Martha. "What else does he have?"

"That's all I've seen."

The man stepped forward and picked up Keres's discarded gun without taking his eyes off Keres. Next, he took two additional sets of plastic cuffs and handed them to the hotel woman. "Put them on each of them and pull them tight."

The woman pulled the cuffs tight enough to bite into Keres's flesh. The man stepped up when she was done and nodded in approval. He frisked Martha then Keres more carefully. He did it quickly and efficiently. Toes to crown. It was not the first time he'd taken prisoners. No doubt a pro. He paused and pulled the crucifix from Keres's pants pocket. He seemed puzzled.

"Have you found your Lord and Savior yet?" Keres said.

The bearded man smirked and held up his gun. "Got the only savior I need right here."

"Won't do you any good in the next life."

"If the next life is full of you jailbirds, I'll take a pass. Keep your salvation." He stuffed the wooden crucifix back in Keres's pocket. "Alright, let's take a walk."

Keres and Martha started to turn for the main building behind them, but the man stopped them. "Uh-uh. Not that way. We're going to a different entrance." He pointed in the opposite direction toward a door partially obscured by landscaping. It looked like a bunker or elevator shaft. Just a discreet door set in the center of a small, brick square.

They walked in a line with the bearded man bringing up the rear.

"Why are you limping?" Beard asked.

"Ask the bitch," Keres replied, but the hotel woman remained quiet. Keres turned and looked at her. "How's your dog?" He saw her stiffen and her jaw clench, but she didn't take the bait and Beard let the question drop.

The parking lot and surrounding grounds remained quiet

and empty. Keres wondered if they were holding people inside until the three of them were out of sight.

As they approached the door, Keres could make out a small placard placed next to the door that read 'Buildings and Grounds. Authorized Personnel Only.' Then he noticed the keycard and retinal scanner. What kind of maintenance shed needed that kind of security? He felt an uneasiness creep into his gut. What kind of lab was this?

They descended in a neat line. Cobb first, then Max, then Lisa. The stairs were wide enough to accommodate two abreast with room to spare, but some unspoken organizing principle kept them separated. The stairwell was plain and utilitarian. The stairs circled and clung to the outer shaft's wall. There was a hole down the center. A gray railing at staggered heights ran along the outside as a handhold and nominal protection from tripping and falling through the center.

Each time Cobb passed or stepped on some hidden sensor, more lights clicked on to illuminate the next floor down. No one spoke, but at one point Max glanced back at Lisa and could read her thoughts. They matched his. They were underground. Deep and getting deeper. Max looked over the railing. He couldn't see the bottom in the dark, but he could sense it wasn't close.

Cobb stopped after eight flights at a gray door with the words 'Control' stenciled in black at eye level.

"We're here." The words bounced and echoed around the shaft. He took a plain unadorned keycard from his pocket and held it in front of a six-by-six black plastic square mounted next to the door's handle. Then he looked up at a black hemisphere mounted above the door and said, "Bradley

Cobb." There was a pause and then a light snick sound as the lock disengaged.

"Welcome to the future," Cobb said as he opened the door and waved them inside.

The lights were off, and Max couldn't see beyond the first few feet. He looked again at Lisa.

"I didn't come this far to turn around now."

Max nodded and stepped through the door.

Just like in the stairwell, movement triggered the lights. They were standing at the top of some sort of viewing room. It felt almost like a movie theater. Three pitched rows of seats faced a large set of floor-to-ceiling windows. The windows were currently black and opaque. The first two rows held four staggered seats. The final row, at the front, was the nerve center. There were two chairs tucked under a long desk that held various monitors, keyboards, switches, and other equipment.

"Please, have a seat. It will take a moment to get things set up."

"Cobb, why are we here?" Lisa asked. "Is this necessary?"

"You said this wasn't a negotiation. Fine. I accept that. This is my stipulation, call it whatever you want, for completing the deal and giving you what you want." A button lit up on the console and a tone sounded. "Ah, right on time. Please, have a seat. I need you to understand."

Cobb went and sat in one of the chairs in the first row and started flipping switches and turning on monitors. Max didn't want to sit. He followed Cobb down and stood behind him. He wanted to be close enough to grab him. He felt Lisa at his elbow. He was about to ask her to call Vic, she might be worried, when the lights on the other side of the glass snapped on and he could see into the other room.

CHAPTER SIXTY-SIX

The guard keyed the brick bunker door open by waving a card hooked to his belt over the sensor. It swung open noiselessly to reveal the inside of an elevator car.

"Get in, stand facing the rear wall. Study that wall. Don't turn around."

They all marched in and stood shoulder to shoulder. Keres glanced at the panel as he limped inside. Just two buttons, stacked on top of each other, neither marked. He took the left corner. Martha took the middle and the hotel woman filled in the opposite side, as far from Keres as she could get. The elevator door slid shut and they began to descend. They descended for 15 seconds, then 20. The only sound was the creaking of the cables, their shuffling feet, and soft breathing. They kept going. Far longer than Keres thought possible. This wasn't a quick trip to a basement or even a sub-basement holding area. This was deep underground. Finally, they jerked to a stop and Keres heard the door open.

"Okay, come on out."

Keres turned around, stepped out, and then stopped. "What the hell?"

He was standing on a bright city sidewalk. He held an arm up to shield his eyes. There was a tall, glass-fronted office building across the street. The street itself was empty. No cars. Or buses. Or taxis. But it looked like a slice of street from any mid-sized city in the country. There was a crushed coffee cup in the gutter, and Keres could see oil stains and cracks in the asphalt. He glanced up and down the street. There were smaller shops alongside the tall office building. A convenience store, an electronics or mobile phone store, a bar, a restaurant named Kelley's. He could sense the confusion in the two women as well. He glanced over his shoulder. On this end, they made the bunker look like a subway station entrance. Holloway Street Station was on a sign affixed over the doors. The city continued on the opposite side of the street, too. A dry cleaner, liquor store, pawnshop, a national bank branch. Keres had a moment of vertigo and thought maybe his leg wound was worse than he thought. Maybe it was causing him to hallucinate. He looked across the street again and forced himself to look beyond the obvious ornaments. He looked at the edges and it was like those magic eye books that became so popular even the Stanhope library had a few, at least until a few prisoners got frustrated when they couldn't 'see' the image and destroyed them. Keres saw now. It was all a ruse. Or stage dressing.

"Is this a movie set?" he asked.

The bearded man had stepped off the sidewalk and stood in the street. He had a bemused smile on his lips. "Something like that." Then his eyes lost focus and he touched a hand to his ear. Keres realized he was wearing an earpiece radio. The man nodded. "Roger that."

The man's focus snapped back to his prisoners. Keres had

to admit now that was what they were. It was a familiar feeling for Keres.

"If you'll please step this way," Beard said and held a hand out toward the doors of the glass office building.

"This is Control," Cobb said. He smiled up at them from his chair.

"What is it?" Lisa asked.

"It's a lab. It's where I'm field testing the Dactyls."

"Dactyls?"

"Greek mythical beings," Max said.

Cobb glanced at him, maybe seeing him for the first time. "Not just the muscle, huh? That's right. The Dactyls were an ancient mythical race that acted as smiths and healing magicians. I thought it was an appropriate name for a technology that will revolutionize how we build and heal."

"Every scientist, engineer, or inventor thinks they are going to change the world," Max said.

"True. I'd argue that type of hubris is our most important characteristic. Anything less than total commitment and belief, and you'll fall short. You might make an impact in your field or even in the world, but it will be fleeting. You need to have the vision to see and the conviction to do what is necessary to truly write your name in the history books."

"And you think that describes you?"

Another smile. "I don't just think it anymore. I know. Soon the world will know it too, but right now this is just talk. Always better to show, not just tell, right?" He turned around, pressed a button, and spoke into a microphone. "Have them walk across the street and stop near the revolving doors."

He turned slightly to address them again while typing and adjusting settings on the panel in front of him. "It just so happens we have some available subjects for a demo. Typically, we do a larger field test, for reasons that will become clear in a moment, but I think this smaller group will suffice for today."

A moment later, Max watched far below, as Vic crossed the street.

They stepped off the curb and into the street in the same order as they'd entered the elevator. First Keres, then Martha, then the hotel woman. The guard stood in the middle, slightly off to the left, eyes covering all of them. Keres wasn't sure what was going on but felt like it had gone on long enough. The guard was good. Much better than most of the brainless mokes at Stanhope. But he wasn't perfect. He should have bound Keres's hands behind him. He slipped his hand into his front pocket. Keres had no intention of entering the building in front of him. Some primitive, atavistic instinct told him that if he went through those revolving doors, he'd never come back out. Not on his own two feet.

"Why is she down there?"

"Martha?" Cobb asked.

"Who?"

"Oh, the other woman? She's with you? My security found her sitting in a car in the parking lot. I honestly don't know who she is, but she will be the perfect control and further point of demonstration for the Dactyls."

"She better not get hurt in this experiment."

Max tried to keep his voice steady, but Cobb picked up on something and smiled over his shoulder.

"She'll be okay."

Max realized okay was not the same thing as not getting hurt.

"Now watch closely," Cobb said. He tapped a touchscreen in front of him and three monitors on the far left lit up. He then hit a series of buttons before sitting back in his chair. Nothing happened for 15 seconds. The four people below made it across the street and stepped up on the far curb. The guard must have said something as the party regrouped and reoriented toward the main entrance to the office building. Max now recognized the security guard as Beard, the leader of the crew that had attacked him, or tried to, at The Night Owl. This had gone too far.

He wasn't sure what he was going to do, but he took a step forward, when in doubt move forward, and reached a hand out toward Cobb. But then Cobb turned around quickly and looked at both of them. If he noticed Max's movement, he didn't comment, instead, he said, "Did you see it?"

Max flicked his eyes back out the large viewing window. Nothing appeared to have changed. The group was 15 feet from the revolving entrance doors. They walked behind a plastic bus enclosure and passed a fire hydrant.

"See what?" Lisa finally said.

"Exactly," Cobb said. He smiled wide, like a schoolboy proud to show off his work. He tapped the keyboard again and data began to display on the monitors. EKG, blood pressure, heart rate, oxygen levels, and other things Max couldn't discern. "They didn't notice down there either. Infiltration was undetected."

"Infiltration?" Max said. "You injected them with something?"

"No, not injected. Not exactly. But the Dactyls are inside their bodies and transmitting basic patient health monitoring information." He waved a hand at the screens. "And you can see, they are all okay, other than elevated heart rates, at least for the women, which I'd say was to be expected."

"But that's not all it does, right?" Lisa said.

Cobb smiled. But this smile was different. "Wireless remote monitoring with nanotech will revolutionize health care."

"True, but that's on the benign end of the spectrum and wouldn't get the Pentagon interested."

"You've done your homework."

"Know thy enemy."

"Okay. You're right. By default, the Dactyls simply relay basic biodata, like being hooked up to a monitor in the hospital. But they can do other things, too." He turned back to the control panel and leaned over the gooseneck mic. "Grady, have them stop and sit at the bus stop for a moment." Down below, Grady relayed the instructions and the group diverted back to the plastic bus enclosure.

"Okay." Two of the monitors changed to show two different high-definition video views. One looked like a close-up drone shot of the bus stop, but Max didn't see any drone flying around. The second video appeared to be a first-person point of view shown directly from one person sitting on the bench. But that was impossible...

Cobb stayed silent and watched them process the new information.

"The tech tapped into their ocular nerves? Without them feeling it?" Lisa said. Despite her personal feelings, she couldn't keep the awe out of her voice.

"That's right," Cobb said. "Just the tip of the iceberg. Watch this."

CHAPTER SIXTY-SEVEN

Keres needed to get close. He didn't think the restraints would be a problem, but the distance would be. The guard wasn't holding the gun on them, it was down at his side, but he had his eyes up and alert. He was standing 10 feet away, out in the street. He needed to time this right.

Keres edged forward on the bench and tensed his legs to move, then a moment of vertigo swept over him. The scene in front of him went soft and fuzzy. He heard low mumbling whispers. It sounded like words, but he couldn't make them out. He suddenly felt like a passenger in his own body. Like he was watching his own life on a movie screen. He wasn't outside his body, he was tethered but disconnected. He didn't like it. He shook his head to try to clear it. Then it was gone. Or it faded. Or maybe it was never there at all. He looked at the two women, but they gave no indication of feeling it. They still seemed in shock by the fake city scene.

He refocused on the guard. He had a habit of touching his ear and looking away for a moment when he was listening to his earpiece. That was the time. That was the moment. Keres edged forward a little more and dug his toes into the pavement. His calf burned where the damn dog had gouged his flesh. He ignored it. He couldn't let it slow him down. He felt Martha shift on his left. She'd noticed his movement, but he didn't care. As long as the guard didn't notice. He stared down at the guard's left hand. It twitched and then started moving.

Keres lunged.

Or, tried to.

Max watched as Keres stood and began to... dance.

"Viennese waltz. Faster and more elegant, in my opinion, than the traditional English waltz. A test program that demonstrates coordination and complexity of movement. It's also one of my best, and only, memories of my parents. They belonged to a local German club that would have monthly dances. They took me along, gave me some sweets, shooed me off to the side."

Max watched Keres swoop and spin into the street. Something was wrong with his leg. He was limping and favoring his left side, but his feet moved in time to some unheard music. He stumbled and fell out of sync at times, but not for long. He always returned to the steps like a compass recognizing north. He even paused and held up his arm as if spinning a partner.

"Amazing." Cobb was hunched over the terminal, studying the data flowing across the screen. Rather than seem concerned with how his demo was disintegrating, he seemed intrigued. "This has never happened. I wonder..."

He also appeared to have forgotten that Lisa and Max were in the room. Max stepped up next to the glass. He banged on it. He had no idea if Vic could hear or see him. There was no response from the street. He didn't like that

Vic was down there. Keres was a loose cannon before, now with untested nanotech in his body, he was even more unpredictable and dangerous.

Max watched as Keres spun across the yellow divider lines in the road and then reversed back toward the bus stop. He stumbled again as he approached the guard and went to a knee and then he was back up again. Something flashed in the light. Then there was blood and chaos.

Keres was a passenger again, but this time was different. He felt not just disconnected, but as if he'd taken a step back and relinquished control of his own body. It was the strangest feeling. He heard more whispers. He could still feel his muscles and body moving and responding. It just wasn't him giving the commands. He was on his feet now. He stepped off the curb and continued into the street. He passed near the guard, close enough to touch, but he didn't. He saw a wry smile on the guard's face. Keres moved away, wheeling and whirling farther into the street. This was insane! What was going on? He bore down and tried to regain control, but hit a wall, not literally but figuratively. That tethered feeling returned. He felt walled in and handcuffed. He was bound inside his body just like he was with the flex cuffs outside his body.

He relaxed and regrouped. Kicking and screaming weren't going to work. He could sense that. Whatever was going on, brute force would not break the hold. It would only exhaust him and make him easier to control. He closed his eyes. Not really, he couldn't even control his eyelids, but he stopped paying attention to the scene he could see from his eyes. He pictured himself instead as a passenger in a car, not just pictured it, but really put himself there. It was his first car. A 1961 Chevy Impala. He bought it off Creeger, his boss at the salvage yard, after working two back-breaking summers. It was nothing to look at. A beater with faded black paint, ripped upholstery, and a missing side mirror. It wasn't a cool car by 1970. Creeger knew how to squeeze pennies from scrap, but he knew shit about cars or he would've never let Keres buy it. Cool or not, it had a beast of a stock engine. It was a dragstrip warrior and he won a lot of money on Friday and Saturday nights out at the abandoned airfield. He loved that car.

He could smell the tang of the exhaust and the sweat caked into the seats. He reached out and rubbed a hand along the dash. He felt the cracks and pocks and peeling edges. He looked over at the driver's seat and saw only a dark, slightly translucent shadow. He reached out, grabbed the steering wheel, and wrenched it to the right. Outside in the fake street, he felt himself stumble and fall. Inside, the shadow threw him back against the passenger door. But it worked. Sort of. It did not, or could not, completely lock him out. He had some free will. But he'd been too tentative. He tried again with the same result, but this time felt more resistance. The shadow was ready, but Keres wasn't totally at his mercy. Maybe he could still make his plan work.

He let go of the vision of the interior of the Impala for a moment and looked out through his own eyes. He was moving back across the empty street headed toward the guard. The guard still looked bemused. It was clearly not the first time he'd seen this sideshow. The two women in the bus shelter, on the other hand, had their mouths hanging agape. You think you're surprised now? Watch this.

He swung his legs up out of the footwell and kicked out with all this strength. There was no dog bite now. His legs felt tough and strong, and he drove them into the shadow like twin pistons. The shadow disappeared, but Keres could feel it nearby. There was no time to waste. He slid into the driver's seat and took control.

It would have been easier without his hands being bound. Or without someone else in his head, but Keres thought he was doing okay, all things considered. He'd spun around so his back was to the guard, he'd tried to make it look like part of this insane dance, and then slid his hand into his front pocket and grabbed the crucifix. The shadow was pressing against him. It wanted control. Keres was going to have to fight himself and the guard at the same time.

He twisted the lower wooden part of the shaft off. Ice pick crucifix shivs had been a cottage industry for three years at Stanhope before the prison staff caught on. Keres managed to keep ahold of one. It was practically an antique now, but still plenty sharp.

He did a spin. The guard was right there. The gun still down at his side. Keres reversed his grip on the crucifix. Everything snapped to a stark black and white. He did a stumbling pirouette and brought the sharpened blade up in a short vicious arc. It caught the guard under the jaw and angled up and exited back out through the bridge of his nose. Keres ripped the blade out and made three quick secondary jabs to the guard's chest. He felt one blow nick off bone, maybe the ribcage or sternum, but the other two went clean through into soft tissue and vital organs. Keres felt warm blood flow over his hand. The man's mouth was open in an O of surprise.

"Say hello to all those jailbirds for me, will ya?" Keres pushed him away and he fell over backward and landed face up. Keres stood over him for a moment, catching his breath. He could hear a whistling sound as the man tried to draw a breath. Then a beautiful gush of blood poured out of his mouth. Keres wiped his bloody hands on his pants. Yes, he'd hit something vital.

He turned around and faced the two women. He took a step and then stopped. The shadow was gone. Or maybe not gone but it was no longer fighting him. It had retreated. Or maybe he'd hallucinated the whole thing? No, he'd seen their faces. He'd been fucking dancing in the streets. That wasn't a mirage. That had happened. But how?

The sound of a door opening and then the hinges sucking the door closed made him turn. He watched three people walk out of the narrow alley between the dry cleaner and the bank. He didn't recognize the two men, but he knew the woman. After the last hour, nothing was surprising. He leaned over and picked up the guard's gun.

"How did you do that?" The man in front was older and carrying a tablet in one hand.

"Do what?"

"Stay in control?"

"What did you do to me?" Keres asked. "Who are you?"

"My name is Bradley Cobb. I run this place."

"What is it?"

"A lab. Of sorts."

"A lab for what?"

Cobb glanced down at the tablet. "Let me ask you something. How does your leg feel?"

Keres paused and did a little hop and jump on his leg. It felt better. A lot better than it had 15 minutes ago. He pulled his pant leg up. The streaks of red around the wound were fading. He could almost feel the skin knitting and tightening under the makeshift bandage.

"It feels alright."

"Good. I'm glad to hear it. That's the Dactyls. They are actively working to heal that open wound."

"Dactyls? I never took anything besides aspirin."

"You did. You just didn't know it. Your body is currently full of the latest generation of my medical nanotech machines called Dactyls. They are working to heal your body."

"But that's not all they're doing, is it?"

"No, that's not all they're capable of."

"Those fucking things took over my body. Medical advancements are one thing. Mind control is another."

"Mind control might be a bit of an exaggeration. We just watched you overrule them and take back command. You killed Grady when they wanted you to dance. I'm interested in that. No prior test subject has ever shown that capacity. What did you do?"

Keres was about to tell him about the Impala and then stopped. Leverage. Maybe he could have his cake and eat it, too. He'd come all this way because he thought he'd lost his last chance at Lisa, and he still needed cash. If this man ran all this, he had money. And Lisa was standing right behind him. "I'll tell you how I did it, but I have a request first. Actually, two."

"What?"

"I assume you paid prior test subjects."

"Yes, we compensated them for their time."

"I want money and I want Lisa Sullivan. Give me that and I'll tell you exactly what I did to get around your mind bots."

"How much?"

"Two million."

"Okay."

Shit. The guy answered too fast. He'd sold himself too low.

"You tell me what you did and do it again, not the killing, but display the same dominance over the Dactyls and I'll give you $2,000,000."

"And Sullivan."

Cobb looked over his shoulder. "Sure, and Sullivan."

"I don't think so," The guy standing next to Lisa stepped forward. "I could care less about the money, but you're not taking Lisa."

Keres looked at him. "Who are you? I don't know you, but I've seen you."

"I'm just a guy."

"Brave guy."

The guy shrugged. "Bravery? Madness? Is there a difference?"

Keres smiled. "Yeah, I know you. I've never met you, but I've met your father. Isn't that right?" He looked over at Lisa. "But maybe you're right. Maybe I don't need to take her. Maybe having her watch me shoot you like I shot her husband will be enough."

He pointed the gun at the man's chest and pulled the trigger.

CHAPTER SIXTY-EIGHT

Eddie slowly chewed down the length of a Red Vine and watched the video feed on one of his monitors. He gulped down half a can of soda and tapped a key. The screen changed. He could see the body again by the man's feet and the pool of blood. He didn't like looking at that and tapped the key again. The next view was better. He could still see some blood and a bit of a foot, but off to the side and easy to ignore. He preferred not to think about death. It reminded him of Mama and that always made him feel weird and sad.

The people on the screen were still talking. Eddie had full control of the system if he wanted it, both audio and video, but Eddie wasn't paying attention to the words. He didn't care about the talk. He was only watching because Lawrence had asked him to keep an eye on Max. Eddie wasn't sure what that meant and Lawrence explained it to him. So, Eddie needed to watch, but not necessarily listen.

He used the mouse and zoomed the camera in closer. He wondered if the bloody guy was the hacker who had been inside Eddie's system. Eddie felt a hot flash across his neck thinking about the smudge. That memory also made him feel strange, but not in the same way as Mama. Plus, he'd done something about the smudge. He couldn't do anything about Mama.

He studied the bloody man. He didn't appear to be a hacker. Or to be in charge. His hands were tied up. He just appeared to be old. Maybe it was the other guy, the one holding the tablet and also talking. His hands weren't tied. But he was old, too. Did everyone suddenly get old? Eddie had the sudden urge to go into the bathroom and check the mirror, but Lawrence had told him not to move until he came back. But everyone wasn't old. He looked at Max. Max looked the same and Eddie relaxed a fraction.

Eddie didn't recognize anyone other than Max. That was okay. He didn't need any more friends. Max and Lawrence were enough. And maybe the boy down at the corner store. Eddie needed him. Did that mean he couldn't be a friend? He wasn't sure. He was getting bored. His fingers itched to get on the keyboard and explore this new system, but Lawrence said it was very important to wait. He did his best. He'd only poked around a little. He spun around in lazy circles in his chair and let the background chatter from the feed wash over him.

Then he heard Max's voice. He put out a hand and stopped the chair. The bloody guy was no longer talking to the other old guy. He was talking to Max. He tried to concentrate and listen, but the words got scrambled up. Nothing made sense. He looked over his shoulder, but the room was empty. Where was Lawrence? He needed his brother to tell him what to do. He went back to the screen and zoomed the camera in as far as it would go. He listened to the words and watched the man's face like Lawrence had taught him, but it still made little sense. It was all gibberish.

Then the bloody man pointed the gun at Max and things made more sense.

CHAPTER SIXTY-NINE

Max watched the gun come up. The pistol had a short barrel and a longer grip. Max guessed it was the civilian version of the military's Sig Sauer M17 or M18. Most of the military used some variant of it now. Max guessed the guard had used it in the service, was comfortable with it, and continued to use the same weapon when he started working for Cobb. All this flashed through Max's mind as the gun came level and he looked into the black hole of the bore.

How to save his family and friends? Ending up here, at the mercy of a lunatic like Keres, had not been the plan. Keres being here at all was unexpected. They'd deal with Cobb now and Keres later. That had been the plan, but now they were both here in the same room. He and Lisa knew they'd be searched on the way into Cobb's lab and had left anything remotely resembling a weapon in the SUV. They had taken only the USB drive. It had served its purpose. After that, Max was left only with the clothes on his back.

The effective range of a handgun was 50 meters. Theoretically. With a perfectly maintained gun, an experienced and skilled marksman in a stable shooting position, aiming at a motionless target in perfect environmental conditions. Here and now? Keres was 15 yards away, bleeding, chock full of nanotech, under stress, and using an unfamiliar gun. Max guessed he'd fired a gun before, but he'd just gotten out of prison. How much recent practice did he have? Max thought his odds of taking a bullet were 50/50. A lethal shot? Much lower. If he didn't remain motionless? Even better. He ducked low and launched himself at Keres.

It was like running in chest-high mud. His legs churned, but he didn't feel like he was making any progress. He saw Keres's arm jerk to the side just as he fired. He heard the boom of shots but knew they'd missed. Then his shoulder finally connected with Keres's sternum and sent both of them sprawling to the ground. They lay there, stunned by the impact, before slowly getting back to their feet. Keres tried to throw a short left into Max's ribs, but Keres was still catching his breath and the punch had little impact. Max batted it away and swung an elbow at Keres's face. Keres dodged back and the blow only grazed the top his head. Keres tried to move again, get more space and time. His breath was heavy. Max grabbed him and didn't let go. He threw two quick jabs to Keres's mid-section. Keres punched back. This wrestling and grappling felt familiar. This was a down and dirty hockey fight. Clutching, grabbing, bodies tight, rabbit punches that would bruise but not stagger. Max ducked his chin and let the blows glance off. He held on and let Keres tire himself out.

As Keres's punches slowed, then stopped, Max thought about his next move. Disengage, push the man back, get some distance, aim a kick at that damaged leg. Put him down. Max was about to step back when he realized Keres hadn't stopped fighting because he was tired. He'd stopped fighting because he was reaching for something. And now he had it. Max's desperate tackle had put them near the guard's body. And the shiv. Max watched as Keres's arm swung up toward his chin. There was no time to dodge. Keres knew it, too. Max could see his smile, crooked teeth rimmed with blood. Max brought his arm up in a last-ditch effort to deflect the strike.

The sharpened steel pierced his arm, went through the muscle and bone of his forearm, and stopped an inch from his eye.

There was no pain yet. And no blood.

Keres's smile transformed to a look of shock and surprise. Then it changed again and became feral. The look of a weasel. Keres hadn't only found the crucifix. He'd also found the gun. He hadn't used it because he wanted to use the shiv. He wanted to make it personal. He wanted Lisa to watch Max die painfully from a gruesome wound. But he was nothing if not fluid in his plans. He was a survivor. He brought the gun up.

Max brought his forearm down and across Keres's neck. There wasn't a lot of blade showing but there was enough.

Keres dropped the gun and put both hands to his neck. He tried to look down and see the wound, but then gave up. His head fell back, and he died with a strange smile on his lips.

Max stood and kicked the gun away. He looked at the blade sticking out of his arm. He didn't pull it out. He wanted to make sure he had bandages ready when he did. The pain was still manageable. It was building, but the adrenaline was keeping it at bay. The entire fight had lasted less than 30 seconds. He looked around. No one had moved. Then he looked again. That wasn't true. Someone had. Lisa stood in the same spot, but her arms were clamped over her stomach. Blood leeched through her fingers.

"Michael," she said, then fell to the floor.

"Help her," Max said.

The wound looked like nothing, just a small, bruised hole to the left side of her stomach, but Max knew that wasn't true. A bullet's path could cause a wide swath of collateral destruction and there were so many vital organs in the lower abdomen. A trickle of blood bubbled up each time she breathed. Her eyes were open, but Max knew she wasn't seeing Max or Cobb huddled over her. Her eyes were filled only with pain.

"Why?" Cobb responded.

"Why?" Max looked at the man and realized Lisa had been right all along. No one who asked that question with a bleeding woman in front of them deserved to wield that kind of power. But Lisa needed it now. Right now. "Consider it another test. Have you tested this scenario?"

"No, not like this."

"We're wasting time. Do something."

Cobb took a small aerosol tube, the size of a lipstick tube, out of his pocket and sprayed it first over Lisa's wound and then over her face. Next, he lifted the tablet and started tapping on the screen. "For the data."

Max wanted to hit him. He wanted to put everything he had into a punch that would shatter the man's jaw. Lisa was not data. He wanted to punch the smug certainty right out of him, but he didn't. He was their only option. They would never make it to a hospital.

Instead, he took Lisa's hand and leaned over, close to her head. "If you go down in the woods today, you're sure of a big surprise. If you go down in the woods today, you'd better go in disguise. For every bear that ever there was will gather there for certain because today's the day the teddy bears have their picnic."

"Too much damage," Cobb said. He slid his finger along the tablet, then Lisa started convulsing.

The gun skidded across the floor and stopped near the bus bench. She nudged it with her foot. Martha stood and walked over to where the others huddled around Lisa.

Vic felt as if she was rising from a deep, cold pool. She was alive. She took a shuddering breath and it hit her that she hadn't expected to live until tomorrow. Not after Keres had shown up with his ugly smile. Not after they'd been herded into that elevator and down to this underground city. Her goal had been to make it to the next minute, the next second. That was it. She looked at Max and Cobb kneeling over Lisa. From the moment Keres reappeared, she knew it was only a matter of time before more blood was spilled. Keres was a tornado of ruin that left a path of butchery in his wake. She was sure this was not the first bleeding body he'd left behind.

But no more.

She looked at his crumpled body.

She was alive and he was dead.

Only.

She frowned. Had his hand just twitched? No. The stress was making her see things that weren't there. She rubbed her face and stood. She should see if she could help with Lisa. But she looked again.

Another tremor. Slight but there. She wasn't imagining things. It was the goddam nanotech. The Dactyls were fighting to keep their host alive. She glanced over at the others. They were focused on Lisa. Vic stood. She picked up the gun. It surprised her how light something so deadly could be.

His eyes were open. And alert. "Throw me off a bridge. Send me into the woods. Stab me. You can't kill me."

"You're not special. Anyone can die."

She put the first shot through his ruined teeth and then pulled the trigger until it was empty and then kept on pulling until someone gently took the gun away.

CHAPTER SEVENTY

It was not clear if they were free to leave. None of them had tried. Martha had disappeared, so presumably they could go, but the door at the end of the hall was locked. Then again, maybe it always was. This facility dealt with a lot of secrets. Max didn't know for sure either way. So far, it hadn't been an issue.

He looked down at Lisa. Tubes and wires snaked off the bed and connected to beeping equipment. She hadn't regained consciousness since the seizure. There were two nurses and a doctor tending to her. The nurses sat at a desk in an adjoining room. The doctor came in three times a day to look at the notes left by the nursing staff. She was a short woman with short hair and Eastern European features. She was brisk and blunt. She told them Lisa was stable and needed rest. Max had tried to read the chart to fill in the blanks but couldn't decipher it.

They hadn't seen Cobb. Max stood and moved to the windows. He rubbed at his bandaged arm. It ached, but the doctor said he would be fine once it healed. Some stiffness occasionally, maybe sensitivity loss in the fingertips, but no loss of motion. He looked out over the grounds. Construction crews had assembled the temporary bleachers and stage for Cobb's big Dactyls demo. The one that would showcase the future of war for the senators and the other DoD bigwigs who held the lucrative government purse strings. The first domino to fall in Cobb's plan to leave a mark on the world.

But plenty of people left a mark on the world. A mark wasn't a sign of genius or generosity. A mark could be callous and cold and leave a devastating impact. A mark could wound the world in irreparable ways.

He turned back to the bed. But it could also save. The world was full of gray spaces.

He thought back to the conversation around Vic's kitchen table. Was it too late? Would it be better or worse if the entire world had Cobb's technology?

The world was already a dangerous place.

Would the Dactyls heal it or hurry along its destruction?

The next day, Lisa opened her eyes. "Did it work?" she whispered.

The doctor didn't want to let them leave, but she couldn't stop them either. She told them Lisa was stable and well enough to make the trip. That was all Lisa needed to hear. Despite what Cobb and his Dactyls had done to save her life, she didn't trust him. She wanted to get as far away from Cobb and his lab as she could.

Before they left, the doctor came into the room. Vic was helping Lisa slowly get out of bed and ready for the trip. "Can I speak to you for a minute?" she said to Max.

"Sure."

They stepped out into the hall.

"We're going," Max said, expecting another argument. He knew the doctor thought a few more days of rest would be prudent. He didn't disagree. But he also didn't disagree with Lisa. They needed to get away from Cobb.

The doctor held up her hands. "I'm not going to debate that again. You are free to go."

Max nodded. "Okay, good. Then what did you want to talk about?"

"There's something else you need to know about your mother."

CHAPTER SEVENTY-ONE

Cobb smiled. It was going better than he could have predicted.

Cobb looked at the faces sitting in the bleachers and then moved his gaze closer and looked at the generals and two senators sitting on the dais with him. Each face was the same. Each face showed a mixture of wonder, fear, and greed. They wanted the Dactyls. They wanted them badly. Everyone could see the potential. Everyone wanted to be part of history, even if it was only a minor footnote.

As workers removed the previous targets from the field, he stood once more and moved back to the lectern.

"Thank you again for your attendance here today. I trust we have not wasted your time, and I sincerely hope we have not disappointed you. We have one last demonstration for you today. If you'll direct your attention to the left quadrant of the field. We will use unmanned drones and show you how the Dactyls can be deployed to strengthen defense capabilities against a variety of incoming aerial attacks."

The crowd shifted away from him to the left so they could see the drone as it lifted off from the field. Cobb had ordered enormous video screens installed and all the Dactyls sprayed with phosphoresce so they would be easier to see. He wanted it to be mysterious, almost magical, but he also didn't want it to appear to be a trick. The DoD would pay for mysterious but might balk at something that smelled like a con. It had worked out beautifully. The Dactyls looked like miniature-sized lightning bugs and were easily seen on the high-definition screens.

Cobb stayed at the dais to watch and wrap up the proceedings when this last demo was complete.

The drone lifted off, hovered over the field, and then moved in a pre-programmed pattern. The incoming ground fire started up, but the Dactyls never appeared. Cobb frowned and looked around. Then he caught movement to the right. He turned and saw a shimmer in the air headed not toward the field but the stage. He touched the tablet sitting on the lectern in front of him and tapped the screen to redirect the swarm. They didn't change course. He tried again. They kept coming.

Now, Cobb jabbed at the tablet with increasing alarm. He appeared to be locked out of the system. But that wasn't possible. He glanced up. They were coming. The generals now noticed something was, if not wrong, not quite right. Cobb stepped to the front of the stage. The incoming shimmer adjusted.

He felt a surge of panic. He needed to get away. He needed to get inside. He could figure this out if he could get inside. He jumped off the stage and started running across the grass toward the brick bunker. If he could get to Control, he could salvage this.

He felt a slight tickle near his ear. Something brushed lightly against his neck. He felt himself slow to a stop. It was the strangest thing.

He heard whispers in his head.

CHAPTER SEVENTY-TWO

Martha left immediately. She didn't have a dog in this fight. She just wanted to get away. From Cobb, his guards, his tech. All of it. She removed the keycard from the guard's belt, retraced her steps to the elevator, and took it back up to the parking lot. No one stopped her. No one followed her. She drove out the gate and didn't look back.

Four hours later, she returned the rental to the Newark airport. She left Keres's bags in the back seat. She didn't want to touch them. With any luck, they'd end up in a landfill within a week. She took a rickety shuttle bus to long-term parking and retrieved her Subaru.

Back at her apartment, she hesitated at the elevator, but didn't have the energy to walk up the stairs. She did have the energy to grab a bottle of red wine, strip off her clothes, and slide into a hot bath.

She was too tired to read, almost too tired to open the wine, thank God it was a screw top, and just sat in the steaming water. Eventually, her back unknotted and the tightness between her shoulder blades relaxed. She slowly emerged from the tub, wrapped herself in a robe, and collapsed into bed.

She woke up 18 hours later, finally feeling a bit like her old self. It would take a few more days and probably a few more bottles of red wine, but she'd get there. She padded to the kitchen and started the coffeemaker. She looked out the window. Her apartment was on the fifth floor and, if she leaned over just right, she could see across the Hudson to the city skyline. She was a city girl through and through. Give her 2:00 a.m. horns, asphalt, subway steam, and street cart pretzels over fresh air and mountain views.

She poured a cup of coffee, took her bag from where she'd dropped it last night, and carried everything into the second bedroom that she used as an office. She worked her way through the notes and various receipts for Cobb and typed it up into a one-page summary. She wasn't sure if anyone would ever read it, but she always liked to finish a case with a one-page rundown as a way of literally and figuratively turning the page. Case closed.

She spent the next two days in her robe with her wine and books and takeout containers from Siam Thai and Grand Sichuan. By the third day, she felt ready to restart the life she'd put on pause when she'd driven up to Stanhope Penitentiary in Maine.

She walked back to the kitchen and took out the French press and Stumptown beans. Might as well treat herself. It could be bumpy reentry, better to face it with good coffee. She turned on the television while she waited for the water to boil. She glanced at it and then stopped, hand extended toward the beans. She flipped from the local station to CNN. Same story. She jumped to MSNBC. Same thing. The video was too compelling to talk about anything else. She could see the gleam of excitement in the anchors' eyes as they recounted the details. She caught different snippets on different channels. She put the remote down now and watched it all the way through.

Every channel had the same angle. It was a static high shot taken from a camera mounted on a pole or support beam near the stage. It was crisp and clear but without sound. The lower left edge showed part of the stage and bleachers, but mostly a grassy field. Martha recognized the facade of a brick building off to the right. As the video started, the field was empty, then a man scrambled off the stage and walked fully into view. She didn't need the graphic at the bottom of the screen to tell he it was Bradley Cobb. He carried a tablet and looked over his shoulder, as if looking to see if anyone was following. He began to walk more quickly. Then run. Each time he turned toward the camera he looked more terrified. He dropped the tablet and started waving his arms and ducking his head. He looked like he was being attacked by a swarm of bees or insects, but nothing was visible on screen. He continued to thrash around and then he suddenly stopped. He turned and began walking back toward the camera at a normal pace. His face was blank. He stopped again. He just stood there. A few other people cautiously inched into the frame from the bottom. Cobb opened his mouth to speak, but no words came out, only bloody foam that ran down his chin and neck. Blood hemorrhaged from his eyes before he fell forward face first, no effort to put his arms out and break his fall, into the grass and lay still. People started running toward him and then the video cut out.

She changed channels and watched it again. Some stations blurred out or cut the end completely. Others did not, following the old news mantra, if it bleeds, it leads. No one had answers. She turned off the television and walked back into the office. She put the Cobb file in a locked drawer.

She picked up her phone and called her brother in New Mexico. She could hear her nephews in the background shouting and getting ready for school. She smiled. She would be okay.

CHAPTER SEVENTY-THREE

Joyce called three weeks later. He'd been expecting it. He knew it would be fast. She didn't want to go into the hospital. Both he and Joyce had argued with her, but not too strongly. They didn't like it, but they understood.

The view across the tidal basin to Route 93 and the iconic rainbow gas tank wasn't much, but the golden afternoon light softened the edges and gave it all a dream-like quality. Lisa was in bed. She had somehow grown smaller in the days since he'd last visited. Her cheekbones were sharper, her skin looked papery thin.

She smiled when he entered the room. He smiled back, but he could see it in her eyes. It was time. He pulled a chair over.

"My son."

Suddenly, he couldn't find any words. His throat constricted to a narrow point. Yes, her son. He nodded.

She covered his hand with hers. He felt the bones and the brittleness.

"I have one more lie to confess," Lisa said.

He looked at her. They had had many long talks since Cobb's doctor had told them the Dactyls had only temporarily saved her life. They'd also shown advanced renal failure. Too advanced and pervasive for the current version of the Dactyls to cure. They had their limits. The doctor had suggested immediately getting on the transplant list. It was a long shot, but her best chance. Lisa had said no.

"Why am I not surprised?" Max replied.

Her smile stretched her skin even tighter. "I lied to Keres. I did have the warehouse money. Not all of it, but some of it. I used a lot to hide and to help Joyce, like I told you, but I also invested some of it."

She reached out and took an envelope off the side table. It was on top of a large pile of papers. Most of them were about him. She had wanted to know his story. He had told her much of it, but she had wanted all of it. True and not true. Good and bad.

"The details are in here."

He opened it and raised his eyebrows. It was just a handful of stocks, but they had performed well. Really well. She noticed his reaction. "Got lucky."

"We make our own luck," he replied.

"That's something your father would have said."

"You know I don't need this."

She nodded. "Take care of Joyce and do some good with it."

He realized something in the stillness. "You didn't call the first time because of Keres, did you? It was before he found you. You knew before you got shot, didn't you? You called—"

"To say goodbye."

After a pause, Max said, "I'm glad you did."

They fell silent after that and watched the traffic build out on the highway and the sun dip lower. She closed her eyes and he watched her breathe. The pauses became longer. It was dark when she opened her eyes again. The faint light in the room came from the streetlights outside.

"Are you as bad as they say you are?"

He glanced again at the side table and the papers. His story. He wanted to say no. His family history was laced with lies. What was one more at the very end? But maybe it was never too late for the truth. "Sometimes."

She closed her eyes. "Good."

CHAPTER SEVENTY-FOUR

Lawrence reached for the clippers to finish Deshawn's fade when he noticed the silence. He looked in the mirror that ran the length of the shop's walls. A man in a black suit was standing in the doorway. A white man in a black suit. The three other people waiting for cuts had stopped talking. Lawrence clocked him. White people weren't unicorns in the shop but they were rare, and this guy didn't look like he needed a haircut. Well-tailored, maybe bespoke suit, solid tie with a silver pin. Thick leather English shoes. And a haircut that likely cost five times what Lawrence charged. He was not here for a haircut.

There was also something else about him. Maybe that's why Bobby, Clarke, and the others fell silent. They sensed it, too. Lawrence kept the scissors in his hand.

"Help you?" he asked.

"Lawrence Jackson?"

"That's right."

"May I have a word?"

Something told Lawrence saying no wasn't an option.

Plus, he was curious. Too fancy to be a cop. Too alone to be a rival.

"Sure, just let me finish this up."

He grabbed the clippers. Lawrence kept one eye on the man as he worked. Conversations resumed with sidelong glances. The man in black didn't appear to notice. He took a seat and waited. Lawrence took his time finishing up with Deshawn and tried to figure out what the man wanted. Lawrence had his fingers in a lot of different pies, but he couldn't think of anything that might have brought this man, or this type of man at least, to his door. Unless... Max.

He swept the cape off Deshawn and collected his money. "Guys, can you give us a few minutes?" The shop emptied and, to Lawrence's surprise, the man stepped up and sat in the chair.

"You want a cut?"

"You do shaves?"

"Sure."

"Just a shave then." The man sat back and closed his eyes.

"Thought you wanted to talk?"

"I do, but I just cost you three customers, the least I can do is pay for your time."

"Those guys will be back. They spend most of their days here. They're not really here for a shave and a cut. They're here to fill up their day."

"Still, I never pass up a hot shave. One of life's small pleasures."

"Suit yourself."

Lawrence took a towel from the hot box, laid it over the man's face, and then prepped his razor and mixed up some fresh cream. When he removed the towel, the man nodded at the television mounted in a corner, playing mutely. "You pay attention to the news?"

"Not too much. Never feels like it has much impact on my day-to-day."

The man nodded. Lawrence lathered his cheeks and ran the straight razor over his already smooth cheeks.

"But you pay some attention, right? You noticed the big story last month about the weapons demo that went wrong down in D.C.?"

Lawrence wiped the last bits of cream from the man's neck. He tried to keep his hands steady. "No, can't say that I did."

"No?"

"I'm a Black man in America. There's not much good news for me coming from Washington unless the Wizards are going to trade a couple of their all-stars to the Celtics."

The man touched his cheeks and looked at himself in the mirror, then stood. "A man got killed. It was quite a spectacle. I'm sure it made the news up here."

Lawrence shook his head. "Sorry. I run a barbershop. We mostly talk sports and women. Weapons and nanotech and politics don't interest me."

The man tilted his head. "Nanotech?"

Lawrence felt his stomach knot. He'd walked right into it. "I might have caught a few headlines. Didn't they blame it on foreign hackers? Chinese? The whole system got corrupted, right?"

"That's right. All the source code was fried. But it wasn't the Chinese."

"No? Well, whoever did it probably did the world a favor."

"Maybe." The man stood and straightened his tie. He placed a $20 by the register and then moved toward the door but stopped short. "Or they just delayed the inevitable and put our national interests at risk."

Lawrence shrugged. "The world's a dangerous place and

my concerns don't go much beyond this shop's door. I'm just a barber."

The man smiled. "We both know that's not all you are, Mr. Jackson."

"What's that mean?"

But the man ignored the question. "Maybe we'll talk again."

"Yeah? And who are you?"

"Don't ask a question you don't want an answer to," he said, and pushed open the door. "I'm just a bureaucrat."

CHAPTER SEVENTY-FIVE

Max set his bag down and pulled the door shut.

"There's more in the cooler if Bailey approves."

Vic was sitting on the hood of her truck in frayed jeans and a Bruins Winter Classic t-shirt. She must have been there for a little while. There was one empty already balanced on the hood. He hadn't heard her pull in. The sun was a sinking orange ball over the Berkshires to the west. She leaned back against the windshield and took a long pull from the sweating bottle. Winters were cold and the summers were hot. Chepstow did everything to the extreme. He went around the passenger side and pulled a beer from the cooler. He gave the napping dog a quick rub behind the ears.

"You're leaving?" she asked.

"Not much left for me to do. Randy's gonna finish the electrical later this week. That just leaves some touch-up painting. Even you can handle that."

"Very funny. And I'm the boss, remember? I subcontract those types of tasks. But you won't be available?"

"I think I need to get my head straight."

"Don't we all." She didn't look at him. "Running to something or running away?"

"I'm not sure. Does it matter? I can't seem to stop."

"You okay? I know you didn't get all the answers you wanted."

"Am I okay? I think if I could answer that, I wouldn't have to keep moving." Max looked around at the ramshackle motel, now with patches of fresh wood and shingling, to the tall, unnecessary sign, then out to the cracked road running west through the trees. He could feel it pulling at him.

He hated to admit it, but the episode with Cobb and Keres had given him purpose. It had sandblasted him clean and left his mind still and empty. He flexed his arm, but now he could feel the doubts and questions tiptoeing back.

"Maybe I don't want those answers."

"How's that feel?"

"Guess I'm going to find out."

"You're a good man, Max."

"Am I? Sometimes I lose track."

She gave a crooked smile. "More good than bad, I think. Try to find some peace."

"Easier said than done."

"But not impossible. And maybe not as hard as you think."

She slid off the hood of her truck, climbed in, and started it up. Bailey roused from his nap in the passenger seat and sniffed the air before settling back down.

"If you ever get tired of running, we'll be here."

Max watched her turn right and head back to town toward her frilly house and lumpy sofa. Her taillights flared once, but she never looked back.

He sat in one of the old, weathered Adirondack chairs

they'd dragged around front from the courtyard and finished his beer, then he sat some more. The moon swapped places with the sun. He looked out at the mountains. They're all out there, he thought. All my ghosts. His mother now, too. Waiting and watching. Had he done enough? Had he made amends? Could he stop running? He listened to the hot summer wind, but there was no answer. Not one that he could hear.

He tossed his bag in the car and got behind the wheel. Left was the unknown. More roads and more small towns. Maybe more problems and more ways to help. Right was Chepstow and The Night Owl. And maybe Vic.

He turned.

ABOUT THE AUTHOR

Mike Donohue is the author of five previous novels in the Max Strong series. He lives with his wife, two daughters, and Dashiell Hammett outside Boston. Dash is the family dog.

Mike doesn't think reading during meals is particularly rude. Quite the opposite.

You can find him online at mikedonohuebooks.com.

 facebook.com/mikedonohuebooks

 twitter.com/miked_mystery

www.ingramcontent.com/pod-product-compliance
Lightning Source LLC
Chambersburg PA
CBHW061344190726
48288CB00005B/1587